THE FABERGÉ SECRET

THE FABERGÉ
SECRET

Charles Belfoure

This first world edition published 2020
in Great Britain and 2021 in the USA by
SEVERN HOUSE PUBLISHERS LTD of
Eardley House, 4 Uxbridge Street, London W8 7SY.
Trade paperback edition first published
in Great Britain and the USA 2021 by
SEVERN HOUSE PUBLISHERS LTD.

British Library Cataloguing in Publication Data
A CIP catalogue record for this title is available from the British Library.

ISBN-13: 978-0-7278-9086-3 (cased)
ISBN-13: 978-1-78029-725-5 (trade paper)
ISBN-13: 978-1-4483-0446-2 (e-book)

All Severn House titles are printed on acid-free paper.

Severn House Publishers support the Forest Stewardship Council™ [FSC™],
the leading international forest certification organisation.
All our titles that are printed on FSC certified paper carry the FSC logo.

Typeset by Palimpsest Book Production Ltd.,
Falkirk, Stirlingshire, Scotland.
Printed and bound in Great Britain by
TJ Books Limited, Padstow, Cornwall.

IMPERIAL RUSSIA
1903

PROLOGUE

The Tsar stood up from the dinner table and smiled at Dimitri.

'We have a new gramophone disk. It's Tchaikovsky's "Fantasy Overture" from *Romeo and Juliet*. Will you join us in the study, Dimitri?'

'Oh, please come,' Grand Duchess Tatiana cried, as she took the last bite of her raspberry tart. 'We can play cards while we listen.'

Dimitri bent over and kissed Tatiana on her cheek.

'As you wish, my little Highness. I'll be along in a few minutes.'

There was still enough light coming from the window, so Dimitri could see everything on the shelves in the display room very clearly. He pursed his lips, then made his decision. This time it would be the 'Coronation Egg,' the third Fabergé Easter Egg Nicholas had given to Alexandra. He picked it up and opened the hinged yellow-enameled shell. Inside was an exact gold and diamond-encrusted replica of the carriage the Imperial Couple rode in for their coronation. Pulling it carefully out of the egg, he marveled at the incredible workmanship. Even the platinum wheels and the strawberry-red upholstery were exactly like the real thing. He opened its little door and placed a tiny piece of folded paper on the floor of the carriage, then put it back into the egg. As usual, he set it slightly forward from the line of the other eggs and gifts to let his fellow agents know which object held the message. He opened the door of the display room a crack to see if anyone was about, then hurried down the marble hallway to the Tsar's study.

ONE

'What a beautiful Easter day,' Grand Prince Dimitri Sergeyevich Markhov commented.

He was sipping a *zubrovka* on the veranda of his host, Count Yuri Bykov.

The Count, who was standing next to Dimitri, closed his eyes and raised his face to bask in the brilliant sunshine.

'Much nicer weather here than in St Petersburg, eh, Dimitri?' He took a sip of his vodka and walked back into the mansion.

Dimitri watched him pass through the wide French doors that opened onto the veranda of the south wing. He admired this detail, as well as the rest of the beautiful house which he had designed two years ago. The seventy-five-room mansion, executed in the classical manner after the great Italian architect Palladio, was clad in whitish-gray Pentelic marble – the same marble that was used in the Parthenon in ancient Greece. He had created a small kingdom for the Count, who had demolished the original eighteenth-century manor house on his 38,000-acre country estate to build a more magnificent one with electricity, modern bathrooms, and central heating.

Dimitri turned around to face the magnificent verdant landscape that spread out before him. It was a wonderfully hilly countryside in Bessarabia, a province in the south-west corner of the Imperial Russian Empire near the Rumanian border. Easter, the holiest feast day of all in Imperial Russia, was a holiday of great happiness for all in the Empire. Accompanying Bykov's family, Dimitri and his wife of ten years, Princess Lara Pavlovna Markhov, had attended midnight mass last night at Kishinev's main Russian Orthodox cathedral. At the end of the service, the long-bearded priest had proclaimed, 'Christ has risen.' Behind the religious procession led by the priests, people poured out of the cathedral holding their flickering candles, creating rivers of light through the dark streets as they headed home for the great midnight feast.

Some made a detour to the cemetery to wish dead relatives a joyous Easter.

The seven long weeks of fasting during Lent, when no butter, milk, eggs, and meat could be eaten, had ended at midnight, and Dimitri was starving for good food. After the Easter service, there was a tremendous supper waiting at Count Bykov's mansion. The symbols of the Easter feast – *kulich*, a cylindrical cake topped with white icing, and *pashka*, a cheese curd packed with preserved fruits and vanilla baked in the shape of a truncated pyramid – lined the long linen-covered table in the big banquet room. Everyone cheered when the traditional suckling pig with its drowsy, half-closed eyes, brown crispy skin, and an Easter egg stuck in his mouth was set upon the table. The feast lasted until the early morning with the intention of staying up to watch the Easter sunrise, but most guests collapsed drunk into bed.

It was now the afternoon on Easter Sunday. The Orthodox Church did not have services on Easter, but the city's church bells still pealed all day long. Dimitri could hear them ever so faintly in the distance. Princess Lara came up alongside her husband.

'I'm *so* glad Lent is over,' Princess Lara said.

After years of loveless marriage, Dimitri had to admit that he was still dazzled by his wife's incredible beauty. Lara looked stunning in her lavender and white lace dress accented by a brilliant diamond necklace with a large heart-shaped pendant.

'I know what you mean, I've been famished for weeks,' Dimitri replied.

'I didn't mean that, silly,' Lara said with disdain. 'During Lent, you know that a woman can't wear velvets or satins, and jewelry's limited to one measly string of pearls. Now I can wear my best clothes and jewels again.'

'Princess Lara, is there anything I may get you?' asked Baron Boris Savarin, a portly man of about fifty with a broad, flat ruddy face. Every time Lara went to a social event, the men fawned over her and begged to fetch her food and drink. She loved it; Dimitri knew that she lived to be admired.

'You're so sweet, Baron. May I have a glass of champagne?'

'Why of course, Your Highness. It would be an honor.'

Easter Sundays were reserved for visits. Men and women hurried through the city from one house to the next making social calls to wish friends a happy Easter. Being a nobleman, Count Bykov didn't have to do any visiting; people came to call on him.

One of the most distinguished visitors here was Bishop Iakov, the highest priest in the Orthodox Church in Kishinev. As a courtesy to noblemen, he paid calls to bless the household and its food. In the corner of the veranda, the bishop was speaking to Count Krijitski. Bykov had returned to the veranda with a fresh glass of vodka and was speaking to Vassily Kulgin, a wealthy merchant, and General Léon Demin.

As Dimitri and Lara walked over to join them, he noticed smoke on the horizon.

'It looks like something's going on in Kishinev,' Dimitri said loudly to the men.

Off in the distance, isolated towers of curling gray smoke stretched up into a blue sky strewn with fat puffy clouds.

'I heard there's a riot in the Jewish quarter,' Kulgin said in a matter-of-fact voice, then continued talking to Bykov about this year's wheat harvest.

'What are you handsome men chattering about?' asked Princess Lara in a sly seductive tone. Dimitri had seen his wife use that line many times before at the countless parties at Court and in St Petersburg society. Coming from an incredibly attractive aristocratic woman, it flattered the hell out of men, especially those fat and well up in years. It was particularly effective with provincial types, some of whom who actually blushed bright red. Even back when they had been in love, he never minded her flirting; it had amused him. It was when Lara had eventually followed up on several of her admirers' interest that the heartbreak began. Savarin handed Lara her champagne, and she gave him a peck on his fat cheek as a reward.

Before anyone could reply, Lara snapped, 'Well, I hope it's about the Imperial ballerina Elizaveta Roerich's new lover, Prince Gorky.'

Dimitri wasn't surprised by this news. Many Russian

aristocrats had their own favorite dancer from the Imperial Ballet as a mistress, as if they owned a prized thoroughbred racehorse. In exchange for sex and companionship, the 'patron' lavished jewels, money, and houses upon the ballerina. The dancers cooperated because they put away the gifts as retirement funds for when they became too old to dance.

Countess Elena Bykov, a still ravishing woman in her sixties, walked up to the group with Princess Tremenisky, a forty-year-old of stunning beauty and grace who wore a magnificent 'dog collar' of pearls and diamonds. Other Court ladies who had broken out their best jewelry and dresses, as Lara had, followed them. Except for the military officers, male guests were dressed the same in black cut-away coats with tails and gray trousers.

'Prince Gorky!' the Countess exclaimed. 'That old duffer? He's the size of a polar bear. In bed, he'll roll over and squish her like a bug!'

'He's become so fat, I heard he's now wearing a custom-made corset,' exclaimed Count Krijitski.

The group roared with laughter – except Dimitri.

'Let the old Prince have his fun, he has problems at home,' Lara said gravely. 'His oldest son and heir, Vladimir, has been dressing up like a woman and picking up men in the bars along the Nevsky.'

'Vlad has such feminine features and a trim figure. I'll wager he makes a very convincing woman with some rouge and powder!' the Countess replied.

'You know,' exclaimed Princess Tremenisky, 'at the last ball of the season, he asked me where I got my gown. I told it was from Worth.'

'Well, at least he is a moral degenerate with excellent taste in clothes,' said Lara.

Dimitri shot them a furtive look of disdain as he stepped away from the group. He liked Prince Gorky – he was an old fool but he was kind-hearted. Dimitri knew that gossip was the mother tongue of the Russian aristocracy. Lara and these shallow foolish people spoke it fluently – and constantly. He was sick of it. He was no prig, he always enjoyed a little gossip. But lately, he had a great longing for an intelligent conversation. And he knew was not going to find such a thing at Court.

'Your Highness, tea is served,' announced a scarlet and gold liveried servant who had crept up on them. All servants wore soft-soled shoes to silence their footsteps.

The Countess led a dozen guests into the drawing room with its barrel-vaulted plaster ceiling and blue damask walls divided by pink marble pilasters. Like a good English hostess, the Countess poured the tea from a bubbling silver samovar which servants in powdered wigs handed out along with plates piled high with pastries. They sat on upholstered chairs and sofas each with a white Louis XIV-style tea table. Servants were scurrying about refilling glasses and removing empty plates. Bykov had an army of four hundred servants just for this estate; some with extraordinarily specific jobs, like one man just to take care of Bykov's hunting boots. On some estates, two footmen were there just to carry the mistress up and down the grand staircase, but Dimitri had ingeniously designed a closet for a small Otis elevator to take care of that job. While he ate, Dimitri could see servants in the ballroom across the hall with felt pads on their feet skating across the parquet floor to buff it to a glossy shine.

'Yuri, what's going on in Kishinev?' he asked.

'This stupid peasant boy was stabbed to death back in February. A crazy rumor got started that Jews did it as a ritual murder. It turned out that the boy's cousin killed him to be in line for an inheritance. But these ignorant peasants still believe the Jews did it for the blood of a Christian to make matzah for their Passover holiday. Now, they're attacking them,' Bykov answered as he took another large cream cake from the silver plate a servant was holding.

Dimitri grimaced. Although he found this news quite disconcerting, it made no impression on the party. Everyone went on chattering and gobbling sweets as before.

'Yuri, slow down! You've already eaten more than the entire city of Kiev,' the Countess scolded. She then shifted the conversation to a more agreeable topic.

'I can't wait to see what the Fabergé Imperial Eggs will look like this Easter,' the Countess said enthusiastically.

'Last year's "Cover Leaf Egg" was just extraordinary,' gushed Princess Tremenisky. The egg, which had translucent green enameling, held a surprise inside of four miniature portraits of the Tsar's little daughters. The frames were encrusted with tiny blue diamonds.

'The egg the Tsar gave his mother with the gold miniature of her palace in Gatchina was amazing,' the Countess declared. 'It was so accurate, down to the statue of Paul I.'

'My favorite is the "Cuckoo Egg" with the red rooster. It pops up, flaps its wings, and sings,' chimed in General Demin.

'The beauty of Fabergé's eggs is almost too overwhelming for the eye,' added Dimitri. 'It stuns you.' He loved anything Fabergé and went to their shop in St Petersburg frequently to buy gifts. Peter Carl Fabergé, the official jeweler to the Imperial Court, set the taste of St Petersburg society.

Speaking more to her tea glass than the guests, Lara said, 'This year's egg is a Peter the Great design.'

'Nonsense,' snapped Dimitri. 'How would you know? That's the most closely guarded secret in the Russian Empire.'

Lara just smiled and bit into her honey tart.

'Larissa, must you leave today? I wanted to show you the palm trees in the new conservatory,' the Countess wailed in a disappointed voice. 'And hear much more delicious, malicious gossip.'

'I really must, *ma chère amie*. I have a fitting for a new gown I'm wearing to the ballet on Thursday. But we still have time before our train to St Petersburg, Elena. Time enough to tell you the details about Baron Volkonsky's *ménage à trois* with his wife, Natasha, and his brother.' Her revelation brought a hush over the guests, then they immediately exchanged coy looks and began talking between themselves in low voices.

'His *brother*, Kirill?' Princess Tremenisky said.

'As you know, the Baron was brought up to share *everything* with his brother,' Lara retorted.

'Hurry and finish your tea, Larissa. We want the minutest details, we want diagrams!' the Countess said in a giddy voice.

Dimitri rolled his eyes.

'Our train leaves at seven, Lara. Please have the two hundred trunks you brought packed and ready to leave,' he ordered in a stern voice. 'The team of ten oxen to pull the wagon will be waiting.'

His remark got a good laugh from the guests as Lara shot him a withering look.

Bykov clapped his hands and stood to make an announcement. 'Now for some entertainment!'

Aristocratic estate owners had their own private ballet companies along with resident orchestras and small theatrical troupes. Bykov motioned for the group to follow him to a palatial private theater Dimitri had designed in red and green granites with a huge white marble proscenium arch and a scarlet velvet curtain.

'The "Lake in the Moonlight" scene from *Swan Lake* will start us off,' Bykov bellowed. The curtains parted, the music began, and six pretty ballerinas started dancing.

The Count's open landau carriage bringing Dimitri and Lara to the train station rumbled along the stone-paved streets of Kishinev, the capital city of Bessarabia. The province also happened to be in the Pale of Settlement, where all Jews in Russia were required to live. A carriage with the valet, the lady's maid, and baggage followed behind. It was nine hundred miles from their home in St Petersburg. The train trip took a whole day, but they would travel in a very comfortable sleeping compartment with a sitting room and a bathroom. On the journey, Dimitri would work on some sketches for a summer palace for his cousin, Prince Andrei Mikhailovich Markhov.

Everything looked so quiet and normal in Kishinev. The gas lights were being lit in the streets, and people strolled along the boulevards looking in store windows. Their carriage came up behind a slow-moving wagon pulled by a tired-looking horse. To his astonishment, Dimitri saw that the wagon bed was piled with dead bodies carelessly covered by a canvas tarp. When the edge of the tarp shifted, revealing the body of a toddler, Dimitri's eyes widened in horror and he sprang up from his seat to look at the corpse. The child was a boy of about two and had thick black curly hair. There was a large patch of dried blood on the side of his head. As his carriage passed the wagon, Dimitri twisted his body so he could still

catch a glimpse of the boy. When the body was out of sight,
he kept standing in the carriage with an expression of revul-
sion and shock. Lara looked up at him.

'Dimitri, you look as if you're going to pass out. Sit down
at once.'

TWO

'Their Imperial Majesties!'

The great fourteen-foot-high gilt double doors of
the Malachite Hall in the Winter Palace swung open.
There stood Tsar Nicholas II and his Tsarina, Alexandra
Feodorovna, the emperor and empress of the Romanov dynasty.
Nicholas, the wealthiest man on earth, was the divine autocrat
of one hundred and thirty million people living on one sixth of
the planet's surface.

A shiver went up Dimitri's spine, and a smile came over
his face; he loved this magical fairytale world in which he
lived. No court in all of Europe could match the wealth and
splendor of the Russian Imperial Court. The magnificent
procession about to begin displayed all the majesty and glory
of the Romanov throne.

Arm in arm, the Imperial Couple slowly walked forward.
In unison, every male member of the Court in uniform or
formal dress bowed. Every female in her beautiful flowing
gown executed a deep rustling curtsey, then they all separated
to provide a wide path for the royals. The Tsar smiled and
nodded at courtiers calling out, 'Greetings, children.' In chorus
they replied, 'Good health, Your Imperial Majesty.' The Tsarina
nodded as well and the slightest of smiles crossed her thin
lips. A tall, slender woman, she was dressed in a gown of
silver brocade embroidered with gold thread. Atop her beautiful
reddish-gold hair was a pearl and diamond tiara with a red
ruby at its center. The Tsar was a lean handsome man with a
beard and mustache and clear blue eyes.

'The Tsar always looks good in white.'

'Nicholas is an attractive man – if you like short men,' Lara added, which made Dimitri frown. He never could tolerate mean cracks about his best friend, whom he'd known since he was ten.

Walking backward and holding his ten-foot ebony staff crowned with gold double eagles, the Grand Marshal led the procession which would parade through the Winter Palace's Great Enfilade, a series of giant interconnected halls to the Palace Cathedral, and back again. Behind Nicholas and Alexandra in the order of succession to the throne came the members of the Imperial Family – the Grand Dukes and Grand Duchesses, the Tsar's blood relations. They were followed by the top hierarchy of the Court led by the head Minister of the Imperial Court. The Emperor's military entourage came next, then the ladies-in-waiting who served the Tsarina, all dressed in gowns of white silk with white jackets and green velvet trains. Her maids-of-honor who followed wore crimson velvet jackets.

'I'm surprised Grand Duke Alexis showed up after all he drank last night,' Lara said under her breath to her best friend, Princess Betsey, who with her husband, Prince Paul, was standing next to her.

'He's not human. He could drink the entire Black Sea and still get up in the morning,' Princess Betsey giggled.

Dimitri ignored the women's comments. He loved watching this incredible spectacle. It was part of an unbreakable court protocol: since the reign of Catherine the Great, the trappings of palace life had stayed *exactly* the same. Dimitri's father, grandfather, great- and great-great-grandfathers were all part of the exact same Imperial Court that now consisted of fifteen thousand people in seven palaces.

'Look who's here,' Dimitri whispered happily to Lara, who in turn smiled.

The Imperial Couple's oldest child, Grand Duchess Olga, who was eight years old, followed right behind her parents. She wore a white silk dress trimmed with lace and with a pale-blue sash, and she smiled at the crowd who were delighted by her appearance.

'I bet she had asked to be part of the court ceremony today

because she made her first communion,' Dimitri said. 'Olga thinks she's a big girl now.'

As the Tsar came nearer, Dimitri could see his friend was tired. And why wouldn't he be? On Easter Monday, the Tsar and Tsarina had to give Easter greetings to five thousand soldiers in the Winter Palace. On Easter Sunday, the Tsar kissed every male of the Imperial household on both cheeks, and the Tsarina did the same with all the women. They had to do it because it was a tradition.

When the Tsar passed Dimitri and Lara, he smiled broadly and silently mouthed the words, 'Come for lunch.' When the Tsarina's eyes rested on Lara, a slight frown came over her usually impassive face. Dimitri knew what she was thinking. Although he was a childhood friend of her husband's, she disapproved of Lara because she thought her a frivolous courtier who wasn't at all religious and gossiped too much. He returned the Tsar's smile and bowed.

Lara leaned close to Dimitri's ear and whispered, 'I suppose I have to change into something simple for the luncheon like a nun's habit or a peasant's sarafan for the Mother Superior.'

'Don't worry about it. You're not going.'

'What wonderful news!'

Lara disliked Alexandra intensely. The Tsarina, the former Princess Alix of the grand duchy of Hesse-Darmstadt, was a Lutheran who had converted to the Russian Orthodox faith upon marrying Nicholas. Alexandra threw herself into her new religion with a zeal that Lara and the rest of the Court thought ridiculous: collecting rare ikons, voraciously reading about Church history, and consulting holy hermits. Lara and the men and women of the Court criticized Alexandra for being cold and distant, speaking rotten Russian, and worst of all, being a prude – especially because she didn't approve of the Court's tradition of extra-marital affairs. She also hated low décolletage. Lara and the Court treated Alexandra unfairly, Dimitri thought. She was unpopular because she was a preternaturally shy person not suited at all for a royal life. But Dimitri knew she actually had a sweet, charming personality in private, and he admired her greatly. She was also very thoughtful. Last year, she had heard that Lara was quite ill with typhoid fever, and she personally brought to their St Petersburg mansion a gift of holy water from Sarov, a greatly venerated site. After she left, Lara got out of her sick bed and flushed it down the toilet. The water was useless, but Dimitri thought what Lara did was outrageous and ungrateful.

Dimitri winked at Olga, who giggled, then caught herself. She loved Dimitri and called him her 'handsome fairy tale prince.' He enjoyed playing games with her and her three younger sisters, Tatiana, Marie, and Anastasia, who were all two years apart in age. Collectively, they were known to the court as 'OTMA.' Dimitri knew that part of his attraction to the Tsar's family was because he and Lara could not have children: one reason the Tsar let him be on such intimate terms with the Imperial Family. At the outdoor court functions where children were sometimes allowed, he always beamed when observing the boys and girls at play. Watching them made him both happy and sad. Their good cheer and boisterousness delighted him, but every time, it drove a stake into his heart – he would never have any children of his own or an heir. His mansions and country estates would never be filled with the noise of happy children.

Princess Betsey smirked as Grand Duchess Ella Feodorovna passed in the procession with her husband Grand Duke Sergei, an uncle of the Tsar. She wore a white silk gown with huge diamond buttons down the front and a necklace of brilliant red rubies.

'Poor Ella, the only woman in Russia who doesn't know her husband's a homosexual,' Lara whispered.

'Sergei went a bit far buggering that handsome priest. One has to draw the line at the Church,' Princess Betsey replied disdainfully.

'Going after his nephew, Pavel, was the limit, but you're right, the Church is out of bounds, *ma chère*,' Lara agreed.

'Goddamn it, woman, do you ever stop?' Dimitri hissed. He was quite fond of Ella, who like her younger sister, Alexandra, had a heart of gold.

When the Imperial Couple and the entourage moved on to the next room, the members of the Court again filled up the room, talking and laughing. Lara chattered away in French to

Princess Betsey, Countesses Eugenia and Nadia, reminding Dimitri of magpies. Although Nicholas preferred Russian, the official court language had always been French. That was the great irony of the Russian Court, they adored everything French. They lived in villas in France for part of the year, had French chefs, French tutors and governesses for their children, and preferred speaking French at home. At least the aristocrats preferred Russian music and song.

Count Alexis Zubov came up to Dimitri. A long-time servant of the Empire, there was not a square inch of empty space on his ribbon-and-medal-covered breast.

'Will you be dining with His Majesty today, Prince Dimitri?' Zubov asked.

Dimitri smiled. There were two problems with his friendship with the Tsar. Many members of the Court were bitterly jealous of the relationship, and second, many tried to get Dimitri to influence His Majesty on a favorite project of theirs.

'Yes, Your Excellency.' He knew what Zubov was going to ask.

'An Imperial charter for a concrete company in Kiev would be most beneficial to the Empire. As an esteemed architect and engineer, you know the possibilities of this material.'

They always throw in some flattery in their request, Dimitri thought.

'Yes, I do. There have been great strides with concrete. I read that the Americans are constructing a skyscraper of rein-forced concrete.'

'Exactly. This is a new material we need to use for Russian factories. None of this wood nonsense anymore. Russia needs to modernize.'

'I agree wholeheartedly, Count Zubov. I may mention it to his Majesty.'

'Wonderful. You must come to my villa in Peterhof. It has become much too small for my family; maybe we can discuss designing a more suitable one.'

'Thank you. I'm always looking for new architectural challenges.'

And he was. Dimitri was one of the rare members of the noble families in Russia who actually knew how to do something. Almost all the aristocracy did was attend the ballet and opera, have sexual affairs, go to endless parties and balls, and above all, gossip. Typically, it was beneath contempt for a nobleman to engage in anything resembling real work, but Dimitri was raised differently. His father, Prince Sergei, didn't want his son to become the usual aristocratic wastrel, and when he saw Dimitri's artistic talent, he encouraged it. When Alexander Kaminsky was designing a new villa for the Markhovs overlooking the Black Sea, Dimitri's father asked him to look at his son's drawings. Dimitri was flattered by Kaminsky's praise and from then on took a keen interest in architecture. When he was of age, his father enrolled him in the Imperial Academy of Arts in St Petersburg to study painting and architecture. To complement his studies, he took classes at the Institute of Civil Engineering to understand the new iron and steel structures used in building and bridge construction. During his education, he still found time for aristocratic fun. He attended his share of parties, hunts, balls, and theater mainly because of the beautiful females present. He adored his gay social world of privilege, but it came a close second to architecture.

After apprenticing a year with Kaminsky, Dimitri wanted to try his own hand at designing. His father had no problem with this, as long as he took no money for his work. A nobleman *never* asked for payment, so Dimitri had worked for free for Kaminsky. While many Russian aristocratic fortunes had melted away like the winter snows in the spring, Dimitri's family was still immensely rich. So, starting with a small pavilion for the niece of Count Bobrinsky, Dimitri began his career as a gentleman architect, though he did insist on payment for his assistants. Villas, estates, libraries, and a bank came his way through his social connections. Because of his engineering training, he also designed bridges and a railway station shed. The Tsar greatly admired his abilities. No one else in Court had such talents, so Nicholas came to rely on him for architectural and engineering advice especially for the Trans-Siberian Railway that was under construction. The Tsar once told him, 'You can train me to be an architect and engineer, Dimitri.'

Dimitri had been disappointed that he wasn't able to spend Easter with the Tsar's family this year like he always did. Anxious to see the girls and his old friend, he rushed back to his St Petersburg mansion to change into something more comfortable. Luncheon with the Tsar's family was always an informal, casual affair which he loved attending.

THREE

N ow dressed in his favorite brown three-piece tweed suit, Dimitri was led to a door of the Imperial Couple's private apartments in the Winter Palace. He was always punctual because Nicholas was a man of strict habits. There before the door stood a huge black servant dressed in scarlet trousers, gold-embroidered jacket, pointed silver slippers, and a fez with a gilded tassel, one of four 'Abyssinians' who silently stood guard before the doors of the private apartments. Their only job was to open and close the doors; they were a left-over from the days of Catherine the Great, when dwarves and exotics played a big part in court ceremony.

'Hello, Jim,' Dimitri said in English.

Jim beamed a white toothy smile. 'Good day to you, sir.'

Jim Hercules was not actually from Abyssinia, but from the Alabama province of America. Originally a servant of Alexander III, the Tsar's father, he was totally loyal to the Imperial Family. Each year, he brought back jars of guava jelly from his vacation in America for the Tsar's daughters. He opened the ten-foot-high door for Dimitri to enter.

The Winter Palace was the symbol of the Tsar's power. Used as the center for the ceremonies of the Russian Court and military parades, it contained one thousand cold empty rooms. But the Tsar's private apartments on the first floor had exactly the opposite feel; warm and homey, crammed with over-stuffed furniture and personal mementoes. Lunch was always served at one o'clock in the White Dining Room.

Dimitri walked into the room and bowed to the Tsar, who was standing alone by the sideboard.

'Dimitri, so good to see you. Let me pour you a glass of vodka.' Nicholas always drank one glass before sitting down to lunch, and Dimitri joined him.

'The procession was magnificent as usual, Nicky,' Dimitri said. Only when they were alone could Dimitri address his friend by his Christian name. The same with the Tsarina, whom he called Alix.

'Oh, that. Whenever we have those, I miss my morning walk with my dogs,' Nicholas replied with a frown. The Tsar had ten magnificent English collies with whom he loved to romp about.

He let out a loud whistle that sounded like a warbling bird call. This was his way of calling for his children and the Tsarina, whom he called 'Sunny.' Within a minute, Alexandra appeared with her black Scotch terrier, Eire, under her arm. She welcomed Dimitri with a radiant smile few people ever saw. Lara hated the dog because it nipped at people under the table, and once ripped her silk stocking. Olga, Tatiana, Marie, and Anastasia, in white linen jumpers with blue sashes, skipped along behind their mother. They ran over to Dimitri to get hugs. To the distress of Monsieur Cubat, their master French chef, the Tsar preferred very simple food like borscht and fish. His favorite meal, roasted suckling pig with horseradish, was being served for lunch today.

'We missed you at Easter, Dimitri,' said the Tsar.

'You should not have gone away,' Grand Duchess Olga scolded him. 'Bad boy!'

Dimitri laughed. Olga was the wittiest child, but also the naughtiest.

'Your little Highness, I promised Count Bykov to come down to look at the completed mansion and make a few revisions.' When talking to the children, the parents spoke in Russian, as did Dimitri. But the Imperial Couple always spoke English to each other, so Dimitri did as well. This habit had to do with the fact that the Tsarina was a granddaughter of Queen Victoria of England. Alexandra had lived with her after her mother died when she was six and she was English to the bone. Alexandra had only been in Russia a month when she married Nicky, so she was at a great disadvantage from the start and still spoke Russian with great difficulty.

Dimitri always felt so happy being with the family. Maybe because this was where his friend Nicky was happiest and completely at ease. Away from the public, the Tsar wore a simple cotton peasant blouse with baggy breeches tucked in soft leather boots. He preferred to be Russian in all aspects of his private life. He once told Dimitri that he had disdain for Peter the Great having built St Petersburg as a city of Western architecture, and making his subjects adopt Western dress and ways or be punished.

As Dimitri ate his lunch, the Grand Duchesses chattered on telling him what they did for Easter.

'I ate the biggest piece of *pashka*,' Marie boasted to Dimitri.

'But I won the Easter egg game,' Tatiana crowed. The family played a game where one struck an Easter egg of another with theirs. The one whose eggshell was broken was out of the game.

'Anastasia bit the ears off my chocolate rabbit when I wasn't looking,' Olga complained. Anastasia giggled at Dimitri.

'Here, my love,' Nicholas said as he handed Alexandra a piece of black bread he'd buttered for her. Dimitri smiled when he saw their exchange of warm looks over such a simple act. Unlike most aristocratic marriages which were arranged for political and financial reasons, theirs was a marriage based on true love. Nicholas had been in love with Alexandra for five years before their marriage in 1894. Now, in 1903, they still acted like young lovers. 'Real love,' Dimitri remembered Nicholas telling him, 'is a gift from God that becomes stronger and purer by the day.'

Dimitri both admired and envied this. He and Lara had been truly in love when they married ten years ago. Their passion for each other was intense as Nicholas and Alexandra's. No one had to force Dimitri and Lara into an arranged marriage. But then the exact opposite of the Tsar's marriage happened to them. He remembered the precise moment when everything had changed.

'Colonel Dorogyn, Larissa?' Dimitri had asked, standing in a state of confusion and disbelief in the middle of the bedroom.

Lara didn't reply, and just kept brushing her hair in front of the mirror of her dressing table. She finally turned in her seat to face him. Her expression was blank.

'Yes, we've been having an affair for almost two months, Dimitri.'

'I didn't believe the gossip, but it wouldn't let up. I had to see for myself. I stood outside Dorogyn's flat, and you came out before midnight.'

'I'm sorry to have hurt you.'

'But do you still love me? Because I still love you with all my heart, Larissa.'

Lara didn't reply, she just looked down at the carpet.

'Answer me!' Dimitri ordered. Tears were burning his eyes.

There was just a deafening silence in their bedroom. Like a crushing blow to his stomach, he realized it was her answer.

'I was always so proud of you for never succumbing to the advances of all these men. Because I was your *special* love, and you'd always be faithful to me, like I was faithful to you.'

'Don't be so provincial, Dimitri. Everyone has affairs. So many men admire me; surely you understand. And you're free to play around too, of course,' she said dismissively.

Dimitri was stunned by Lara's response. In a complete daze, he staggered out of the room and down into the street. For three hours, he drifted like a somnambulist along the quay overlooking the Neva. When he returned home, Lara's maid told him she'd gone out for the evening.

Since divorce was not an option for aristocrats, Dimitri eventually strayed. His affair with his first lover, the young Marya Belyi, was intensely passionate but devoid of any love. It left him sexually satisfied, but empty inside. The next affair, with Countess Sigorsky, lasted a month and gave him the same feeling, as did the scores of them over the past eight years. Only the affair with Princess Betsey, which lasted almost a year, came close to feeling like love.

So, like most couples in the Imperial Court, Lara and Dimitri led two lives, an outwardly proper aristocratic marriage with separate bedrooms, and a second life of discreet sexual affairs.

Dimitri was so lost in this bitter memory that he didn't

realize that Nicky was talking to him. 'Dimitri, who is Russia's greatest composer?' asked the Tsar.

Dimitri snapped out of his reverie. 'That's easy, Nicky – the one and only Tchaikovsky.'

'Our very favorite Russian composer. Don't you think it's time for the Empire to build a memorial to honor the late genius?'

'Long overdue.'

'Then my friend, you will design Tchaikovsky a great memorial – not just a statue but a great complex that has a grand concert hall, a music conservatory, and a music library housing all his work,' said the Tsar excitedly.

'What a tremendous honor, Your Majesty! Thank you so much!' Dimitri replied, almost shouting.

'It will be on a site just off the Nevsky Prospect on the Griboedova Canal, millions will visit it,' said the Tsar grinning from ear to ear.

Dimitri was completely bowled over by the announcement. Throughout the years, Nicholas had personally given him commissions for libraries, public buildings like the Imperial Tax Office, and bridges because of his engineering training. But this was far and away his most prestigious commission.

'I'll start design sketches at once,' he said excitedly. He felt like bolting out of the dining room to his drawing board.

The Grand Duchesses clapped their hands and cheered. 'You are the Tchaikovsky of architects,' shouted Olga.

'You're the only person we thought of for the job,' said the Tsarina, patting Dimitri's hand.

Dimitri smiled at her. If Alexandra didn't act like an empress in the cruel eyes of the Court, she certainly looked like one. Dimitri thought her quite beautiful with her large gray eyes, lovely white complexion, and that red-golden hair. She always wore high-collared dresses that accentuated her graceful long neck. Sometimes, he thought he was a tiny bit in love with her.

'I want this building to be Russian not Western in style. This Art Nouveau style from Paris is quite lovely,' said the Tsar. 'Some architects are doing a Russian version of it. Maybe you could, too, and include some old Muscovite and Kievian symbols.' The Tsar was the leading patron of the arts in Russia, and up on all the latest trends, so he enjoyed giving Dimitri unsolicited design advice. He loved everything in the arts to be Russian-inspired.

'Yes, Your Majesty, it is a most interesting trend.' Dimitri knew of the style, which had come from Paris in the 1890s and now had taken root in Russia. Trends and fashion always arrived late to Russia. He had seen photographs of the work in magazines by its leading architects, Henry van de Velde and Victor Horta. He had visited the Paris World Exhibition in 1900, when the style was first presented internationally. He didn't think much of the facile style; he was a devoted classicist.

'When someone says a thing is "interesting," that means they don't like it, but are too polite to say so.'

Dimitri and Nicholas exchanged grins.

As they finished lunch, the Tsar raised his hand. 'I must go back to work, but first let us show you something special.' He motioned for Dimitri to follow him and the children tagged along. The Tsarina bid Dimitri goodbye, and Jim opened the door to let her out. From the dining room they walked into the Tsar's study. Dimitri's eyes lit up when he saw what was standing on Nicholas's desk.

'Here is this year's Fabergé Easter egg I gave to Sunny. It's called the "Peter the Great Egg."'

Was there anything in Russia that Lara didn't know about? She should be running the Okhrana, Russia's secret police. The newest Easter egg was set in its own three-legged stand. Its outside had intricate detailing of gold cattails surrounding a miniature painting of the Winter Palace that was outlined in little diamonds. The Tsar lifted the hinged lid on the egg. Inside was a miniature gold statue of Peter the Great on a horse atop a black boulder; a copy of the one that stood by the Winter Palace. It was not more than an inch high. As usual, the workmanship was incredible, every detail impeccable.

'Superb!' Dimitri bent over to take a closer look, circling the egg to take in every detail. 'Peter Carl Fabergé is such a genius in everything he designs.'

Fabergé employed two hundred craftsmen in St Petersburg alone, with branches in London, Paris, and Moscow. He also provided exquisite jewelry to the royalty of Europe, including the Tsar's uncle, King Edward VII. The Russian of French descent produced not just the Imperial Eggs but an astounding array of beautifully designed pieces – brooches, cigarette cases, necklaces, clocks, cufflinks, and picture frames. One could even buy pearl and diamond-encrusted knitting needles. No aristocratic Russian celebration was complete without Fabergé gifts to hand out.

'Ah, but Fabergé's greatest act of creativity was the Imperial Easter Eggs – started by my father,' the Tsar said proudly.

Nicholas had continued the tradition begun by his father, Alexander III, in 1885 by commissioning Fabergé to create two Easter eggs each year: one for his mother, the Dowager Empress, and one for the Tsarina. The design and choice of materials was left up to Fabergé, who hid the annual designs under a cloak of secrecy. His brilliant idea was to use the egg as a shell which would be opened to reveal a 'surprise.' The very first was the 'Hen Egg,' a white enameled egg lined with gold that, when opened, held a little golden hen. But Fabergé didn't design the eggs, he only provided the basic idea every year then let his master designers carry it out to the most minute detail.

'You know, Nicky, before they were exhibited for the first time in Paris three years ago, the world outside of the Court didn't know the Imperial Easter Eggs even existed,' Dimitri said, while still examining the egg. 'It sort of angers me that it's no longer our special secret.'

Nicholas patted Dimitri on the back and nodded in agreement.

'Mama feels the same way.'

'What treasure did she receive this Easter?'

'I sent her the "Royal Danish Egg." It's done in blue and white enamel, and the surprise is a double portrait of her mother and father.'

'Ah, she'll love that.'

The Dowager Empress Maria Feodorovna had been a Danish princess. She lived in Anichkov Palace in St Petersburg, but spent part of the year in Copenhagen, where she was now.

'I'm looking forward to seeing it.' Dimitri liked the Dowager, but she, too, harshly criticized Alexandra and drove the Court against her.

'I'll wager you still think the "Trans-Siberian Railway Egg" is the best of all.'

Nicholas was absolutely right. That egg from 1901 was made in honor of the Trans-Siberian Railway that was under construction. On the outside was a map of Russia with the route of the railway to the Pacific Ocean engraved in silver. But it was its surprise inside that was so incredible. Inside was a scale model of the locomotive and five cars of the Siberian Express. When connected together, they measured one foot in length. A few turns of a golden key and the loco-motive of gold and platinum actually pulled the train. It was an unbelievable piece of workmanship. Dimitri didn't envy Fabergé; every year's masterpiece made the next egg more difficult to surpass.

'Yes, *that* is my very favorite. I've gone into the display room to look at it many times.' Most of the Fabergé items were kept in a special room at the Alexander Palace at Tsarskoe Selo, the Tsar's retreat outside the city. The Tsarina and the Dowager Empress kept a few in their private apartments. Olga tugged on Dimitri's arm. 'The "Lilies of the Valley Egg" is my favorite because it has a picture of me that pops up,' she exclaimed. 'And *me*,' shouted Tatiana in indignation. That was an unusual Art Nouveau design with the pink enameled egg covered in lilies of the valley, each made of a pearl crested by tiny diamonds.

Dimitri affectionately put his hand behind Tatiana's head and pulled her toward him. She hugged his thigh tightly. What a wonderful feeling, he thought as he stroked her soft dark hair. She didn't let go, and he didn't want her to. To hug a child, to caress its hair, to watch it sleep were sensations he desperately wanted to experience. But it was never to be. After two years of trying, Lara did not get pregnant. After his wife's first infidelity, they never shared a bed again.

'Give Dimitri his gift, Papa,' Olga cried. Tatiana released her grasp and began jumping up and down clapping her hands with glee.

'Dimitri Sergeyevich, this is our Easter gift to you from

Sunny and the family.' He held out a gorgeous cigarette box
enameled in light blue that was lined with tiny diamonds in
an X-pattern. It had a little gold Russian eagle mounted in its
middle. As an architect, he liked the fact that Fabergé never
went in for an ostentatious display of precious gems but
subordinated them to the overall design of the piece and
focused on the incredible enameled finishes. Enamels were
applied by fusing a thin layer of powdered glass, heated to
600 degrees centigrade, on a metal surface. Fabergé's genius
was creating a hundred colors – blues, purples, pinks, and
greens with an amazing translucent depth made possible by
multiple applications.

'We had them filled with your favorite Turkish cigarettes,'
Olga said excitedly.

'Thank you so much, Your Majesty. And to Your Highnesses,'
Dimitri said, bowing to Olga and her sister. 'You know I'll be
using my gift immediately.'

'You smoke too much, Dimitri,' Tatiana scolded him. Her
nickname for him was 'Old Smokestack.'

'Don't you dare leave without taking our gift for Larissa,'
commanded Olga.

'A beautiful blue Fabergé hairbrush and comb that *I* picked
out,' Tatiana said proudly.

'Now I must return to running the Empire. There's been
such a fuss about the riot in Kishinev. Everyone's in a fury
over it,' said the Tsar in an annoyed tone. 'Even Teddy
Roosevelt and the United States are angry.'

Dimitri was just about to blurt out that he'd seen a wagon
of dead bodies in Kishinev, but he held his tongue. On the
train ride home to St Petersburg, the image of the curly-haired
baby kept running through his mind. But since he'd gotten
back, he had thought less and less about it. Nicky's mention
of the riot jolted his memory, and the image vividly returned.
It occurred to Dimitri that nobody had explained the extent
of bloodshed of the riot to Nicky.

'Yes, on the way home we saw—' he began, but Nicky
interrupted him.

'The Jews are money-lenders who take advantage of the
simple peasant. They are tavern-keepers who get their

customers drunk, causing widespread resentment. No wonder we have these occasional attacks,' Nicholas said testily.

The Tsar swung Tatiana into his arms and gave her a big kiss on her rosy cheek. The children ran off to the nursery.

'Ah, von Plehve has arrived.'

Vyacheslav von Plehve, the Minister of the Interior, bowed when he entered the study. A stout man with bushy receding hair and a walrus mustache, he handled the Empire's domestic affairs, and was also director of the Imperial Police. He said nothing because court etiquette dictated that one never spoke first to the Emperor.

'Von Plehve here says the Jews stand in the forefront of the revolutionary movement. You remember, Dimitri, Jews killed my grandfather.'

As a young boy, Dimitri remembered the assassination of Alexander II, the 'Tsar Liberator' who freed the serfs and had just eased the restrictions on Jews. Blown to bits by a bomb in the street in 1881, they brought him back to the palace literally in pieces. He died on a blood-soaked sofa as his thirteen-year-old grandson, Nicholas, looked on in horror. Nicky had never recovered emotionally from the event.

'Here is the survey of the land where the Memorial will go,' the Tsar said handing Dimitri a rolled drawing.

As the Tsar was about to address von Plehve, a servant entered carrying his personal mail on a large silver platter.

'There may be a letter from Mama about her Easter egg,' said the Tsar excitedly as he sifted through the mail. 'What's this? It's marked "private." He held up a small flat parcel. 'It's postmarked from Suez.' When he opened it, inside was a dirty piece of blue cloth. A puzzled look came over his face.

'Suez, Egypt!? Don't touch it, Your Majesty. Drop it on the floor!' screamed von Plehve. 'For God's sake, don't touch it!' Nicholas did as he was told.

'It's infected with plague germs!' von Plehve cried out.

Dimitri fought back his panic-stricken urge to run out of the study. He frantically looked about and saw a large pair of scissors on the Tsar's desk. Using them like tongs, he carefully lifted up the filthy piece of cloth. Von Plehve had picked up a metal waste basket, and Dimitri dropped the cloth in it. The Minister shouted for his Imperial police officers to come in.

'The Okhrana's laboratory will test this, but I know it's plague.'

The officer to whom he handed the can, widened his eyes in horror and swallowed hard. Holding the can away from his body as if there was a king cobra inside, he slowly walked out.

'This is deadlier than any bomb,' Nicholas shouted. 'The entire palace – the children could have been infected.'

Dimitri shook his head in disbelief. Who would want to kill the Tsar and his family in such a horrible way? What had Nicholas done to deserve this?

FOUR

'Welcome home, Mistress Katya.'

Doctor Katya Alexandrovna Golitsyn was so glad to be home. When the *droshky* pulled in front of the great house on Konnogvardeysky Boulevard, her heart had soared. The three-story yellow stone mansion had eleven tall windows overlooking a little park, and all were ablaze with light like a welcoming beacon.

The ancient wrinkled face of Sasha, the family servant standing in the glowing entrance hall in his rumpled sack of a black suit, was a cherished sight after her long journey. There had been two kinds of slaves, or serfs, when they were emancipated back in 1861: field serfs who worked the land; and house serfs working as servants. But to gain their freedom, house serfs had to pay their master thirty rubles, or guarantee personal service for two more years. Sasha chose the latter and had stayed with the family now for fifty-two years. He was as loyal to Katya as he had been to her grandfather.

'My Sasha,' she cried out, and gave him a kiss on the cheek. Sasha ordered the coachman standing behind her to bring the luggage into the entrance hall. As she was taking off her coat, a black and white cat bounded up to her.

'Noskey missed you very much. He slept on your pillow every night,' Sasha said.

'My darling Noskey!'

Katya swooped up the cat and cuddled him, pressing him against her face. The smell and feel of his soft fur were wonderful after so long a trip. She and her friend, Dr Clara Deverenko, had been in Bucharest for a medical conference on infections of the stomach lining during the week after Easter. They enjoyed the lectures, despite the fact that they were the only female doctors who attended. While Russia could proudly boast that it had more women lawyers and doctors than any other European country, the male doctors who came from all over Europe were unimpressed. They made jest of female doctors and treated them as they would servant girls, often implying that a woman didn't have the brains or disposition to be a doctor. Clara, who was quite pretty, had an especially hard time fending off advances and lewd remarks. But despite the insulting treatment, the trip had been worth it.

'You're just in time for dinner, Mistress Katya,' Sasha said.

'There's my doctor!' boomed a voice from the top of the staircase.

Katya's father, Aleksandr Vassilievitch Golitsyn, marched down the marble steps of the great curving staircase. A stout pink-faced man in his fifties, he was dressed in a black suit with a waistcoat. He had a reddish-brown beard and held a cigarette in an ivory holder.

'Katya, my love!' he cried out. He threw his arms around his daughter, giving her a long embrace. She loved the smell of his sweet-flavored Turkish cigarettes that hung about him, as if it were a cologne.

'Hello, my delightful papa.' From the great dining room to her right came her sister, Yelena, a pale girl of twenty-five. She held her four-year-old, Irina, by the hand. Her husband, Fydor Erorovitch, a partner in her father's textile business, followed them. Yelena and Fydor lived with them in the great house. Then came Boris, her eighteen-year-old brother, in his black high-school uniform with high collar. Waddling along with them was Valentina, the family's *nyanya*, holding Natasha, Yelena's four-month-old infant. Katya rushed into the nanny's arms, then kissed the baby on the head. This devoted, illiterate, superstitious peasant had taken care of every child in the family for the last forty years, wiping noses, telling bedtime stories, and keeping them in line. Only for the most serious offenses of behavior did she consult the parents. Since Katya's mother had died from cholera when she was seven, Valentina had been her real mother.

'My dear *nyanya*, how are you?'

'Ah, my knees again. My little Katya, could you take a look at them after the meal?' One of the drawbacks of being the doctor in the family was that everyone wanted medical attention.

Another person emerged into the grand entry. Ivan Pavlovitch Telegin also worked for her father, as the chief financial officer. Katya knew immediately why he was here tonight, as well as many other nights.

'So good to see you, Katya Alexandrovna. I hope you had a pleasant journey, the train ride from Bucharest to St Petersburg is very long.' Ivan clicked his heels then bowed to kiss her hand.

'Yes, I'm quite worn out,' Katya replied, almost withdrawing her hand before Ivan completed his kiss.

Though incredibly proud of his daughter, Aleksandr Vassilievitch thought it was time for her to get married. Ivan was the main candidate for a husband, but Katya would have none of it. He was cultured and intelligent, but she had no desire to raise a family yet. She wasn't her sister. Her profession came first.

'I'm starving,' Katya added with a laugh. 'I've had nothing but train-station food.' Her father took her arm and escorted her, leading the family into the big, bright dining room lined with dark green marble paneling.

Valentina handed the baby to Sonya, the family wet-nurse. Unlike most *nyanyas*, Valentina was welcome to eat at the table with the family.

'Time for the little one's dinner, too,' Valentina said. Looking at Sonya's huge breasts, Katya could imagine her feeding an entire regiment of the Tsar's Guard.

'Sit down, let's eat,' came the command from her father.

There on the sideboard was a feast of *zakuski*, fresh caviar, herring filets, smoked sturgeon, *balyk*, suckling pig, roast chicken, cucumbers in brine, cold salmon, and pâtés of meat and cabbage. Bottles of iced vodka, ordinary white to peppered, were also in abundance. For a Russian, iced vodka had to have needles of ice formed inside the bottle not merely chilled in an ice bucket the way the French did. The family chattered away over the meal.

'There's a performance of *The Seagull* next week, would you allow me the pleasure of taking you, Katya Alexandrovna?' Ivan asked in an eager tone of voice.

'What night would that be, Ivan Pavlovitch?'

'Wednesday, but it's playing every night next week, if that's more convenient for you.'

'I'm so sorry, I must work the evening shift at the hospital. Come to think of it, I work every night next week.'

Katya washed down each mouthful of food with a glass of vodka, sending a bolt of fire down her throat and into the stomach. Vodka, her father taught her, called for food, and food called for vodka.

'The vodka in Bucharest was like rubbing alcohol. So good to taste the world's best vodka again,' Katya said, raising her glass. The family lifted their glasses in agreement.

The servants dressed in black suits with white cravats and gloves brought in the main courses, including her favorite quail pies with truffles à la Perigueux. Like all wealthy Russian households, hers boasted a French chef. The wines were French except for one fine Crimean vintage.

'What did you think of the Somov exhibit, Katya Alexandrovna?' asked Ivan.

'It didn't impress me for some reason,' she replied with a frown, not wanting to encourage him. She took a big bite of her quail pie.

Coffee was served after the dessert of pineapple jelly whipped with champagne and topped with fruit. The after-dinner conversation always dwelt on the same topic, St Petersburg versus Moscow.

'St Petersburg is the new Russia, the "the window on Europe,"' Aleksandr Vassilievitch boasted. 'The Muscovites are coarse and puerile. And St Petersburg definitely has the best theater.'

'They may have Chekhov, but we have the greatest ballerinas, Pavlova and Kschessinska,' said Yelena.

'They hate our Western ways,' added Katya, blowing a smoke ring into the air. Her niece, Irina, tried to poke her hand through it. 'They say we're Western, not Russian, hah! We are the *new* Russians – with *new* ideas.'

'And we have the most creative painters,' Ivan added enthusiastically.

'We love the arts more than they,' said her father, who winked at Katya. The new patrons of arts in Russia today were the great industrialists like her father. They supported the actors, painters, poets, composers, and dancers in both St Petersburg and Moscow. Aleksandr Vassilievitch was the second largest textile industrialist in Russia after the Morozov family. As a young man, he had gone abroad and studied the textile industry in Manchester, England. He'd brought back new ideas and machinery to advance the Russian textile industry, turning the modest business his father, Pyotr, had begun into a great fortune. He was also proud that he treated his workers better and paid them more than the Morozovs. Katya wanted to believe she had a part in that decision.

'And does Moscow have the Pavlov State Medical University? No!' he added.

A cheer went up at his pronouncement. It was the first medical college for women in the Empire, and Katya was in its first graduation class in 1900. Unlike most Russian fathers, Aleksandr Vassilievitch believed in educating women beyond high school. Both Katya and Yelena had sharp intellects which he insisted on expanding, though her sister's main goal in life was to be a mother. Their brother, Boris, was also very smart, but he was lazier than a peasant, which constantly infuriated their father.

It was getting late, and Valentina gathered up little Irina for bed. She fell asleep in the *nyanya*'s arms as she was carried up the grand staircase.

Her father ordered Boris upstairs to finish his schoolwork. Yelena and Fydor bid them good night. Ivan Pavlovitch also took his leave, extracting a reluctant promise from Katya to go to the Théatre Français next month. Before Katya started the climb, she hugged her father good night.

'Come stay with me for a bit in the study,' asked her father in an almost pleading tone. 'I missed you so.'

Katya was exhausted, but she followed him to the great mahogany-paneled library with the polished parquet floors. The fire was crackling in the wide fireplace. Aleksandr Vassilievitch lit a cigarette for his daughter and for himself, then plopped down in his tall leather chair behind his desk. With a full stomach of food and vodka, Katya collapsed into a chair. Many times, she had sat here talking with her father into the night. They both found each other good company, trading stories, jokes, and opinions about everything under the Russian sun. Katya remembered fondly how grown-up she felt the first time her father offered her a cigarette. Aleksandr Vassilievitch loved his family, Russia, and his textile business, in that order.

'Back to the clinic tomorrow, eh? Dr Trofimov called this morning, wondering where you were.'

'We were a bit late leaving Kishinev. Bad business there, they say. Fifty dead and over five hundred injured in a pogrom.' Katya blew a smoke ring and watched it disappear.

'The Jews are a smart but unfortunate people,' mused Aleksandr Vassilievitch, picking out bits of tobacco from his tongue.

Katya nodded, tossed her cigarette into the fire, then stood up to kiss her father good night.

FIVE

At exactly 9 p.m., the Grand Master of Ceremonies struck his ebony staff embossed in gold with the double-headed eagle three times. The taps on the floor of the Great Gallery in the Catherine Palace always sounded like pistol reports. 'Their Imperial Majesties!' he cried out.

A complete hush fell over the three thousand people milling about in the gigantic ball room. All men bowed and ladies curtsied in unison. Dimitri, wearing formal white tie and tails, bedecked with medals for service to Russia, surveyed the crowd and smiled. The beauty and splendor of the scene were magical to him. He had been to hundreds and hundreds of Imperial Balls in all the palaces, but the incredible spectacle always sent a bolt of excitement through him. Before him stood Lara and thousands of women with jewels covering every neck, head, ear, wrist, and finger. The men also wore diamonds on their cuff links and shirt studs. Because the room was lined with fourteen-foot-high mirrors on both sides, it gave the impression that the ballroom went on forever, and that there were thousands more guests.

As Nicholas and Alexandra appeared, and the orchestra struck up 'God Save the Tsar,' Dimitri saw that his friend was wearing his usual public expression of smiling warmth and confidence – despite the fact that he and his entire family could have been murdered by plague less than two months ago. Dimitri was still terribly shaken by the assassination attempt, which had been kept secret from the public. What an incredibly evil thing to do! For weeks, he couldn't help thinking about it. No one could hate the Tsar that much. A madman must have sent that cloth to the palace. Who else would do such a heinous act? Dimitri was impressed that Nicky's face didn't betray a single trace of worry. He looked the brave supreme leader he was.

Alexandra, whom Nicky told nothing of the incident, wore her usual severe expression but looked magnificent. She was wearing a silver brocade gown embroidered with gold thread. Adorning her neck was the Imperial Rivière Necklace, with thirty-six diamonds totaling 470 carats; the largest diamond necklace in the world. The Tsar was in the uniform of the Hussar Guards, a crimson jacket and black trousers with a red stripe. As tradition dictated, the emperor and empress led a polonaise, then one quadrille. After finishing the dances, the Imperial Couple moved through the ballroom to greet guests. Dimitri saw that this was an excruciating experience for Alexandra.

'Here come the blotches,' announced Princess Betsey.

Alexandra's skin always broke out in red blotches when she had to greet the Court. Her beautiful face had blotches on her cheeks and forehead, as well as parts of her arms. She barely said a word to the guests and scarcely looked at them, making her seem cold and haughty.

'Still have to admit she's got great taste in clothes – blotchy skin and all,' Lara said.

A mazurka began, Dimitri bowed to Princess Betsy, and they joined the floor. As usual, Lara had no lack of partners, and she chose Grand Duke Michael, the Tsar's brother. As Betsey chattered away, Dimitri smiled but blanked out everything she said. What a lot of nonsense, he thought. How could he have been in love with this woman for almost a year? These damn men and women never seemed to have an intelligent thought in their heads. Then he let out a sigh; this was the privileged world of outrageous vanity and mendacity into which he was born and, there was no escape. But how nice it would be to have a real conversation with someone for a change!

It was very unusual to have a ball out of season, especially in June and at the Catherine Palace. Normally, the Imperial Family would be spending the month at Spała, their beautiful estate in central Poland. Dimitri had heard through the rumor mill that the Minister of the Interior von Plehve urged the Tsar to hold a ball to invite ambassadors and dignitaries from the foreign countries who'd criticized Russia about the Kishinev incident in order to placate them. Dimitri could make out who those people were in the ballroom. Many were from the Asiatic countries like China and Siam. Except for their eyes and darker tone of skin color, they looked exactly like everyone else. Some ambassadors were being introduced to the Imperial Couple. Dimitri noticed that all the Court women were displaying even more décolletage than usual, in defiance of the Tsarina.

Lara had made sure the neckline of her scarlet and gold gown was especially low tonight. She had already danced two mazurkas and four waltzes before she caught up with her husband, who had finished his dance with the Countess Trigorin.

'And how is our beautiful Countess Trigorin tonight . . . you wicked boy?'

The Countess was Dimitri's current lover and knew his wife didn't care just as he didn't care about her affairs – as long as they were done with discretion.

'You should tell Prince Gayev to resist the temptation to put his hand on your ass when you're dancing, no matter how perfect it is.'

Lara shrieked with laughter, putting her scarlet-gloved hand over her mouth to stifle the outburst. 'Oh yes, I'll be sure to do that. But several of my partners have already beat him to it.'

Dimitri gave a sardonic smile. At least his wife had a sense of humor to match her beauty. It was one of the very few pleasant things left in their marriage; at times they amused each other. On the dance floor young officers with brilliant decorations on their tunics whirled young girls around on the polished wood floor. The officers had to make sure their spurs didn't get caught up in their partners' gowns in the excitement. Couples seemed to glide on air, producing a brilliant effect of color mixed with sparkling of diamonds, rubies, and emeralds. They looked as though they had their heads up in the stars and were soaring in their own separate universe. To Dimitri, they seemed to have wings on their heels. That was the feeling he'd had at that wonderful age. The dancers' faces were flushed pink from exertion.

Along the mirrored and gilt walls were the old doyennes in white satin gowns flitting their fans and watching the goings-on. These crones were always sizing up the young girls and gossiping about their chances for a choice marriage, like men examining the stock at a horse auction. At midnight, a buffet supper would be served in an adjoining room of the enfilade. The luxurious feast would have red, black, and gray caviar, blini with sour cream, lamb, roast beef, and chicken. Vodka and champagne would be chilled in blocks of ice.

'So many commoners invited tonight,' Lara said, whipping her scarlet and gold fan about. As usual, she looked stunning. Her blonde hair was decorated with a diadem set with two rows of diamonds. A *ferronière* with a single diamond of one square inch crossed her forehead.

'But extremely rich commoners,' replied Dimitri.

Before Lara could reply, she was swept onto the floor by Sir John Sinclair, a British diplomat to the Imperial Court. Dimitri looked to his right and saw General Zamansky, an eighty-year-old in the Lancers Regiment.

'Damn hot in here, Prince Dimitri,' bellowed the general.

'Yes, it is rather uncomfortable.'

'The Tsar invites too many damn people, like all these diplomatic fellows. Useless bunch, those. I was talking to one, and he had the gall to say . . .'

Not wanting to be stuck talking to an old windbag like Zamansky, Dimitri bowed and excused himself. He walked into the long corridor that connected the ballroom to other rooms of the enfilades. Stationed at ten-yard intervals like statues along the corridor were soldiers of the Chevalier Guards with silver breastplates and eagle-crested helmets. On one side of the corridor were tall French doors that opened onto a park. Dimitri took a cigarette from his new Fabergé case and walked out. The night air was cool and refreshing after the closeness of the great ballroom. The fragrance of the poplars and roses was quite strong, and the light from the Catherine Palace cast a golden glow over the park's lawn. He was surprised to see a woman standing by herself. It was odd to see a young woman just standing around, looking off into the moonless night, and not in perpetual motion on the dance floor. He decided to stroll over.

'Beautiful evening,' he called out. The woman didn't seem startled by his words. She turned to face him. He could see in an instant why she wasn't dancing. She wasn't at all homely, but rather plain. Her hair was piled à la mode, and she wore expensive earrings and a becoming diamond necklace. Her trim little figure looked good in a lilac gown spotted with little rubies. Because of the thousands of women he had met over the years, Dimitri instinctively made these judgements. He had been tutored by the master of criticism, Lara. She could evaluate a female in a millisecond. Lara would deem this woman too plain to be wearing such an expensive gown and fancy jewelry. 'A mule in horse's harness' was the expression she liked to use. Women who looked like that usually stood by a wall watching the dancing. Lara would say she wasn't a wallflower; she *was* the wall. But Dimitri found the woman's wide eyes very striking; they were of an extraordinary corn-flower-blue. It was a pleasure to look her straight in the eyes because they were so remarkable.

'Not as humid as a regular summer night,' replied the woman. Her voice immediately told Dimitri she was well-bred and educated.

Because it seemed all women nowadays smoked, he offered her a cigarette from his Fabergé case, and she accepted it.

'I'm Dimitri Sergeyevich.' He gave a slight bow.

'Katya Alexandrovna. Beautiful Fabergé case.'

'Thank you, it was an Easter gift. Yes, the summer heat can be quite harsh,' Dimitri said, adding to her comment about the weather; a safe conversation topic at a ball. 'I was inspecting the construction of a new villa near Krasnoe Selo, and I was quite bowled over by the sun. I had to sit in the shade a bit.'

'Even the healthiest person can get sunstroke very quickly. You were wise to take shelter. I've seen many people especially, the elderly, suffer and even die from exposure in the sun. You must also drink plenty of water.'

'Ah, so you volunteer to minister to the sick? How noble to use your time that way. I wish more society women did that.'

The woman was clearly amused by his comment.

'I hope not. I'm paid a salary for being a doctor – but then, I'd probably do it for free.'

Dimitri turned to face her.

'A doctor, you say? What a fine thing!' He was genuinely impressed. He threw away his cigarette.

'You've never met a female doctor?' Katya had a bemused look on her little heart-shaped face.

Dimitri thought for a second, then shook his head.

'You're the very first.'

'Doctor Katya Alexandrovna Golitsyn of the St Igor Hospital – by way of the Pavlov Medical College,' she announced, extending her hand.

'Prince Dimitri Sergeyevich Markhov of the St Petersburg Imperial Academy of the Arts and the Institute of Civil

Engineering,' he replied, clicking his heels, bowing, and kissing her hand.

'A *woman* doctor! What times we live in,' he added.

'A *prince* with a university degree – and one that actually knows how to do something! What times we live in.'

They both laughed. As they strolled through the park promenade lined with lime trees, he found out that tonight she had accompanied her father, Aleksandr Vassilievitch Golitsyn, an immensely wealthy textile industrialist, one of the very richest men in Russia – everyone in Court knew him. Katya said with no embarrassment that she had danced with her father twice, but other than that she'd had only three requests to dance, and that was due to her father's money and influence. Dimitri admired her candor. While he knew that would crush many girls, it didn't seem to make the slightest bit of difference to Katya. As they walked, the music from the ballroom filled the summer night.

'Listen!' she said. 'They're playing the polonaise from *Eugene Onegin*!'

'You're an admirer of Tchaikovsky?'

'The greatest composer ever. Mozart, Bach, and Beethoven step aside!' Her eyes lit up.

'My opinion exactly!' He didn't want to brag that he was designing a memorial building for the composer.

'Of course, my next question will be, what's your favorite piece?' she asked.

'That's an easy one. The *Capriccio Italien*,' Dimitri said.

'Mine is the Concerto Number One in B-Flat Minor for Piano and Orchestra. The *Capriccio Italien* has such a marvelous middle section but the beginning is so loud and military,' Katya said in a critical tone.

Dimitri nodded. He liked her forthrightness. Most women never spoke their mind unless gossiping.

'Well, there's a reason for that opening. Tchaikovsky was on holiday in Italy, and the villa he was staying in was right next to a military garrison that woke him up every morning with bugles. So, he worked it into the piece,' he said.

'Really?'

'He told me that.'

'You met Tchaikovsky?' Katya stared at him, her lips slightly parted.

'Yes, a few times. He was a great favorite of the Tsar. A fine fellow.'

'It's sad he died so young from cholera. Think of all the music he could have written.'

'Yes, suicide is especially tragic.'

'Suicide?' she asked in an astounded voice.

'Yes, Tchaikovsky was tormented because he was cursed with "the unspeakable vice of the ancient Greeks." Couldn't live with it any longer.'

The doctor's eyes widened in surprise. They had a very inviting, warm quality to them.

'Is that true?' she asked under her breath, looking around to see if anyone was listening.

Dimitri nodded and grinned at the doctor's reaction. He enjoyed sharing a little gossip with an intelligent person.

'Prince Dimitri, you're *scandalizing* me,' she said in mock horror. 'Tell me more!' They both burst out laughing.

'God's truth, I could spend an entire afternoon shocking you with stories from the Court – sordid affairs, ménages, incest . . .'

'I may just take you up on that offer. But first, tell me about this villa design you suffered in the sun for. What is the style?'

Whenever Dimitri was asked about his designs, he launched into feverish descriptions of the buildings, their design, and the materials they used. Tonight was no exception. Katya listened with great interest; not the usual bored attitude he received from his wife and fellow courtiers.

'Ah, you sound like a committed classicist with your Corinthian capitals and pilasters. But my arts circle says the Russian Style Moderne, or what they call the Art Nouveau, is the current style. Are you interested in that mode, Prince Dimitri?'

'No . . . not really. It seems rather superficial and . . .'

'Have you seen Fedor Schechtel's Levenson Printshop in Moscow? It just pops with creativity, the colors, shapes of the windows; so marvelous,' Katya interrupted with great enthusiasm.

'Well, no, I . . .'

'You know of course he did the Yaroslavsky Rail Terminal there, it's almost finished. I saw it when I was at a conference in Moscow last fall. That incredible arch in the tower.'

'You seem quite up to date on the vanguards of the artistic movement.'

'St Petersburg is definitely the center of all that's advanced in the arts – except for architecture, maybe,' Katya said, then immediately regretted the last part of her reply.

'Yes, Russia is definitely undergoing a creative renaissance.'

'Our Silver Age,' said Katya proudly, 'the new Russian cultural rebirth with Sergei Diaghilev, Mikhail Vrubel, Leon Bakst, Gorky, Valentin Serov, Fabergé, Pavlova, and of course, Chekhov. Oh, so many! And I didn't even name one composer. Rimsky-Korsakov – there!'

'And of course, Glazunov,' Dimitri added.

'No one loves the arts more than a Russian,' she said enthusiastically.

'I'll wager you've seen all of Chekhov's plays at the Moscow Art Theater.'

'Of course – with its new interior designed by Shekhtel and Ivanov Fomin. Have you been there? Well, you should,' said Katya without waiting for an answer. 'You'll see real human drama, not papier-mâché pastiche and melodramatic make-believe. *The Cherry Orchard* will be premiering soon.'

'It sounds like I really must see it,' Dimitri said, intrigued by her enthusiasm.

'Oh my, we've walked so far,' said Katya in a surprised voice. The music coming from the Catherine Palace was very faint now. 'I must get back, Prince Dimitri. My father will think I've run off with one of the Cossack Guards.'

They both did an about-face and strolled back to the palace, talking about Tchaikovsky's *Nutcracker Suite*. Katya wondered if a hundred years from now it would still be played every Christmas; she hoped so because it was so brilliant. As they neared the row of glass doors, a black and white object skittered out the shrubbery and raced by them.

'Oh, I adore cats. I have one,' Katya said, turning to watch it disappear in the shadows.

'I love them too. I always had one or two when I was growing up, but my wife hates cats. We have a dog, a borzoi named Fedor,' Dimitri said.

Katya brought her hand to her heart. 'I love cats, especially when they sleep cuddled up to you.'

Dimitri was touched by her lack of artifice. It was such a contrast to ladies of the Court, who never said anything they really meant. When they reached the ballroom, she turned to him.

'My arts circle meets every Thursday night at seven. The address is at 23 Tverskaya. You must come sometime, Prince Dimitri,' Katya said, spotting her father in the vast crowd and waving to him.

The orchestra broke into a waltz, and she and Dimitri exchanged big smiles.

'Tchaikovsky's waltz from *Eugene Onegin*,' Dimitri exclaimed.

'My favorite waltz,' Katya added.

'And *mine*. Doctor Golitsyn, may I have this dance?' Dimitri asked with a bow.

'You most certainly may.' They glided onto the dance floor and whirled skillfully among the other scores of couples. Dimitri noticed that despite tonight's lack of partners, Katya was an excellent dancer. Her petite, lithe body moved gracefully through the steps. She really was quite attractive, he realized, noting her flushed cheeks and sparkling blue eyes as he twirled her around.

When the dance was finished, Dimitri bowed to her again, and they bid each good night. As he walked up to Lara, who had finished dancing with General Sorokin, she crinkled her nose.

'My God, Dimitri! Was that a *pity* dance? *Who* were you dancing with?'

SIX

Katya pulled the thermometer from Pyotr's mouth and nodded with great satisfaction. *This new Bayer aspirin is a miracle drug*, she thought. *It's true, Germans are the best scientists in the world.*

'You see, I told you that if you rested and took the pills, your fever would go down.'

The little boy looked up at her with watery blue eyes in a thin pale face. Katya took the red stuffed bear off the nightstand and danced it on his blanket. She got a wan smile out of the six-year-old.

'Visiting hours are almost here. Guess who's coming to see you? *Mama!*'

That got a bigger smile. Katya recorded the temperature on his chart and watched him play with the bear. She waved to him and moved on to the next patient four beds down. It annoyed her that St Igor Hospital had no separate children's section. Adults and the little ones were all lumped together in men's and women's wards.

'Mr Yevgeny Victorivitch Kazimirov, roll over and let me see the stitches on your back,' Katya ordered in a friendly voice. She had quickly learned being a woman doctor brought resistance from the more modest male patients who didn't like being examined, especially near their private areas. Kazimirov's incision was on his lower back, perilously close to his derrière, which embarrassed him. The fat forty-year-old businessman grumbled then slowly rolled over. Katya yanked up his white linen nightshirt.

'Mmm, doing nicely,' she said prodding the wound. 'We need more salve to help heal it, then we can remove those cat-gut stitches. Next time, you won't ride your horse after so much vodka.' That brought a laugh out of Kazimirov. She marked his chart and moved on.

'My friend, Vladimir Ivanovich Prigozhin, stick out that leg and show me your dog bite. He probably thought it was a nice delicious bone, your legs are so skinny.' Katya had also learned that you could catch more flies with honey than with vinegar.

Prigozhin chuckled and extended a white bony leg with a big bandage on it. Katya gingerly pulled the bandage away. 'It's still red, but it's not infected, and that's what's most important. Sister! Come apply some petroleum ointment to Mr Prigozhin's wound here.' Infection was by far the biggest killer in the hospital. But Katya had trained under the new germ theory that bacteria caused disease and infection. Now that hand-washing and sterile bandaging were standard practice in the hospital, infections had plummeted.

A nurse in a white nun's habit came up and did as she was ordered. Katya walked down the long aisle between the beds, and she went through the glass and wood doors in the women's ward. Like the men's area, it had a high open ceiling supported by white cast iron trusses with side walls of out-swinging glass windows.

'Madame Sviazhsky, how is that stomach of yours doing?'

'Oh doctor, it feels that a dozen Cossacks are dancing inside me, kicking their legs out.'

'You Cossack devils in there! Stop that dancing!' Katya said, poking her finger in Madame Sviazhsky's plump belly under her nightshirt. The patient started a fit of giggling.

'Sister, fetch the Bromo-Seltzer!' When Katya's father had returned from his trip to the United States, he'd brought these blue bottles of medicine. They really eased his stomach troubles, so she ordered some for the hospital. One mixed the granules with water to make a fizzy concoction. Like many of the well-to-do women in the hospital, Madame Sviazhsky's ailments were largely in her head. Why were so many women here like that? Were they bored, and needed imaginary sicknesses to devote their time to? Or did they do it to get the attention of their husbands, which had the exact opposite reaction? They *wanted* to be gravely ill. All Madame Sviazhsky had was simple indigestion.

'We will prepare you a nice hot-water bottle and get the old samovar boiling for a nice glass of tea with some mint. How would that be, madame?'

'Oh, thank you. I am so glad I have a woman doctor to attend me. You really listen to my complaints and respond – not like these fool male doctors.'

Katya smiled at her patient and wrote some remarks on her chart. The next bed over was Madame Ravenskaya, who never talked to Madame Sviazhsky because she thought she was on a higher social plane.

'Madame Doctor, could you please tell that old crone, Madame Sviazhsky, to stop moaning and groaning so?'

'Yes, madame, I will see to it.'

Madame Ravenskaya had a genuine reason for being here; she had cancer of the liver that seemed to be spreading. Katya knew that when it came to cancer, she or any other doctor was quite powerless to stop it. It was like standing on a railroad track and trying to stop an oncoming locomotive. She only could try to ease Madame Ravenskaya's pain, which meant injections of morphine.

'How is the pain today, madame?'

'It hurts terribly, but I'll get by.' Katya had nothing but admiration for her patient, who took on the excruciating pain with great dignity and courage. She knew Madame Ravenskaya would be dead within two months, so she planned to have her moved home with a private nurse and an ample supply of morphine to spend her final days with her family.

'You'll be getting your injection at eleven,' said Katya in a gentle voice while taking Madame Ravenskaya's pulse, which was on the faint side. 'Then just nod off and have good dreams of all the pleasurable times you've enjoyed.'

'Thank you, Madame Doctor. I have had some good times in my life.'

'A beautiful lady like you must have had wonderful fun.'

Katya finished her rounds, tending to three more female patients. Then Doctor Orlinsky, her supervisor, came up to her.

'Doctor, I'd like your opinion on one of my patients.'

It pleased Katya to be asked her professional opinion by Orlinsky because it meant she had become accepted in a hospital run by men – often very hostile men. He led her to a separate ward on the third floor, for intensive treatment and reserved for the sickest patients. They walked to the bedside of a thin, pale man in his seventies. Katya could imagine how handsome he would have looked like in the picture of health, but now he seemed cadaver-like, a living corpse.

'Mr Shamrayev is suffering from a congenital heart ailment, the left ventricle is not performing properly,' explained Orlinsky in a cold clinical manner, as if there was no sick person lying there. Like most of the male doctors, Orlinsky had no bedside manner; just brusqueness, which Katya always hated. The doctors seemed like meat inspectors impassively examining a side of beef. In their cruel manner, they would explain to families the harsh truth of the situation causing mothers and sisters to break into tears or fall to their knees. Then the doctors would turn their backs on them and walk away. Katya had vowed that when she became a doctor, she would never ever emulate that behavior. Orlinsky gestured for her to listen to his heart with her single-ear stethoscope.

'Yes, the irregularity is quite apparent,' Katya said.

'When you've given it some thought, tell me if the nitro-glycerin would be preferred and the dosage.' He turned on his heels and quickly walked away.

Katya smiled at Shamrayev. 'Is there anything I can get you?' He shook his head weakly and did not return the smile. Although Katya was immensely proud she was a female doctor, she secretly wished she was as pretty as Clara Deverenko, who always seemed to get a more positive reaction from the male patients. She checked her timepiece pinned to the lapel of her white smock. She would be off duty in thirty minutes but since she'd finished seeing her patients, she could do a little checking on Mr Shamrayev.

As she walked down to the basement where the patients' files were stored, she thought about the ball. In particular, Prince Dimitri. What a charming, intelligent fellow. In addi-tion, he was incredibly handsome; she couldn't help but be mesmerized by his good looks. But what impressed her most was how easy it was to talk with him. Like they'd been friends for five years. She had never met another man like him, let alone an aristocrat. So unexpectedly unassuming and friendly. She smiled as she thought about her dance with him. It had been so effortless and exhilarating. Then she grimaced; she hoped she hadn't chattered too much, or come off as too opinionated. Men hated that.

All the patients' files were kept in paper folders, which were stored in a recent invention called the 'filing cabinet.' Instead of stuffing the papers in pigeonholes, one could store them vertically in stacked wooden drawers, so much easier to find. The files were kept in a long, low basement room lit with bare Edison bulbs. The fronts of the cabinets were marked alphabetically; she opened the drawer 'S,' then found Shamrayev's folder. It held his complete medical history; his prior illnesses, and as she could see, his long history of heart ailments. It also had the ages of his father, mother, and grandparents when they died, an important indicator for his own mortality. Katya then noticed a red dot next to the grandfather's name, but she didn't understand what that meant. When she finished, she put the file back in its proper alphabetical place. The red dot came to mind again. Before she closed the drawer, she fanned the rest of the 'S' files. Toward the back, a man named Stolypin also had a red dot. She moved over to the 'T' files and found three more marked with the dots.

Kerensky, a stooped hospital porter who tended to the big room, entered with a sheaf of papers to be filed.

'Kerensky, what does it mean when a name has a red dot next to it?'

'Madame Doctor, in the old days, the government required us to mark the people who had converted from Judaism to the Orthodox Church.'

'Thank you,' Katya replied. 'I would have never thought of that.'

'Oh, it's never done much anymore, Madame Doctor,' he said shutting a drawer and opening another.

As Katya walked back upstairs, she thought of what old Kerensky had just said then remembered the pogrom in Kishinev. Being a Jew these days seemed to be a dangerous occupation.

SEVEN

The sidewalks along the Nevsky Prospect were empty as Dimitri and Lara's carriage clip-clopped down its center. It was going on eight, and everyone was sitting down to supper. Or like them, on their way to the ballet. Because it was a warm night, Dimitri had the carriage windows lowered and was looking out onto the street. Lara, on the seat opposite, scanned the society page for mention of her and her friends.

'I can't believe they'd waste the ink writing about an old hag like Madame Laviska,' she said, shaking her head.

'Larissa, my sweet. Did you ever think that one day you'll look like Madame Laviska?' Dimitri asked contemptuously.

'Promise me to shoot me like a horse if I do.'

As Dimitri continued gazing out the window, a smile came over his face; he was thinking of the ball at the Catherine Palace. For the first time in ages, he had had fun at a ball. The scores and scores of them he had attended over the years had blurred into one boring routine. But Katya had made it special. What a refreshing change to meet such an intelligent, well-informed woman. He could have talked with her another twelve hours; he was enjoying himself that much. She was so easy to talk to. She was opinionated, but that didn't bother him at all. He liked her candor, because she knew what she was talking about. He always compared a friendship to a hand fitting into a glove. If two people hit it off, the hand slipped effortlessly into the glove for a perfect fit. That's how he felt about meeting Katya. The doctor was of course quite plain in comparison with Lara (all women were), but she had such glowing blue eyes, and that warm, comforting smile on her heart-shaped face drew him in. Maybe because they both loved the waltz from *Eugene Onegin*, they were in their own world on the dance floor. He grimaced; he hoped he didn't seem like a puffed-up aristocrat to her.

There were still a few stragglers on the Nevsky this time of night. Men with their heads down, and hands stuffed in their jacket pockets hurrying home. He saw a woman, probably a governess, pulling along a chain of four nicely dressed children. He grinned; it was way past their bedtime, and she was rushing to get them home. The last child, probably the youngest, was slowing them down.

'Stop dragging me,' he heard the little one wail.

Lara looked out the window at the children, then at Dimitri's face.

'Forget about it, Dimitri,' Lara said, returning to the society page. 'Your brother, Ivan, has two sons to carry on the Markhov name,' she added without looking up from her newspaper. Dimitri glowered at her.

The carriage slowed, joining a line pulling up to the front of the theater. Dimitri and Lara climbed out.

'Doesn't General Protopopov look absolutely ancient,' said Princess Lara with a giggle. 'Wasn't he on the general staff of Peter the Great?'

Dimitri wasn't listening to her chatter. He was looking up at the main facade of the theater. He always believed the beautiful aqua-green and gold Mariinsky Theater looked more magnificent at night when it was all lit up. Its tall arched front windows glowed with a magic golden light. In the flickering lights of the carriage lamps, footmen in livery were helping guests get down in front of the theater, including the white-side-whiskered General Protopopov in his heavily medaled black-and-gold uniform. He seemed as stiff as a board as he tried to step down to the sidewalk. But no matter how ill or infirm a Russian was, they would make it from their deathbed to the ballet especially if it was a gala performance. The footman in a top hat held Lara's hand as she got out. She looked splendid in her red evening gown, a silk shawl covering her bare ivory-white shoulders and the diamonds on her tiara and on her Cartier necklace sparkling.

The vestibule buzzed like a beehive, with men in uniforms of all regiments or formal black evening wear, and women in gowns in a dazzling array of colors. Jewels of every description smothered the necks, chests, and wrists of the female patrons, who sported scandalously low décolletages trimmed with sable, mink, and ermine. Stars made of diamonds, emeralds, and rubies held up hairdos. It was a magnificent blaze of splendor. The ladies of the Court and St Petersburg society were really here to be seen, not to see the ballet. Season-ticket holders exchanged greetings, kisses, and handshakes like old friends before they proceeded through the glass doors to the auditorium. Princess Zagovna wore a gown of light blue dappled all over with tiny diamonds. Around her long slender neck was her famous necklace of square-cut green emeralds and oval-cut diamonds. She walked over to Lara and Dimitri.

'*Comment vas-tu, ma chère?*' gushed Princess Zagovna.

He knew the two women were instinctively eyeing each other's gowns. *Who looks better?* They exchanged kisses on the cheeks in the French manner.

'Larissa, *ma chère*, we're going to the Restaurant L'Hiver afterwards. But don't you dare come if you don't have gobs of malicious gossip.'

'Varya, when have I ever let you down?' replied Lara with a sly smile. Princess Zagovna shrieked with laughter. Dimitri rolled his eyes, but she was speaking the truth, no one beat Lara when it came to gossip. If the Tsar had a Minister of Gossip, Lara would be the person most qualified for the job. The two women bent their heads together and began their heartless critique, conspiratorially looking over the other women and whispering about hairstyles and jewelry. The performance began at eight, and an usher in a red-and-gold uniform led Princess Zagovna, Lara, and Dimitri up a short red-carpeted staircase. Their private boxes were down a long curving hallway, its walls covered in purple damask. The ceiling was completely mirrored, making the passage seem bigger than it was. They passed the open doors of the other boxes where patrons were settling in. As they went by the box of Count Trigorin, the Countess standing in the doorway made a slight gesture for Dimitri to stop. Lara and Varya kept walking, chattering away.

'Dimitri, my sweet, try to be at my place by two tonight,' whispered the Countess. 'You're always late.' She extended her white-gloved hand, and Dimitri gave it a quick squeeze and walked on.

Before Lara and Varya went into their respective boxes, they paused in an alcove with a mirror, as Dimitri went on ahead. They both attended to their hair one last time. As Lara came out of the alcove, she met Prince Gayev on the way to his box.

'Alexi,' Lara whispered, 'come at one tomorrow. I have a fitting at four.' Prince Gayev smiled conspiratorially and lightly touched Lara's bare shoulder.

From their box, Dimitri and Lara took in the five tiers of the horseshoe-shaped balconies faced with beautiful plaster detailing and bright electric globe lights. The great domed ceiling with its enormous crystal chandelier hung above the auditorium like a sun. Their box was on the second tier over-looking the orchestra pit and the stage. This position, Dimitri believed, gave them a much better angle of view than a ground-floor box. Lara was using her new Fabergé opera glasses like a ship's captain, going up and down every row of the orchestra stalls, inspecting the women and making comments. The opera glasses were finished in a translucent turquoise guilloche enamel and encrusted with tiny diamonds, and came with a matching ostrich-plume fan with silk tassels. The Tsar's sister, Grand Duchess Xenia, had one in salmon that Lara greatly admired. She wanted one just like it. Every woman in Court adored Xenia's taste.

'Countess Rodzianko looks as though she has a five-pound bag of flour under her chin,' Lara announced to Dimitri. 'How disappointing. Princess Anna's gown is such a rag. Hardly any diamonds and gold embroidery . . . Good God! The new wrin-kles on Alenya.'

Dimitri scowled at these observations. 'You have a sharp tongue, Larissa. Someday, it will cut you.'

Still peering through her opera glasses, Lara smiled.

'Pfff, mind your own business. Why don't you wave to your latest lover, Trigorin?'

People were engaged in animated conversation and waving to friends in the balconies whom they were probably insulting. Lara knew almost every single person in the auditorium tonight, and she could memorize what every woman was wearing including her jewelry. Dimitri was constantly amazed by her memory. She could recall what shoes the Grand Duchess Ella wore at the 1901 performance of *Sleeping Beauty*, or what ring Princess Orlinka wore on her right hand at a performance of *Boris Godinov* last spring. In the boxes directly across the auditorium, women wearing elbow-length white gloves and bedecked with jewels twinkling in the chandelier light flirted with their fans. On the second tier directly facing the stage was the Imperial Box with its two-headed eagle emblazoned on its rail. It was empty tonight, which pleased Dimitri. After the assassination attempt, he didn't like the Tsar and Tsarina to go out too much in public. He now worried for his friends' lives – and their children's.

While Dimitri was scanning the crowd, he suddenly realized that Katya might be in the audience tonight. The possibility filled him with delight.

'Give me those glasses,' Dimitri said, reaching over and pulling them away Lara's face. She resisted at first but then gave them up. 'Be quick about it,' she snarled, 'I wasn't done with them.'

He slowly checked all the boxes then the orchestra seats below but didn't see her, which disappointed him. If she had been here, he would have gone over to talk to her at the interval. Maybe he missed her and would bump into her in the lobby as everyone was leaving.

The orchestra pit was filled with musicians in white tie and tails, adjusting the black metal stands of the musical scores and warming up. The auditorium hummed with conversation, but when the lights dimmed and the conductor came to the rostrum and tapped his baton, a deafening silence enveloped the space. The crimson curtain lit by electric footlights rose.

Tonight's performance by the Imperial Ballet was *Giselle*, the story of the peasant girl who died from a broken heart because her lover was untrue. A group of supernatural women, the 'Wilis,' who danced men to death, summoned Giselle from the grave and wanted to kill her lover. They are all virgins who died of broken hearts before they were married and thus carried an insane hatred of men. Dimitri was always amused by the plot of the ballet; the 'Wilis' would be busy day and night if they had to deal with the infidelity of the Imperial Court.

A few minutes into the production, the auditorium erupted in cheers for the ballerina who danced the part of *Giselle* – Anna Pavlova. She had joined the Imperial Ballet School at age ten in 1891 under the tutelage of the grand master, Marius Petipa, and was now on her way to becoming a legend in her own time. She had become Petipa's favorite and was selected for many choice roles in his ballets. She was sure to become a *prima ballerina* ranking with the *prima ballerina assoluta*, Mathilde Kschessinska, who was also famous for being a special favorite of Nicholas before he met Alexandra.

The audience sat transfixed by Pavlova's sensational perform-ance tonight. It wasn't just her incredible physical dancing talent; she had the unique ability to throw her entire soul into a role. Pavlova *was* Giselle. Spellbound, Lara did not once use her glasses to spy on another woman, although she did the whole time during the interval, ignoring the champagne and chocolates that were served in their box.

'Anya is having her way with the son of Prince Zablotsky – age sixteen,' announced Lara after draining her wine glass. A waiter immediately refilled her glass without her asking.

Around the great table in a private room at the Restaurant L'Hiver sat a group of their friends, enjoying three different types of caviar that accompanied the eight courses of French cuisine and iced champagne. The room had a tall bay window where traditional Russian singers with balalaikas stood singing.

'Well, I don't blame her,' exclaimed Princess Maria. 'Mikhail is gorgeous, why wouldn't he be? His mother and father are gorgeous! He must look like a Greek god naked! He's getting a marvelous sexual initiation.'

Dimitri looked over at Maria and frowned. She was such a silly woman. He did not approve of dalliances with such young boys. It was beneath contempt. He believed that such affairs should be strictly forbidden, as was sex with servants.

'I believe that the Moscow dancers sacrifice tradition to facile effects,' announced Dimitri.

Lara threw down her forkful of lobster a la crème and gave her husband a slit-eyed look.

'Damn you, Dimitri, don't you dare try to change the subject. We're exchanging delicious gossip here. If you don't like it, then get the *likatch* to drive you home,' she snarled. 'No one wants to discuss the differences between dancers in Moscow and St Petersburg.'

The table erupted in laughter, but Dimitri knew his wife was dead serious.

'*Oui, ma chère.*'

'Varya, tell us something spiteful but *très amusant*,' commanded Lara, glaring at her husband.

'Madame Tushkevich knows about the Muscovite actress,' Varya said, with a wink of the eye.

The comment ignited heaps of ridicule and scorn for Madame Tushkevich, whom Dimitri liked. True, she had become an old hag tarted up with rouge and powder, but she had a jolly nature. He remembered as a boy how beautiful she was. Lara didn't realize that she could end up looking like that in old age.

'And she ordered a gown in tangerine orange. Can you believe it?' added Varya.

'I *don't* believe it,' cried Madame Grabbe. 'She always had a sense of style so *à la mode.*'

'Now, this is all *very* indiscreet,' said Lara, 'so I *won't* mention any names. When Count Petrisky took off his trousers and . . .'

'I thought you weren't going to mention any names,' interrupted Dimitri.

'Ooops,' gasped Lara putting her hand over her grinning mouth causing others to convulse with laughter.

For the next two hours, the conversation sizzled and popped. Every word was pure evil gossip, maligning man and woman equally. If they didn't like a particular person, they set about destroying him or her with their most effective weapons: lies and vicious rumors. They even made fun of Baron Saroka's dog. Dimitri hated it, but it was part of his existence. Russian high society never had the guts to say what they thought to a person's face; it was always praise to their face then knives to their back. He had seen people driven out of Court by Lara's malicious rumors. His wife was correct when she said the Tsar and Tsarina never gossiped or cruelly ridiculed anyone. Maybe that was why Dimitri liked being with them.

An orchestra in the main room played Viennese waltzes, and Dimitri danced with everyone but his wife, which was the correct thing to do. A group of officers in dark green tunics with epaulettes dined at a table, and every one of them danced with Lara, some twice. As usual with after-theater suppers, most people did not leave before 4 a.m. Dimitri had to leave early. Lara was the last to leave, with General Dolgorousky.

EIGHT

'Dimitri, you're magnificent,' purred Baroness Ekaterina Moncransky. 'You know how to treat a lady like a tart.'

Dimitri, who was smoking a cigarette, turned and smiled at Ekaterina, who snuggled against him.

They were in Ekaterina's brother's house. He had just left for the south of France, so the place was empty, with white dust covers on the furniture. Dimitri stroked Ekaterina's sandy blonde hair, which was undone. He loved to see the hairdos of Court women unpinned and tumbling down onto their shoulders. It made them so much more alluring and seductive. It was ironic, he thought, because the ladies of the Court took immense pride in their hairstyles, and had a hairdresser come in every morning to get their hair piled up with pads for the day.

'I wanted to see you before you went off to Italy. Where are you staying?' he asked.

'Palazzo Volpi in Venice.' Ekaterina propped herself on one elbow. The white silk sheet slid away, showing her beautiful full breasts.

'Ah, yes, a wonderful place. We stopped there the year before last on the way to Nice,' Dimitri said approvingly. 'Then will you go on to your villa in Capri with the Baron?'

'Yes, the eunuch will be coming down later on. But you *must* come by for a visit.' Ekaterina kissed him full on the lips. 'I love the taste of tobacco on a man.' Dimitri snuffed out his cigarette and lay on his stomach. Ekaterina pulled the sheet off him to expose his naked body. Straddling his thighs, she began to run her hands over his back, starting at the shoulders. He had a muscular V-shaped torso that pinched down to a narrow waist.

'Mm, that feels so good,' Dimitri murmured.

'You have the most wonderful body, Prince Dimitri. The part I love best is your little rock-hard buns,' said Ekaterina as she clenched his buttocks with both hands. 'I wish I could take them home with me, but I know that Countess Trigorin admires them also. How is she doing these days?'

Russian aristocrats had a main lover, but they could also have a few auxiliary lovers at the same time. Illicit Court love was like a game of musical chairs, but with plush beds – round and round you went.

'I'm seeing her this coming Saturday. I'll give her your regards,' replied Dimitri cheerfully. He meant it, too.

Ekaterina got off the bed to start dressing. 'I saw Lara at Worth's last week. My old Smolny classmate is still so beautiful, and you know she was top of the class *every* year?'

This remark jolted Dimitri's memory. Lara, along with other daughters of the aristocracy, attended the Smolny Institute for Young Ladies of Noble Birth in St Petersburg, Russia's most prestigious girls' school, founded by Catherine the Great. The image of his wife dressed in a plain white cotton jumper with starched navy-blue shoulder capes brought a smile to his face. Girls learned all the necessary skills to be a society lady, such as riding, dancing, archery, and tennis. They were also taught languages, science, mathematics, and classical subjects. When they first married, Lara impressed him so with discussions about literature, history, and philosophy. He'd forgotten how smart and well-read she'd been. That happy memory had long vanished along with her fidelity. He missed it. Despite her sharp intelligence, Lara was now as idle as any Court lady who started each day with a massage while gossiping on the telephone. The gossiping continued through the morning with her manicurist and then her personal hairdresser. When she was finally dressed, she'd shop on the Nevsky Prospect with her friends or go for a carriage ride. Back home, she'd dress for a ball or the opera. Dimitri and Lara never talked about anything except their social schedule, and she didn't read anything except the society news to make sure she was mentioned.

'Yes, I do remember she was an excellent student,' Dimitri muttered.

Ekaterina slipped on a yellow satin morning dress embroidered with white lace, a loose dress with flowing skirts and sleeves. When she returned home, she would change into a day dress for her afternoon carriage ride and shopping, then a tea dress, and then an evening gown. Court women changed clothes about four times a day, six during the season. Dimitri was glad he wasn't a woman. He got out of bed to change into a comfortable dark gray three-piece tweed suit he always wore on days when he was doing his architectural work.

He was ready to leave. He gave Ekaterina a passionate kiss.

'*Au revoir, ma chère*. Have a good time in Venice and Capri. But before I go, I realized that I never gave you your Easter present.' He pulled a tiny box out of his side pocket. 'It's a few months late, but I think you'll like it.'

Ekaterina opened it. 'Oh, Dimitri, it's darling!'

Not all Fabergé eggs were Imperial Easter Eggs; the firm designed many miniature eggs, like the 'Raspberry Egg' Ekaterina held up to the morning light. It looked exactly like a red raspberry, but it was made up of dozens of tiny red rubies set in gold. All the little eggs had a gold loop at the top to attach to a simple gold necklace.

'You not only have a great ass, Dimitri, but you're the most thoughtful person I know. You remembered raspberries are my favorite fruit.' She blew him a kiss, and he left.

Out on the street, he could feel the heat of the day coming on. There was barely any spring in St Petersburg, summer engulfed the city so quickly. He didn't have far to walk to his mansion on the Quay overlooking the Neva River. Fifteen minutes later, the Baroness emerged onto the street and headed home. She didn't notice that far down the street a carriage waited. In it, her husband Baron General Igor Moncransky was smoking a cigar.

Moncransky had unfastened a few buttons of his scarlet and gold-braided tunic because it had gotten uncomfortably close in the carriage. He was a general in the Hussars Regiment of the His Majesty's Life Guards and head of the Okhrana, the feared Imperial Russian Secret Police. The general was formally addressed as 'Your Super-Excellency,' and God help the officer who didn't use the proper salutation. Once he challenged a man to a duel for the slip in etiquette. He watched his wife turn the corner on the way back to their house on the Moika Canal. It was by accident that he discovered that she and Markhov were lovers when he went to his dacha on the shore of the Gulf of Finland in the early spring, and saw them leaving together.

Moncransky always had an intense dislike for Prince Dimitri, which he expertly disguised in Court because Dimitri was the Tsar's closest friend. Moncransky hated and envied him for his closeness to the Imperial Family. He also despised the prince because of his good looks and trim physique. Moncransky believed *he* should be a close friend and confidant to Nicholas, who was always very cold and formal with him. Markhov wasn't even a career military man; just a dilettante architect and engineer. An aristocrat who worked was an abomination, he believed. Once when Moncransky criticized a bridge Markhov had designed, he replied it was designed specially to hold the weight of the cannon of supporting artillery units, thus embarrassing him in front of the Tsar. Moncransky *never* forgot an insult.

The general puffed away on the cigar. He didn't mind his wife taking lovers. Under the Court's unwritten rules, she was allowed to because she'd produced a male heir for him. After that, she was a free agent if she acted with discretion. He was a soldier, and it was expected that he take lovers and frequent the best class of brothels. But he bitterly hated the fact that Markhov was her lover. He tossed away his cigar and growled at the young fresh-faced soldier driving his carriage.

'I have an appointment at the Winter Palace in ten minutes, so move it, son!'

The front west wing of the Winter Palace was where the government ministers' offices were located. Moncransky left his carriage and went in through a side entrance. A liveried footman opened a door to an office suite. There sitting and smoking were von Plehve, the Minister of the Interior; Grand Duke Sergei, the Tsar's uncle; General Isvoltsky, the Okhrana's second in command; and several other under-ministers and officers.

'You're late,' growled Grand Duke Sergei.

Looking contrite, Moncransky bowed, then took a seat. Isvoltsky was the first to speak. He opened a large brown envelope and removed a piece of white paper.

'The next pogrom will be in Gomel next Wednesday. Our people are in place, and the police have been instructed not to interfere. These flyers will be scattered throughout the city and the peasant villages the week before.' He held the paper up for all to see.

Printed in big letters was '*Kill the Jews & Save Russia.*' A sentence under it said, '*Revolutionary Jews are overthrowing our Empire and want to kill the Tsar and his family.*'

'I hope this doesn't cause a big stink like the one we put on in Kishinev,' muttered Grand Duke Sergei to no one in particular.

'Have your men kill a Christian,' von Plehve ordered Isvoltsky. 'That really riles the peasants. We want to be sure this pogrom will be a success.'

NINE

Ivan Plechenko stuck his head through the broken glass of the window.

'*Kill the Jews and save Russia!*' he shouted at the top of his lungs.

A great cheer rose up from the street below. Plechenko was delighted to see a mass of men throwing rocks through windows and running out of houses with their arms full of looted silverware and linen. Directly across from him, two young men were taking turns with a rusty crowbar bashing in the head of a bearded middle-aged man. Fire was pouring out of the first floor of a house at the end of Kirov Street in the Jewish quarter of Gomel.

Plechenko felt a wonderful sense of elation that seemed to lift him a finger's breadth off the floor. And it wasn't because of the copious amounts of vodka he had already drunk this morning. No, it was the sight of the blind senseless carnage going on around him. To be caught up in this great frenzy, to be able to go completely wild and destroy anything that could be broken, smashed, set on fire, or killed without consequence – that made his heart soar. It made him feel so alive and happy to be part of such a business.

Smiling, he turned and faced the room. He repositioned his visor cap atop his mop of unruly sandy-blond hair and smoothed out his white cotton blouse that buttoned up the side and hung outside his baggy wool pants. He bent down and wiped off the dust off his most prized possession, his black knee-length boots. Leather boots were a sign of status; peasants usually wore crude sandals made of bark from lime trees. He had pulled these fine boots off a passed-out drunk in Orgeev a year ago. In front of him, the woman lay on the floor sobbing hysterically over her husband whom Plechenko had just savagely beaten.

A door opened to his right, and the clean-shaven face of a lean sunburnt peasant poked out.

'Ivan Sergeyevich, come see what we've found,' shouted the young man. As he was pulling his head back from the door, he took notice of the young woman on the floor.

'Say, these Jewesses aren't bad-looking, are they? Where'd she come from?'

As Plechenko walked into the room, the moujik named Iyla whom he had met a few hours before in Zuniski Square slid by him unbuttoning his fly. Iyla straddled the woman, who looked up at him and started screaming.

When Plechenko entered the small room, he began to laugh uncontrollably. The entire room was filled with floating white feathers. It was like it was snowing inside the house, and he understood why. Across the room was a stout, red-haired man ripping apart a mattress with a short-bladed knife. Billows and billows of the tiny goose-down feathers spewed out. They stuck to his hair and clothes.

'Look!' yelled the man with glee as he held up a leather pouch. He shook it, and it jingled. 'I knew the Jews hoarded their rubles in their mattresses, I just knew it!' He continued his hunt, ripping apart the rest of the cotton covering. Plechenko's eyes lit up when he heard the jingle of coins. There was another bed in the corner of the room. He pulled out his jack-knife and leapt on its mattress, slashing it apart in a fury. He howled with pleasure when he found a pouch. Delirious with joy and covered in feathers, he ran out of the room and into the street, where the chaos had escalated. Wafting from the windows and doors of the houses he passed were goose feathers. Flames were licking out of the front windows of more houses on the street. One was totally engulfed in fire. The family who must have lived there was silently watching the inferno from the middle of the street. The white-bearded elder was clutching in the crook of his black coat sleeve one of those candelabras the Yids used for that holiday around Christmas. Right at the very moment Plechenko was watching, a skinny boy of about thirteen struck the old man in the back of the head with a piece of firewood and snatched the candelabra from his grasp. Plechenko convulsed with laughter and offered the boy a salute of admiration, which the kid enthusiastically acknowledged. The boy pointed to his booty and shouted proudly, 'This is *pure gold*!'

Plechenko realized he was covered head to toe in feathers. 'It looks like I've slept in a chicken coop,' he said with a laugh and began brushing the feathers from his hair and blouse. He pulled off his tunic and shook it like a blanket to get the feathers off. They seemed to be glued to his clothes. Once he was tidied up, he walked down the street bouncing the dark-brown leather pouch of coins in the palm of his right hand. He passed at least three buildings that had crosses or Orthodox ikons in their windows, a very smart move, he thought, to keep the rioters away.

He passed some local policemen smoking and leaning

against a brick wall of a house occasionally looking left and right but mostly looking straight ahead. They were all dressed in ill-fitting light-blue uniforms with short yellow epaulets and caps with scarlet banding.

An ancient woman in a black shawl limped up to them. 'Aren't you going to stop this?' she screamed.

'It's none of our business, cabbage-face,' mumbled an officer whose big belly was about to burst out of his tunic.

'The Tsar himself ordered this, grandmother!' yelled Plechenko, briskly walking down the street.

TEN

'What do you mean, you're not going? You've never missed Prince Kovrin's party. He has that spicy Black Sea sturgeon you love so much.'

With a quizzical look on her face, Lara stood with her hands on her hips at the doorway of Dimitri's bedroom.

'Like I said, I'm not going.' Dimitri was sitting in an armchair, smoking a cigarette and reading a magazine. Instead of evening attire, he was wearing his three-piece tweed suit.

'Your little Countess Trigorin will be there – without the Count,' Lara said in a devious tone.

'You can go without me.'

'You know damn well I will,' she growled. 'I didn't buy this gown to stay home with you.'

'Tell them I wasn't feeling well. Anyway, no one will miss me,' Dimitri said in a weary voice. It was true; they went to a party or a ball every night of the week, no one would notice his absence. Sophie, Lara's lady's maid and confidante, came up behind her and put a wrap around her shoulders and handed her a pearl-embroidered silk purse. A big brown and white borzoi trotted into the room.

'There's my handsome boy! You've come to say good night to your mama, Fedor?' Lara knelt down and wrapped her arms around the dog. She kissed Fedor on his snout, and he wagged his tail furiously. 'My baby, I wish I could take you with me. But you go sleep on mama's bed.'

A young girl in her twenties wearing a black dress stood at the door.

'Varinka, please make sure Fedor gets his treat after I leave,' Lara said. 'The *fresh* duck.' Varinka's sole duty as a house servant was to take care of the dog.

'Yes, Your Highness,' Varinka squeaked.

'So, what will you be doing tonight, if you're not seeing your Countess or gorging on sturgeon?'

'I'll be working on the drawings for the Tchaikovsky Memorial,' Dimitri responded, trying not to show his irritation.

'Don't wait up, I'll probably be horribly late,' Lara said with a wink. 'You know what Kovrin's parties are like.'

'I know what *you're* like,' he said.

'Everything in moderation,' he added without looking up from his magazine.

'Including moderation, said Oscar Wilde.' Lara waved goodbye.

Dimitri took another cigarette out of his case and lit up. He coughed and picked a piece of tobacco from the tip of his tongue. Little Olga was right, he smoked too much. Fedor walked over to Dimitri's armchair and curled up to sleep. Gazing into the fireplace, he was glad he wasn't going to Kovrin's. It all seemed so silly, compared to real life where people were intent on murdering someone. The attempt on the Tsar's life with the plague-infected cloth; he could not understand what the Tsar had done to deserve this. Then he remembered the child in Kishinev. What had he done to deserve a bashed-in skull?

He went over to the window that looked over the Neva, and watched Lara drive off in the night in their carriage. As he threw his unfinished cigarette into the fireplace, Dimitri checked the time on the Fabergé mantel clock.

'Alexsandr,' he shouted to the ceiling, 'fetch me a *droshky.*'

'Oh, come now, Russian modernism acknowledges the art and science of the West, but it definitely tailors them to Russian tradition and symbolism. We're producing our own special kind of painting and literature,' said Katya. She was wearing a green silk dress, standing in front of the great fireplace, waving her cigarette to emphasize her point.

The other men and women in the room seated in plush sofas and armchairs were nodding and holding glasses of tea. Before them, on a table set with a white lace cloth, a silver samovar was bubbling away.

A young man in a navy-blue suit with a waistcoat leaned forward to pour himself more tea. 'It's a cultural rebirth – but a *Russian* one,' he said enthusiastically.

'Just look at the Moscow Arts Theater,' exclaimed a middle-aged woman. 'That in itself set the Russian standard for the arts for the world.'

The dozen or so people turned in unison when the doorbell chimed. Off in the entry was a mumbling of voices, then footsteps on the marble steps were heard.

Katya looked up in surprise.

'Prince Dimitri, how good of you to come,' she said.

All eyes set upon the tall, handsome aristocrat holding his hat and walking stick in hand. The butler came up, and Dimitri threw his gloves in the hat and handed it and the stick to the servant.

He smiled at Katya and bowed. 'I remembered that you met on Thursday nights, and so I happened to be free tonight.'

'Everyone, may I present Prince Dimitri Markhov. He's an architect.'

She went around the room with introductions.

An attractive woman in a white lace dress offered Dimitri a glass of tea with a little white frosted cake. Her name was Clara; she was also a doctor and she worked with Katya at the hospital.

'Prince Dimitri,' said Olenka, a pretty blonde girl, 'we were just talking about native Russian influences in the new modernist arts we have in Russia today.'

'We must get your thoughts on the "Style Moderne" in architecture, the "Russian" Art Nouveau. One sees so much of it nowadays. You of course have seen Minash's Vitebsk Railroad Station in the city here. Those unbelievable sinuous curves!' Clara exclaimed.

'Yes,' answered Dimitri. 'Many around the world are enamored with this new style because they feel architecture has to change with the times.' He and Katya exchanged grins.

'Architectural styles come late to Russia. It's the Art Nouveau in Paris and Brussels, and Jugendstil in Germany,' said Grigory, the fellow in the natty blue suit.

'And that Spanish chap, Gaudí, in Barcelona,' Olenka added.

'Korolyov identifies the Art Nouveau as a philistine taste, with a lack of stylistic integrity that denotes vulgarity,' Alina Medvedena announced.

'Korolyov may be right,' Dimitri replied, wanting to impress Katya even though he didn't know who the hell Korolyov was. 'The classical language of the ancients is still the standard by which we judge all architecture.'

'But Your Highness, we live in modern times, and we need buildings of our time,' Grigory pleaded.

'Dimitri,' Markhov corrected him. He liked being addressed as Your Highness, but this definitely wasn't the place for that salutation. He wanted to be part of the group.

'You don't think the Style Moderne is facile and fleeting, while the classical principles are eternal?' he added in an earnest tone.

'Dimitri, that's so retrograde. We live in a new age of the automobile and wireless communication,' Clara said in a dismissive voice.

'We don't need these white temples anymore, Dimitri,' the hostess, Evigenia, said. 'What did you think of Schechtel's Levenson Printshop in Moscow?'

Dimitri's eyes met Katya's because she had asked him the same question. When she smiled in acknowledgment, he felt a surprising jolt of pleasure.

The spirited discussion continued past midnight. He couldn't believe it was so late; Lara might get home before him. Instead of running out of steam, the group seemed more invigorated. Literature, Chekhov and his plays, Vrubel and Somov paintings were all appraised.

'The arts can play a critical role in the revolution that's coming,' said Grigory, 'to help end this terrible nightmare that's been oppressing Russia for centuries.' Dimitri learned that Grigory was a professor of literature at the St Petersburg University.

'The peasants can't take this kind of treatment any longer,' Olenka said.

'Did you hear that thirty-two Jews were killed in the pogrom in Gomel yesterday? With millions of rubles in property damage?' Katya asked.

'The Jews are treated worst of all – like animals,' Grigory exclaimed.

Everyone shook their head in disapproval. Dimitri hadn't heard about this; the news jolted him, but he kept a calm expression. He imagined that among those thirty-two dead bodies there had to be a dead child or two like he'd seen in Kishinev.

'The workers in those miserable factories have no rights at all,' added Grigory. 'Some have to sleep under the machines they use.'

'Russia needs a constitution like England has. With freedom of speech,' Evigenia exclaimed.

'And an uncensored press,' Clara added.

'The peasants and workers are helpless to ignite a revolution in Russia. It's up to the intelligentsia and professional classes to bring about change,' Grigory said.

For the next hour, the group talked of the oppression in Russia, and how it had to be stamped out. Land had to be given to the peasants, factory owners must improve working conditions, and Jews had to be given their basic civil rights. Dimitri just sat and listened. This was all a revelation to him. No one ever discussed these kinds of things in Court. He had met a few Jews over the years; they seemed rich and quite content with life. And he had never been inside a factory. Why would I? he thought.

Katya stood up. 'Well, it's been a very stimulating discussion tonight, but it's late and I must be off. Thank you again, Evigenia, for your hospitality.'

Dimitri quickly said his goodbyes so he could walk outside with her.

'I hope you are well, Katya. In the heat of the discussion, I didn't get to inquire after you. Thank you so much for inviting me. I haven't had such an enjoyable evening in years; I'd like to come again.' He saw once more what wonderful blue eyes Katya had. Her face as he had remembered was plain, but it had a great warmth about it, something very appealing. And when she smiled, she seemed to light up from inside.

'Oh, our little evening discussions are probably nothing compared to the gay life you lead every day. But thank you so much for coming tonight; your presence really livened up the group.'

Dimitri waved goodbye to Clara, Grigory, and the others who were coming out of the mansion. As his carriage started off, he was feeling so happy he had come. His mind and body felt invigorated, like when he rolled in the snow after a sauna. When he entered the sitting room tonight, he experienced a pang of happiness in his chest at seeing Katya again. At the Catherine Palace ball, he had found her to be very captivating and interesting. As she talked during the evening, he found her even more fascinating and intelligent. He couldn't help himself from constantly glancing over at her.

Suddenly, he ordered the carriage to halt, and he hopped out. Just as Katya was getting into her carriage, he waved to catch her attention.

'Do you know Mrs McIntosh's Authentic English Tea Shop?' he asked, trotting up to her. 'Maybe we could have tea together sometime soon.'

Katya looked out at the deserted streets as her carriage rumbled along. She considered herself a good judge of character, and her first impression of Dimitri that night at the Catherine Palace was that he was refreshingly unassuming and did not have an exalted opinion of himself. But she thought she'd never see him again after the ball and was shocked to see him turn up at her arts circle tonight. She never thought he'd take her up on the offer to come. At the same time, she was delighted and thrilled to see him there. When he came into the drawing room, his height and good looks seemed even more apparent than the night they met. When he entered the room, it wasn't with a prince's commanding air, but with the disarming shyness of a little boy. That tugged at her heart and brought a smile to her face.

Professor Grigory Pahlen had extra time before his first class started this morning, so he thought he would run a few errands. He paid his bill at the butcher's, bought writing paper at the stationer's, and picked up some fruit for his lunch. That left just one last thing. He strolled down Strogonoff Street and entered a nondescript brick building. Taking the lift to the fourth floor, he rapped on an office door.

'Enter!' came a gruff command.

Colonel Tipev looked up at the professor in his rumpled olive suit.

'Oh, it's you,' the colonel said with disdain. 'Just leave the report and get the hell out of here.'

Grigory frowned. Nine months working as an agent for the Okhrana had brought him no respect in the eyes of Tipev. He deliberately handed the report to him instead of dropping it into the box. Tipev grunted and scanned the paper. Grigory had to leave to make it to class on time so he went toward the door.

'Wait!' Tipev shouted. 'Sit down.'

Tipev quickly made a telephone call. Twenty minutes later, General Moncransky, head of the Okhrana, appeared at the door. The burly general faced Grigory, who stood up and bowed.

'Tell me everything Prince Dimitri said last night.' The general wore an expression of great pleasure.

ELEVEN

'Little Father, please grant me this special request to help my son who's dying. I have no money to pay a doctor, and he will die.'

The Tsar always went riding in the afternoon when the family was staying at Tsarskoe Selo, their country palace. He liked to ride in the countryside accompanied by an adjutant officer or a close friend like Dimitri. Often, he talked to the peasants in the villages along the way, asking them about their families, their crops, and their problems. Sometimes, a peasant like this one pleaded for help.

'What is your son's name?'

'Vassily Andreivitch Fedorov from Perekyula, Little Father.'

'I will send someone later this afternoon,' the Tsar said with a smile. 'Dimitri, do you have a coin I could give to this fellow?'

Dimitri was amused that the man with the largest private gold reserve in the entire world never carried any money. He handed Nicholas a one-ruble coin, and they rode on.

Without turning his head to Dimitri, the Tsar spoke as if to the road.

'Dimitri, at the coronation when the Metropolitan of St Petersburg placed the crown on my head, he said that it was Christ Himself who was irrevocably crowning me as the divine authority over the Russian people. My sovereignty is absolute, and I swore in my coronation oath to uphold the principle of autocracy. They are my children, and I am ordained by God to take care of them – like that poor devil.'

Dimitri already knew this. Nicholas was an intensely devout member of the Orthodox Church, and he absolutely believed he had inherited a profound sacred responsibility for the welfare of his people. It was no false promise he'd given the peasant; a doctor would be showing up at his son's bedside today.

'You are our divine leader,' said Dimitri solemnly. He wasn't flattering the Tsar. He really meant it, as his family had believed in this fundamental truth for almost three centuries of Romanov rule.

'There is no burden so wearisome as the duty of the Tsar, Nicky,' he continued, 'especially that damn nine-pound crown.'

The Tsar laughed. 'Yes, that awful crown.'

The Tsar hated wearing his crown of gold and diamonds. It pressed on his brow at the very spot where a Japanese madman stabbed him when he was the Tsarevich on a tour of the Far East. After wearing it for a few hours at a royal function, it gave him an excruciating headache.

In the hot sun, they rode slowly on the dusty road. Twenty yards in front and behind were pairs of Cossacks dressed in their distinctive long scarlet coats trimmed in black. Called the 'fists of the Tsar,' they were armed with a *shashka*, a curved sword, and a long lance called a *pika*. The Cossack Konvoi Regiment and the Garde Equipage were assigned to protect the Imperial Family. In addition to them, a permanent five-thousand-man army garrison was stationed at Tsarskoe Selo.

It was teatime when they returned. The Romanov family did not like living in the Winter Palace and much preferred Tsarskoe Selo, 'the Tsar's village,' which they thought of as their real home. Located fifteen miles south of St Petersburg, it was a beautiful eight-hundred-acre estate with parks, fantastic pavilions, monuments, gardens, artificial lakes, and winding paths, built by Catherine the Great and the Empress Elizabeth. It had two palaces. The Imperial Family lived in the Palladian-style Alexander Palace, which was smaller than the great Catherine Palace, with just one hundred rooms. It was separated from the rest of the estate by canals and lakes, spanned by lacy ironwork bridges. Their private apartments were on the first floor of the east wing, with the children's rooms on the second floor directly above their parents. Dimitri and the rest of the Court also lived there in great pastel-colored mansions lining the tree-shaded boulevard, which ran from the railway station to the gates of the Imperial Park. Tsarskoe Selo was arcadia to Dimitri; an enchanted fairyland in which few people were allowed to live or even visit.

The Alexander Palace had rooms designed by the Italian Baroque architect Quarenghi, with walls of white and cream. The family's wing had been redecorated by the Tsarina, and it reminded one of a comfortable English country house with overstuffed armchairs and sofas done in mauve, her favorite color. She had the rooms supplied daily with fresh flowers, giving it a wonderful never-ending sweet fragrance. The Imperial Anteroom had an unusual feature, a huge wooden slide called the Russian Mountain on which children (and Nicky) slid down.

When Dimitri entered the Rosewood Drawing Room for

tea, the Tsar had changed from his uniform into a simple white cotton tunic. Before he sat down, he let out his familiar bird whistle to summon the Tsarina and the children. A stout, doughy-looking woman of about twenty named Anna Vyrubova was also present. Although not a maid of honor, she came from an old distinguished Court family. The Tsarina enjoyed her company, especially playing two-handed piano and singing duets. This woman's increasing presence around the Tsarina had started tongues wagging, especially Lara's, who ridiculed Vyrubova's dumpy body and puffy face.

Because of the time-honored tradition, tea was always exactly the same, hot bread and English biscuits, with white table linen, although to Dimitri's disappointment, never was any frosted cake served. The Tsarina complained she was powerless to change the rigid routine. While the children played on the floor with their toys, the Tsar drank his usual two glasses of tea and ate a piece of buttered bread. He looked over the newspapers and would tell Dimitri if he saw something funny.

'Dimitri, listen to this. In a London music hall, one of the monkeys in an act ran into the audience. It stole a feathered hat off a woman's head, then bolted out the exit.'

His cheery mood turned sour. '*The Times* of London is still harping on the Kishinev violence.'

'What came of the meeting between von Plehve and that Zionist Jew, Herzl?'

'Herzl told von Plehve that he wants all his people to leave Russia to establish a homeland in Palestine, which is just fine with me. Then our "Jewish Question" would go away for good.'

The Tsarina was petting her dog and giving him bits of bread. She looked over at Dimitri and smiled.

'Dimitri, come with me, I want to show you something. Excuse us for a moment, Nicky.'

'I'll wait for your return,' Nicholas replied without looking up from the newspaper.

Dimitri followed her through to the bedroom. Unlike most royal couples, the Tsar and Tsarina actually shared a bed. The walls were hung with a light floral silk with a pattern of green wreaths tied with pink ribbons. Every square inch of the walls and shelves was covered with Victorian bric-a-brac, framed family photos, and ikons of all description. Then they entered her boudoir where the curtains, carpet, and furniture were done in light gray or mauve. Fresh bowls of purple and white lilacs and bunches of violets scented the air to an intoxicating effect. The room was filled with religious mementos and family photos, including one of her grandmother, Queen Victoria. The Mauve Boudoir was the family's inner sanctum and most private space.

The Tsarina went to a glass cabinet and took something from the top shelf, then turned to face Dimitri.

'I want you have this ikon of St George, Nicky's favorite saint.'

Dimitri took the ikon and ran his hand over it. On a six-inch-square wooden panel was painted a magnificent haloed St George in a red cape slaying the black dragon at the feet of his white charger, with the towers of the Kremlin in the background. It was painted in the most minute detail with gold foil.

'It is so beautiful, Your Majesty. Thank you so much.' Dimitri took her hand and kissed it.

'The men who surround my husband are false and insincere. No one does their duty for duty's sake or for Russia. Just for their own selfish interests and own advancement. But you are Nicky's true and sincere friend, who wants what's best for him. I love you for that.'

Dimitri was genuinely touched by her gesture. To a Russian, an ikon was an object full of divine energy, power, and grace. This shy woman who appeared cold and unapproachable to the Court was beaming a great smile. The room was filled with afternoon light that made her reddish-gold hair even more radiant.

But Dimitri knew he wasn't any saint like the one depicted on this ikon, especially when it came to his married life. He expertly played the Court's game of musical beds. But he truly cherished his long friendship with the Tsar. The Tsarina was absolutely right that those in the highest ranks in Court were only out for themselves. They constantly flattered Nicky, never offering advice they thought would anger him. One's inclusion in the Court was totally dependent on the good graces of the Tsar. Nicholas could cast them forever from Court, so they made sure they never rocked the boat. The Church, whose senior leaders were appointed by the Tsar, did nothing either.

The Tsarina walked over to a window that overlooked a garden and stared out.

'St Petersburg is a rotten town and not one atom Russian,' she said in a voice seared with bitterness. 'Even our beloved Tsarskoe Selo is too close to it. I wish we could leave and never come back. My granny Victoria was right; there's a total want of principle, from the Grand Dukes downward.'

Dimitri knew she hated Court life. Alexandra had pressured Nicholas to greatly reduce the number of court functions and receptions which the nobility (and especially Lara) were quite fond of. That move had made the Tsarina even more unpopular.

Dimitri followed the Tsarina back to the drawing room. There, the children's nanny, Miss Constance O'Brian, a tall, lean woman in her fifties, was rounding up the Grand Duchesses for the next activity. She was from England, another symbol of the Imperial Couple's anglophile tendencies like the English collies. Miss O'Brian had her hat and coat on.

'Please, Nanny, please bring us back some of those bon-bons from the shop on the Nevsky,' Olga cried out. Her sisters jumped up and down in agreement.

'I most certainly will, but you now go with Nurse Daria to your dancing lessons.' Miss O'Brian curtsied in the presence of the Tsar, then backed away as she was leaving. No one except the Tsarina and the children ever turned their back to him; another strict rule.

The Tsar waved goodbye to Miss O'Brian, then turned to Dimitri. 'Please come ride with me tomorrow.'

Miss O'Brian enjoyed walking down Kanimov Street. The great avenues of St Petersburg were alive with greenery, and the air was unusually fresh and cool for a summer afternoon. Though 'Petro' was a brilliant Western architectural creation, she hated its usual dank, misty climate. The weather was far worse than London's, where she had grown up. There it rained during the winter, while here it snowed and was bitterly cold. The city called the 'Venice of the North' was built on nineteen islands connected by stone bridges over winding canals. Along with the Neva River that ran down its center, the canals froze so solid streetcar tracks could be laid on them. Then the city became a humid inferno in the summer. This was an odd world to her, especially the people. Not a bit like the English, the Russians were a strange enigmatic group who all seemed fatalistic and depressed to her. Yet they had the habit of painting their buildings in cheerful bright colors of red, yellow, blue, and aqua-green. And though it seemed humanly impossible, they drank more than Englishmen.

The nanny turned down an alley lined with tall brick walls with wooden gates. She pushed one open and walked to the paint-blistered rear door of a small, shabby brick building. She rapped on it, three quick sharp knocks. The door creaked open, and there stood a tall, middle-aged man with a full beard and mustache. He smiled at Miss O'Brian.

'Welcome, Comrade. So good to see you again,' he said.

TWELVE

'Ssshhh! Have respect for the dead!'

'The only way to get our civil rights is to use *violence*,' said Asher Blokh, lowering his voice to a whisper. 'Peaceful methods of protest are worthless.'

He was standing in one of two rows of university and Yeshiva students that lined both sides of the road leading to the Jewish cemetery in Kishinev. Passing by him just at that moment were five stretchers, covered in black cloth embroidered with gold thread depicting the Ten Commandments. On each stretcher borne by two men were two urns under the black cover holding shreds of the Torah that had been desecrated in a pogrom in Kishinev last Easter. Behind the stretchers walked over ten thousand Jews in total silence.

'Or we can emigrate to Palestine,' whispered Isaac Hersch, standing next to him.

'To hell with that. We'd be playing into the hands of the Tsar by running away. Emigration is a goddamn escape not a solution. I'm a *Russian*, and this is *my* homeland. I'm not going anywhere!'

Hersch smiled at his classmate's stubbornness; Blokh had always had a hard head.

'Herzl says that Jews will never be safe until they have a homeland of their own – in Palestine. Don't you see? Jews are *guests* in whatever land they're living in. Their asses can be kicked out in a second, like they did to us in Spain,' replied Hersch. The procession now passed them, and he felt he could talk in a louder voice.

'Ha, think the Turks that control that little corner of the world are going to want a bunch of Yids squatting there and taking over? They're even bigger anti-Semites than the Russians. These Zionists are idiots.'

Hersch rolled his eyes.

'St Petersburg is orchestrating these massacres. The police just stand by. Some even direct the mob to Jewish-owned property,' Blokh continued, his voice becoming angrier.

Once the funeral procession had passed them, the two lines of men broke up, joining the huge crowd heading to the cemetery. Blokh and Hersch walked side by side. They were third-year students in the university in Odessa. Although Jewish enrollment was severely restricted, both young men were admitted because of their brilliant academic records and the large bribes paid by their families to university officials. In Jewish families, there was no sacrifice too great for educating the children. While ninety-nine percent of Christian Russian peasants were illiterate, the same percentage of Jews were literate. But in the Pale of Settlement, it was religion that drove education, with the grammar school ending at age thirteen, then the yeshiva for more advanced studies of the Talmud. From five in the morning until ten at night, young men studied at long wooden tables in a large room. These Yeshiva students were the most admired men of all, because wisdom of the Talmud was seen as the highest attainment.

But Jewish university students like Blokh and Pesach were a different breed altogether. Those men who studied secular subjects in the universities were looked on as heretical; it was something for the 'goy,' but not for Jews. Blokh and Hersch in turn looked on the religious Jews as hopelessly old-fashioned and ridiculous. Their dress, Yiddish language, and obstinate isolation made them even more alien to the Christians, fanning the flames of anti-Semitism and making things worse for all Jews, especially the ones who were 'Russified.' The two students may have admitted that the study of the Talmud as youths sharpened their minds, but they felt Jews needed to move with the times and study sciences, arts, and literature – to become *modern*.

'Anyway, this isn't just about the Jews,' Blokh snarled. '*All* people have suffered under the tyranny of the Tsar, tens of millions of gentile peasants. The first uprising last year was by the Christian peasants in Poltava, remember? To capture political power for the masses, there's no other alternative than violent mass revolution.'

'But our Little Father, the Tsar, knows what's best. He'll take care of us,' replied Hersch, knowing full well this would ignite an outburst from his friend.

'The Tsar? That bastard can . . .' Blokh halted his speech, realizing his leg was being pulled. He started laughing, then stopped because of solemnity of the crowd.

The procession was almost to the cemetery.

'Don't forget that those gentile masses you'll be fighting alongside still think of us as Christ-killers that collect blood to make our matzoh,' said Hersch, and he wasn't joking this time. 'Three centuries of Jew-hating isn't going to go away just like that.'

'I may be a fool, but I think fighting for political freedom will transcend that hatred. People will be different after the revolution.'

'You *are* a fool,' said Hersch in a friendly tone. 'Remember the saying: the lion and the lamb may lie together down in green pastures, but the lamb isn't going to get much sleep.'

Blokh smiled at his friend whom he'd known since the Russian grammar school they attended together.

'And keep your voice down, the Okhrana are everywhere,' added Hersch. 'They're probably walking next to us in this crowd.'

Blokh instinctively looked around him, searching for anyone that didn't look Jewish. But the crowd was all black-garbed people with stricken expressions. It was if they were attending a funeral for a family member. In a way, they were. When the Torah was vandalized and desecrated, it had to be buried in a holy ceremony. Although Blokh wasn't a believer anymore, he understood the emotion surrounding him. To gentiles, it might seem stupid to bury torn and burnt paper in such a solemn manner, but these people were devastated with grief, and would mourn for the next year with the same intensity as over a dead child. Jews were killed and maimed in the Easter pogrom; violating the sanctity of the beloved Torah was just as brutal and shocking. The violence in Kishinev, Blokh was delighted to discover, had awakened more Jews to the revolutionary movement and some had armed themselves for self-defense.

The stretchers reached the open iron double gates with Stars of David affixed on their pickets. At the exact moment they entered the cemetery, a collective groan arose from the crowd as though on cue, and it startled Blokh. It was a cry of anguish that lasted for a few seconds, then evaporated into the sunny blue sky above. Blokh looked up at the telephone wires that stretched between wooden poles along the edge of the cemetery, and saw they were lined with silent shiny black crows. It was if they were gathered in mourning too.

A crypt had been prepared for the burial, and the procession stopped before it.

A rabbi cried up to the sky in a loud stentorian voice:

'*It is enough, O Eternal Father! We are Thy children and Thou art our shepherd. Yet we feel abandoned, helpless orphans. God of our fathers, like unto Job, no tribulation will ever shake our faith in Thee, but why then must our faith in Thee be eternally tested?*'

The ten urns were gently placed inside the crypt and covered with moist black earth. Then the crowd turned away and walked home in silence. Blokh and Hersch walked by themselves behind the crowd.

'We will kill the Tsar,' said Blokh confidently. 'With the information from our new inside source, we'll succeed.'

THIRTEEN

K atya and Clara turned onto the Nevsky Prospect by the Alexander Garden.

'Are you on call this Thursday night?' Katya asked.

'No, Popov will cover as long as I can do Friday.'

'Wonderful, then you can come to the circle. The discussion is Repin versus Somov, who is the better portrait painter,' Katya said.

'Repin,' Clara exclaimed. 'I'd love to have my portrait painted by him.'

'He did mine, so maybe Father could arrange it,' Katya replied in an enthusiastic voice.

Her father had commissioned the famous Ilya Repin, who did the Tsar's portrait after his coronation, to paint her. He was a charming gentleman who tried his hardest to paint a flattering picture of her, making her far more attractive than she was in real life. Now Clara's portrait would be radiant. Yes, her father would easily set it up with Repin.

'So, do you think Prince Dimitri will come again? Quite a handsome man!' Clara giggled.

'Maybe. The prince seemed very interested in our discussion,' Katya replied.

'Interested in *you*,' Clara teased.

'Don't be silly. What a thing to say,' Katya said testily.

'So how is your favorite suitor doing?' Clara asked, referring to Ivan Pavlovitch. 'Has he finally gotten the message?'

'I think he understands that he is not going to marry the boss's daughter – I hope.'

When they passed over the Moika Canal, Katya called out, 'We're almost to our little peasant country church.'

Standing before them on the Nevsky Prospect was the Lady of Kazan Cathedral, a copy of St Peter's in Rome. The city's main Orthodox Church, it had curving wings of open columns that defined a vast semi-circular courtyard just like St Peter's Square. Church-goers were streaming in, and Katya and Clara joined them.

Because Katya and Clara considered themselves modern women of science, to them, religion was nonsense. They definitely agreed with Karl Marx that religion was the opiate of the masses. At the hospital, the two doctors felt sorry for the relatives of dying patients who brought holy water and smoke-blackened ikons to their bedsides in hopes of God granting them a miracle. Only a breakthrough in medicine, not God, would help people survive cancer and heart disease. Researchers bent over microscopes were the ones to ease humanity's miseries. Pasteur's germ theory, once laughed at, was now universally accepted, and mere hand-washing and better sanitation had saved millions from bacterial infection. One day, Katya hoped, there would be a pill to defeat one of the world's biggest killers, tuberculosis.

So, for Katya, coming to church on Sundays and feast days was a pretend exercise. She was only going through the religious motions that every Russian Christian had been taught since childhood. A well-bred Russian was expected to worship for the sake of appearance. She remembered her late mother, Anna, being devout; she often brought home bread rolls that had been blessed, and the family made the sign of the cross over them. To Katya, praying to ikons lit by red glass lamps was as primitive as a native praying to an image carved from a log.

In the Russian Orthodox Church, sitting down before God was seen as disrespectful, so worshippers stood for the whole service. Katya and Clara joined shoulder-to-shoulder with the throng stuffed into the majestic space, a tall barrel-vaulted ceiling supported by polished granite columns with gilt capitals, the air thick with incense. The mass began. All around her with their heads bowed were all classes of society, from the most refined and educated to the coarsest peasants. The church was the only place in Russia where the population mixed so intimately. Instead of being deep in prayer, Katya looked at the great frescoes on the wall, for there was no sculpture allowed in the Orthodox Church. She loved the choir, their voices so well blended that the singing seemed to come from a single mouth. Although no musical accompaniment was permitted, the singing resonated joyfully within the great cathedral. Like wound-up automatons, she and Clara always took communion, as they had since childhood.

At the end of the long service, the priest in his caftan and flowing beard dismissed the congregants. Many went up to kiss the crucifix he held in his hand. Katya and Clara refused to do this on the grounds it was most unhygienic: a child would kiss it after a slobbery tubercular old man. At the corner of Bolshaya Morskaya Street, the women bid each other goodbye.

When Katya got home, the Sunday dinner was about to begin. Her sister and her family just arrived before her, as they attended another church. She could hear her father, who had not gone to church this morning because of an undisclosed ailment, yelling his head off in his study. There was only one person he'd be that upset with: her brother Boris. He'd skipped church, and his father was letting him have it. Katya decided to intervene so dinner would not be delayed. She hadn't eaten breakfast, and she was hungry.

Her father was at his desk, which had a large gray metal box sitting on it. Boris was standing across from him, slump-shouldered with his usual sheepish expression.

'Why didn't you let me know earlier you needed your baptismal certificate? Now you've missed the deadline for the examinations. What's to become of you, boy? You've had every advantage in life, but you're lazier than a goddamn peasant.'

Aleksandr Vassilievitch halted his tirade when he saw his daughter. Then he pointed his finger at Boris.

'This blockhead failed to get his baptismal certificate in on time,' fumed her father, his face beet-red. Katya took action, as she always worried about him getting a heart attack. It was impossible to legally exist in Russia without a baptismal certificate issued by the Church. She frowned at her brother, who looked away.

'Is it in there?' Katya pointed to the box. She had never seen it before.

'Yes, all the family papers are in there,' her father snapped.

'Both of you go into the dining room,' she commanded, and they obeyed. Katya knew she had to find the certificate herself to calm her father down, so she needed peace and quiet.

She undid the latch and looked inside to see a jumble of papers that her father had stuffed in over the years. She rummaged through the mess, but was quickly frustrated so she dumped the entire contents on the desk and began sorting through it, creating one neatly stacked pile. Her stomach was rumbling from hunger now. The papers went back to the early nineteenth century. She stopped cold when she found her mother's death certificate. It said she died of cholera and was signed by a doctor. It was sadly ironic to Katya that now she signed a few of these each week.

She continued sorting and was about to place a paper on the stack when something caught her eye. Next to the name of Leonid Alexandrovitch Golitsyn was a red dot. She looked at the date, 1801, and mentally did a family tree, mumbling out the names of ancestors – Leonid was her great-grandfather. She set that paper aside and continued looking until it slowly dawned on her where she'd seen that red dot before – in the hospital files – and what Krensky the clerk had told her. Her eyes widened in disbelief. She tore through the pile on the desk. She found Boris's baptismal certificate but kept looking until she found what she was really after: *a baptismal certificate for a Jewish convert to the Orthodox Church in Leonid's name.*

Katya put her hand to her mouth in astonishment. She stared at the yellowed paper for over a minute, her mind spinning like she was on an out-of-control carousel. Steadying herself against the desk, she folded the document and slid it in her skirt pocket. As if in a trance, she slowly put all the other papers back in the box and shut it, then walked into the dining room with Boris's certificate in hand. The meal had already begun.

'You look like you've seen a ghost,' Yelena said.

FOURTEEN

'Yes, Minister, I think we will follow your guidance on the new army-issue pistol. Thank you very much for seeing me.'

Von Dalek, the Minister of War, bowed and backed out of the Tsar's study at Tsarskoe Selo and into the antechamber where other officials were waiting their turn to see the Tsar. It reminded Dimitri of a doctor's waiting room, furnished with tables, chairs, and magazines. It led to a small courtyard where more men waited.

Dimitri stood by the Tsar's Fabergé-appointed desk. It was as orderly as Nicky was. Every pen and piece of paper, as well as the calendar with appointments written in by the Tsar's hand, was always exactly in the same place. Nicky had told Dimitri that he wanted to be able go into the study in the pitch dark and place his hand on any object. The Tsar was unlike any other monarch because he had no private secretary, he preferred to handle things himself. Even the Tsarina had a secretary to help her with her mountains of correspondence. When official papers arrived on Nicky's big writing desk, he opened, read, and signed each one of them.

Three men in dress uniforms filed in and bowed. These were the Grand Dukes and Nicky's uncles – Vladimir, Commander of the Imperial Guard; Alexis, Grand Admiral of the Navy; and Sergei, the Governor-General of Moscow. The brothers of Alexander III exerted an intimidating bullying influence on Nicky, who hated to be left alone with them. That was why Dimitri was in the study, although they barely acknowledged his presence. All of the uncles were huge, bearish men who towered over the slim, five-foot-seven-inch Tsar. They all wanted special favors and considered their requests as orders to their thirty-five-year-old nephew.

'Nicky, the French-made pistol is far superior to the one von Dalek wants,' bellowed Grand Duke Vladimir. He went on for five minutes denigrating the Minister of War's choice of the weapon. Nicky sat and listened in silence.

When the Grand Duke finished, the Tsar smiled at him and said, 'Then, Uncle, we shall have the French pistol.' Both Dimitri and Nicky knew that his uncle probably had a financial arrangement with the French arms manufacturer.

To everyone's dismay, the Tsar had trouble making decisions of any kind. Then when he did, he changed his mind. The only constant about Nicky was his inconsistency. He was slow about almost everything he did, whether it was writing a letter or pasting a photograph in an album. The Tsarina was the exact opposite; quick and decisive. Nicky had the peculiar habit of basing his final decision on the advice of the very last minister or relative he met with. That was why so many jockeyed to get the last word in. He especially hated confrontations of any kind and would never tell someone he disagreed with their opinion, especially his uncles. Upon the early death of his father, Nicky had ascended the throne totally unprepared at the young age of twenty-six. His father had taught him absolutely nothing about governing the Empire. Dimitri remembered him saying, 'What is going to happen to me and to all of Russia? I am not prepared to be a Tsar. I never wanted to become one.'

Now, it was the Grand Admiral's turn. Uncle Alexis was round as a barrel at two hundred and fifty pounds, and a notorious *bon vivant*. He unrolled a sheath of maps onto the desk.

'We have done more mapping of the terrain around Port Arthur for the gun emplacements, Nicky.' Port Arthur was a naval station on the Pacific coast that Russia had wrested control of from China, to the dismay of Japan. It was ice-free the whole year and was the headquarters of Russia's Pacific Fleet. Nicky, who didn't like clutter on his desk, moved the maps aside. The Grand Admiral then began a ten-minute plea for Danchenko to be promoted over Lyvoko for vice-admiral for the Tenth Squadron.

When Uncle Sergei's turn came, he began by slamming his ham-sized fist onto Nicky's desk.

'Goddamn it, Nicky, why do you let so many Jews live in

St Petersburg? *All* Jews belong in the Pale. The Jews lead the revolutionary movement to overthrow us.' The Tsar listened without a trace of emotion. In 1891, as Governor-General, Sergei had kicked every Jew out of Moscow. In addition to being a vicious anti-Semite, he was a comically narrow-minded man. He had forbidden his wife, Ella, to read *Anna Karenina* because it aroused 'unhealthy curiosity.'

Sergei changed the subject to something he felt was far more important.

'Nicky, I'll be needing about sixty thousand rubles for the alteration of my villa in Livadia,' he said as if he were asking for a cigarette. He avoided eye contact with Dimitri because he wasn't the architect for the renovation.

Money was a sensitive subject. As head of the house of Romanov, Nicholas was responsible for managing a fortune of twenty-four million gold rubles. There was another forty million in the form of Imperial jewelry, like the 194-carat 'Orlov Diamond' and the 'Moon of the Mountain Diamond' of 120 carats. But these riches were drained by the upkeep of all the palaces, yachts, and trains, the salaries for servants, the Imperial charities, and the Imperial Theaters, including the Imperial Ballet. These expenses left the Tsar almost penniless by the end of every year. Each of the Grand Dukes including his cousins, who were also called grand dukes, received one hundred thousand rubles a year. They ran through that quickly and were constantly pestering him for more money.

The uncles spent another fifteen minutes giving unsolicited advice, then they took their leave. The Tsar smiled at his friend and shrugged his shoulders. Nicholas began going through the stack of official envelopes from his ministers. He came to a small card that was stuck in between them and held it up for Dimitri to see. Written in block letters in pen, it read: *YOU SHALL DIE.* Dimitri was shocked and started to speak, but the Tsar held up his hand. He didn't seem disturbed by the discovery at all.

'Lately, death threats have been slipped into the ministerial pile. I just hand them over to the Okhrana.'

'But to get into that pile, someone inside the household must do it,' Dimitri cried.

'An emperor must expect such things. Remember that dirty cloth I was sent? The Okhrana laboratory tested it, and it was infected with plague germs like von Plehve said. That was a far more cunning, almost ingenious attempt on my life.'

Dimitri still thought of that blue swatch of cloth. If it hadn't been intercepted, it would have spread death throughout the palace killing not only the Tsar's family but many others in the household including himself. There was no medicine to cure the plague. Impressed by Nicky's courage and demeanor, Dimitri knew his friend had accepted the fact that there were people who wanted him dead.

The children bounded into the study during the brief interval between ministerial visits. They were accompanied by Miss O'Brian, who was carrying a Kodak Brownie.

Dimitri liked the gray-haired nanny because the girls adored her. Although she had a very severe English-looking face with a pointy chin, Miss O'Brian was the opposite of British reserve with a wide toothy smile and a jolly nature.

'Nanny has been taking snaps of us with her new camera, Papa,' said Olga in a giddy voice. 'We'll have ever so many more pictures for the albums. We made funny faces and Nanny snapped them. Come, Dimitri, pose with us!'

The Tsar loved pictures of his family, and he kept his many photo albums in the adjoining billiards room. They were all bound in green Moroccan leather and embossed with gold double-headed eagles. An official photographer printed the pictures, and the family loved to sit together on rainy days to paste them in the albums. But Miss O'Brian's photos were far more fun and informal. Dimitri was delighted to join in, and so was the Tsar, who got up from his desk to pose. Any fun family event took precedence over his work.

Miss O'Brian, who was by the Tsar's desk, snapped the camera twice by mistake.

'Oh, Nanny, you took snaps of Papa's desk, that won't do,' chided Marie as her sisters burst into laughter.

'Oh, dear, wasn't that foolish of Nanny?' Miss O'Brian said with a giggle.

'Don't let it bother you, Miss O'Brian,' Dimitri said. 'I've ruined a few snaps in my time.'

Dimitri bowed to the Tsar and waved goodbye to the children.

'Come back tomorrow for tea, Dimitri,' Tatiana shouted.

As Dimitri was walking down the hallway, he checked his pocket watch and saw that he had plenty of time to dress for the theater. He backtracked a few yards and opened a door to a room on his right. It was the Alexander Palace's display room for the Fabergé items. Dimitri loved to go in the room and look at the collection. Like a child playing with toys, he always opened the 'Trans-Siberian Railway Egg' first and wound up the foot-long miniature train inside. The incredible detail and craftsmanship never failed to amaze him. Each time he looked at an egg, he found another wonderful detail to marvel over. These things weren't valuable; they were one-of-a-kind priceless. He took out the surprise from his next favorite egg, the tiny exquisite gold carriage in the yellow enamel 'Coronation Egg,' and wheeled it back and forth. Then he opened a gold and blue egg to reveal a miniature solid-gold model of the former Imperial Yacht, the *Azova*. Suddenly realizing time had flown by, he closed the yacht egg. Lara would kill him if he were late. He didn't notice a tiny folded paper tucked under the golden yacht.

FIFTEEN

'Y ou'd look smashing in that hat.'

Dimitri and Katya were walking up the Nevsky Prospect, looking at storefront displays after their tea.

'I'm afraid I couldn't do it justice.'

'Nonsense. Go ahead and buy it.'

'I'm a practical girl and don't shop on impulse. Let me think about it,' she said with the cute smile that he found so charming.

As usual in the mid-afternoon, both sides of the Nevsky were jam-packed with people visiting the expensive shops that lined the great thoroughfare. A bobbing sea of men in black suits and women in colorful day dresses made up a tide of human beings. If one wanted to stop and talk with another, they had to step to the side against a building to avoid being swept away. Soldiers in their uniforms were scattered throughout the crowd. An endless parade of single- and double-horse open carriages was driven by coachmen in top hats. In the middle of the cobblestone street were iron tracks; in each direction came trams full of people pulled by lumbering horses.

'It would be easier to swim across the Neva than cross the Nevsky,' Katya said.

Dimitri laughed. 'Yes, it's impossible to get to the other side.' He loved this bustle of life in the center of St Petersburg, the incredible variety of people walking along – Poles, Armenians, Muslims, Finns, Tartars, Circassians, Cossacks, and Mongols.

As they walked, Dimitri and Katya were deep in discussion about the last arts circle meeting. It was now late October, and Dimitri had been attending them every week since the summer. He had also been having tea or lunch with Katya each week; the time always had to work around Katya's hospital schedule. The more he was with her, the fonder he grew of her, but in the last month, he'd sensed a tiny change in her buoyant personality. It was like one note in a musical piece that was ever so slightly off.

'I was shocked by Ilya's photos. I can't seem to get them out of my mind,' Dimitri said. The arts circle discussions would always start out about the arts then veer into politics. The intellectuals had story after story about the miserable lives of peasants on the estates and the workers in the factories. At first, he thought it all hogwash, having never heard of such things at Court. Factory workers who lived in company housing filthier than pigsties? Children getting their hands and arms ripped off by the machines they operated?

But at the last meeting, an art instructor named Ilya Nicolay brought photographs he had taken of workers around St Petersburg. He said he was using the camera for social reform, as a man named Jacob Riis had done in America. The photos showed first-hand the suffering Russia. Dimitri was shocked by the filth and poverty of the workers in the pictures. Using flash photography, Ilya could shoot in the darkest hovels and factory barracks. Poor dirty people packed thirty in a room looked at the camera with dead eyes. Half-alive workers in rags slept on slimy floors. Emaciated child workers peered out from under the dangerous-looking machines where they slept. A mother with a shriveled breast fed a pathetically thin baby. Ilya had also traveled to villages to capture peasant life, which was almost as filthy and destitute as in the city. The shacks were like pigsties. He had a lot of pictures of dead rotting animals and wilted crops from a recent famine. Dimitri hadn't heard of any famine. Shaking his head, he just couldn't believe these pictures were taken in Russia. It was unbelievable to him, but everyone in the circle said they were real. If so, he thought, how could people be allowed to live like that?

As he shuffled through the dozens of photos, he wondered if the Tsar knew about this. Maybe he knew, but never mentioned it to Dimitri. It certainly wasn't some isolated circumstance. If things were this bad in St Petersburg, the grandest city in Russia, they must be worse in out-of-the-way places in the Empire. Dimitri owned country estates; were the peasants there living in shit?

'Yes, there it was in black and white; all the suffering and injustice,' Katya said gravely. 'He's bringing more pictures for the next meeting. He's thinking of publishing a book of them, but he doesn't have the money to do it. It doesn't matter, the government would ban it anyway. There's no freedom of expression in this country.'

Dimitri was puzzled. 'They would? But people should know about all this.'

'The intelligentsia has to improve society through practical reforms like education, public health, and political freedom. Science is the key to overcoming Russia's economic and social backwardness.' Katya caught herself speechifying and looked embarrassed. 'Sorry, I'll get down from my soapbox,' she said.

'Some people want to use violence to bring about change,' Dimitri said sadly. He was thinking of the plague cloth. Then there were the death threats in the ministerial pile; more had showed up over the past months, but thankfully, there had been no more assassination attempts.

'Marxism rejects violence as an instrument of revolution. But some revolutionaries insist that violence is the only way to overthrow the Tsar.'

Dimitri enjoyed the arts circle including the political discussion but always felt uncomfortable when talk turned to replacing the Tsar's rule with a democracy and a parliament. But no one, not even Grigory, the most rabid of the bunch, had proposed using violence. If anyone had, Dimitri would have walked out then and there. He couldn't bear the thought of hurting the Imperial Couple and their children.

'Are you a Marxist?' Dimitri asked, hoping Katya had chosen the non-violent path.

Katya laughed. 'I don't know what I am. But I'm a doctor who saves lives not takes life so I could never be a terrorist.'

'I know I could never kill anyone,' Dimitri said in a firm voice.

'But there has to be change in Russia,' Katya insisted.

'The Romanovs have been Russia's divine rulers for almost three hundred years. They feel they know what's best for their people, not a parliament.'

Katya stopped in mid-step, faced Dimitri, and scowled. 'After seeing those pictures, do you actually believe that?'

Her cornflower-blue gaze bored into him. Taken back by her ferocity, he had no reply. Then her expression softened.

'Please forgive me for snapping at you.'

He saw a convenient way to change the topic.

'See that lot over there? That's where the Tchaikovsky Memorial I'm designing will go.' The brick and stone building on the site was beginning to be demolished. He had shared some of the preliminary drawings with Katya, who was very excited by the project. He liked the fact that she didn't hold back criticism of the design. Most architects would have been deeply offended.

Katya's mood completely changed.

'It must be wonderful to see a building you've designed get built. It goes from a drawing to a huge three-dimensional object.' Briefly she placed her hand on his arm. The sensation of her warm touch was wonderful, and he was sorry when she removed it.

'It is. I remember the first commission I had, a little pavilion in the Crimea, and the incredible feeling of elation when it was completed.'

'You have great passion for your art. I like that,' Katya said, her eyes glowing.

Dimitri liked looking directly into Katya's eyes; they and her enchanting personality were like magnets that drew him. Her interest was such a contrast to Lara's boredom when he used to excitedly describe a new project. Dimitri hadn't bothered to tell his wife about his commissions for years.

'Ah, but I always hear the passion in your voice when you talk about your patients,' Dimitri said. 'Like that little boy you brought back from the brink of death.'

Katya gave him a bashful smile which he found very charming.

'Now, Mr Classicist, I want to show *you* something just down the street,' she said, taking him by the arm.

They joined the torrent of humanity and walked west over the Fontanka Canal bridge. As they strolled, they looked in the plate-glass windows of haberdashers, dressmakers, confectioners, and druggists. Then Dimitri paused for a beat when he spotted Lara with some other people looking at displays in the showroom of a women's clothes shop. With her female friends, including Princess Betsey, was General Vladimir Pevear. Pointing at a hat, he made a comment that convulsed the ladies in hysterics. He was the epitome of the tall, dashing military man with ramrod-straight posture and dark almost exotic good looks. It was said that his great-grandmother was a Tartar princess. Lara held his arm while she slowly walked about, perusing the merchandise. Men often accompanied aristocratic women while shopping, especially if they were beautiful. The women insisted that they wanted a man's opinion on a selection, while in truth they couldn't care less. What did a man know about ladies' fashion? The men in Court, Lara always said, preferred seeing the females out of their clothes.

The fact that she was in the company of a man didn't bother him a bit. Except for social and Court functions, he and Lara spent very little time together. She liked to say about a husband,

'Give me a husband who, like the moon, won't appear in my sky every day.'

Dimitri's instinctive reaction was that he didn't want her to see Katya, so he switched positions to block her out of view. There was nothing wrong with being seen in public with someone of a lower social class, especially if they were from a rich family, but Lara had ridiculed him for days after for dancing with the plain-looking Katya at the Catherine Palace ball. She wouldn't let up. Dimitri had kept their weekly arts circle meetings and teas secret. If she saw Katya with him, he'd be in for a new round of abuse. He pretended to want a closer look at something in the window. Katya continued talking, and Lara never spotted them as they walked on.

'This is the Eliseyev Emporium, just finished,' Katya called out at the corner, pointing to a stone building with a great shallow arch. At each corner stood a bronze statue. Dimitri already knew about the new store but didn't want to let on and spoil Katya's excitement over showing him.

'Isn't it beautiful? And don't you dare say it's "interesting!"' she cried.

He burst into laughter. 'It is bold, and I do like the way the storefront transoms are detailed. The wrought-iron balconies are well done.'

'You're not placating me? I won't stand for it.'

'No,' he replied, looking up at the building. 'It has a classical proportion with a base, shaft, and top, but with very imaginative detailing. It reminds me of work by an American, Louis Sullivan.'

They continued walking and turned right on Konnogvardeysky Boulevard toward her house. They talked about the ballet, and how Pavlova's long lithe figure had changed the body type of Russia's ballerinas. They wouldn't be short and voluptuous like Kschessinska anymore. Dimitri and Katya could discuss any topic under the sun. He was disappointed when they reached her front door.

They said their polite goodbyes. As Katya's elderly servant was opening the door for her, and she turned to go inside, Dimitri touched her shoulder lightly.

'Please forgive me for asking, but you seemed to be troubled by something lately. Is everything all right?'

Katya looked up into his concerned eyes and gave him a shy smile.

'You're a very intuitive and thoughtful man,' she replied slowly. She looked genuinely touched. 'No, it's just a small family matter, nothing bad.'

'Oh, good. Then are you available for tea tomorrow afternoon?'

'Yes, my shift is over at three. I'd love to have tea.'

'At three then,' Dimitri said with a bow. 'My carriage will be waiting.'

Before Katya turned to go inside, she stopped and faced him.

'I came across the oddest story,' she said with a perplexed expression. 'It was about these Jewish boys conscripted into the army who were coerced into converting to Christianity. To please Tsar Alexander I, who was to inspect the camp, the commanding officer arranged for a group of twenty Jewish recruits to be baptized by a priest in the river. But when they were submerged, they had made a pact to not come up. They drowned themselves – still holding hands. You have to have a very strong faith to make that kind of sacrifice.'

Dimitri was puzzled by this. It came out of nowhere, and he didn't know how to respond.

'Yes . . . the Hebrews are a strange race,' he said.

Katya's expression froze, and she darted into the house.

SIXTEEN

Miss O'Brian checked the time by looking at the little watch pinned to her blouse. Her four charges would be starting their dancing lessons now. They all danced very gracefully; even two-year-old Anastasia was getting the hang of it. With all the balls they would have to attend, the earlier they learned to dance, the better. In addition to their regular school lessons, the Tsarina also sat in and observed their dancing lessons while doing embroidery work. Coming from a small German court where royalty occupied themselves usefully, she hated the idleness of the Imperial Court. She wanted to stay busy, even when she was with the children. Miss O'Brian could remember her holding her infant babies while reading and signing papers of state. A woman of exceptional intelligence, the Tsarina wanted her daughters to have well-developed minds and intellectual interests, unlike the ladies of the Court – especially that silly Lara Markhov. All the young women in Court, the Tsarina said, seem to have nothing in their heads but officers and parties. She dreaded for her daughters the companionship of the women of the aristocracy, who would fill their heads with vicious gossip and wicked values.

Miss O'Brian checked her watch again and decided she had time to make a detour across the Moika Canal to the Nevsky Prospect, to buy the raspberry-filled chocolates the girls loved so much. It wasn't as though they were continually spoiled. On the contrary, she was shocked to find that the Grand Duchesses slept on hard camp beds without a pillow and covered by one plain blanket. They had cold baths every morning, and warm ones at night. Only porridge and bread were served at breakfast. This was all due to the fact that their father, Nicholas, had been raised the same Spartan way by his father Alexander III, a bear of a man who prided himself on living a simple rigorous life reminiscent of a peasant's. But the reason she was making the trip for the candy was because she truly loved her girls. As with many nannies, if not biologically, these were her own children. Eight-year-old Olga had grace, wit, and good looks, but she also had a temper; six-year-old Tatiana looked like her mother and also inherited her kind disposition. Four-year-old Marie, the most beautiful, had wonderful wide eyes and red-rose cheeks. Anastasia was turning into a clever child with a penchant for mischief. They all had a tomboy inclination, which pleased Nicholas, who loved to roughhouse with them. The Tsar was an exceptionally loving father who spent every spare minute he had with them and his wife. He was nothing like Miss O'Brian's father, a stern, gruff factory worker in London, a Marxist agitator who lived for the overthrow of the capitalists the world over. The man breathed revolution like a dragon breathes fire. From the time she was a toddler, Constance O'Brian had been indoctrinated in the revolutionary movement. It became her religion and passion. And now she had the opportunity to help topple an autocracy.

'You're doing the revolution a great service, Comrade.'

Every two weeks at an appointed time, Miss O'Brian met her revolutionary contact, Ivan Azref, on the second floor of a rundown building off an alley behind Krasnova Avenue.

Miss O'Brian handed her Kodak Brownie camera to the dashing fellow, who had a hawk-like nose and high cheekbones. Azref had been a captain in the Tsar's Household Guard for eight years. Now, he dedicated his life to the overthrow of the Tsar. Azref was quite pleased to hold the little black box camera.

'Why do you need maps of Port Arthur?' she asked.

Azref put the camera on the desk and motioned for Miss O'Brian to take a seat. He sat on the desk and pulled out a cigarette.

'Russia wants to take Korea away from Japan. Japan doesn't want to give it up and will go to war with Russia to stop them. They'll attack Port Arthur first to destroy the fleet,' Azref said in the slow measured tone a schoolmaster would use.

'Go to war with the Russian Empire? That's ridiculous, they'll be crushed,' Miss O'Brian said with disdain.

'That's what most Russians would say. That the Empire would never be defeated by a bunch of "yellow monkeys," as they call the Japanese.'

'But isn't it true?'

'No, because the Japanese have been modernizing their military in the last ten years and now have a far superior army and navy.'

'So, a Russian defeat would *help* the revolution,' Miss O'Brian said in an astonished voice.

'Exactly. We have to make that defeat happen to bring about the civil dissent to fuel the revolution. All the men who'll die needlessly in the war will be peasants who will be quite angry with the Tsar and the government. Your help, Comrade, is absolutely critical to our mission.'

'Yes,' the nanny replied excitedly.

'We need every scrap of information about Russia's plans in the Far East. The Tsar meets with his military advisors and ministers in his study in the Alexander Palace, and you have access to that study. You must commit to memory any information you can find.'

'A fifty-year-old nanny is as invisible as the servants. No adult pays her any attention or even realizes she's in the room,' replied Miss O'Brian with a wan smile.

'Another reason Russia will lose is that it has to transport every man and piece of equipment over four thousand miles on a single track of the Trans-Siberian Railway. Japan is only two hundred miles from Korea.'

'I'll be proud to be an agent if it helps bring about revolution,' she said earnestly. Then, suddenly, she scowled at Azref. 'But I'll have nothing to do with violence, do you understand? Marx rejected violence! I won't do *anything* that will harm the Imperial Family!'

Azref got up and placed his hand on her shoulder.

'No, Comrade. We don't believe in violence either. There is a rogue faction called the Combat Group that does believe in terrorism, but we have nothing to do with them.'

The angry look on Miss O'Brian's face disappeared.

'You are our most important *agent provocateur* in the Imperial household.'

A puzzled look came over her face.

'You have other agents in the household – in the palaces?'

'Yes,' Azref said in a matter-of-fact voice. 'But for your own protection, you can't know who they are. The Okhrana would torture you to get their names.'

As Miss O'Brian's mind was forming images of such a thing, Azref handed her a tiny folded note.

'You will always deliver your war information directly to me. But you'll also be our new postman delivering messages to our inside agents via the Fabergé "mailboxes." Put this note inside any Imperial Egg in the display room in the Alexander

Palace, then move the egg slightly forward of the others. And when *you* see an egg that's been moved, you'll bring its message back to me so I can decode it.' He showed her a small leather-bound notebook that was filled with columns of letters of the alphabet next to columns of different letters. She immediately understood the system, an A for example was transposed into a C.

Miss O'Brian's somber expression changed into a big smile.

'The freedom of movement that comes with your position makes it far easier and safer to make a delivery than with the other agents we've been using,' Azref explained.

The nanny tucked the note carefully in her jacket pocket. As she was leaving, Azref noticed there was a pronounced bounce in her step.

SEVENTEEN

D imitri was standing on the deck of the *Standart*, the sleek black-hulled Imperial Yacht, where Nicholas and Alexandra could escape from the Court and the demands of government. At four million rubles, it was the most luxurious private yacht in the world. Steaming on the calm blue waters of the Gulf of Finland, a constant cool breeze swept over the ship as the bright summer sun shone on its gleaming teak decks. Under white canvas awnings were wicker tables and chairs where Alexandra would sit, knitting, reading, or just looking out to sea, especially at sunset. The Tsar would join her for a while, but he preferred to move about the ship in his white naval uniform talking to the captain and crew. He would sometimes row ashore and take walks by himself in the Finnish forests or take the children to pick berries and wildflowers. The girls loved the yacht because it meant uninter-rupted time with their father.

Unlike the palaces, life on the *Standart* was extremely informal. The family mingled freely with the crew, and they were on a first-name basis with the sailors and officers. The girls could go about the deck as they pleased, but Anastasia had a sailor assigned to her to make sure she didn't fall overboard. The other three children had learned to swim. At the end of the cruise, he would be awarded a gold watch for his service by the Tsar. The ship was a thirty-room floating palace with imperial cabins and staterooms. Below were the galleys, the officers, the crew, a platoon of Marine Guards, and a brass band and balalaika orchestra. There was even a stall for a cow to provide fresh milk for the girls. For all its incredible opulence, the *Standart* was constantly plagued with rats, which the family had become used to as though they were members of the crew. If a rat entered a guest's cabin, they were instructed to throw a shoe at it.

Nicholas hated working onboard the yacht, but he had to keep up with government matters. Although he banned his ministers and police security from the *Standart*, courier boats powered by the new gasoline outboard motors carried official documents from St Petersburg daily to the ship. Whenever the tsar was on a cruise, an escort destroyer was off on the horizon and two small navy torpedo boats were a few hundred yards away. Today was the same relaxing routine – swimming, fishing, exploring the beach, then supper at nine. After tonight's meal, the family was entertained by the ship's balalaika orchestra playing Russian folk songs in the state dining saloon. Dimitri sat by Alexandra.

'Look, Dimitri, at my little happy family,' she said.

He reached into the pocket of his white tunic. 'I left my cigarette case up on deck,' he said in an irritated voice. It was the Fabergé case the Tsar had given to him for Easter, and he panicked when he thought he might have lost it.

'Excuse me for a moment, Your Majesty.'

'Leave it, Dimitri. You smoke too much,' scolded Olga. Dimitri winked at the Grand Duchess and went up on deck. He found the case on a wicker table. Taking out a cigarette, he looked up into the evening sky. At these northern latitudes in the summer, its color was a milky haze of pearl, so he could still see out to sea very clearly. The *Standart* was at anchor, and the only sound in the night was the lapping of the sea against the hull. Dimitri heard a low motor from the direction of the coast. As he tossed the cigarette into the sea, he realized the noise was getting louder. In the evening light, he could make out an Imperial courier boat coming toward the yacht. He went back to the saloon and passed an officer, Captain Oneff.

'There's a courier boat coming alongside,' Dimitri said.

'At this late hour, it must be an urgent dispatch,' Oneff said. Both men went up on deck.

Oneff had brought a pair of binoculars and scanned the direction.

'It's odd there's no helmsman at the rudder,' he said.

'Call out the Marine Guard!' Dimitri yelled suddenly. Oneff blew the whistle around his neck repeatedly until a dozen soldiers in white and red tunics came running on deck.

'Rapid fire at that boat – and don't let up!' Oneff screamed.

The night air was filled with non-stop rifle fire. The boat was about fifty yards away now. The naval officers joined them and fired their revolvers.

Now only thirty yards from the hull of the *Standart*, the courier boat, riddled with bullets, exploded in a ball of fire lighting up the sky like the sun. Pieces of wood hurled into the air, and burning wood floated on the water. Then there was complete silence. Dimitri heard footsteps, the Tsar ran up on deck with a look of shock.

'Goddamn it,' yelled Blokh. In a fury, he hurled his cap to the ground and started pacing around it. He leaned against a birch tree and with a stunned expression, looked out from the edge of the forest at the burning debris in the Gulf of Finland.

'Come on, we have to get the hell out of here,' said Hersch, tugging on his friend's sleeve.

EIGHTEEN

'We'll have a wide red granite arch as the entryway. Within it, the words "Tchaikovsky Memorial" will be carved and the date of construction.'

'That will be impressive, Dimitri. We should have two great staircases, one for the conservatory students, and the other for concertgoers to get to the balconies. I've decided that nothing but Tchaikovsky's works will be played here,' the Tsar said excitedly.

The Imperial Family had just returned from a religious ceremony in Sarov, and Dimitri had been invited to supper. Afterward, he joined the family in Alexandra's boudoir. The Tsarina was stretched out on her mauve chaise longue doing embroidery. Marie and Anastasia were spread out on the carpet playing with toys, and the two oldest were reading. As he did every week, Dimitri went over the latest sketches of the Tchaikovsky Memorial with Nicholas, laying out the basic spaces. The plan of the building would be just about final when Nicholas, like all clients, decided to add or change something.

'There should be a niche in the center of the lobby for the portrait of Tchaikovsky.'

'We have it centered in the outer foyer now.'

'The lobby would be better. More room to look at it,' Nicky replied.

'You should put in an ice-cream parlor, Dimitri,' said Marie. Her sisters chimed in in agreement, which made Nicky laugh.

'I hope you enjoyed yourself at Sarov, Alix,' Dimitri said, not looking up from the sketch he was doing.

'I prayed to St Seraphim for divine intercession to grant us a son, Dimitri.'

Dimitri met Alexandra's gaze. He knew how she felt. After two years of trying to have a child, Dimitri, while not a religious man, had even tried praying to God to grant his most fervent wish. He craved to be a father, but nothing had happened. He actually began to believe God was punishing him for something he'd done by making them unable to conceive.

When Anastasia was born in 1901, Dimitri knew that beneath the joy was great disappointment on the Tsarina's part. Being brought up by Queen Victoria, Alexandra was familiar with women being heads of state. But Russia was different. Tsar Paul I, who had so hated his mother Catherine the Great, had decreed that no woman would ever sit on the throne. When Nicky almost died in 1900 of cholera, the heir was his brother, Michael – not Olga, their oldest child. The dream of providing a son and heir for Russia had become an obsession for Alexandra.

'You and Nicky were quite moved by the ceremony in Sarov, weren't you?' Dimitri said gently.

The Imperial Couple along with clergy, bishops, and Grand Dukes had participated in the canonization of St Seraphim of Sarov, a holy man linked with miraculous healings. Because ancestors of the Tsars were said to have been healed by him, Nicholas had initiated the proceedings, which delighted the Tsarina.

'It was an incredibly touching experience, I'll never forget it,' Nicky replied.

'At night, I bathed in the holy pond while Nicky sat on the bank. St Seraphim is my intercessor before God, and I entrust my will to Him. He will provide us a son.'

Dimitri smiled and nodded. Lara constantly ridiculed the Tsarina's faith, and Dimitri, who genuinely liked the Empress, had to agree that she took it to a ridiculous level. But nonetheless, he admired her unwavering piety. It was her nature; if she believed in something, she believed with all her heart without reservation.

'Our Tsarina *will* have her son.' Anna Vyrubova was sitting in an armchair doing needlework. This young woman had become the Tsarina's closest confidante, visiting with her daily. Anna worshipped the Tsarina. She lived in her own cottage at Tsarskoe Selo. She wasn't a member of Court because Alexandra didn't want a friend in the Court that she hated so much. To Dimitri, she seemed like a bootlicker. The Court, which was quite envious of Anna's access, spread ridiculous lies about her, like she was sleeping with all the black Abyssinian Guards, or appeared in the nude in her window which was across from a sentry box. This was total nonsense, though one of the children's nurses was caught in bed with a Cossack a couple months ago. Alexandra had sacked her on the spot.

'The crowd was wonderful, Dimitri. Fifteen thousand people

were at the monastery, all cheering me. I moved amongst them, and they reached out to touch me,' Nicky explained with great emotion. 'The police did not hold them back. The people *blanketed* me with their affection.'

'They worshipped St Seraphim – and our Tsar,' Anna added in a reverential tone.

'These were my people who love me with all their heart. That is why as their divine emperor, I must take care of them. I am their Little Father, and they are my children. I alone know what's best for them.'

'You are anointed by God,' Alexandra added at which the Tsar nodded.

'You'll see, Dimitri. God will grant us a son and heir,' Alix said.

A tall footman dressed in scarlet and gold livery brought in the evening tea and set it down on the table next to the Tsarina.

'Thank you, Leonid,' said Alexandra.

'Time for bed, my little bears,' announced Miss O'Brian, standing at the door to the boudoir. The girls collectively groaned. 'Just a while longer?' Tatiana pleaded.

'I forgot to fill my cigarette case,' the Tsar said testily, starting to rise from his chair.

'Your Majesty, kindly allow me to get them for you,' the nanny said.

'Thank you. The cigarettes are in the mahogany humidor on my desk in the study,' Nicky said as he handed Miss O'Brian the case.

Nicky's words 'blanketed me with affection' stayed with Dimitri as he walked home to his Tsarskoe Selo mansion. This certainly didn't agree with the opinion of those in his arts circle who kept insisting that all Russians hated the Tsar and the autocracy. And those poor devils in Ilya's photos probably didn't have any love for their Tsar either. The terrorists who sent the motorboat into the *Standart* certainly didn't. Who were these people would kill at any cost? The members of the circle knew that violence against the Empire was useless – not to mention being morally wrong. Dimitri was still quite shaken by the attempt on the yacht. Not because he'd could have been killed, but because the children would have perished. That thought sent a shiver through him every time.

He couldn't believe Nicky could be hated so. But maybe it was true; those pictures didn't lie. An emperor who allowed so many to live that way was bound to be hated – not by a few terrorists but millions of Russians. But Nicky was a kind, gentle man; not capable of such brutality. The Tsar loved Russia. Dimitri was greatly troubled by all this. His first instinct was to make excuses for his friend, that the ministers of the Court knew all about this. They hid it from the Tsar so they wouldn't incur his wrath. He would never stand for his 'children' to live like animals. The minute Nicky found out about this travesty, he would issue an *ukase*, an imperial proclamation having the force of law, to stop such a thing. He must bring the matter to his attention – in a subtle manner.

As Dimitri walked up the marble steps of his home, he was met by Fedor, which meant Lara was here. As he kneeled to rub the borzoi's head, suddenly a shocking thought occurred to him: Fedor had a better life than millions of Russians.

NINETEEN

'When a people lose their nation, they disappear. But contrary to that rule, Jews continue to survive all over the world where they're considered strangers. We've survived since the destruction of the Temple in Jerusalem in AD 70, and that's why we're special,' Baron Jacob Grunberg explained.

Katya had never really had a conversation with a Jew. There were only a tiny number living in St Petersburg. They were of a special class like the Baron, a very wealthy merchant. These Jews were the elite and were allowed to live outside the Pale. Many Jewish doctors and surgeons, including those at St Igor's, were also part of this class. One of Katya's patients was the baron's niece, and she'd met him while he was visiting her and struck up a conversation.

Katya was greatly troubled by the discovery about her family. It had sent a bolt of shame through her. It was silly because she was a baptized member of the Russian Orthodox Church. She was as Jewish as the light fixture above her head. But her family's hidden past scared her. She felt as though she had a Star of David stuck on her back for all to see. She lived in a constant state of fear of being found out by her Christian world – and worse, the government. Jews were hated and persecuted in Russia; the recent pogroms had indiscriminately slaughtered scores of them and no one in Russia gave a damn. It wouldn't just be her that would suffer but her entire family. Suppose her father's beloved textile business was taken from him? Would friends abandon her because she had Jewish ancestry? Maybe they would take away her job she loved so much. That thought was unbearable. Then what if Dimitri found out and shunned her?

Dozens of horrible scenarios raced through her mind each day. She couldn't keep all this inside any longer and had to talk to someone. The irony was that she was frightened to death but at the same time was intrigued by her Jewish roots and wanted to find out more about them.

The Baron was a cheerful rotund man in his fifties. He had a walrus mustache, slicked-back black-dyed hair, and gentle brown eyes. Some Jews had been so successful that the Empire bestowed the title of baron upon them. But it was for a very few, because some gentile barons felt insulted.

The Baron seemed amused about her questions about Judaism. He was puffing away on a large cigar as they sat in the visitors' lounge.

'Your religion seems to have a strong set of beliefs,' Katya said.

'But what's most important is not just believing in those beliefs but acting upon them. Doing good things. So, tell me, why does a young Christian girl want to know so much about us Christ-killers?' The Baron raised his thick eyebrows and smiled.

'Just intellectual curiosity. Jews are such a force in Russia's new cultural revival. It's very impressive to me. I greatly admire them,' Katya replied in an uncertain voice. 'And the

ones in the medical profession are the best in their fields, like
our doctors here at St Igor's,' she added hastily.

'You have an enlightened view, my dear. Most, including
the Tsar, think we're parasites and exploiters.'

Katya frowned. 'I think the intellectual class of Russia
doesn't see it that way.'

'Ah, it's wonderful to be young and naive,' he exclaimed.
'To have ideals before the harsh reality of life wipes them
away.'

'But the intellectuals aren't Jew-haters.'

'What people say and what people think are two completely
different things, my dear. Trust me,' the Baron said in a jolly
voice.

'Then what is the answer to Jew-hating in Russia?' Katya
asked in an almost inaudible voice.

'Men like Theodor Herzl say that a homeland in Palestine
is the only answer. But unfortunately, that's owned by the
Ottoman Empire. The United States is actually the land of
milk and honey – the new promised land, where a Russian
Jew can seek refuge from massacre and persecution. There,
they treat men as human beings who can practice their religion
without fear. Jews go there, write home how wonderful it is,
and more emigrate.'

'But if you've been treated in such an unjust way, why
haven't you gone, Baron?'

The Baron chuckled. 'My treatment here in St Petersburg is
nothing compared to the hardship of my people stuck in the
Pale. My wealth insulates me and my family from anti-Semitism.
But contrary to popular opinion, not all Jews are rich.'

'Those poor people in Kishinev and Gomel, how can they
stay after such a bloodbath?' asked Katya.

'This is very hard for gentiles to understand, but many
generations of Jews were born in Russia and consider themselves Russian first, Jews second. Russia is *their* homeland.
Their ancestors fought and died defending the Motherland
against Napoleon, and they won't be driven out.'

'I never thought of it in those terms,' Katya said.

'You're genuinely interested in all this, aren't you?' he
added in a tone of admiration. 'All right, here is a quick

primer on the Jewish faith. The Torah is like your Bible but just the Old Testament part. The first five books are written in the scrolls they read in the temple every week. But the big difference is that Christians worship Jesus as the Messiah, but Jews are still waiting for their savior to come.'

'And your Sabbath runs from sunset Friday to sunset Saturday,' added Katya, to show him she wasn't entirely ignorant.

'That is called Shabbat. And there are some high holy days, but not nearly the dozens you have for every single saint in the Orthodox Church, plus the patron saint's day of the Emperor, the Empress, the Dowager Empress, and on and on. With all these feast days and Sundays, there's a hundred non-working days. No wonder Russia is so backwards. No work ever gets done,' he said with a laugh. Katya joined in.

'Doctor, please join us at supper tonight so we can continue our discussion.'

'Thank you, but I have an engagement tonight. I'm free on Wednesday.'

'Delighted. We'll see you at 14 Vernovsky Street at eight.'

Katya had greatly enjoyed the Baron's company, and she was determined to learn more about her ancestors' religion. It was risky to be seen associating openly with Jews; it heightened the possibility of her being found out. But she would show up Wednesday night. An hour later, when she left the hospital, she looked behind her to see if any Okhrana agents were following.

TWENTY

Katya unwrapped the paper to find a three-inch-tall black enameled figure of a cat in a sitting position. There were two tiny diamonds for the eyes. It had the marque of Fabergé on the cat's back leg.

'I remember you said you were fond of cats,' Dimitri said. 'It's a black cat, but I didn't think you were the superstitious type.'

'This is very special. It's not the actual gift, but that you remembered that I love cats. It was just an off-the-cuff remark that night at the ball.'

'I thought you'd like it. After all, you're a cat-lover.'

'So it is. Thank you so much, Dimitri. You're so thoughtful.' She held up the figure to admire it. The cat's diamond eyes sparkled. She tucked it away in her pearl-beaded bag.

Tonight, they were standing under the cast-iron and glass entry canopy of one of the grand mansions on Plekhanova Avenue, where Katya was taking Dimitri to a party.

'Prince Dimitri and Doctor Golitsyn,' she announced to the servant, who opened the great bronze and glass doors.

'Yes, Your Highness and Madame Doctor, I will announce you,' said the tall servant.

Before he could turn to lead the way, a short slender woman dressed in a gold and blue Japanese kimono rushed up to them. She wore a gold-colored turban and held a long ivory and diamond cigarette holder in her hand as though it was a magic wand.

'Katya, I'm so happy you came. Ah, this must be the architect prince you've been telling me about.'

'Prince Dimitri Markhov, may I introduce you to Princess Maria Tenisheva.'

Dimitri bowed and kissed her hand. He had heard of this eccentric aristocrat who shunned the Imperial Court.

'The Princess is an artist of great talent,' Katya announced proudly. 'She has just designed the church and the interiors of her chapel on her estate, Talashkino. In, of course, the Style Moderne.' Katya directed Dimitri's attention to the walls of the vast entry hall they stood in. 'And she's responsible for the interior decoration of her home.'

The first thing that caught his attention was the great serpentine stair, which reminded him of a flowering vine ascending upstairs. It didn't have straight balusters, but curving sinuous wrought-iron work that flowed up under a curved wood railing. It was like it was a living organism not an inanimate object. Along the walls were painted swirling vines with flowers in orange and gold. The hall floor had a stone pattern that mimicked the wall's design with curving red and white granite.

'I can see that Prince Dimitri is transfixed by my design,' said the Princess.

'Ah, the Prince is a recent convert. He was committed to the glories of Rome and Greece,' Katya said, in a mock-scolding tone that made Dimitri laugh. 'But he's making good progress.'

'Well, we'll have to help him, won't we?' The Princess took Dimitri by the arm and escorted them to a grand drawing room. It was high-ceilinged and brightly lit; its walls were ablaze with painted, curving organic and botanical forms. At least two dozen men and women were drinking and chatting and servants in powdered wigs flitted about with trays of food and caviar.

'You see, Prince Dimitri, the Style Moderne, or what they call the "Art Nouveau" in Paris, is a complete art form. The furniture, fabrics, rugs, and even the electric lamps are designed to complement the style.' She was correct; every single object in the room was designed in the same manner. Dimitri was quite impressed a woman from the aristocracy did this. Then to his astonishment, he saw a leopard in a cage near the corner. It just sat there, observing the goings-on. The Princess saw Dimitri's eyes riveted to it.

'Yes, even my dear Xenia adores the Style Moderne.' Instead of regular bars, the cage had intertwined wrought-iron vines. Dimitri wondered if Xenia could squeeze out through them.

'Katya, you must take the prince to Fedor Schechtel's Riabushinsky House in Moscow. Now, there's a complete work of art.'

'We must,' Katya said in a gay voice.

'Stepan is a great friend and would be glad to have you as his guests. He's most proud of his house. Now, let me intro-duce you to some most stimulating people, Prince Dimitri.'

Three men talking immediately turned their attention to the Princess. They looked like dandified artistic types that one would never see at Court. Their cravats were of color instead of the accepted black, something that would be seen as scan-dalous and ridiculed by Lara and her cronies.

'Prince Dimitri, may I introduce Leon Bakst, Konstantin Somov, and this big fellow is Sergei Diaghilev.'

'A great pleasure to know such influential members of the world of art,' said Dimitri.

'We were just discussing the need for art to touch the Russian heart,' Diaghilev said enthusiastically.

'Tchaikovsky's String Concerto Number One was based on a Russian folk tune he heard whistled by a decorator painting the inside of his house one afternoon,' said Dimitri.

'Marvelous,' shouted the Princess. 'Tchaikovsky wanted a *Russian* music.'

'Dimitri is designing the Tchaikovsky Memorial for the Tsar,' Katya said proudly. 'In the Russian spirit, I may add.'

The group was genuinely impressed by this announcement, some clapped.

Arm in arm, Dimitri and Katya circulated through the great drawing room, stopping to talk to painters, playwrights, and authors. Other than Bakst, Diaghilev, and Somov, Dimitri had never heard of most of them. But he wasn't in the least bored. These people believed as Dimitri did, in 'art for art's sake,' and they shared a love of St Petersburg. He met women artists like Elena Polenova, who had illustrated children's books, some of which he'd read to the Tsar's daughters at bedtime. He persuaded her to scribble a little sketch of a duck and sign it as a gift for them.

The party sat down to supper in a large dining room lined with murals depicting nature in abstract patterns; the ceiling had a back-lit stained-glass skylight pulsating with sinuous vine-like leaded glass. Even the place settings of silver plates and cups had a flowing Style Moderne motif. As was the practice of the nobility, a gift was waiting on the plate for the guests. Dimitri found a Fabergé ashtray in gold, white, and green enamel with rubies. Katya received a *kovsh*, a small traditional Russian oval drinking cup, with a long handle made of gold encrusted with pearls and moonstones by Fabergé.

The supper was an energetic affair, with Diaghilev leading the conversation. As at the arts circle, the subject of revolution came up; how the arts could transform Russian society and uplift the peasants and workers.

'The workers live like animals,' exclaimed Somov. 'One day they'll rise up, you'll see.'

'Then it's the responsibility of the educated intelligentsia to lead them to revolution,' said Princess Tenisheva, and everyone vigorously agreed. The talk continued on and on through the sumptuous dessert of pastries, frosted cakes, and fruit-flavored ice creams. Servants filled glasses with champagne, French and Crimean wines, cognac, and sherry. A haze of cigarette smoke hung over the table like a storm cloud.

The Princess's house wasn't on the quay, but from an elaborate wrought-iron balcony one could see a part of the Neva flowing by. Katya and Dimitri stepped out into the cool night, refreshing after the dining room. Katya placed her hands on the railing and leaned forward, deeply inhaling the cold November night air. The moon was full and clear, and its reflection bounced off the river. Dimitri stood next to her.

Suddenly, Katya shivered.

'Oh, you're cold. Here, please take my jacket,' Dimitri insisted. He placed it on her shoulders then vigorously rubbed her back and arms.

'Yes, that feels much better,' Katya replied, pulling the jacket lapels together across her chest.

'Thank you for bringing me tonight, Katya. I'm having a wonderful time. To think that there are all these incredible artistic minds in this city,' he said.

'For even such a hide-bound aristocrat, I thought you might enjoy yourself.'

'It's nothing like this at Court. To even be the tiniest bit different from the norm brings scandal and ridicule raining down on one's head. I've seen it so many times. But these people revel in being different, even if a few come off as blowhards.'

'Ah, you're referring to Mr Diaghilev,' Katya said with a chuckle. 'That was sweet of you to get a drawing for the Tsar's daughters. You spend a lot of time with his family.'

'Yes, I do,' he said. 'I love the little Grand Duchesses.'

'I like children, too,' Katya replied, looking into the distance. 'They're the favorite part of my practice. It crushes me when some die so young, and I can't help them.'

'I thought doctors had to divorce their emotions from their professional practice.'

'In that regard, I'm a failure as a doctor,' Katya replied. She looked up into his eyes with a sad earnest expression that touched him. At that moment, a very wonderful sensation gripped at his heart. Despite being irresistibly drawn to her, he was a married aristocrat and she was a young single woman of the upper middle class. Unlike the women at Court, an open affair with a married man would compromise her reputation and could ruin her life. He was playing with fire and had to be careful. He knew that she also understood the rules of the game.

'You must constantly see life and death at battle with each other, not an easy sight to bear,' he said admiringly. He patted her hand resting on the railing and kept it there.

'We'd better go back in. Savva Mamontov is going to play the piano, and the Princess will sing,' Katya said. She placed her other hand on top of his. 'By the way, thank you again for my little cat. You must come to my home for dinner and meet my darling kitty, Noskey,' she added.

Katya rose up on tiptoes, and kissed Dimitri's cheek. Having her warm body so close to his was intoxicating; he couldn't hold back any longer. He looked about to see they were alone then in one fluid motion, he drew her to him, and gave her a kiss full on the lips. Katya responded, opening to him like a flower.

Breathlessly they parted. 'I – I guess we'd better get back inside,' she stammered.

Dimitri nodded. 'Yes, we should,' he said, and followed her back to the mansion. He felt like he could float up into the night sky and soar over St Petersburg.

TWENTY-ONE

D imitri did all his work in his St Petersburg mansion. There was no need for a separate office when the house was so huge that he could devote a suite of rooms to architecture. Built by his grandfather in the early 1800s, the studio was palatial, and done in the neo-classical style with white scagliola walls framed between green malachite pilasters. The white coffered ceiling was picked out in crimson and gold, with a huge crystal chandelier in the center. His two assistants, Vassily Kuzka and Mikhail Semyon, both graduates of the Institute of Civil Engineering, had large drafting tables with long side tables. They had been his employees (he never treated educated men as servants) for eight years, and they had been most dependable. Both could draw well, but Semyon had a special talent for construction administration – seeing that the building got built to the drawings. He paid them far more than they would get in an ordinary office, and they appreciated his high regard for them. In addition, few architects worked in a palace with servants to wait on them. Typically, architects' offices were dreary affairs with tables in a cold, threadbare room. Sitting on the plush furniture in Dimitri's office, they smoked, drank tea, and discussed architecture theory in general. They worked well as a team.

Dimitri had an extraordinary talent for drawing. He enjoyed doing the renderings and elevations himself instead of asking his staff to do them. Using pen and ink, he drew his designs with the finest detail. They were works of art unto themselves. After assembling the drawings he'd done for the Tchaikovsky Memorial, he called his men to join him. Semyon and Kuzka sat in high-backed armchairs in front of Dimitri's wide desk. Behind it was his own drafting table. Shelves filled with architectural tomes lined the walls.

'Here are the initial Tchaikovsky elevations and plans,' Dimitri announced. 'Tell me what you think.'

A puzzled look came over Kuzka's smooth baby-face. He handed the sketches to Semyon, whose eyes widened.

'These are quite different, Dimitri,' Semyon exclaimed. The young men exchanged grins.

'Not in the classical vein at all. This is the Style Moderne – so organic and flowing!' Kuzka cried.

'What a wonderful entry hall you've designed,' Semyon added in an enthusiastic voice. 'Very much like Victor Horta's work, "Hôtel Tassel" in Brussels.'

'Yes, I admire Horta's work very much,' Dimitri said in a matter-of-fact voice.

'It's the use of plant motifs on the stair that is so original,' Kuzka said pointing out the sinuous linework. 'The pattern in the lobby floor is marvelous.'

'And you carry the same motif onto the lobby walls, brilliantly,' Semyon added. 'Against that orange-red color.'

'Look at the detailing of the barrel-vaulted skylight in the lobby,' Kuzka said almost shouting. He paused, so he wouldn't embarrass himself with his excitement. 'So many colors of glass,' he said in a calmer tone of voice.

The two men kept flipping through the sheets of the preliminary drawings, each finding something that delighted them. 'The railings of the balconies look like vines that would spread out and engulf the audience,' Semyon said with a laugh.

'Will you design all the door hardware in Style Moderne, Dimitri?' asked Kuzka, who then realized it was a dumb question.

'Yes, everything down to urinals in the men's room will be designed to harmonize,' Dimitri answered as he pulled a cigarette from his Fabergé case.

Dimitri was secretly delighted that they were pleased. In the eight years Semyon and Kuzka had worked for him, the two men had always been honest in their criticism of his work. If they didn't like it, he encouraged them to tell him flat-out. He didn't want them to feel as if they had to please him just because he was an aristocrat.

He tried to downplay the new design direction he was taking, as if it was no big deal.

'Yes, this is a different, freer design approach that I'm trying out. The Tsar likes this direction as well,' he said in an offhand manner, puffing away.

The two young men were beaming, and he understood why. It was natural for the young to experiment, and try new things, especially if it was for the Tsar himself.

'So off you go and draw the preliminary floor plans.'

He smiled as they bounded out of his office. Once it was announced that he was designing the Memorial, more commissions had come in. This was a natural occurrence in architectural practice; one prestigious project led to another.

Everyone wanted to use a fashionable architect. He would
have to hire more men.

He flipped through the elevations, mentally noting little
changes he would make. His staff didn't understand how
difficult it was for him to try something so new. At first, he
was scared to leave the familiar classicism, he'd grown up
with – like a frightened, crying child parting from his mother
on his first day of school. When he did make his decision to
change, he was like a diver at the edge of a lake hesitating
to plunge into the cold water.

Then, the other night at Princess Tenisheva's convinced him
he was going in the right creative direction. He was overwhelmed with the design she had done. What a talent!
Everything worked seamlessly as a whole work of art. The
Princess's design had inspired him, and Dimitri went home
and worked through the night and into the next day, improving
his design. The problem had been that he was too cautious; he
had to cut loose and couldn't hold back. Looking through the
drawing set, he realized what a sense of creative liberation
the Style Moderne had given him. A wonderful sense of
freedom. The feeling was as exhilarating as kissing Katya on
the balcony that night. He couldn't hold back his emotions and
wanted her with all his heart. He was worried that he'd come
off as being too forward. The thought that he'd frightened her
away scared the hell out of him.

Firs, an elderly house servant, entered the room, snapping
him out of the upsetting thought.

'Peter Carl Fabergé is downstairs and wishes to see you,
Your Highness.' Oleg handed Dimitri the visitor's calling card.
'He apologizes that he came with no invitation.'

'Ask him in and have tea sent up, Firs.'

This was both a puzzle and an honor for Dimitri. He had
met the famous jeweler only a few times over the years at his
store.

A slight, bald, middle-aged man with a full gray beard
strode confidently into Dimitri's office and bowed.

'A great pleasure to see you again, Monsieur Fabergé. It's
always a pleasure to meet true genius face-to-face,' Dimitri
said.

'Thank you, Your Highness. It's my pleasure to meet someone of your varied talents – architect, artist, scenic designer.'

'Please sit down. How can I be of service to you?'

'It's your artistic talent that I wish to tap. All of Russia knows you are designing the Tchaikovsky Memorial for the Tsar.'

Dimitri nodded as a footman brought in tea with cakes and set it down on a side table.

'The Tsarina wishes you to design an *objet d'art* inspired by this project, which my shop will produce. It will be presented to the Tsar at the laying of the cornerstone,' explained Fabergé in a low baritone. 'It is to be a surprise from you and the Tsarina.'

'This is a great honor to design for Fabergé,' Dimitri exclaimed. His excitement seemed to elevate him above his chair.

'This will not be an egg or piece of jewelry, but a presentation commission of your own design. The Tsarina will be paying for it, so needless to say cost is of no consequence.'

'I'm overwhelmed, Monsieur Fabergé. My first thought, is how will I ever measure up to your extraordinary artistry?' There were stories that upon inspecting an almost finished piece, Fabergé would place it on an anvil and smash it with a hammer, telling his craftsmen in a kindly voice, 'You can do better.'

'Her Majesty expressly wanted you to design the present. *You* will present the gift personally to the Tsar. It is indeed a great honor.'

'We must discuss the timing of all this, especially how long you will need to fabricate the gift,' Dimitri said excitedly. He couldn't wait to tell Katya.

'Once you have a preliminary design, we can go into all that. My studio prefers a pen and ink drawing with watercolor. You are joining a select group of artists – including Alexandre Benois and Nikolai Roerich – to design for us, Prince Dimitri. If this effort is successful, we may come to a long-term arrangement to take advantage of your vast creativity.'

'Tea, Monsieur Fabergé?'

TWENTY-TWO

'Remember, women go upstairs,' the Baron said.

Katya blushed in embarrassment for having forgotten. He smiled at her and continued on to the main sanctuary, where the men sat. She had never in her life been in synagogue, but had passed this one on Lermontovsky Street many times. It had always seemed to her a very exotic building from the Levant, with its high copper dome flanked by slender domed towers. The temple's most distinctive feature was its exterior of alternating bands of red and yellow ocher stone, giving it an even more oriental feel. She could almost imagine Aladdin on his flying carpet swooping over the structure.

Because of her budding interest in Judaism, Katya had been invited by the Baron to see the inside of his synagogue while a service was going on. She might find it interesting, he said, to compare it to what goes on in the Russian Orthodox Church. Afraid of offending him, Katya didn't tell the Baron that she thought all religion was superstitious nonsense. At his insistence, she came, telling herself that there was no harm in watching what went on. After all, it wasn't against the law for a Christian to enter a synagogue.

Katya joined in the flow of women ascending the rear stair. They were all very well dressed, but none wore jewelry, and all had their heads covered by hats or scarves. The stained wooden stair led to a three-sided gallery that overlooked the main space. She was surprised to see it had long wooden pews, as the Russian Orthodox churches had no seats at all. One thing that struck her was unlike in her church, there were no religious images or ikons painted on the walls, which were just a creamy yellow. The half-dome over what looked like an altar was painted a sky blue. She was impressed; since very few Jews lived in St Petersburg, it must have been difficult to raise the great amount of money for such a grand structure. Although not as bad as Moscow, where they had been driven

out by the Tsar's uncle, Grand Duke Sergei, this city had
grown far more intolerant of Jews. The Baron said the authori-
ties threw many obstacles in the way of a building permit. But
St Petersburg Jews didn't want to meet in rented rooms any
longer, and desired a true temple of architectural quality. The
first design was rejected by the government because it was
too fancy, so a more modest design had to be submitted by
the architects. Getting the land was also hard because it
couldn't be near a Christian church, nor on any routes the
Tsar's carriage traveled. Katya would be interested in asking
Dimitri what he thought of the building.

Finding a seat in a pew at the rear, Katya looked at the
women who were filling up the seats. Funny, she thought,
they looked no different than any other fashionably dressed
woman strolling along the Nevsky Prospect. The men below
all looked like prosperous businessmen like her father, with
their round bellies and graying beards. Most were formally
dressed and wore top hats, giving the space an air of elegance.
Some had black and white prayer shawls, which the Baron
called a *tallis*. Katya had half-expected to see men wearing
black wide-brimmed hats with full beards and corkscrew
dreadlocks as did Jews in the Pale. An elderly man, probably
the rabbi, entered from the side, and another man came
from the opposite door. The women picked up books from the
seats and opened them as the rabbi began the service. Katya
did the same, but she was surprised that the book was printed
backwards. Maybe she had a misprinted one. So she picked
up another, but it was the same. Didn't the printer catch such
a mistake? she thought. Her row had filled up, so she glanced
over to see their books. They also were backwards, but no one
seemed bothered by this. One side of the book was printed in
Hebrew, and the matching page in Russian.

'This is called the *Siddur*,' the elderly lady next to her
explained in a low, kind voice, pointing at her prayer book.

Katya smiled and nodded, then the woman patted her hand
and said, 'Welcome to our temple.' The lady on her other side
said the same thing and directed her to the right page.

Katya had come to just observe and experience what this
world was all about. Her biggest fear was that she would look

out of place, like a zebra walking into a cathedral. She felt she had a sign attached to her chest saying, 'I'm a goy,' which the Baron told her was the word for gentile. She had imagined that if they discovered a Christian among them, the Jews would scream at her and drive her out of the place, maybe stone her to death. In Russia, Jews were considered strangers, even though they had lived in the Fatherland for centuries. Now the tables were turned, and *she* was the stranger. But because the women were so friendly, Katya felt much more relaxed.

'Under that dome at the end of the room, behind those curtains, is where we store the Torah,' whispered the woman to her right. 'And that is the eastern wall.'

'That platform where the rabbi is standing and talking is called the *bima*,' explained the lady to her left. The service was in Hebrew, but she guided Katya in turning the pages of the Siddur, like turning pages of sheet music for someone playing the piano. Then a man with a beautiful deep voice began singing.

'That's our cantor.'

A choir of men and boys started singing along with him. It was as beautiful a sound as in Kazan Cathedral. The service was unusual because people seemed to come and go instead of staying in one place for a set amount of time until the clergy dismissed them. Each man down there seemed to be having their personal religious service, slightly bowing back and forth, mumbling to themselves. When the women in the gallery stood, so did Katya and when they sat, she sat. Then they switched books, and handed her the correct one.

For the women up in the gallery, the service seemed more of a meditation. They closed their eyes and internally prayed to themselves. Some covered their eyes with their hands.

Throughout the service, the two women whispered to her what was going on. Katya felt a bit guilty about interrupting their prayers. When the service was over, one of the women squeezed Katya's hand. 'Thank you so much for coming.'

Katya waited until the gallery emptied and looked down into the sanctuary. It was like she had just visited an exotic foreign country. She wasn't sorry she came, on the contrary; she was more intrigued with all this. When she made her way to the entry, she saw the Baron sitting in his carriage at the curb.

'I'll wager that was all very strange to you. It must have sounded like Chinese,' he called out.

'I enjoyed it, and I even started making head and tails of the whole thing.'

'May I drive you home, Doctor?' the Baron asked.

'No thank you, Baron. I'd like to walk. Thank you again for inviting me.'

He tipped his hat, and his carriage drove off.

Before taking a step out of the doorway, Katya scanned both sides of the street to see if anyone was watching her. She stayed in the same spot for almost a minute then walked down the granite steps to the street. She hugged the building line trying to stay out of sight.

Deep in thought, she walked on. She had done some reading about the Jews – not their religious practices, but about their history. She hadn't known a thing about them. The Jews were a tormented people and had been so for two thousand years wherever they had lived. But here in their temple, they felt safe and comfortable praying to their god. It was their refuge from the cruelty and injustice of Russia.

Because she trusted him, Katya eventually told the Baron about her discovery in the gray metal box. She then deluged him with questions about Jewish conversions. The Baron explained that almost all Jews in the nineteenth century converted for practical gain: to enter the professions, to live in the cities outside the Pale, or to succeed in business. He had never heard of a conversion because of a truly religious conviction for Christianity. Many did it for love, he said. A Jewish girl in the shtetl who fell in love with a gentile would convert and get married. Often, these young women were the daughters of innkeepers who had met gentiles while serving them drink and food.

The Baron went on to describe the tragedy that came as a result of conversions. A mother killed her daughter before she converted, so she'd be buried a Jew. But the worst outcome, the Baron said, was a Jew who converted and although successful in business was tormented the rest of his life for his decision to forsake his people. The Baron had also known the story of the drowned Jewish soldiers who refused to convert.

All of this talk of conversion had reminded Katya of a pressing question she'd wanted to ask the Baron. Mustering all her courage, she said haltingly, 'I have a question . . . something of a personal nature. I'm good friends with a man named Dimitri. He's an aristocrat, and I feel that I need to tell him about my heritage – but maybe it will change his feelings for me. What should I do? Should I just keep it a secret?'

'I sense that you're more than friends with this Dimitri fellow.' The Baron nodded sagely. 'If he really loves you, your Jewish blood won't matter. And if it does, it's better to find out now.'

Still mulling over their conversation, Katya reached the Nevsky Prospect, where she planned to do some shopping. She was scared to follow the Baron's advice. Suppose Dimitri had to follow the strict rules of his class and spurned her. That was more terrible than losing her job. No, she wouldn't tell him yet. That evening on the balcony at Princess Tenisheva's was the happiest in her entire life. If it was to end then let it last as long as possible. She would keep her secret hidden for now.

As she walked along, she reminded herself that the red dot meant she had descended from these same people she'd just met in the temple. Her ancestors had worshipped in the same manner, using the backward-printed books. And they probably suffered the same prejudice and barbaric violence as those Jews had in the Kishinev and Gomel pogroms. Discovering her real background captivated her. It was like going into the attic, opening an old cobweb-covered trunk, and finding life-changing secrets buried inside.

All other religions were looked down upon by the Orthodox Church, but Jews were despised as an evil race. Even the Russian Muslims, of which there were twenty million, were held in a higher regard. She couldn't understand why Jews were hated so. Back in the temple, she didn't undergo some wonderous epiphany telling her to convert to Judaism (it was also illegal to do so). But by the end of the service, a wave of empathy, compassion, and admiration for these special people had swept over her.

TWENTY-THREE

'Can't the train go any faster, Papa? It's taking forever to get home.'

'Olga, we only went to Volgovo, that's not far,' the Tsar said, glancing up from his paperwork.

Dimitri was sitting with Olga and Tatiana looking at the wintry landscape pass by. The snow was made blindingly white by the sun. He agreed that the Imperial Train was poking along, and wanted to get back soon to work on the Memorial drawings. It was the beginning of December, and Dimitri had promised the Grand Duchesses he would go with them to Volgovo for the Tsar's Christmas blessing of the village. Now they were heading back to Tsarskoe Selo. A Tsar's blessing was a great Russian tradition, and an honor for the village. The Imperial Train would stop at the station and thousands of peasants would greet him. Whenever a Tsar visited, a deputation of village elders would present the Emperor with bread and salt on a gold plate. When Nicholas ascended to the throne, he discovered that some villages couldn't afford the gold plate, but unable to bear being outdone by richer villages, they still bore the huge expense. The Tsar decreed that henceforth, bread and salt would be presented on wood or china plates. That gesture said a lot about the Tsar's kind character. He had a gentle humanity about him that made him a good-hearted man, but not necessarily a strong Tsar. Dimitri didn't like to be confronted with his friend's faults, so he just ignored them.

'I wish we were there,' Tatiana said.

'Look for places where we could go tobogganing,' said the Tsar in jolly manner. The Tsarina, who was sitting in an armchair across from him doing her needlework, smiled at her husband. Dimitri noted the silent exchange of affection. When Dimitri was alone with the Tsarina in her boudoir at the Alexander Palace last week, and Nicky's bird whistle was heard, he saw the happiness flash in her eyes. Seeing their contentment only underscored the emptiness of his own marriage.

If the Imperial Yacht the *Standart* was a floating palace, then the Imperial Train was a thousand-foot-long palace on wheels, a string of royal-blue cars adorned with golden double-eagles pulled by a gleaming black locomotive. The interiors were finished in oak with floral English cretonne, silk and leather panels inlaid with tortoiseshell and mother of pearl. The third car held a dining room seating sixteen, the fourth was the drawing room, the fifth held private compartments for the Imperial Couple including a mauve and gray boudoir for Alexandra, and the sixth was reserved for the children and members of the Tsarina's household. Then came two luggage and staff carriages. The very last car contained a power station to provide the train with electricity, and a chapel topped with a little belfry.

A servant knocked on the door of the boudoir, then brought in tea.

'You may butter me a scone, my sweet Olga, it'll make the time go quicker,' Alexandra said.

'Just a few more minutes,' said Asher Blokh in a voice brimming with excitement.

'I don't see why we have to wait here. The place will be swarming with Cossacks in no time. They'll ride us down in an instant.'

'Shut your damn mouth, Svirskii, you fucking coward. I want to be here to see this,' snapped Blokh.

Blokh, Isaac Hersch, and Roman Svirskii, a short stocky man with a bullet-shaped head and squinty blue eyes, stood in a grove of pines on a hill a half-mile away overlooking the train track. They were bundled up against the bitter cold.

'There!' cried Hersch, pointing. 'They're coming!'

The smile vanished as Blokh's gaze shifted to the left.

Would the bomb go off as planned? The precise timing of the mechanism was critical to success. Sometimes bombs wouldn't go off on time, or at all. Once when they were walking up to a test bomb they thought was a dud, it exploded. They could have been killed had they been fifty feet closer.

Svirskii held out a pocket watch that reflected in the bright winter sun. The train and all its cars were in sight now, but it was traveling much slower than they calculated. They focused all their attention on a point ahead on the tracks.

'Just ten seconds,' cried Svirskii.

A puff of black smoke accompanied the sound of a low thud under the locomotive. They heard the squeal of the brakes, but it was useless; the train could not stop in time. The shiny black locomotive and its carriages went flying off the tracks. The sound of bending metal and crushing of wood was amazingly loud. Every car shattered into pieces when it hit the ground. The locomotive was on its side, sliding through the snow, reminding Blokh of a sled. Svirskii put away his watch and ran. 'Come on, you fools,' he shouted behind him.

'We killed the Tsar!' screamed Blokh. He pounded Hersch on the back.

The wreckage of the train came to a rest and all was silent. Blokh could see the bodies of the engineers, who had been thrown from the train into the snow. Steam belched from the locomotive. A man staggered from one of the cars and collapsed on the ground.

'One last time again, Papa, before we go home,' Marie cried. 'Please!'

The Tsar smiled at his daughter. Dimitri knew he wouldn't say no because he was having so much fun. The train always carried toboggans in the winter, in case the family found a good hill for sledding. This one was a steep embankment right next to the tracks. On the way to the Crimea in the summers, the Tsar would stop the train at the top of a hill and use silver trays from the kitchen pantry to slide down its sandy slope. Nicholas couldn't resist another sled ride down the hill where they had stopped. He had a child's heart for fun.

'This will be the last time. We must be getting back,' replied the Tsar. He tried to use his sternest voice, but his daughters who were trudging up the hill saw through it. Anastasia was having trouble climbing, so Miss O'Brian had to carry her up.

As Dimitri and the girls were arranging themselves in the bright red toboggans, an officer of the Palace Command ran up to the Tsar and whispered into his ear. A shocked expression came over Nicholas's normally placid face.

'Children, come at once!' he shouted in an unusually harsh voice. The girls knew to obey without question.

Dimitri got off the sled, and the Tsar walked up to him with a grave look on his face.

'The decoy train was blown up.'

Whenever the Tsar took a trip in the Imperial Train, a second train was dispatched as a decoy to confuse terrorist bombers. The ruse worked, but six men were killed.

'Comrade, you know you're only supposed to come here on the appointed day and hour,' Azref said crossly.

'To hell with that! Who is trying to kill the Tsar and his family!? I told you I won't be a part of any violence,' yelled Miss O'Brian, her face beet-red. 'The yacht, and now the train!'

'And I told you that there are revolutionaries who are committed to the violent overthrow of the autocracy. *Terrorists* with whom we have *no* connection,' Azref shouted back at her. 'It's madness to use violence against an empire with one million soldiers plus regiments of Cossacks.'

'The Combat Group *must* have agents inside the household. And they must be found!' Miss O'Brian turned and stomped out.

TWENTY-FOUR

'This isn't just about peasants and workers. The autocracy must treat the professional classes and intellectuals as citizens, not subjects, by giving us civil and political rights,' said Evigenia in a passionate voice.

'Nonsense. Over ninety percent of the population are peasants. When they were emancipated, they felt cheated by the land settlement. They wanted the land for free, not to pay for it in installments for forty-nine years!' countered Val Taganstev, a geography professor. 'They're the angriest and should be in the vanguard of the revolution.'

Each week the arts circle was given even more to politics. Often, the meetings were rife with arguments.

'What do you think, Dimitri? Who should lead the revolution? The peasantry or the workers?' Grigory asked eagerly.

Dimitri didn't know what to think. All his life, he'd been given full rights to do whatever he wanted; a prince had a great life with nothing to complain about. But now his entire world view had been turned upside down. The appalling photos had stayed vivid in his mind. Ilya had shown them dozens more. Then there was the dead boy in the wagon.

He hesitated before he spoke. 'The extent of the misery of the lower classes, as well as these pogroms, shows there's something fundamentally wrong in Russia.' A part of him didn't want to believe it. He still refused to accept that Nicky had anything to do with this. A good man like his old friend would never allow such a horrible thing to exist.

'But you think there should be a revolution to overthrow the autocracy, don't you?' hectored Grigory. 'There are some revolutionaries out there who feel that only all-out violence will change things. You think that's the method to use, Dimitri?'

'Absolutely not!' Dimitri replied in a loud voice that caught everyone's attention. 'We're all in agreement, violence is out of the question, right?' he snapped. All the group nodded including Grigory. The attempts on the yacht and train had outraged him. But because the government kept the incidents secret including the plague cloth, he could not tell the group about them. 'But something has to change,' he said sadly while looking straight into Katya's eyes. 'People can't be treated like this – that I believe.'

'The government would sooner listen to the monied educated and professional classes about political change than peasants or servants whom they consider their social inferiors,' Katya said.

Dimitri stood up. 'You must forgive me for leaving so early. I must go home to write my political manifesto, then saddle my horse and charge the Winter Palace.'

The group burst into laughter, and the meeting broke up.

Katya walked out to the street with Dimitri. It was mid-December and a new layer of snow had covered the sidewalk. A sharp wind cut through them, and Katya huddled against Dimitri as he helped her into his waiting carriage.

On the ride to her house, they sparred over what Tchaikovsky's best work was (it was a never-ending argument), and chatted about the state of medical treatment for the poor and her patients. As she talked, Dimitri fastened his eyes on to hers and drank in her voice. Each time they met, the more she talked, the more attracted he was to her. At tea or lunch, they would talk and talk. The time always raced by, each saying almost in unison, 'Where did the time go?'

'I've seen so many people die,' Katya said as she gazed out the window. 'I always wonder if they had had a meaningful, fulfilling life. Because you only get one shot at life.'

'If having a meaningful life means doing something you love, then you certainly have one, Katya,' Dimitri said with admiration. 'You love being a doctor, don't you?'

Katya nodded. 'Yes, it's my own universe when I step inside the hospital. All my own worries and problems disappear when I care for my patients. But I'll wager that's the same feeling when you do your architecture. Or don't princes have worries or problems?'

She always teased him about being an aristocrat. 'Does your castle in the Crimea have one or two dragons? Do you use the solid gold plates at every meal or just at supper?'

'We certainly do have problems,' Dimitri replied indignantly. 'Like what is the proper vintage French wine to accompany my horse's dinner. An 1892 or 1898? It's a very vexing problem.'

Katya burst out laughing. Her laugh was always like a little song. Dimitri liked its charming high-pitched trill.

'Yes, I feel the same way about architecture.'

'To do something one loves is most important,' Katya said.

'But what about love?' he asked in a quiet, soft voice.

'Love?'

'Love itself.'

'Why . . . yes . . . Dimitri, that's very important,' Katya replied uncertainly.

'Not to have a passion for something, but to love someone with all one's heart. Isn't that the highest attainment in life?'

'If a person is lucky enough to find that someone,' said Katya, looking straight into Dimitri's eyes. 'Has that happened to . . . you?'

'It just has.' Dimitri got up and sat next to her. He placed his hand at the back of her neck and gently pulled her toward him. He gave her a long, deep kiss. Their lips melted together, and the kiss seemed to last an eternity. When they finally pulled apart, Katya rested her head on his shoulder, and he wrapped his arm around her, clenching her tightly to him. The moment was absolute bliss; he had never had such a sensation of closeness. There was complete silence, only the wheels of the carriage rattling along the street. He drew her even closer and began kissing her cheek and forehead. When the carriage stopped in front of her house, he gave her another long kiss.

Katya turned to him before leaving the carriage. Before she could say anything, Dimitri leaned forward to take her into his arms and kiss her again. She held on to him for a moment, not wanting to let go. Then she forced herself to move away and smiled at him.

'You know we're playing with dynamite, here,' she said quietly.

'Yes,' Dimitri responded in a serious voice. 'If we're caught, we'll both be cast out by our respective tribes. My love for you could destroy you – and me. How do you feel about that?'

'Tea tomorrow at Mrs McIntosh's?' she asked. 'I'll have finished my shift at four.'

'My carriage will be waiting at the hospital.'

Dimitri waved goodbye. His body literally ached to watch her leave. He wanted to run out and hold her just one more time. But that wouldn't have been enough, he thought, feeling deliriously happy.

As the carriage made its way home, he came back down to earth, and thought of a few revisions he should make to the front facade of the Memorial. He realized that he was more concerned that Katya liked his design than the Tsar.

*   *   *

Katya watched from her doorway until the carriage was out of sight. Instead of going inside, she walked across the street to the narrow park and sat down on a bench. The happiest, most magical moment of her entire life had just taken place. Her heart seemed to be floating above her head. She had to gather her wits.

Katya was stunned when it dawned upon her that Dimitri might be falling in love with her that night at Princess Tenisheva's. It had been just a quick kiss, but its effect had levitated her several inches above the floor. When she went home to bed, she couldn't sleep and stayed up all night thinking about that wonderful fraction of a second.

Then Katya thought she was deceiving herself, convinced it was absolutely absurd. It was just a simple kiss. He had probably kissed a million women like that in his time. She was terrified when she realized that she was falling in love with him. There was a magnetic field between them, pulling them together. She wanted desperately to break away, but she was aroused and desirous at the same time. Tonight in the carriage sealed her decision: she wanted him with all her heart. The passion overwhelmed her, and she was going to surrender to it. The best part of kissing him was the drawing of their faces close together, right before their lips met.

But it filled her with anguish to think how this would all play out. Nothing but unhappiness and heartbreak could come of it – because Dimitri was married. Divorces in the Orthodox Church were rare. The Church believed marriage a holy sacrament not to be broken. One's spouse must be exiled to Siberia or disappear for five years before a divorce could be granted. Even a woman beaten to pulp every day by her husband could not obtain one. In addition to the Church's restrictions, there was the scandal of a divorce in Russian high society. Katya didn't fool herself into thinking Dimitri was a babe in the woods; he'd had countless affairs, which were acceptable because they were discreet. But he would be exiled from his peers if he divorced. Society would turn his back on him.

And even if he could obtain a divorce, could a man like Dimitri, who'd had many sexual liaisons, really love one woman for the rest of his life? She wouldn't bet on it. He'd grow bored and restless after a short time. How could she compete with all of the beautiful, stylish women throwing themselves at him? She would be in a constant dread about whether he was cheating on her.

Then there was the difference in their looks: handsome princes in real life didn't fall in love with plain-looking girls like her. His friends, including the Tsar, would think he'd gone mad. She let her imagination run away, believing that this was all a great joke being played on her, orchestrated by Lara. A handsome aristocrat leading a girl on, then breaking her heart. She could hear the courtiers in their mansions ridiculing her to no end. They would call Dimitri the Beauty and her the Beast.

His beauty wasn't skin-deep, she thought. People always assumed beautiful men and women had shallow, selfish characters. But it was what was underneath his handsome looks that she loved best. His uncommon sweetness of disposition was what touched her heart most. He could be a product of his class – supercilious, a snob at times – but he was a kind-hearted man. The thing that Katya was most impressed with was that he took a genuine interest in whomever he was talking to. Most people just pretended to. Although he was a rich prince of the realm, he made her feel like she was the most important person in the world. One would assume a prince was born to be selfish, but he wasn't that way at all. Another thing had won her heart: just after she found the conversion document, he'd sensed that something was troubling her. She had been bowled over by the revelation about her heritage, and he had been sensitive enough to her mood to pick up on it.

Katya decided then and there that despite the heartbreak that might lay ahead, it would be worth suffering for the incredible bliss she would experience. She was glad to be allowed to enjoy the greatest happiness a human being could know, even if it were only for a short time. She also knew that her reputation would be ruined if their love for each other was discovered – but she didn't give a damn. Getting up from the bench, she slowly walked across the street to her home.

TWENTY-FIVE

Miss O'Brian waited in the doorway until the hall was clear of any servants. The Alexander Palace was always swarming with every kind of servant. Like the tutors and nurses, nannies existed in their own separate worlds, neither part of the Court nor servants in the household. But now each servant could be an enemy willing to turn her in, if they caught her spying. After the train and yacht bombings, she realized that one of them could also be a revolutionary agent intent on killing Nicholas and his family.

Once inside the display room, she quickly reached for the nearest egg. The 'Pelican Egg' was made of engraved red gold topped with a pelican in her nest with her brood. The egg itself ingeniously unfolded into eight oval ivory miniatures of the institutions of which the Dowager was the patron. Miss O'Brian was about to place the note on top of one of the miniatures when she stopped and drew her hand back. She stared at the little folded piece of paper, then unfolded it. As she had predicted, it had a series of random letters, which she knew was a code. She hid it in the egg and moved it slightly forward of the others. She then scanned the shelves and saw that an egg at the far end had been moved forward. She walked over to it and picked it up. It was the 'Danish Palaces Egg,' pink and mauve outlined in enameled gold. Opening the top, she found the surprise to be a folding screen of ten miniature watercolors of the palaces and yachts owned by the Imperial Family. Between one of the panels was a folded piece of paper exactly like the one she had just delivered. Miss O'Brian quickly tucked it up the right sleeve of her day dress. When she started being a postman, she often wondered who her confederates in the household were. But being a good agent, she didn't want or need to know.

Before she left the room, her eyes glanced over the rest of the Fabergé objects, which included cigarette cases, jewelry, miniature figures like dancing moujiks, and frames. The pink 'Lilies of the Valley Egg' was her favorite, with its swirling pearl and diamond buds. But she was both fascinated and repelled by the objects. While marveling at their brilliant artistry and beauty, she couldn't ignore the contrast of these riches with the abject misery of the Russian people. How could the Romanovs have such treasures when the workers were treated like dogs with no rights? Or when the peasants lived in abject poverty and filth? She imagined her father coming into this room. The old revolutionary would take a hammer and smash these treasures to bits because of the inequity they represented. Their incredible beauty be damned, he would shout. And he would be right. Opening the door a crack to make sure the hallway was clear, Miss O'Brian slipped out and walked to the private apartments.

'Hello, Jim.'

'Hello, Miss O'Brian. You look in mighty fine spirits today.'

'I am indeed. Christmas is coming.'

Miss O'Brian liked speaking to Jim. He was one of the few people with whom she could have a conversation in her native language. The Tsarina spoke English because of her upbringing with her 'Granny,' Queen Victoria, and the Tsar was brilliantly fluent in French, German, and English. He could have passed as an Oxford graduate, he spoke the language so perfectly. But she didn't get to have real conversations with the Imperial Couple.

'When are you going back to America for a visit, Jim?'

'In two months, ma'am. I can't wait,' Jim replied as he opened the door to the apartments.

'One day when you're off-duty, you must describe this Alabama place you come from.'

'It's nice . . . and warm, ma'am.'

Miss O'Brian laughed. Winter had enveloped St Petersburg in a deep blanket of snow, and sleighs now replaced carriages for getting about. The Neva River had frozen over and become another crowded avenue in the city. The bitter cold had driven everyone inside into a kind of hibernation. When people had to go out, they were wrapped head to foot like mummies. An

American black man like Jim must have a very hard time adapting to Russian winters.

Christmas meant the start of the 'season' on New Year's Day for the Court and Russian high society. An incredible succession of balls, banquets, ballets, operas, midnight suppers, and parties would go on day and night until the beginning of Lent. Ballrooms in great private mansions and in the Winter Palace would be filled with officers in brilliant uniforms, men in elegant evening dress, and women in billowing low-cut satin gowns. There would be a continuous river of food and drink. Music would never stop with waltzes, quadrilles, polonaises, and gypsy music. The Court never seemed to sleep during this whirlwind of gaiety, every minute was taken up by a social engagement. They were constantly on the move, bundled up in furs and sable blankets in their fancy sleighs pulled by strong fleet horses to the next party or concert. The Russians made the English look like paupers when it came to giving parties and balls.

It was just two weeks before Christmas, and the Alexander Palace was decorated throughout with eight tall Christmas trees that easily fit in the huge spaces of the palace.

Christmas was the favorite holiday of the Imperial Family, with much attention paid to the festivities. The Tsarina trimmed all the trees as well as choosing the presents for each member of her personal household, including the officers, which numbered close to five hundred. Jim always got a nice present, and she did too. In the nursery, the children and Miss O'Brian had their own glittering tree, which was fixed into a rotating music box which played 'Silent Night.' It was an object of great interest and admiration for the girls. All the presents were laid out on white covered tables. One would think the dozens of gifts here were all for the children, but except for two or three apiece, the vast majority of the toys went to the children of members of the household including the lowliest ones like the gardeners' and the grooms' children. The nanny was always touched by this, Nicholas and Alexandra had instilled in the girls at an early age that they were to share and be kind to others. The idea the public had that the girls were spoiled and pampered was sheer nonsense.

Miss O'Brian entered the mauve boudoir of the Tsarina. Even in winter, it smelled of lilacs. The girls had finished their lessons and were having tea with their mother. She was talking to Baroness Sophie Gurka, but she motioned for the nanny to help herself. Miss O'Brian settled into an armchair with her tea next to the irritating Anna Vyrubova and watched her charges. Unlike the children of the English aristocracy, the Grand Duchesses saw their mother and father almost every day and were perfectly at ease with them. They were always so happy together; there was never a sharp word exchanged between parent and child. In the household of the Duke of Weston, where Miss O'Brian had worked for many years, the Duke, who was a cold man, gave more love to his horses, hounds, and whores than his children. The Duchess had almost no contact with her children. The Tsarina basically brought up her daughters herself. Miss O'Brian wanted to tell her colleagues how wonderful a job the Tsarina did, but strict Court rules forbade her from joining the English Governesses' Club in St Petersburg to avoid the temptation of gossip. She understood this, but it made her life even lonelier.

'Mama has a special Christmas gift for us, Nanny,' Olga exclaimed with glee.

'For all of Russia,' Anna added with a great smile.

'With God's help, Russia will have an heir born in August. It will be a son,' the Tsarina said proudly.

Miss O'Brian knew that after four daughters, the Tsarina hoped heart and soul for a son.

She stood up, bowed, and went over to kiss Alexandra's slender hand. 'May God grant you a son, Your Majesty.'

'It *will* be a son,' said Anna.

Miss O'Brian smiled. She hoped the child would eventually live in a very different Russia than the current one.

TWENTY-SIX

'What a wonderful view of the Peter and Paul Fortress,' Katya said, drawing aside the lace curtain covering the tall French window. The snow was falling steadily on a dark gray afternoon. 'Your apartment is so charming.'

Looking over her shoulder, Dimitri wrapped his arms around her waist. As he began kissing her neck, she bent her head back and sighed.

'*Our* apartment. I got it for us – our own special world where we can escape,' he murmured in her ear.

With his arms still around her, she turned to face him.

'Our private oasis?' Her eyes sparkled, and she cocked an eyebrow.

He nodded. Her lips met his, and she gave him a long, passionate kiss.

Still kissing, he slid his arms down and lifted her up as she wrapped her legs around his waist. He walked her to the bedroom, where a fire was roaring. Laying her down gently on the bed, they began to undress each other; at first with restraint, but then impatiently ripping buttons as they went. As more of her was revealed, he became even more aroused by her perfectly formed breasts and tiny waist.

Their bare bodies finally touching, she ran her hands up and down his muscular back. 'I'm so happy,' she sighed.

A moan escaped her as he kissed her breasts. He glanced up at her. 'You don't know how I've longed for this day.'

'Me too,' she said, and she gave herself up to his caresses.

Dimitri watched Katya breathe slowly while she slept. Her tousled brown hair framed her heart-shaped face on the fluffy down pillow. He reached out to stroke a chestnut strand. She looked so alluring with her hair undone. He slipped out of bed to stoke the fire, feeling its warmth on his bare thighs, then scooted back under the blanket. He wanted to stay right next to her, not wanting to miss her opening her beautiful blue eyes when she awoke.

He was head over heels; something he hadn't felt in quite a long time, since his courtship with Lara. His love for Katya was almost volcanic, it moved him so. He had been swept away by her. After his marriage disintegrated, he never thought he'd experience that kind of emotion again. But now his feelings were ten times more intense. He had sensed that when they made love for the first time, it would be sensual and feel entirely natural – and it had. Their lovemaking was the final piece of a puzzle that clicked into place.

As she slept, he thought it amazing how the trajectory of one's life can change in an instant upon a chance meeting – that night at the Catherine Palace ball.

'When we met, I felt my life begin again,' he said to her in a soft voice.

He smiled, remembering the day he'd gotten to the hospital early to pick her up. On a whim, he'd sneaked in to watch her at work. Because of her strict professionalism, he knew that she would never let him, but he had been curious to observe her in her medical world. He was glad he did, as it gave him great pleasure to watch her on her rounds. He had never been a patient in a hospital, but he had visited friends and relatives many times and always noticed how brusque, almost cruel the doctors were with patients, barely showing a trace of emotion. Katya, on the other hand, spent time with each person, making some small gesture of concern such as pulling up their blankets or playing with a child to make them smile. As she approached her patients, their dour expressions brightened at the sight of her. He really liked the fact that she was able to bring sunshine to them. Each time he saw her, she had that effect on him, too. Whenever she came out of the brightly lit hospital foyer, a wave of happiness seemed to lift him above the carriage seat and brought a great smile to his face.

He was hoping she would wake up soon so they could do what he liked best – talk about topics ranging from poetry to architecture. Saying goodbye to her was wrenching. Back at home, trying to fall asleep, he would lie wide awake for hours, thinking about her. Now with the flat, they would have much more freedom, including spending nights together.

Katya stirred, then opened her eyes. When she saw he was looking down at her, she smiled and stretched out her arms. He leaned over and gave her a long kiss.

'How did I exist without your love?' She grinned drowsily.

'Hello, sleepy head,' he said in a quiet voice. He pulled her tighter to him and nestled his face in her hair. It smelled wonderful. He rubbed his face back and forth, and she giggled.

They sat up against their pillows, and he lit cigarettes for them. She cuddled against him and pulled the blanket up under her chin.

'Mmm . . . there's no more comforting feeling to be snuggling after making love under thick fur blankets, before a fireplace on a frigid day,' she said.

'There's cold salmon, caviar, sliced meats, and plenty of ice-cold pepper vodka in the larder,' he said.

'Oh, I'm famished!' She jumped out of bed, put on Dimitri's tweed jacket over her naked body, and bounded out of the room. She came back with a tray of food.

'You've a well-stocked kitchen, Prince Dimitri.'

'This is our home now,' Dimitri said proudly.

'This looks so delicious. But I'll be sure to save some of the caviar for your horse,' she said with a serious expression.

For the next three hours, they talked about everything. They had gone to see Chekhov's new play, *The Cherry Orchard*. She loved it, but he didn't, because it portrayed aristocrats as silly and helpless. She teased him mercilessly about it.

'The aristocrats were able to put their shoes on themselves. And I think Madame Ranevskaya opened a door for herself once,' she said mischievously.

'I'm not as helpless as that.' He pretended to be insulted.

'No . . . there's at least one thing you're extremely good at.' She reached under the covers, and he gave a gasp of pleasure.

They made love again, slowly, taking their time. Bodies damp with perspiration, entirely sated, they drifted off into a blissful sleep.

TWENTY-SEVEN

'That's all? He just said, "Something must change?"'

'Yes, Your Super-Excellency, that's all Prince Dimitri said,' the professor replied.

General Moncransky stood up from the chair in Grigory's parlor. He began pacing in front of Grigory, who was still seated. The General thought it best to meet Grigory in his flat, instead of having him come to his office at the Winter Palace. Dimitri might be there and see his friend from the arts circle and know something was up.

'So, Professor, are your parents fond of frigid weather? Are *you* fond of frigid weather?'

From Grigory's pained expression, the General could see that he knew where the conversation was heading.

'Your Super-Excellency, the Prince has spoken of no intention overthrowing the Tsar by violent means . . . I swear to you. At all these meetings, he just listens and never really says anything.'

The General frowned at Grigory, which made him squirm in his seat.

'In fact, no one in the group is committed to violence.'

'In six months, you don't have a damn thing on him!' growled the General.

Grigory remained silent.

'You must try harder, my friend. Try to incite him to violence with your revolutionary fervor. Speak about the workers' and peasants' misery, and the two pogroms. I must have concrete proof that Markhov is a revolutionary – and that means *action* not words.'

'I'll try, Your Super-Excellency,' said Grigory meekly.

'You bet you will, or you'll be teaching in Siberia!' The General nodded at his adjutant that he was leaving.

'This is such a nice flat. Maybe you can bring some of this furniture to the log shack you'll be living in,' said the General as he was going out the door. 'And be sure to bring some bear-fur underdrawers.'

Grigory put his hands over his face and groaned.

As General Moncransky stepped into his sled, he thought about what would happen if he accused Dimitri of being a traitor to the Tsar's face. Nicholas would think he was mad as a hatter and laugh at him as though he were an idiot child. No, mere words overheard at an intellectual soirée wouldn't be enough to convince him. He needed absolute proof – to catch him red-handed in a revolutionary act. So, he had to be patient. He couldn't have him followed because the bastard might be still sleeping with his wife, and his officers would find out, subjecting him to humiliation and gossip. He couldn't bear that.

The sled glided to a stop in front of Grand Duke Sergei's St Petersburg Palace. A servant led him to the Grand Duke's study.

'The meeting was supposed to start at 10. It's now 10:03, Moncransky,' hissed the Grand Duke. The General nodded to General Isvoltsky to begin.

'The next incident will be in Sebezh in the Pale.'

'Where's that?' the Grand Duke asked.

'In the Vitebsk Province, Your Highness,' replied Isvoltsky.

'I heard that some of the Jews in Gomel actually fought back,' said General Gromeko, an officer in the Chevalier Guards. 'Is that true, Isvoltsky?'

'Yes, Your Excellency. Jews throughout the Pale have formed self-defense leagues after the Kishinev affair – with guns and clubs.'

'Well, that's not fair. If the Hebrews have guns, then our people should have some guns, too,' barked General Gromeko.

'I'll see to it, Your Excellency.'

'Some Jews aren't going to have a very happy Hanukah this year,' Moncransky said.

TWENTY-EIGHT

'**K**atya! Katya! Wait!'
As Dimitri trotted up the marble steps of St Igor's Hospital, Katya had come crashing out of the entry doors and run down the stair past him. It was only when she was about to cross the street that she heard his shouts and turned.

'Whooa . . . Is the hospital on fire?' he said. But the look on Katya's face wiped off his smile.

'Dimitri, there's been a pogrom in Sebezh! Dozens have been killed!' she yelled frantically. People walking along the street looked at her. Dimitri ran down the steps and grabbed her by the arm.

'Take a breath, then tell me from the beginning.'

She inhaled slowly and set her doctor's bag on the sidewalk.

'Dr Tchinarova received a wire from his sister, who has an estate near there. She was afraid the pogromists would come on their land and kill their Jewish steward,' she said in a panic-stricken voice. 'I have to go there. The hospital there has put out a call for doctors!'

Dimitri had never seen her act this way. She was always so level-headed. It alarmed him to see her in such a state.

'Calm down. You can't go there.' Sebezh was just inside the border of the Pale of Settlement, at least a three-hour train ride. 'It's too dangerous!'

Katya's face reddened. 'Damn you, I'm telling you I'm going. I *have* to help those people. I'm going straight to the train station.'

'But why?'

'Because I have sympathy for these outcasts, that's why!' she shouted. 'And I'm a doctor who took an oath to save lives.'

Her anger made Dimitri step back. It reminded him of opening a door to a stove, and the heat of the red-hot fire bursting in his face.

'Then I'll come with you,' he said in a calm voice.

Katya's expression was transformed. She reached out and squeezed his gloved hand.

'Oh God!'

It wasn't the dead body lying in the street that was so shocking to Dimitri but the blood that had spilled from the hole in its head onto the snow. The contrast of the dark scarlet-colored liquid against the pure white snow mesmerized him.

'I warned Your Honor this place was a goddamn mess.'

He frowned at the driver of the coach and waved him away. He had to be paid triple his usual fare to bring them to this part of town. Katya rushed up to the body, her boots sliding in the snow, the blood turning it a pinkish hue. She turned the man face up. He had a full beard and looked about forty. His eyes were wide open, as though he was gazing at the gray cloudy sky above. When she saw he was beyond help, Katya walked down the middle of the street to another body lying about twenty yards away. This one had a sobbing woman crouching over it. When she saw Katya approaching, she stood up.

'Please, mistress, please help my poor husband,' wailed the woman. She spoke as though in a trance. 'My husband, Mottel Greenspoon. He was a glazier. I just returned this morning from visiting my sister in Drissa. A neighbor said he was hiding in the shed in the back. He was dragged out and beaten by the peasants – one of them he knew.'

Katya just patted the woman's shoulder. She knelt down to examine him, and found the side of his head had been bashed in. She could see the purple-pink brain inside in the skull.

'I'm very sorry, there's nothing I can do now,' said Katya. The wife began screaming uncontrollably. Dimitri was now standing next to Katya. He saw that on both sides of the streets, all the windows had been smashed in. Just outside the open doors were trails of debris that were now being covered by a light snowfall. Clothes and silverware were strewn out of doorways, along with a curious coating of white feathers. One building had smoke pouring out of the second-floor window. He walked into a house, and was taken aback by the extent of the carnage. The room was completely destroyed, with broken furniture and smashed glass. When he saw the feathers from ripped mattresses covering the floor, he now understood where they came from. Even the pictures on the walls had been stolen. He heard someone moaning in pain and shouted for Katya. They found a young woman crumpled up in the corner of a side room. Her face was terribly bruised, and there was a gash across her forehead. Dimitri noticed her black flannel skirt was bunched up at her waist, and there were bloodstains in her underwear. He understood what had happened. The semi-conscious girl didn't acknowledge their presence and just stared off into space. Katya opened her bag and began to dress the wound. Dimitri walked up the plank stairs and saw another body that looked dead.

When he and Katya left the house, three scarlet-coated Cossacks abreast rode past them, and Katya shouted at them to halt. One turned and bowed politely to her.

'A girl in there needs to go to the hospital,' ordered Katya. 'I'm a doctor,' she added in a loud voice to make the Cossacks take her command seriously.

'The Jews will take care of their own, Doctor. Don't worry,' replied the Cossack in a jovial voice.

His answer surprised Katya. Before she replied, the soldier spoke.

'All is under control, we've dispersed the rioters,' he said proudly as if he'd done his duty well.

'What caused all this?' asked Dimitri.

'Oh, the usual circumstances, Your Honor. A Jew cheats a peasant. A Christian gets killed by a Jew, and things get out of hand.' He saluted and rode off.

As they walked down the street, they found three more bodies. All of them had their heads bashed in. The violence reminded Dimitri of when he was a child, smashing all the melons in a garden on his father's estate, for the pure fun of it. There were also more wounded lying about, and one by one Katya tended to them while Dimitri assisted. He noticed something off to his right. The new snowfall was covering up a piece of paper. After he tied off a bandage, he went over to pick it up.

'*Kill the Jews & Save Russia*,' it read. He tucked the flier into his pocket. After an hour, people appeared like mice cautiously emerging from their holes. All were Jews, out to survey the damage. He watched as they picked through the rubble, setting aside possessions that were spared and going right to work beginning the cleanup. Several more injured people, including a limping child, came out of the building, and Katya gathered them in one spot to treat them. Finally, the doctor and two nurses from the Jewish hospital arrived in a *droshky* and consulted with Katya. The wounded were piled into the carriage, and the doctor drove off, saying he would be back for another load. A wagon had arrived, and people began piling the dead like cordwood into it. The image of the dead child in Kishinev came back to him. It was twilight when Katya saw the last victim.

Dimitri's boot crunched on something. He bent down and picked up a little piece of metal about a half-inch wide and four inches long. It had an engraving of a little house with a symbol rising above it like a sun. On both ends, it had holes with tiny nails still in them.

An old woman was outside a house cleaning up broken glass.

'Excuse me, does this belong to you?' asked Dimitri.

The crone walked slowly up to Dimitri and took the metal from him. She wiped the dirt off it with the hem of her long black skirt.

'Why yes, thank you, Your Honor,' she croaked.

She then fastened the object to the right side of the door frame, touched it lightly with two fingers and muttered,

'*Hear, O Israel,*
The Lord is our God,
The Lord is one.'

'Is that your house number?'

'In a way, Your Honor.'

Dimitri walked in another building, a grocery store which had been looted to the last morsel of bread. An old man was sweeping up broken glass from the storefront that had been completely smashed in. He looked up at Dimitri, then continued.

'Here, this will help you get back on your feet, old fellow,' said Dimitri as he handed the man some ruble notes.

'Thank you, Your Honor, this will be of much help,' said the old man in a quiet voice. He bowed slightly and went on sweeping. When Dimitri turned to leave, he saw Katya standing in the doorway. She glowered at him.

'You think giving him a hand-out will solve things,' she snarled. Dimitri, puzzled, said nothing. 'You think everything can be put right with money! These people need their civil rights and freedom – to be treated as human beings,' she said loudly, catching the old man's attention. 'Not money!'

Dimitri was now ashamed for his gesture, but then he became annoyed.

'So, what do you expect *me* to do?'

'Fight for justice for these wretched people. Change the way they're treated! Didn't you see first-hand these atrocities? Persuade your chum, the Tsar, to make Russia a constitutional monarchy,' she said acidly.

Dimitri shook his head.

'You mean, tell Nicholas II that he's a tyrant, and not ordained by God Himself to rule his people as he sees fit?'

'Exactly,' she said.

'Sometimes you remind me of a four-year-old who can't get her way.'

'You're the child who lives in his own nursery. Open your eyes, Dimitri. Look at this suffering. But it's not just here in this shtetl, but throughout an entire empire of a hundred thirty million people – except for you, Lara, and the Tsar.'

'You and your father live pretty well, I've noticed.'

She narrowed her eyes and took a step forward.

'And I'm ashamed of that, do you hear? It kills me to live in privilege while children live in shit. I'd give that up for a free Russia any day. At least my father treats his workers well and pays them fairly.'

Before Dimitri could answer, Katya held up her blood-stained hand to end the discussion.

'We have to get to the hospital,' she said as she walked back into the street.

The Jews were milling about, some carting debris out of

the buildings. Katya asked a man where the hospital was, and he offered to walk her there. The people had seen her on her knees treating the injured and were eager to oblige her. Two old women had wanted her to come in and have tea, but she wouldn't hear of it with so much work to do.

'We can walk, it's only a mile,' she said grimly.

Dimitri instinctively looked around for a carriage, but there were none in sight. He took her arm, and they started walking.

After about five minutes, a wagon pulled by a half-dead gray horse appeared at the end of the road. It picked up the pace and came toward them. A peasant woman bundled up in rags was driving. When it pulled alongside of them, she hopped out with surprising agility.

'Are you the lady doctor?' she wailed.

Katya just nodded. The woman took hold of her fur sleeve.

'My boy has been crushed under a pine he was felling, his leg is broken badly. The bone is sticking out through his trousers, there's blood all over. Please come, I beg you, mistress.'

'I'm on my way to the hospital to tend to the wounded of the pogrom,' replied Katya calmly.

'I beg you to come and save him. We'll go in the wagon. It is not far. Please,' pleaded the woman.

'But I must go to the hospital.'

'Mistress Doctor, he is a good Christian boy. Those people are just *Jews*, they can wait.'

Dimitri could see anger flush Katya's face red. He expected her to start shouting at the peasant. But she said nothing, and only stared at the woman's wrinkled, weather-beaten face that was racked with panic and desperation.

'Take us to him.'

The woman kissed Katya's hand and quickly ushered her into the back of the wagon. Dimitri followed and sat next to her. The peasant whipped the hell out of the poor horse to get it to move faster. Dimitri thought it would keel over at any second. The village, which wasn't that close by, was a collection of sagging shacks, their roofs heavy with snow. Pulling up to a rough plank door, the woman jumped off and ran to the back of the wagon to help Katya out.

Dimitri was almost knocked down by the stench when he

entered the one-room space. Except for a dim red glow coming from the big five-foot-high brick stove, the room was pitch-dark. Its one window was covered with canvas to keep the cold out, but Dimitri soon realized it wasn't much warmer inside. As his eyes got used to the darkness, the woman lit a candle and beckoned Katya over to a corner. There under a tattered blood-stained blue blanket was a shivering boy of about twelve.

'Stoke the fire,' Katya commanded Dimitri. 'His teeth are chattering.'

When Dimitri got the fire going, it threw more light in the room. Two dirt-covered, hollow-cheeked children wrapped in rags were leaning against the log wall staring at him. He took in the whole space they were in; a filthy sty with a wet bare dirt floor. It was like looking into a cesspool. Disgusted by the sight, he walked over to Katya, who had pulled the blanket off. There, protruding through his pants, was the boy's leg bone. With a scalpel, she cut the pants leg off. Dimitri had to turn his head away. It looked like a snapped chicken bone. She asked the mother to fetch some clean water and soap, but the woman said she had no soap.

'Dimitri, you're going to have to help me set his leg. Find some wood for a splint.'

Going to the stove, he found two flat pieces in a pile of wood. While Katya cleaned the wound, the boy moaned loudly.

'What is his name?'

'Georgy, Mistress Doctor.'

'This will hurt like hell, Georgy, but be brave like a Cossack,' Katya said in a kind soothing voice.

'Get hold of his shoulders, Dimitri.'

The boy screamed at the top of his lungs when Katya pushed the broken bone back in place. With deft hands, she quickly applied ointment to the wound, set the splints, and wrapped bandages around them. Impressed by her skill, Dimitri told her so, which elicited a smile from her; the first in twelve hours. By the time she finished, Georgy had calmed down, and Katya gave him some aspirin to ease the pain.

She turned to the mother. 'The bones will knit, but if the wound gets infected, he'll die. Do you understand?'

'Yes, Mistress Doctor, I will change the bandage and wash the wound,' replied the woman.

'Where is your husband?' Dimitri asked, gazing about the filthy room.

'Dead from the typhus, Your Honor. My eldest boy too, may God rest his soul,' said the woman making the sign of the cross. 'The famine was hard on us,' she said, pointing toward the children.

In spite of what Katya would say, Dimitri handed the peasant some coins. Outside the shack, Katya waved her hand in a broad arc toward the village. Crows were pecking away at the carcass of a cow in the snow about twenty yards away.

'Every one of these huts is a shit-hole like hers,' Katya said. 'This is how one hundred million peasants live in this country of ours.' Dimitri didn't attempt to answer as she raged on. 'What did you imagine? Fat happy peasants prancing through the birch groves, singing folk songs and strumming balalaikas?'

Dimitri looked down at his boots. 'I . . . didn't know.'

'Humans have little sympathy for things that do not directly concern them,' replied Katya coldly. 'But don't feel bad, I'm as guilty as you.'

'A boy no older than ten came up to me and said, "Jew, you don't need that other eye." Then he plunged the stick into my only good eye.'

Katya stood over an old man sitting on the floor clutching a dirty rag to his right eye. She could see that the left eye had been blinded for many years. Its lid was fused shut. Katya gently pulled his hand away and saw a blood-filled crater where the other eye had been. She had seen many ghastly wounds in her young career, but this time she reared back – not at the sight of the injury but the story behind it. This poor man was now stone blind. She had learned to control her emotions, but she blurted out, 'Who would do such a terrible thing?' The old man didn't respond.

They were in a large waiting room in the Jewish hospital stuffed with injured people moaning quietly in pain. There seemed to be dozens, and almost all had their heads bandaged.

With Dimitri assisting, she continued to treat wounds. After an hour, she said to Dimitri, 'I need a smoke.' She nodded to the door of an adjoining room, and he followed her.

When they opened the door to what they thought was an empty room, they both stood there dumbstruck. Katya gasped in horror, and the sight paralyzed Dimitri. Corpses were lined neatly with their heads against the base of the wall, their eyes shut like they were asleep. Almost all of them had suffered death by head trauma; heads and faces were caked with dried blood and pieces of brain. One corpse's face was beaten into an unrecognizable pulp. Most of the men were dressed in suits, and all had beards. The few women wore simple white blouses with plain dark skirts. One had no skirt or undergarments left. As Katya walked along the bodies, she came upon rows of murdered children. It was an unbelievable sight. Further down the line, a woman was standing, looking down in silence at a body that had multiple stab wounds in the stomach.

Doctor Slotski walked in. He was head physician of the hospital, in his seventies.

'I knew most of these people. This is Rose Katsup from Gostinnii Street. She was bludgeoned to death while her grandson looked on from his hiding place. And that's Chaim-Leib Goldis. There's the baker, David Drachman; he was thrown off the roof of his building,' the doctor stated calmly.

'For someone who personally knew these people,' Katya blurted out, 'you don't show much emotion.'

The doctor just shrugged. 'This is Russia, and these are Jews.' He left the room.

Dimitri took hold of Katya's arm.

'You're right, Katya. I live in my own fairy-tale world, totally cut off from reality. Until now, I kept telling myself this was none of my concern, and that was how life was – fair to some people, and unfair to most. Each day that reasoning got weaker and weaker. But I can't stand by any longer. I have to do what's right.'

He gazed into her eyes, which were filled with tears. 'This can't go on,' he said. 'We have to do something.'

She threw her arms around him.

*   *   *

As the train raced through the wintry countryside, Dimitri and Katya stared out the large window of their compartment. They had spent the entire night at the hospital treating more victims who had straggled in. Exhausted, Katya had fallen asleep against Dimitri's shoulder for a while. He had nodded off as well. For two people who loved to talk to each other, barely a word had been spoken between them one hour into the journey. It was though their spirits had been broken, and there was nothing left to say. The midday train to St Petersburg was mostly empty, and they had their compartment all to themselves.

'We should each stretch out on a seat, we'd be more comfortable,' Dimitri said.

Katya didn't answer, she was still staring out the window.

'Dimitri,' she said in a quiet almost inaudible voice, 'there's something I must tell you.'

She turned to face him. He saw a frightened look in her eyes, which made him shift uneasily in his seat.

'Out with it. It's best to deliver bad news quickly,' Dimitri said.

'I discovered that my great-grandfather was a Jew who converted to Christianity,' she said haltingly.

Dimitri locked eyes with her and said nothing.

'And?' he said after about fifteen seconds of silence.

'And?' she repeated.

'This is true?'

'Well . . . yes . . . it's true.'

Dimitri looked out the window for a moment, then turned to Katya and crossed his arms. Her heart sank when she saw his frown. She'd been right; this would be the end of their love.

'So . . . did you think I'd toss you off this moving train when you told me?' asked Dimitri gravely.

'I didn't know how . . .'

'I should throw you off, for even thinking for a second that it would matter to me,' he said gruffly. He took her by the arm, drew her to him and kissed her hungrily. 'I don't give a damn what you are. All I know is you're mine,' he said in a husky voice. 'Don't ever forget that.'

Then, they both stretched out on the benches, and he covered her with her fur coat. As Katya floated into a deep sleep, she recalled that the Baron had been right. If he truly loved her, Dimitri wouldn't give a damn.

TWENTY-NINE

'I'd expected more of those damn rioters would die,' the Tsar said. 'Just twenty-five?'

General Drachev looked down in embarrassment at his shiny black boots and cleared his throat.

'When the police couldn't handle them, the Governor-General called in the garrison, and they put a stop to the pogrom,' the General croaked in a shaky voice.

With a frown on his face, Nicholas looked up at him. Dimitri was sitting in an armchair to the right of the Tsar's desk. He was here this morning to go over the Memorial drawings. Drachev was here reporting on the pogrom in Sebezh, the one that Dimitri and Katya had just seen.

Sensing impending criticism, the General bowed his head and started rubbing his hands together nervously.

'These Jews are the revolutionary traitors that want to overthrow Russia,' the Tsar said gravely. 'Next time, don't spare any cartridges.'

A red-hot flash of rage shot up Dimitri's back. His entire body seemed on fire. He sat bolt upright in his chair and glared at Nicky. Right then and there, he decided to join the revolution. Up until now, he had sat passively and listened at the arts circle meetings, now it was time to act. No matter what the consequences, he had to do the right thing.

Von Dalek, the Minister of War, who was in charge of the military, interrupted.

'Your Majesty, the next time the army will be forceful in its punishment of the Jewish radicals. You can count on that.'

'I hope so, because the Jews will be sure to make more trouble,' the Tsar snapped. 'It's the criticism of me by the foreign press that's so maddening. Blaming me for something the Jewish exploiters brought on themselves. Even Tolstoy and Maxim Gorky blamed me.'

Dimitri remained silent, but inside, rage was boiling.

The Minister and the General thought their business with the Tsar was finished and could leave. But Nicholas continued.

'The Jews lead the revolutionary movement. And where are they getting weapons? I heard they were using a portrait of me for target practice.'

Von Dalek interjected, 'The cause of Holy Russia is the extermination of these rebels. Death to the rebels and the Jews.'

Dimitri grimaced; von Dalek was toadying up to the Tsar.

'Your Majesty,' von Dalek went on, 'there are hundreds of loyal, patriotic groups like the Union of Russian People that stand ready to fight the agents of revolution for the House of Romanov.'

The Tsar nodded, meaning the meeting was over. The two men almost ran out of the study. Only the new Minister of the Interior, Mirskii, remained.

'Your Majesty, I'd like to add one last comment,' Mirskii said.

'Go on, Minister.'

'Unless we can solve the Jewish question by drowning all five million of our Jews in the Black Sea, we have no choice but let them live in peace with rights,' Mirskii said in a calm measured tone.

Nicholas glared at Mirskii. Dimitri admired him for having the moral courage to speak for the Jews.

'My grandfather wanted to do that,' the Tsar said angrily, 'then Jewish revolutionaries blew him to bits with a bomb. You know I saw him die with my own eyes.'

'But, Your Majesty . . .'

'The Jews are alien to Russia, with their strange religion, food, clothing, and their Yiddish language. They'll never be Russian!' Nicholas stated in a loud authoritative voice. Another flash of anger shot through Dimitri's body. He clenched the arms of his chair.

'It's in Russia's best interest to leave them alone, Your Majesty.'

Mirskii didn't shrink back as most ministers would have done after a tongue-lashing. Dimitri's respect for him increased exponentially.

'I'll take it under advisement. You may go, Prince Mirskii,' the Tsar said in a pleasant tone. The Minister bowed and left the study.

'Now back to something far more important,' Nicholas said to Dimitri with a smile. 'The toilet facilities of the Memorial must be expanded. The lines at the interval will be far too long. You can't enjoy Tchaikovsky on a full bladder.'

Dimitri stood over the Tsar's shoulder to look at the drawing.

After going over all the revisions, Nicholas gestured for him to sit down and offered him a cigarette.

'This is much more enjoyable than dealing with Jews,' the Tsar said, pointing at the drawings.

'There are some wealthy businessmen and professional Jews in St Petersburg, Nicky, that don't cause the Empire any trouble,' Dimitri said.

'True. They're a tiny number that are "Russified,"' the Tsar replied. 'But they aren't the same kind of Jews in the Pale that take advantage of the peasants by lending money at usurious rates, or getting them drunk on vodka.'

Dimitri's heart sank at his reply, but he forged on.

'So, the Jews in the Pale shouldn't be protected from the peasants' resentment and outright hatred?'

'My dear Dimitri, these riots happen in a blink of an eye. It's just the way things are in Russia.'

'Maybe the peasants have a bad life, too, and they are also part of the revolution. The workers in the factories, too. I've heard the conditions are dreadful.'

'Yes, there probably are peasants and workers in the revolution that have been duped by these Jew radicals,' Nicholas said. 'The peasants are like children who can easily be led astray.'

Dimitri puffed on his cigarette while thinking of what to say. The Tsar was intently studying the first-floor plan of the Memorial. Dimitri stared at him. Now that he knew about Katya's great-grandfather, Nicky's views on the pogrom in Sebezh outraged him. The people cleaning up after the riot, like the old man in the store sweeping up glass, didn't seem like disconnected strangers any longer. It occurred to him that some of Katya's ancestors could have been treated like that for no other reason than that they were Jewish. He imagined Katya being there in Sebezh with her skirt bunched above her waist like the young girl they found. He had grown up in a family that rarely talked about Jews, because there were barely any around. Once he became a member of Court, he was exposed to mild Jew-hating; the courtiers considered Jews clever exploiters, it was in their blood. Nicky, on the other hand, considered Jews as sent from hell to destroy Russia. His grandfather's murder had set his feelings in stone.

'So, you think the Jews are the ones who want to topple the government?'

'I *know* they are, Dimitri,' Nicky said without looking up from the drawing.

'Nicky, I don't think the Jews started this riot. Look at this – a doctor who was in Sebezh found this in the street.' He handed Nicky the 'Kill the Jews' flier.

Nicky simply crumpled up the paper and tossed it into the waste basket. 'Dimitri, my friend, the *Jews* have these printed to make it look like *they're* the victims,' he said with a chuckle. He continued examining the drawings intently.

'We should have a separate waiting area for all members of the Imperial Family, so we can drink and smoke before a performance. And during the interval,' the Tsar announced.

'Maybe Mirskii has a point; if Jews were given full civil rights then we wouldn't have a revolution on our hands,' Dimitri said in a casual manner.

The Tsar looked up at Dimitri with an annoyed expression.

'You're really on a Jewish tear this morning, aren't you?'

'Well . . . I thought that might be a way of derailing a revolution,' Dimitri replied.

Nicky said in the exact kind of voice he used when he tried to reason with his daughters when they were being obstinate.

'The only way to deal with Jews is with bullets and more restrictions to keep those devils in line. These pogroms are actually helpful; they keep the Jews in a constant state of fear.'

Nicky pointed to the drawing.

'And we need our own restrooms. Can't have royals going to the bathroom with regular folk. Can you imagine Sunny doing that?' Nicky laughed at the thought.

Dimitri suddenly felt sick to his stomach.

THIRTY

D imitri was fidgeting in his seat like an impatient child, excited to give Katya her Christmas present. Sitting with her family in their drawing room around the tall, beautifully decorated tree, he couldn't wait his turn. Finally, he handed her a small gift wrapped in gold paper with a red bow. He anxiously watched her tear off the wrapping.

'Oh, Dimitri, this is absolutely wonderful.'

'I thought you'd like it.'

Katya held a framed piece of music written in Tchaikovsky's own hand.

'To think that he sat over this, imagining the music and writing it down in ink. Thank you so much.' She proudly showed the gift to her family.

'I can't read music,' confessed Dimitri.

'Then listen to what it means,' Katya said. She took the frame to the grand piano in the corner and started playing a beautiful tune.

'That was magnificent! It's the middle portion of the Concerto in B-Flat Minor,' Dimitri exclaimed. 'Please don't stop!'

'This fellow knows his Tchaikovsky – that's why the Tsar chose him to design his memorial,' Katya said proudly after she finished.

Her father, sister, and the rest of the family happily nodded in agreement.

Dimitri went over to the piano and picked up the frame.

'It always amazed me that these scratchy black marks can be transformed into something so beautiful to the ears,' he said quietly.

'Your drawings become beautiful three-dimensional objects,' Katya said, placing her hand on his.

Dimitri was so happy when he received Katya's invitation to have lunch the day after Christmas at her home. He had a prior engagement but cancelled it. Back in the fall, he had had tea with her family and really enjoyed their company. The Golitsyn family was such a jolly group that it brought to mind what Tolstoy said: that all happy families were alike, and every unhappy family was unhappy in its own way – as Dimitri was with Lara.

Dimitri had to constantly remind himself not to be too affectionate around Katya in front of her family. He was longing to sit next to her on the sofa and wrap his arm around her so her head would snuggle against his shoulder. He loved the scent of her hair. But he had to keep his distance.

'Another cognac, Dimitri?' asked Aleksandr Vassilievitch.

'Yes, please.'

Katya's brother Boris showed him his new English riding boots, as they both shared a passion for horses. Playing with Katya's two nieces immediately brought to mind the Tsar's daughters. He had been to the Alexander Palace that morning to give the family their gifts. They had given him a magnificent watch inlaid with diamonds with a personal inscription from Nicholas on the back. Each daughter held the watch to her ear to hear it ticking. On Christmas morning, after church, Dimitri gave Lara a *sautoir* of Cartier pearls, and she gave him a little Rembrandt etching for his collection, as she did every Christmas. At noon, saying she was off to visit friends, she vanished from the house and didn't return until early evening. Dimitri assumed she was seeing a lover, but he didn't care.

Aleksandr Vassilievitch dominated the conversation, asking Dimitri questions about the Imperial Family and the Tsar in particular. Like most upper-class Russians, Katya's father held the Tsar in almost religious awe, describing in great detail the one time he met Nicholas at Court. He thought of the Tsar as a forward-thinking leader who understood Russia's need for industrial expansion and the importance of men like him. Yet in all the time Dimitri knew him, the Tsar never once talked about industrial expansion. For a monarch ruling one sixth of the earth, he had little interest in political or economic matters. In fact, he had only *one* interest and that was his family. It was probably Russia's happiest family – though it definitely wasn't like other happy families. If Nicky could be as good a tsar as he was a family man, Dimitri mused as Aleksandr rambled on, Russia might not be in such a fix. And if Nicky cared for all Russians, including the peasants and the Jews, the way he cared about his family – like the 'little father' he claimed to be – he'd never allow his 'children' to live in poverty, or be murdered in pogroms. The carnage of Sebezh was still forefront in his mind. Dimitri wanted to tell Aleksandr how wonderfully Katya had performed tending to the injured there, but their visit had to remain a secret.

The time flew by, and soon Dimitri had to leave. Katya put her hand on his arm.

'You can't leave without your Christmas gift, Dimitri. Wait right there while I fetch it.'

Katya sprang up and ran out of the room. In less than twenty seconds, she was back holding a little basket.

Assuming the basket held a home-baked Christmas treat, Dimitri did as he was told.

'I couldn't wrap it,' she said excitedly. 'Close your eyes, and I'll place it on your lap. No peeking, mind you.'

Dimitri grinned at her family and did as he was told.

'Now, you can open them!'

Inside the basket, curled up on a mound of cloth, was a kitten with black, brown, and white fur. It looked up at Dimitri with round black eyes.

'How wonderful!' he cried out. He picked the kitten up and held him to his cheek, making it purr.

He could see that Aleksandr was disappointed that Katya had given him a cat, when Dimitri had just given her an original manuscript by Russia's most famous composer. But when he saw that Dimitri was as delighted as if she'd had given him a Da Vinci, Aleksandr beamed a smile at his daughter.

'What is that vile creature doing here?'

Lara stood in his bedroom doorway, her beautiful features contorted in a scowl.

'This is Tolstoy, my Christmas gift,' Dimitri replied proudly. He was playing with the kitten on his bed by moving his hand under the blanket and having him pounce on it. 'He thinks there's a mouse under here.'

'I won't have that creature in my home.'

'It's *my* creature and it stays,' he said in an irritated voice.

'No, it doesn't. Anyway, Fedor will kill it.'

'Let's see. Here Fedor, here boy!' Dimitri patted his hand on the bed.

The borzoi rose from his place by the fire and loped over to its master, who rubbed him under the chin.

Dimitri put the kitten in his lap. Fedor began licking the top of Tolstoy's head, and they touched noses. The dog walked back to the fireplace, curled up on the floor, and fell asleep.

'Fedor, you traitor!' Lara stomped her feet, but the dog lay still.

Dimitri looked at his wife and smiled.

'That's two votes to your one. It's what they call democracy. So, the cat stays.'

'Bastard!'

THIRTY-ONE

'Who is that talking to Countess Turgenev, Lara?' Princess Betsey asked.

Lara, taking a quick breather from the dancing, was standing next to her friend. She looked over to see a young woman talking to the old Countess by a stand of palm trees directly across the ballroom.

'Oh, that's the homely daughter of the textile merchant, Golitsyn. He's one of the richest commoners in Russia, so I invited him. I guess because he's a widower, he dragged her along as his escort.'

'Nice petite figure. And that's a Doucet gown with gold thread,' Princess Betsey said, instinctively sizing up a woman.

'She's definitely what they call in America, "plain as a post,"' Lara said fanning herself. It could be twenty degrees below zero outside, but in ballrooms during the season, it was like the tropics.

'Come on, Lara, you promised me this waltz.' Captain Boldyrev of the Lancers bowed before her.

'Fine, but don't let those damn spurs tear my gown. Good thing the officers aren't wearing their swords. Oh, Betsey *ma chère*, remind me to tell you the latest on Anna Vyrubova. I know for a fact that she was caught in bed with two of the Abyssinians at the same time. The Tsarina ignored it because she's her only friend,' Lara said before she was yanked onto the dance floor.

It was mid-January, and the season was in full swing. Dimitri and Lara had been to the mandatory Imperial Balls at the Winter Palace – the Nicholas Ball, the grandest with three thousand guests; three Concert Balls where the guests were serenaded by the St Petersburg Symphony; then five Hermitage Balls, which featured a single act of an opera in the Hermitage Theater followed by a ballet. A ball specifically for debutantes, who only could wear white gowns, was also *de rigueur*. There were more invitations to Court balls, decreasing in size and importance that signaled one's position in society. Because the Markhovs were at the top of the social ladder, they didn't have to attend these. The most exclusive Court ball was the Palm Ball; given at the end of the season; only five hundred were invited. As the name implied, tubs of palm trees from the Imperial conservatories provided the decoration.

Then there were private balls like Dimitri's and Lara's held in their mansion tonight. Lara loved to throw a ball, and she went all-out. The midnight supper in the hall adjoining the ballroom would have her favorite gold place settings for just five courses – consommé with sherry; a fish course of sturgeon; a main course with pheasant, lamb, and asparagus; then oysters and salad; and finally finishing with sorbets and pastries. Bottles of iced vodka flavored with lemon peel, peppercorn, or cranberries were on the long white-linen table next to seltzer bottles and almond-flavored milk. Lara was famous for putting

Havana cigars, French Sobranies, and her favorite American Benson and Hedges cigarettes in crystal holders at each setting. She loved choosing the Fabergé gifts to be put beside each guest's plate. An orchestra hidden in a gallery would play during dinner.

Officers in every type of uniform swirled women around the dance floor; their diamonds, emeralds, and rubies reflected from the four crystal chandeliers. People not dancing stood along the walls taking glasses of champagne from the silver trays held by the liveried servants and gossiping their heads off.

After the third quadrille, Dimitri escorted Countess Trigorin from the shiny parquet floor. The American ambassador to Russia, Robert Wilson, stepped forward and greeted him.

'A beautiful ball, Prince Dimitri. May I have the pleasure of introducing you to Mrs John King of New York City?'

A very attractive woman in her thirties with glossy chestnut hair extended her gloved hand. She had the widest brown eyes and a long neck covered with strands of alternating pearls and tiny diamonds.

'Very glad to meet you, Your Highness,' said Mrs King.

Dimitri had heard about her from Lara, who knew about every rich foreign woman visiting Russia. She was the widow of John King, an American who had owned the biggest paint company in the world. He had died from a fall from a horse while fox-hunting on their estate on Long Island, and his wife was the sole heir to his fortune. Dimitri usually specified King Paint for his projects, as it was a quality brand that didn't skimp on the lead.

Dimitri liked American women. He was always amused at their forthright manner and they didn't seem to be bothered with formality. There were three beautiful American socialites attached to the Court by way of marriage – Julia, the Princess Cantacuzené, the granddaughter of the late U.S. President Grant; Suzanne, the Princess Belozersky of Boston; and Lily Bouton, married to Count Nostitz. Dimitri had had affairs with two of them.

'You must dine with my wife and me while you're in St Petersburg, Mrs King.'

'Call me Kate. I'd be honored.'

Normally, Dimitri would be thinking of a liaison with this attractive woman. But he glanced over at Katya, who was fanning herself by a window that overlooked the Neva.

'And I'm Dimitri. Maybe you have time for a waltz later on.' He bowed to her, then walked over to Katya. He was hoping to sneak in one dance with her tonight – that wouldn't raise any eyebrows. Just as he reached her, Lara came swirling off the dance floor.

All three wound up standing next to each other.

'Lara, allow me the pleasure of introducing Doctor Katya Golitsyn,' Dimitri announced, avoiding an awkward moment.

Katya curtsied and extended her gloved hand. After a moment's hesitation, Lara shook it and grinned. Dimitri knew she remembered her from the Catherine Palace ball last summer. Lara's memory was like a steel trap.

'A pleasure to meet you,' Lara said. 'Thank you and your father for coming tonight. You know, doctor, I envy you. We women of the aristocracy aren't allowed to use our brains; we have to settle for just being beautiful. But in your case, that's not true.'

Katya was trying to figure out if Lara was complimenting her or insulting her.

'Er . . . thank you,' Katya replied.

'Keep up the good work. Someone has to get their hands dirty, and I'm not about to ruin this expensive manicure.' She laughed.

'Princess Lara, our quadrille is coming up,' interrupted General Asmov as he whisked her onto the dance floor.

'See you later,' Lara called over her shoulder.

'Let's go somewhere cooler,' Dimitri suggested, wiping his forehead with his monogramed handkerchief. He led Katya down the grand staircase, which was lined with huge pots of flowers. People were going up and down the stairs like in a train station.

'Nice little hut you have here, Prince Dimitri,' Katya said as they entered the drawing room which they had all to themselves. She eyed the marble inlaid with silver *moiré* panels encased in bronze frames.

'It's not much, but I call it home,' Dimitri said to make her laugh.

They sat on a long sofa in front of a roaring fire.

'I had such a good time with your family at Christmas. It was wonderful.'

Katya's face lit up in the way he found so attractive. 'They loved you. I was so glad you came.'

He fought the urge to put his arms around her.

'Tolstoy is very happy in his new home,' he said. 'He and Fedor have become great chums.'

'I'm so happy you liked my gift,' Katya said, placing her hand on top of his. 'My father said it was unbecoming to give a cat to a prince.'

Dimitri shook his head. 'It was my best Christmas gift of all.' He turned his palm over so they were holding hands. It was intoxicating to have her warm little hand in his. He brought it up to his lips and kissed it.

Katya gave Dimitri's hand a squeeze. Their eyes locked and smiled at each other but they said nothing. His head then started moving ever so closer to hers.

'Listen,' Katya said, cocking her head toward the ceiling. 'The mazurka is starting up. Let's dance.'

'There'll be a lot more mazurkas tonight,' Dimitri replied in a quiet voice. He moved closer, leaned in, and their lips met. The spell of their long passionate kiss was broken by the loud pop of a burning ember in the great fireplace, and they returned upstairs – separately.

THIRTY-TWO

'Such a wonderful design, Dimitri. Congratulations, old boy.'

'Tremendous, Prince Dimitri. Well done.'

Dimitri always felt the best praise came from his fellow architects, and now he was floating on air. On a frigid January night, at the Imperial Academy of Russian Architects, his drawings for the Tchaikovsky Memorial were unveiled. A huge crowd had showed up to view them where they sat on display easels in the rotunda of the IARA on Tenov Street.

'Your work has jumped to a new creative level,' exclaimed Ivgeny Platosky, an architect and old friend from his architecture-school days.

It was true. With a great deal of hesitation and doubt, Dimitri had changed his design direction. He had abandoned his classical ways that he had used for years; it was like abandoning a cherished home and walking into the unknown. From the reaction tonight, he'd been right.

A dapper man with short cropped hair and a full beard walked up to Dimitri, who immediately recognized him.

'A beautiful design, Prince Dimitri,' said Fedor Shekhtel, Russia's leading architect of the Style Moderne. Dimitri tried to look humble, but couldn't suppress a grin.

'Thank you so much for your praise, Monsieur Shekhtel. Thank you for coming tonight.'

'You draw like an angel,' Shekhtel added, nodding to the drawings.

The renderings, in watercolor washes and ink, did indeed look splendid. The main elevation of the building had a huge half-round red granite arch, with tendril-like leaded glass framing pieces of stained glass, between two black granite towers that were topped by glass and steel domes with slender finials. The stone panels had carved bas-relief ornamentation of the Kievian type the Tsar liked so much. The sides of the Memorial were also of stone, with a pattern of oval and square-topped windows giving the facade a lively inventive rhythm for the music conservatory and the music library.

In the middle of the building was the vast concert auditorium, entered from the front lobby whose ornate plaster ceiling in the Style Moderne mirrored the shape of the arch. Dimitri had spent a lot of time on the acoustics, using Carnegie Hall in New York as a guide. It was said that auditorium had the clearest sound in the world. Dimitri knew the Tsar had already decided that the inaugural concert would be led by Nicholai Rimsky-Korsakov, Russia's most famous living composer. He knew the building would be a flop if the acoustics were bad.

People kept showering Dimitri with praise. Grand Duke Vladimir, the Tsar's uncle and President of the Imperial Academy of Arts, came up to him.

'Good show, Markhov,' he bellowed. 'Nicky and Alix are so happy with your design.' Having done his duty as the Imperial Family's official arbiter of the arts, he took the arm of a very young woman and headed for the door.

'Bravo, Dimitri. You're no longer an artistic tight-ass,' Katya said in a low voice. 'I have to get back to the hospital before they know I've skipped out, but I wasn't going to miss this for the world.' She kissed his cheek and walked away. Dimitri knew she would be there tonight.

Two middle-aged men came up and bowed.

'Prince Dimitri, allow me to introduce myself,' said the shorter of the two. 'I am Anatoly Tchaikovsky and this is Ippolit. We are Pyotr's brothers, and would like to congratulate you on your magnificent design. Our family is extremely proud to have the Tsar build this monument. If only Pyotr could have lived to have seen it.'

Dimitri was touched by their words. 'It is only right to build a memorial to Russia's greatest composer.'

The brothers nodded shyly and backed off into the crowd.

'The ambassador said you were a man of many talents, now I believe him,' said a voice directly behind him. 'Where did you learn to draw that way?'

Dimitri turned to face Mrs King, who looked ravishing in an oyster-white gown.

'This is a pleasant surprise. Thank you for coming tonight.'

'So where did you learn to draw?'

'The Imperial Academy of Arts in St Petersburg.'

'Americans are under the impression that all Russian princes do is drink, dance, and carouse with women,' said Mrs King with a big smile.

'Oh, I find the time to do that too.' This made Mrs King laugh loudly. She had a high-pitched laugh that rose above the surrounding buzz of conversation.

Mrs King looked about her. 'So where is the beautiful Princess Lara tonight?'

'Excruciating headache.'

'I've had my share of those – at the right times.'

That comment made Dimitri laugh. She was a witty American woman, something he didn't think existed.

'Well, congratulations – Dimitri. I'll be sure to be at the opening concert,' Mrs King said as she waved and disappeared into the crowd.

An hour went by and the rotunda was emptying. Because of the freezing cold, people went outside when their sleighs pulled up. The drivers laid hot-water bottles on their laps topped with thick sable blankets and off they went, the horses' bells jingling.

Except for the caretaker of the IARA building, Dimitri was the last person to get his coat. As he was bundling up, Mrs King stepped from behind one of the marble columns that lined the rotunda. She wore a full-length black sable coat with a matching hat.

'Dimitri, do me the honor of letting me buy you a drink at my hotel. We can go in my sled,' she said jovially.

Dimitri had expected to have the drink in the lobby bar of the Hotel Metropol, but he now found himself alone in Mrs King's spacious suite. She handed him a tumbler of vodka.

'You are what we girls in Alabama call one swell-lookin' fella,' said Mrs King, raising her glass to him.

'Thanks, very kind of you to say, Kate. You're from Alabama?'

'I'm a real southern belle, honey-pie, didn't you notice my accent?'

'Yes, it had an odd sound. Nothing like the Tsar's Oxford-accented English.'

Mrs King smiled and took no offense at this remark.

'I know someone from Alabama,' announced Dimitri proudly. 'Works in the palace.'

Mrs King crinkled her brow in interest.

'Jim's his name. He's one of the Tsar's "Abyssinians" who open the doors of the Imperial private apartments.'

Mrs King let out a hoot. 'Well, I'd like to meet a fella from back home. I haven't been back to Birmingham in years. We'd have a lot to talk about.'

'In February, he's going home for a visit.'

'Imagine that – a for-real Alabaman right here in St Petersburg.'

'If you're going to be presented to the Emperor and Empress, you might as well kill two birds with one stone and meet Jim.'

'Yes, I'll do that.'

After downing another full glass of vodka, Mrs King was standing right against Dimitri. He looked at the clock on the fireplace mantel; he wanted to leave to catch Katya when she finished her shift. He was feeling sky-high after his success tonight and wanted to tell her about it after they made love.

'Why don't we settle down on the sofa, Your Handsome Highness?' Mrs King purred. She hung on to his arm, tugging on it to get him to sit down.

'I really must be going, Kate.'

'Oh, come on, it's early. I thought you princes stayed up 'til the early hours of the morning,' Mrs King said in a seductive voice. She wrapped her arms around his torso.

'Sometimes, we do, but I have an early appointment, tomorrow,' Dimitri replied earnestly. He tried to step out of her grasp, but she wouldn't let go.

'Ah, please stay a bit longer. Let me get you another drink.'

'No, I haven't finished the first one. Really, Kate, I must go.'

'You wicked boy. Princess Cantacuzené told me you stayed up late with her.'

'Well, that was a while back and . . .'

Mrs King interrupted him by planting a kiss full on his lips. He spread his arms out like an eagle and started inching toward the door.

'You are one damn handsome man,' Mrs King said in a slurred voice. She turned to fetch herself another drink. It was Dimitri's opportunity to escape. When she turned to him, he was at the door.

'Hey, handsome. Where the hell you going?'

'Have to run, Kate,' he said as he was going out the door. 'I promise to call you when I get the chance.'

Out in the corridor, he thought he heard a glass smash against the inside of the door.

THIRTY-THREE

Dimitri and the Tsar had just returned from the theater to the Winter Palace to have some late-night refreshments. Jim opened the door for them to the Tsar's study.

'Zemikov has such a magnificent voice,' Dimitri said.

'I love *Rusalka*,' Nicholas replied enthusiastically.

As they were taking their coats off, an officer came in and handed the Tsar a telegram. Nicholas went pale while reading it.

'The Japanese have attacked the squadron at Port Arthur. They've sunk three ships.'

Nicky handed the telegram to Dimitri. It was from Admiral Alexeiev, Commander-in-Chief in the Far East.

'All this, without a declaration of war,' said the astonished Tsar. 'May God come to our aid.'

The next morning, thousands of people filled the streets of St Petersburg, calling out for Russia's swift victory over the Japanese, the 'Yellow Peril.' Carrying banners and singing 'God Save the Tsar,' patriotic crowds marched to the Winter Palace. When the Tsar went to a window and saluted, they went mad with joy. The rejoicing continued for the rest of the day.

But the Tsar had told Dimitri something that the jubilant crowds didn't know. The Japanese had the Russian fleet completely bottled up by laying mines across the mouth of Port Arthur's harbor. They seemed to know exactly where every ship was moored and launched attacks with torpedo boats. The Japanese set their sights on Port Arthur itself and laid siege with huge eleven-inch cannons. They knew where every fortified position was located, their infantry overwhelmed one spot after another. But the Russian army bravely fought back and held the city. Although Nicholas was quite shaken by the attack, his generals reassured him that everything would be fine. General Teplitski told the Tsar that 'To take the people's mind off revolution, we need a small, victorious war.'

But not everyone was patriotic. Because of the war, the social season and six balls were canceled, to Lara's bitter disappointment. 'We need balls and parties to lift our spirits,' she exclaimed. Alexandra canceled all her social events and began knitting circles for the female members of court in the ballrooms of the Winter Palace. To the consternation of the society ladies, she invited women of all classes to join them. They would make scarves, socks, and bandages for the soldiers at the front. Even the Grand Duchesses, including little Anastasia, worked. The Tsarina came every day and sat down to sew. Lara had no choice to participate; Dimitri demanded that she attend. She was absolutely terrible at sewing and knitting, but showed up daily.

It amused Dimitri to see Lara stuck in such a situation, but it was better than volunteering to be a nurse. Many society women went to work in hospitals in St Petersburg, to allow the trained nurses to go to the front in the Far East. It wasn't long before wounded Russian soldiers were sent back to the west. Katya soon had beds full of men at St Igor's to be cared for. Seeing the maimed bodies made her furious over what seemed an unnecessary war. When she and Dimitri were together, she always cursed the Tsar for trying to steal Korea from the Japanese, and getting Russia into this fix.

In April, when the Far East fleet tried to move out of Port Arthur, Admiral Makarov's flagship was sunk, killing him and seven hundred men. The Russian navy was completely bottled up. It was the first inkling that victory for Russia wasn't guaranteed. Although the newspapers were heavily censored, over the next months, Russians could tell from the constant stream of wounded and dead that things weren't going well. The Tsar felt guilty for staying in St Petersburg. He wanted to go to the front and be at the head of army, but his uncles and his mother dissuaded him. He toured military camps, reviewed troops, and handed out images of St Seraphim to departing soldiers at the train station.

The spring brought news from the Far East of defeat after

defeat for the Russian army fighting the Japanese on the Chinese mainland which they had invaded. Dimitri saw how sad the Tsar was, and tried to keep him involved in the Tchaikovsky Memorial. His feelings for Nicky were complicated; he couldn't dismiss his long friendship with him and his closeness to his family, but he had lost all respect for Nicholas as a ruler. He hoped that by remaining close, he could eventually talk some reason into him regarding treatment of the workers and the Jews.

'Nicky, did you see Lara's latest pair of socks she knitted for the soldiers?' he asked as they had tea in the Tsar's study.

'No, what did they look like this time?'

'Well, she knitted one for a man who must have a three-foot-long foot. The matching one was two feet long.' This got the Tsar laughing. 'They can use them for mittens,' he said.

'Remember the first ones? They were size of baby booties.' Nicky laughed even harder.

As the Tsarina entered the study, she heard this and frowned. 'Lara's doing the best she knows how,' she said testily. 'But it's the effort that counts most. Look at these beautiful pair of socks our Miss O'Brian knitted in her spare time. Even she does her bit.' The nanny had come up behind her, smiling proudly.

THIRTY-FOUR

'The time for talk is over,' said Evigenia in a grave voice. The arts circle sat still as statues in her drawing room. Only the crackling of the fire was heard. Dimitri glanced over at Katya, who wore a serious expression.

'The Social Democratic Party has given me permission to create a revolutionary cell. All of you are welcome as members. Only a united assault on the autocracy will bring victory and rights for all Russians – workers, peasants, and Jews.'

People stood up, clapped, and smiled at each other. Dimitri rose hesitantly, wearing a blank expression. After what he'd seen in Sebezh and after witnessing Nicky's reaction, he couldn't stand by any longer, even if it meant destroying the only kind of life he'd ever known. But part of him wanted to flee the room. Going over to the side of the revolution had very personal consequences – it meant betraying Nicky, his life-long friend, and his wife, Alexandra. He felt like a shit for doing this to the two kindest people in the world. What the hell was he doing? *Maybe I shouldn't do this*, he thought.

Katya came up and hugged him. He held her for a few seconds, then stepped back.

Dimitri swallowed hard and said with a grim expression, 'I guess there are things bigger than oneself. If I do nothing . . . then I am nothing.'

Katya hugged him again as people came up to shake his hand. Grigory affectionately pounded him on the back. 'So glad you're with us,' he cried.

Dimitri knew that the cell liked having an aristocrat on their side, because it gave the cause credibility. He wondered if there were any other aristocrats in other cells, or was he the only one?

Vodka was being poured. Evigenia called for attention.

'Our task is to use mass propaganda and secret meetings to incite revolution. The proletariat must be convinced that they can capture the political power to improve their everyday lives. It's up to us to persuade and guide them. The upper classes must be shaken up as well.'

The group applauded and murmured in agreement.

Evigenia raised her hand. 'There is one more thing to tell you, and it's most important. As a revolutionary, you can never tell anyone of your activities, especially your family members. If they know, the Okhrana will consider them co-conspirators, and if you're caught, they will be exiled to Siberia along with you. The only offense that is punishable by death is assassination of a government official, but we have chosen a non-violent path. From now on, we'll meet in secret apartments in the city.'

Evigenia held up a flyer: *A Constitution for Rights for All*. The text explained the coming new order in Russia.

'We must coat St Petersburg with propaganda like snow.

No inch of the city can go uncovered. Because you can be arrested for distributing subversive material, you must paper the city at night.'

'Excuse me, I must use the men's room.'

Lara turned to Dimitri.

'I warned you about drinking too much vodka before the show, Dimitri. He drank the equivalent of the Baltic.' Princess Betsey and her husband, Prince Paul, giggled along with Lara. They were sitting in a box at the Alexandrinsky Theater watching a performance of *The Hunt*, a Russian drama. Dimitri quickly went down the narrow corridor.

He had learned a lot designing his first concert hall for the Tchaikovsky Memorial. Despite the war with Japan, the project continued, and he was now doing the construction drawings and specifications. Besides acoustics, the most important thing in the design was ventilation. He had become very well-versed in this type of mechanical engineering. Thousands of people watching a concert gave off a lot of heat and humidity that had to be expelled from the space every few minutes. This process happened directly above the audience through vents in the ceiling – which was where he was now.

He stood on a catwalk, one of many that crisscrossed the theater's attic space. He had drunk so much vodka tonight for a good reason; to steady his nerves for what he was about to do. Down on his knees, he stretched out and quietly opened a large ventilation grille close to the center of the ceiling. He could see the tops of the heads of the audience and could hear the actors on stage reciting their lines. Suddenly, his sweaty right hand slipped, and he fell forward. Desperately, he reached out for the other side and caught himself before he plunged into the auditorium. The top of his body was actually hanging below the ceiling. His heart pounding, panicked, he took a deep breath and eased himself up. On the catwalk was a canvas bag he'd hidden in the theater the day before. He reached in and pulled out the pile of flyers that Evigenia had provided. In two batches, he flung them into the ventilation opening. They fluttered down like autumn leaves onto the audience below.

'They wanted me to shake up the upper classes – so I did,' he said out loud while noiselessly shutting the grille. As he ran off, he could hear the murmuring of confusion from the theatergoers.

Back in the box, he saw Princess Betsey was holding a flyer with a puzzled look on her face.

'What the hell's going on?' exclaimed Dimitri, out of breath.

THIRTY-FIVE

'Dimitri, the peasants are the heart and soul of Russia. They are the *real* people of Mother Russia,' Alexandra said. 'There are millions of hardworking, pious, humble people who fall on their knees every day to pray to God and their beloved Tsar. I saw their love for us when we went to Serov.'

Dimitri could see in her eyes that she truly believed what she was saying. His heart sank to the bottom of his stomach. What planet did Nicholas and Alexandra live on?

'Nicky is their "little father," and he knows what's best for them,' she added.

'Sunny is their "little mother," who cares for them,' said the Tsar proudly. 'God *Himself* wants me to rule them; not any parliament or Duma.' He explained this to Dimitri in the patient manner used with a dim-witted child.

'Yes, Your Majesty, I do understand,' Dimitri replied meekly. He knew the conversation about democracy and a constitutional monarchy had ended. Aside from distributing propaganda and attending cell meetings, he had truly believed he could slowly convince Nicholas that Russia must change, because many were suffering. He'd tried to do it in a subtle way. But the Tsar was a person of unchanging conviction. It was hopeless; like talking to a rock. The idea that Russians were in misery was completely alien to his thinking.

The Grand Dukes Sergei and Alexis nodded vigorously in agreement.

'Democracy is all bosh,' growled Alexis, blowing a ring of cigar smoke.

'Total horse manure!' Sergei shouted. 'Nicky is our divine leader, answerable to no one but to his conscience and God!'

The Imperial Family were waiting in a parlor of the Malachite Hall in the Winter Palace for supper to start. But they couldn't go into the Rotunda to be seated because the guest of honor, Prince Henry of Bulgaria, hadn't arrived. Time-honored Court etiquette meant they had no choice but to wait for him.

'His Majesty is absolutely right, Dimitri. Russia doesn't need any democracy,' Lara crowed. His wife was making a rare appearance with him. She'd run out of excuses to back out; one could have only so many stomachaches or headaches. Dimitri knew she'd come tonight to show off her new violet chiffon gown. The Tsar and Lara got along well with each other, often good-naturedly teasing each other, which irritated the Tsarina. But Alexandra was being civil to Lara tonight, telling her about nursing the wounded soldiers from the Far East. Wearing a matron's uniform and cap, Alexandra went to the hospital daily to personally minister to the wounded, giving sponge baths and changing dressings. Russia was getting crushed by Japan, and the country felt humiliated in front of the world, but Lara couldn't care less. She had given up knitting socks; even the Tsarina saw that she was hopeless at the task. Since she was not a lady-in-waiting, Alexandra couldn't force her to do war work.

'It is wonderful of Your Majesty to look after those brave boys. I hear some of them are quite handsome; I just may pay a visit to the wards.' Lara gave a wink at the Tsar, who chuckled. Alexandra frowned.

'Yes, you must go see them, Larissa. The sight of such a beautiful woman will lift their spirits,' said Nicky.

The four children bounded into the Malachite Hall, followed by Miss O'Brian.

The cheerful expression vanished from Nicky's face. 'I pray to God every day for a victory,' he said solemnly. 'We're planning to break through the north-western sector in Port Arthur. I wish I could be there with my troops.'

Dimitri looked down at the floor. He knew the Tsar was in agony over the war. He was so upset that he hadn't commissioned Fabergé to make the Imperial Easter eggs for his mother and wife this year, saying it wasn't right to give such extravagant gifts when Russian soldiers were dying in the Far East. Others in Court didn't feel that way, and had Fabergé continue to make eggs and gifts for themselves. Lara, who wasn't the least bit patriotic, kept buying even more Fabergé *objets*.

'Your daughters would like to say good night, Your Majesty,' said Miss O'Brian. Marie jumped into the Tsar's arms and kissed his cheek.

'We will pray for a victory against the Japs, Papa,' she said.

'Oh, Lara, what a magnificent gown.' Olga came over to touch it. 'You look so beautiful in it, doesn't she, Mama?'

Alexandra nodded.

'Feel how soft it is.' The other girls joined Olga, and Tatiana climbed into Lara's lap to play with her diamond necklace.

'I hope I'll be as beautiful as you when I'm grown up,' said Marie wistfully.

'You're already more beautiful,' Lara replied, stroking her rosy cheek.

The Tsarina felt that Lara was no proper role model. 'Off to bed, my little bears,' she announced.

Olga came up to her mother and placed her ear against her stomach. 'How is my little brother doing in there? Are you getting enough to eat, little one?'

Each girl had to take turns listening. Anastasia said she heard him singing.

The Tsar beckoned a tall blond-haired footman who was holding a gold tray filled with glasses of sherry.

'Thank you, Leonid.'

The servant bowed, then backed slowly away after the Tsar took a glass. Dimitri pictured the elegantly dressed servant standing in the hut of the peasant he and Katya had gone to. Resplendent in his uniform, he made the filth of the room seem even fouler. Katya was right; he had never seen such degradation in his life. Here in this Imperial world, he and Nicholas had been cut off from real life in Russia. The plight of that peasant woman and those injured and dead Jews

remained vivid in his mind. He was still shaken by the experience in Sebezh. He hadn't forgotten the dead child in Kishinev,
either.

'Dimitri, you and Lara come say good night,' Olga cried
out, snapping him out of his thoughts.

'Prince Henry is *never* punctual,' griped Nicholas, checking
his pocket watch. 'He'd be late for his own funeral.'

'I'm as hungry as a bear. We've waited long enough, let's
eat, for God's sake,' said Grand Duke Vladimir.

'You know the rules, Uncle,' replied Nicholas testily. 'He's
the guest of honor; we have to wait.'

Dimitri and Lara went upstairs to say a quick good night
to the children, and then returned to the room. Thirty minutes
had passed the appointed time for supper in the Rotunda.
Dimitri's stomach was now growling.

'I'm sure he will be here any minute now,' Alexandra said
in a reassuring voice. 'Henry may have . . .'

An ear-splitting explosion was heard in the direction of
the Rotunda. Dimitri, the Tsar, and Grand Duke Alexis ran
to the room. A large smoking hole now stood where the
supper table had been. The bodies of several servants could
be seen in the wreckage.

Lara and Alexandra came up to the hole and peered through
the smoke.

In bewilderment, Alexandra put her hand to her mouth.

'Who would want to hurt us?' she gasped.

'Damned Jew revolutionaries,' the Grand Duke exclaimed.

THIRTY-SIX

'This is exquisite, Your Highness. You wouldn't want to
quit the Court and become one of my designers, would
you?' said Peter Carl Fabergé jovially. 'As you know,
my best man, Perkhin, has passed away. He made twenty-eight
Imperial Eggs.'

Dimitri was brimming with pride to get a compliment

from the world's most famous jeweler. He was sitting with Fabergé at the table in his private study in his St Petersburg mansion.

'I worked quite a long time to get it right. I know it doesn't compare to your work, but . . .'

'Oh, but it does. I can help you with the selection of jewels and the enameling.'

'Even though it's not an egg, I wanted it to have a surprise.'

Fabergé ran his fingers across Dimitri's four watercolor sketches, one for each side of the gift. It was to be a ten-inch-high model of the Tchaikovsky Memorial, set on a green marble base, lined with alternating pearls and diamonds. The building itself was simplified in form almost to the point of abstraction. The key color was a deep blue iridescent enameling on engraved gold that Dimitri had designed that mimicked the Style Moderne. The great arch was to be solid gold with the top and bottom edged with tiny square-cut diamonds. The infill below the arch held an oval miniature of Tchaikovsky outlined in tiny pearls. Above the arch in solid gold was the double-headed emblem of the Tsar. The domes of the towers were in white opalescent glass.

A fifth watercolor drawing was a perspective that showed the surprise inside. The roof of the building hinged up and became a music box lined with velvet. The inside of the lid was silver and engraved with all the titles of Tchaikovsky's major works.

'I thought the music box would play the last part of the *1812 Overture*, one of the Tsar's favorite pieces,' Dimitri said.

'That can be easily done. There's more than enough room beneath the compartment for the mechanism. The gift has a nice practical aspect, it's deep enough so that His Majesty can also put things in it,' Fabergé replied. 'Have you shown the Tsarina your sketches?'

'No, I wanted to go over them first with you. You can draw on top of the sketches if you like.'

'Yes, that would make it easier to refine the piece. You have an enormous talent for drawing, Your Highness. I saw the exhibit of the renderings at the IARA. I also heard that they want you to contribute sketches to their weekly publication. Quite an honor. Your father was wise to let you develop your skills at the Academy.'

Dimitri smiled at this comment. Most aristocratic fathers would have dismissed his artistic ability as feminine.

'Yes, he wanted me to have a life of substance and have a skill.'

'He's probably the only aristocratic father to do such a thing. I remember when Prince Korgin displayed special talent in the sciences, his father forbade him to study medicine or train to be a scientist,' said Fabergé disapprovingly.

'The only thing Prince Korgin does these days is drink to excess and gamble.'

'You turned out to be a man of great talent,' Fabergé said.

'Thank you,' Dimitri said ardently.

'Let me take your sketches and mark up some suggestions,' Fabergé said. 'Can we meet in my office in a week? My craftsmen will be there and will have questions for you. Each week, you can come to see the progress of the work.'

Dimitri liked the suggestion. He didn't want to simply hand off the drawings and wait to see the finished product. He wanted to be involved in every step, just as in his architectural work. He had really enjoyed designing the gift for the Tsar, and hoped that Fabergé wasn't just blowing hot air about more opportunities to design. That was the trouble with being an aristocrat, people were always buttering you up.

'Yes, I'd like to do that,' he said.

Fabergé picked up his hat and cane. As he was about to open the door of the study, he frowned. 'That was dreadful what almost happened to the Tsar and Tsarina. They would have been blown to bits.'

'And I and my wife would also be dead,' Dimitri said with a grave expression. 'These terrorists are insane.'

Dimitri was still fuming about the bomb. Their lives were saved only by Prince Henry's tardiness. How one's life could be snuffed out in a fraction of a second amazed him. The vicious assassination attempt made him even more committed to non-violence.

'To think that the bomber was a carpenter who'd worked

at the Winter Palace for twenty-five years. Is there no loyalty anymore?' Fabergé bowed and left the study.

Dimitri knew that it wouldn't be the last attempt. There could be another terrorist inside the palace.

THIRTY-SEVEN

'The bomb was supposed to go off at 8:10,' said Blokh crossly. You're telling me the Imperial Family didn't go in the dining room because a guest was late?'

Leonid glared at him.

'The guest of *honor* – Prince Henry of Bulgaria.'

'That's a load of horseshit,' Blokh said. They were meeting in a secret apartment on Tyushina Street.

'No, that's just good manners. One doesn't sit down to supper unless the guest arrives. I always thought you Jews had good manners. You *are* Jewish, aren't you?'

Blokh was getting angrier by the second. 'Yes, I'm a Jew.'

Leonid frowned and crinkled his brow. 'So . . . how come you're not smart?'

Blokh slammed his fist on the desk. Leonid smiled as the insult got the desired response.

'I'm as disappointed as you,' Leonid explained in a patient voice. 'After all, it was me who assembled the bomb and placed it in the closet of the officers' lounge in the basement. That took quite a while, and a lot of risk. Normally, the family goes in to supper exactly at eight, like clockwork. I even set the timer for a cushion of ten minutes.'

Blokh held his tongue. Leonid knew he wasn't going to shout at him, because recruiting him had been quite an achievement. To have an agent planted in the immediate Imperial household was amazing, and Blokh didn't want to say anything to get him angry and quit. He was too valuable a man to lose – plus Blokh knew full well that Leonid could go to the Okhrana and inform on him.

Blokh sat up straight. 'We are both committed to the

revolution and the overthrow of the Tsar by any means necessary, so we should . . .'

Leonid held up a hand.

'Listen, Monsieur University Intellectual, my grandfather
was a serf who worked like an animal, then was cheated out
of his land at Emancipation. It should have been his for free,
but he was made to pay for it over fifty years, and couldn't
because of the famine. He told me before he died that it would
have been better to remain a serf because the masters did all
the thinking for you. My father and his brothers were treated
like shit as paid workers on the estate. I remember the times
as a boy I watched my father get flogged by the master, once
because he didn't doff his cap and bow to him. I had to put
pieces of wet moss on his back to ease the pain. My mother
worked as hard as a man before she dropped dead in the fields.
The peasants have suffered the most, so *don't* lecture me about
the revolution. No more masters.'

Leonid then looked around the room. 'Say, where's that
other Hebe? Hersch. They didn't arrest him, did they?' he
asked angrily.

'He's probably in Baltimore by now.'

'Where the hell is that?'

'In America. He quit the cause and emigrated,' said Blokh
forlornly.

Leonid started laughing. 'Wasn't he your best friend? So,
he just walked out on you. I bet you were pissed. I thought
all you revolutionary Yids stuck together.'

'So, we will be patient and plan another attempt,' said Blokh,
quick to change the subject.

'We must be extra-careful,' Leonid said in a measured tone.
'The Tsar's Imperial Police have doubled the number of plain-
clothes agents inside and out of all the palaces. They've been
searching all our rooms every week. The Cossack Konvoi
Regiment has also doubled its guard. And the Okhrana must
have at least one plant in the household, but I haven't figured
out who it is.'

'And you're not under suspicion?' Blokh asked. Maybe *he*
was an Okhrana plant.

'Of course not. They've arrested the bomber. I planted some

bomb-making material in Korsof's room, and they got their man. The old carpenter wasn't a bad fellow; a pity he's going to hang.'

'Some lives have to be sacrificed for the cause, and . . .' Blokh chimed in, but Leonid started laughing. He waved his hand in a dismissive way.

'Fucking intellectuals. You'll probably be crueler than the masters.'

THIRTY-EIGHT

'He's on his way to the Mikhailovsky Theater. He could be there already,' Grigory said and hung up the telephone receiver.

The Mikhailovsky's ventilation grilles were much easier to get to than the Alexandrinsky's. They were eight round openings circling the perimeter of the theater. Dimitri was bent down over one in the left rear. The crowd below were laughing at a play by Molière. He'd been to the performance a few days before and had really enjoyed it. The audience burst out laughing again, and at that moment, he lifted the grille and flung out the pile of flyers he'd set next to the opening. He ran to the center grille, opened it, and threw out another stack of papers. Crouching down low to avoid hitting his head on the timber roof beams, he made it to the final grille. After flinging the pile, he paused a few seconds to see if there was any reaction from below. Just like at the Alexandrinsky, there came a confused murmuring. He smiled, then closed the grille. He stood up but forgot about the beam and bumped his head. Rubbing it, he let out a string of curse words as he ran over to the access stair.

At the bottom of the stair, he was shocked to hear the thunder of many footsteps coming in his direction. He didn't need to be told who they were, but he was surprised at how many were coming so soon. He made it through the door at the foot of the stair, which let him out on the third balcony level. The footsteps were a lot louder now. Just as the plain-clothes police came in view along the red-carpeted horseshoe corridor, he slipped into the balcony and found an empty seat. He could hear the police in the attic above the theater. It was quite dark up there, and they would search every nook and cranny for him. The audience in the balcony were reading the flyers calling for a constitutional government. They also were looking at the source of the noise above them.

Dimitri knew that if he had real guts, he would stay in the seat for the whole performance and leave with the crowd, but he didn't. Plus, Katya was outside in a carriage waiting for him. He slipped back into the corridor, but when he saw men in identical dark suits and homburgs gathered down the hall, he went back into the balcony. Walking slowly, he traversed the entire rear aisle of the balcony to get to another door, then slipped out. The corridor was empty, and he made for the side exit stairs. Taking them in leaps and bounds, he suddenly halted when a door at a landing below flung open, and men raced down the stair. When he heard them exit the stairwell, he continued on down. No one was about the rest of the way, and a short corridor at the bottom of the stair would lead him directly to the street. But when he got to the door to the street, he heard men pouring into the stairwell two levels above. Sweat was pouring out of him, as he cracked the door to peek out to see if the police were waiting for him on the sidewalk. There, ten yards to his right on Inzhenernaya Street, was the carriage. A few people were walking along, but Dimitri didn't think they were policemen. Above him and getting closer by the minute was the crash of footsteps on the wooden stairs. He eased out the door and began walking slowly toward the carriage. After seconds that seemed like months, he stepped inside. Men poured out onto the sidewalk and began running in both directions.

'Sasha, get moving,' ordered Katya.

'No! Don't move,' commanded Dimitri.

'Driver, stay where you are!' shouted a policeman, running toward the carriage.

The second before the policeman came up to the side of the carriage, Dimitri took Katya in his arms and gave her a long passionate kiss that went on and on. The policeman glanced in at them, then ran down the street.

Dimitri took a breath from the kiss and said, 'Drive, Sasha.' Then he continued the kiss and as they rode on, their lips had melted into one another's. He held her closer and ran his hand through her hair. Katya sighed quietly with pleasure and felt limp as a rag doll.

The kiss didn't end, but became more passionate as the blocks went by. She felt so wonderful in his arms. The sensation he was experiencing was like floating up and up into a bright blue sky. His heart was soaring.

'Do you think we're safe now?' he murmured.

'No, we can't be too sure,' she replied with a smile. She took his face in her hands and continued the kiss even more passionately.

THIRTY-NINE

'Don't you think he's a beauty?' the Tsar asked. Usually, Dimitri agreed with Lara when she said that all newborn infants looked like baby monkeys, but the Tsar's new son was a beautiful child with blue eyes, rosy cheeks, and golden curls. Nicky was beaming as he held Alexis, his heir, in his arms.

'See, Dimitri, our prayers at Serov were answered,' said the Tsarina, joining them by the baby's crib.

'He's like a little angel,' chimed in Anna Vyrubova.

'I'm so happy for you both – and for Russia,' Dimitri replied. He wasn't just flattering the Imperial Couple; he truly was happy. He knew how Alexandra had longed for a boy to be the heir, and he was elated to hear the news that she had given birth to a son. Throughout Russia, church bells rang, and people down to the lowliest peasant seemed to rejoice. The ongoing tragedy of the war with Japan was forgotten for a while, and there was something to cheer about for a change. Parties across the nation were given in the Tsarevich's honor. August 12 was another special day on the calendar, along with all the countless feast days on which Russians stopped work to celebrate.

Nicholas and Alexandra were glowing with happiness as they gazed at their son. His four sisters bounded into the nursery, followed by Miss O'Brian.

'Let me hold him,' Marie shouted.

'No, me! You held him this morning,' snapped Olga.

'It's my turn! I want to hold him,' Tatiana said, stroking the baby's hair.

The girls all started tugging at Alexis. 'Careful, girls,' admonished Miss O'Brian, 'he's not a doll.'

'*I'm* going to hold him,' the Tsarina said, taking the child from the Tsar, 'because it's time for his bath.'

'I want to bathe him!'

'I want to help, too!'

'The birth of an heir to the throne will cheer up the brave lads fighting in the Far East, Your Majesty,' Miss O'Brian said. The Tsar nodded.

'I'm glad I got to see Alexis before I left,' Dimitri said. He was leaving tomorrow for three weeks in Spała, the Tsar's estate in Poland. He had designed a tennis complex with pavilions and also an iron bridge over a new artificial lake. The Tsar and his daughters loved to play tennis, even little Anastasia who could barely swing her racket. The construction had begun, and he wanted to be there so it was on the right track. When an architect didn't keep an eye on the construction of his design, things could go to hell in a hand basket quickly. His able staff would continue the construction drawings on the Tchaikovsky Memorial, so he had nothing to worry about on that account. He had gone over them with the Tsar this morning, and some revisions were made that he would give to his staff before he left. The Tsar's secret Fabergé gift was under production at the St Petersburg shop, and Monsieur Fabergé hadn't yet smashed it with a hammer. Dimitri was confident it would come off well, having met with Fabergé four times to finalize the design.

As with the Tchaikovsky Memorial, the Tsar had helped him in the design of the tennis complex, wanting it to incorporate Russian native motifs in the new Russian Style Moderne. Normally, Dimitri hated when a client interfered in the design, but Nicky had some good ideas and not because he was the Tsar of Russia. Nicky preferred the way Fabergé's Moscow shop incorporated medieval Muscovite imagery in their designs, unlike the more Western designs of the St Petersburg shop, so they borrowed from that. Dimitri had now switched to a new way of designing in the Russian version of the Art Nouveau style, abandoning the classical style unless clients insisted on it. Katya took full responsibility for having swayed him to a new progressive creative style, but Nicky had a lot to do with it too.

Dimitri kissed Alexis on his cheek and bowed to the Imperial Couple. He was pleased that Russia had an heir now, and it wouldn't be Nicky's brother, Grand Duke Michael. Michael was a bit of a wastrel, and not too bright. Perhaps Alexis would inherit a rule that was a constitutional monarchy – or not inherit a crown at all, Dimitri thought.

'Don't forget to take some snaps of the construction with your Kodak,' the Tsar said.

Katya insisted on seeing Dimitri off at the train station. It killed them both to be away from each other for three weeks. He had begged her to come with him, but she had a patient who was to undergo a complicated surgery. Standing on the platform, they tried to put on brave faces.

'Did you see the new Tsarevich yet?' Katya asked. She wanted to get her mind off his departure, but like everyone else in Russia, she was eager for news about the baby.

'Yes, he's such a beautiful child, like out of a fairy tale. The Tsar and Tsarina are in a state of ecstasy. The baby is the center of the family's life. I'm so happy for them. Even if Nicky is a lousy emperor, he's a good father.'

'She must be thrilled to have given birth to an heir after four daughters.'

'Alexandra is bursting with pride. It seems most of Russia is happy.'

'They're entitled to be, after all this bad news from the Far East.'

The comment made his mind snap back to the revolution.

'But defeat is a certainty, and it will help the cause. People will be angry over the senseless loss of life.'

He then took hold of Katya's hand.

'There's something I want to tell you,' he said solemnly.

A look of fear spread over Katya's face, and her blue eyes widened.

'I don't think it's enough to spread these flyers about in theaters and on the streets where workers walk to the factories. I have another idea that will be more effective. I want to pay to print a book of Ilya's photos, and distribute thousands of copies throughout St Petersburg and Russia. When people, especially the educated, see the pictures, they'll be moved to action. I've told Ilya of my plan. He and I will work on it together in our own secret sub-cell. Only you and Evigenia will know about it.' Dimitri had become more cautious after almost being caught at the Mikhailovsky Theater. He didn't know who had betrayed him.

Katya's face lit up, and she hugged him tightly. 'That's such a wonderful idea, my sweet!'

'Let's face facts. I'm rich, so I can give lots of money to the cause.'

'You're a splendid fellow, my prince. Before you go, tell me exactly what caviar to feed your horse tonight.'

'I'll write it out for you, plus his wines,' he said while checking his pocket watch.

A voice called out.

'Well, there you are, you handsome devil. Seems like I haven't seen you in a coon's age.'

Dimitri turned around and faced Mrs King. She was standing next to a stack of baggage piled on a cart, accompanied by her lady's maid.

He tried to hide his look of disdain. 'Hello, Kate, which direction are you headed?' he asked jovially.

'Down to Moscow to visit Count Borodin. He's going to show me the sights,' answered Mrs King. 'Where're you off to, good-looking?'

'Spała, the Tsar's hunting lodge in Poland. I'm doing some work for him there and have to check on it.'

'How long will all that take?'

'Three weeks or so.'

'Well, I'll be back by then, and we can catch up on things,' Mrs King chirped happily. 'Too bad we're not taking the same train, I've got a private compartment,' she added conspiratorially.

'Mrs King, may I introduce Doctor Katya Golitsyn.'

Katya stepped forward, and the American shook her hand heartily.

'A real woman doctor, eh? You're the first one I've ever met,' exclaimed Mrs King. 'The things you encounter in this fascinating land of yours.'

'Moscow is a very Russian city compared to St Petersburg, which Peter the Great based on a Western model. The cities don't like each other,' said Dimitri, sounding like a tourist guide.

'Must be like New York and Chicago. Both think they're better than the other. I plan to go shopping at the Fabergé store in Moscow. I already bought out the St Petersburg branch. And I figured if Consuelo Vanderbilt can get a copy of an Imperial Easter Egg like her "Pink Serpent Egg," so can I.' Dimitri knew that rich commoners had Fabergé make them versions of Imperial Easter Eggs.

The station attendants had loaded Mrs King's baggage on the train, and her lady's maid touched her shoulder as a sign to depart.

'Well, Dimitri, have to get on board.' Mrs King strode forward and planted a big kiss on his lips then waved goodbye. 'See you when you get back, handsome.'

Dimitri and Katya watched her train chug away from the platform.

'I don't know how I'm going to bear being away from you so long, my love,' he said with a long face, taking hold of both of her hands.

'I know,' she replied sadly. 'It's best to keep one's mind occupied, so throw yourself into your work, and the time will pass by quicker.'

'I'll try,' Dimitri answered unconvincingly. He then gave

her a long kiss and held her in his arms as his train pulled
into the station. It was sheer torture to let go of her; he had
to propel himself onto the train. Standing at the open window
of his compartment, he reached his hand out to Katya, who
grasped it.

'If all Americans are like Mrs King, then I don't ever want
to visit America,' she said with a big smile. He laughed as the
train began to move. He kept waving to her until she was out
of sight.

FORTY

When Dimitri returned from Poland, he was excited
to show the Tsar the progress photos of the tennis
complex and get back to refining the details on
the Tchaikovsky Memorial. The first thing he did was go to
see Katya, but on his way to her house, he left his camera
at the Kodak shop on the Nevsky to get the photos developed.
The next day, the Tsar sent word that he would see him at
the Alexander Palace. Dimitri was looking forward to seeing
baby Alexis again.

When he entered the Tsar's study, he knew immediately
that something was wrong. Over the last year, he could see
the anguish about the Japanese War in Nicholas's face. It gave
him a perpetual troubled and tired look. Today, his expression
looked far sadder: almost grief-stricken. Maybe there had been
another military catastrophe in the Far East. He gave Dimitri
a forced smile, and together they went over the photos at the
conference table. He asked some questions but seemed vaguely
uninterested, not enthusiastic as he normally was when
discussing a design. He didn't even mention the Tchaikovsky
Monument. When they finished, there was an awkward silence.

Without thinking, Dimitri blurted out, 'Tell me what's
happened, Nicky.'

The Tsar seemed relieved that his friend sensed something
was wrong.

'Alexis has hemophilia,' he blurted out.

Dimitri only knew vaguely about the disease.

'He got a cut, and it won't stop bleeding?'

Nicky sighed. 'No, he bled internally from his navel. There was a large dark blue swelling under the skin. Then he bumped against the crib, and another swelling appeared on his arm,' he said in a halting voice.

'What does Dr Botkin say?' He was the Imperial Family's personal physician.

'He brought in a specialist, Dr Petroff, who concurred it was hemophilia.'

'What exactly is this disease?' Dimitri was alarmed.

'His blood doesn't clot. Any rupture of a blood vessel under the skin causes the blood to seep into the muscles and tissue for hours. The skin can swell to the size of a grapefruit before it stops.' Nicky's expression was haggard.

Dimitri thought back to what Alexis looked like. It was hard to imagine that such a child with a happy healthy pink face and golden curls could be cursed with such a horrible disease.

'And there's no cure for it?' he asked anxiously.

'No . . . Surface cuts and scratches aren't the problem; they can be bandaged and pinch off the blood. It's when the blood seeps into joints that it causes terrible pain, the specialist said. Alexis cried non-stop from the bleeding; it's unbearable to hear him, Dimitri. Sunny is in despair. The slightest bump or fall could lead to death. He's what they call a "bleeder."'

Dimitri didn't know how to respond. He just sat there in shock, looking down at the pictures on the table.

Nicky continued, 'Maybe the worst of it is that the boy inherited the disease from Sunny who inherited it from her grandmother, Queen Victoria. She feels so guilty.'

Dimitri met his friend's tired eyes.

'I don't understand.'

'Dr Petroff explained that women transmit the disease but never suffer from it, only males. Queen Victoria's youngest son, Leopold, got the disease, and she also passed it on to her daughter, Alice, Sunny's mother. Her son Frederick died from it when Sunny was a year old. So Sunny in turn got the sickness from her mother and gave it to Alexis. He called it "the royal illness.'"

Dimitri wondered if Nicholas had known that Alexandra carried hemophilia when he married her. Maybe he didn't know or understand the hereditary pattern of the disease in the royal families of Europe. If Queen Victoria carried it, then it must be all over the place since she had nine children who'd married into royalty. But that was water over the dam; now Nicholas and Alexandra had to keep their heir alive. He knew the Tsarina must be in great torment. This baby was the crowning achievement of her marriage – to produce a male heir to the Russian autocracy, the answer to all her prayers. Her face had glowed with joy. She was so proud of such a handsome child. Now she was thrown into endless torture, watching her baby suffer. Unless someone came up with a cure, Alexis would still be suffering twenty years from now, and could die from a bump.

Dimitri sat up straight. 'Nicky, you have to comb the Earth for a doctor who can cure this. I hear that in America, there's a hospital called Johns Hopkins. It's supposed to be one of the most advanced in the world.' Several times, Katya had talked about the hospital and how famous it was.

'Yes,' the Tsar responded sadly. 'We must search everywhere for men of science. But Sunny tells me that Anna Vyrubova has heard of peasant healers who can perform miracles to cure the ill.'

Dimitri raised his eyebrows. The Tsarina was so desperate that she'd consider anyone. Katya would have laughed aloud at that notion. Only modern medicine, she'd say, would save the boy.

'I'll do anything on Earth to help you,' Dimitri said in a reassuring voice.

'Only a very few people know what has happened. Please don't tell anyone,' the Tsar said quietly.

'Of course.' As Dimitri was about to say something else to reassure him, Alexandra burst into the study. He was shocked to see her usually beautiful face the color of a sheet and disfigured with agony.

'He's bleeding again, Nicky!'

*   *   *

Dimitri sat alone on a bench in the middle of Tsarskoe Seloe's park. Usually, he loved walking by himself through the huge, beautiful man-made landscape with its winding paths, meadows, and groves of trees. He had wandered into the park in a trance, still in disbelief over learning about the Tsarevich's sickness.

He felt guilty again for what he was doing.

'Can I betray two people I love, whose son has been cursed with such a horrible thing? What did they do to deserve such an awful punishment?' he said out loud. He still couldn't believe the expression on Alexandra's face when she ran in to tell Nicky that Alexis was bleeding. And he remembered that he was betraying not only the Imperial Couple, but *his people* – the aristocracy. He was a traitor to his class, a goddamn turncoat. He had been brought up to believe that the aristocracy were the chosen rulers of Russia led by the Tsar. His father, grandfather, and great-grandfathers pledged their lives to uphold that rule. Now, he was caught up in a movement that said everyone – down to the dumbest peasant – had a right for self-governance. It went against everything he was taught to believe. He knew he was lucky his father was dead; the old man would have punched him in the nose for such a heinous betrayal. And if a revolution did succeed, what would happen to all the princes, princesses, counts, and countesses? Would their lives and land be taken from them? No more balls, banquets, or summer trips to France? A count and a peasant would have the same social standing? It was a shocking thought. Lara would laugh uncontrollably at such an absurd notion. What had he gotten himself into?

But he had to admit that Ilya's photos had opened his eyes. Then seeing the dead in Sebezh. He'd slowly discovered that he'd been living in a fantasy world. Daily life for most in Russia was pure suffering. It wasn't some isolated occurrence – it was widespread deprivation. So, he'd decided to act. When Katya told him her secret, he'd been even more determined to stand up and fight.

He stood up and started walking home. He imagined telling Katya he didn't want to be part of the revolution anymore. Her big blue eyes would widen in disappointment. She would tell him there was something bigger here, that he couldn't turn back now. Maybe she would start screaming at him, calling him a coward – or worse, say she didn't love him anymore. That last thought stopped him in his tracks.

FORTY-ONE

'You seem to enjoy our rituals,' the Baron said appreciatively.

The Baron was taking Katya home from the Friday-night sabbath meal at his home. It was the fourth she'd attended. She knew she was taking a chance by associating with the Baron and his family so often, but she was irresistibly drawn to them. She had even gone back to the temple one Saturday morning. Well aware of the repercussions from too much contact, she was cautious about her visits – as was the Baron. When he took her home, he always let her off around the block from her mansion. And the Baron and Dimitri were still the only ones who knew of her secret.

'I'll tell you the truth, Baron. I come for the *challah*,' Katya whispered conspiratorially. The Baron laughed heartily. Katya held up the brown paper-wrapped loaf his wife, Miriam, had given her to take home. *Challah* was a golden-brown braided egg bread used for the blessing in the traditional Jewish sabbath meal. Katya found it incredibly delicious.

'I bet my wife has offered to teach you how to bake it yourself.'

'She has, and I refused because I'm a rotten cook. I can heal a gunshot wound, but I can't boil an egg.'

'Well, you're welcome any Friday night. The High Holidays are coming up in the fall. They are special celebration meals I hope you will come to.'

'I had imagined the Friday night celebration to be far more elaborate. But it has a wonderful simple elegance to it. The way the women light the candles, cover their eyes, and say the blessing.'

'Just think, on Friday nights all over the world, Jews are reciting the same blessing,' the Baron said proudly.

'I just realized that my ancestors probably said the same prayer on Friday after sundown.'

The Baron grinned and nodded in agreement.

'You're right,' Katya stated suddenly, 'it's the Jews' faith that has let them survive for two thousand years without their own nation. That says something about a people.'

'And what would that be?'

'That they have an innate resilience that makes them special.'

'It sounds like you've done more reading.'

'I have. At this very minute, Russian Jews are tormented. The government is rounding up any who live outside the Pale and forcing them to relocate there,' she said angrily. 'And they are powerless to check these pogroms. Then there's all the unjust restrictions placed on them.' She stopped because she knew she was shouting from her soapbox again.

'Exactly. There is no one in this country to speak up for the status of Jews,' said the Baron in a voice without any emotion.

'But why do you sit by and take it? An intelligent, good man like you? And those poor innocent souls I saw dead in Sebezh.' Katya immediately regretted saying the last sentence.

'You were in Sebezh?' he asked incredulously. 'After the pogrom happened?'

Katya was caught and had to make a clean breast of it – almost.

'Yes. The hospital there needed help, so I went,' she said quietly.

'I think you are quite a special person to do something like that.'

She nodded. 'The revolution will bring equality for Jews. I know it will.'

'Our Tsar might have something to say about that.'

'But if millions rise up and topple him from power, Russia will be a land of freedom – for everybody.'

The Baron sighed. 'There's a saying we Jews have when we wish for something miraculous: "From my lips to God's ears."'

Katya was ashamed of her outburst, and the Baron could see the embarrassment in her face. He leaned forward and placed his hand on hers.

'Jews are used to the worst oppression a human being can dole out – and can take it. Like you said, it's our resilience that makes us special.'

As usual, the carriage pulled up a block away from Katya's house.

'Please forgive me for being so loud,' she said in a quiet voice. The driver helped her out. Before he shut the door, Katya said to the Baron, 'But I can't watch people being treated that way.'

FORTY-TWO

Dimitri chose his very favorite, the 'Trans-Siberian Railway Egg.' Opening the hinged top of the egg crowned with a gold double-headed eagle, he took out the gold carriages and put them in order. He thought for a moment, then picked up the second to last car, the baggage carriage, and turned it upside down. The workmanship was so incredible; the car actually had a scale-model chassis underneath, which was the perfect place to hide the folded note. He placed the cars back in the egg and slid it slightly forward. Although he often visited the display room and was likely beyond suspicion, he made sure that no one was in the hall before he left. Anyone could be an Okhrana plant.

He had received a message from Evigenia early that morning to go to St Isaac's Cathedral and wait in the rear, by the Madonna and Child Ikon. By the time he got there, there were many worshipers milling about after the service, lighting candles and praying to ikons. It was a good place to meet so as not to arouse attention. He spotted Evigenia kneeling in prayer. He knelt down beside her and held his hands up in prayer.

While still looking up at the ikon, Evigenia whispered, 'You must deliver a message to our agent in the Alexander Palace today. Put this note in an egg in the display room and move it forward of the others. It's under my left knee.'

When she stood up, there was a tiny folded note on the cold stone floor. After crossing herself, she walked away.

Dimitri palmed the note while pushing himself up from kneeling. He decided not to take the train to Tsarskoe Selo, but instead took his carriage for the fifteen-mile trip.

His task now done, he decided that he would visit with the little Tsarevich. He ordered a uniformed equerry to ask if the Tsarina would see him now.

When he entered the Tsarina's boudoir, she was playing four-handed piano with Anna Vyrubova at the upright white piano. Although Dimitri still thought of Anna as a goody-two-shoes, he was happy to see that Alexandra was able to enjoy herself for a few minutes.

'Look who's come to visit us, Alexis!' Alexandra said, walking over to the white wicker bassinette. She held up the smiling baby for Dimitri to hold. Dimitri was getting more confident in holding the infant. After he was told of the boy's illness, he was scared to death he would drop and break a priceless treasure. He took the baby and sat on the carpet next to Alexandra's chaise longue, where she sat and watched them play.

The new baby had brought sunshine into the palace. Alexis was the center of the family's universe: everything revolved around him. The Tsarina was so proud of the boy, she now regularly took him for rides in her carriage and was delighted when people bowed at the sight of him. His father brought him to a review of the Preobrajensky Regiment at the Winter Palace. When the soldiers cheered, Alexis crowed in babyish delight.

'Such a beautiful child,' Anna Vyrubova said fawningly.

'He's going to crawl any day now,' the Tsarina replied.

For most mothers, Dimitri knew, that would be an important milestone, but for the Tsarevich, it meant trouble. A black cloud constantly hung over the poor boy. Hemophilia became even more of a danger the more active the boy became. When the swelling occurred, he cried non-stop. It was heartrending,

but the Tsar and Tsarina had steeled themselves to it. They
didn't dare give him morphine for fear of it becoming habit-
forming. If the pain became too intense, the only relief for
Alexis was fainting. The Tsarina never left the boy's bedside
during an attack, surrounding him with her tender love, trying
anything to alleviate his suffering. The Tsar in a free moment
would come and try to play with him to get his mind off the
excruciating pain. But all the attention and love of his parents
and sisters could not ease it. All they could do was helplessly
witness the effects of this curse.

Because he saw them so often, Dimitri could see the physical
and mental damage that the disease was doing to the parents.
The Tsar looked more haggard, but the Court thought the
disastrous Japanese war was the cause. The beautiful Tsarina
now looked hard and worn as the guilt over giving her son
the disease made her life even more agonizing. The Court
didn't know about the Tsarevich's affliction, so it seemed that
Alexandra had become more aloof, making the aristocracy
hate her even further. More and more Court events were
canceled.

The Tsar strode into the boudoir. Normally, this was his
happiest place to be, but on his face was a fierce-looking scowl.
He was holding what looked like a booklet.

'I found this shoved in the stack of daily ministerial papers,'
he shouted, uncharacteristically. He handed it to Alexandra as
Dimitri stood up to see.

On the cover was the title *The Misery of Russia*, with a photo
of a filth-covered peasant child. The Tsarina slowly turned
the pages, which were filled with black-and-white photos of
people in abject suffering and deprivation. She gasped at one
picture that showed dead beaten bodies laid out on a floor in
a row with a caption – 'Kishinev, 1903.' This wasn't some
crude flyer; the bound booklet looked to be about fifty pages
long, and was professionally done on quality paper. Something
one would see in a bookstore. There was only one short piece
of text on the first page, saying that the Tsar had ignored the
misery of one hundred million peasants and had oppressed two
million Jews, and that there had to be a constitutional monarchy
to right those wrongs.

'This is an outrage,' cried the Tsarina. 'Who is spreading these lies?'

The Tsar was visibly shaken and angry.

'The Jews, that's who,' he snapped.

When Nicky said that, a flash of rage shot through Dimitri's body. But he'd become accustomed to suppressing his anger whenever such things were said by the Tsar.

Dimitri took the book from Alexandra and fanned through it, with Anna looking beside him.

'No one lives like that,' the Tsarina cried. 'It's obviously a fabrication, Nicky.'

'Lies, all lies. Of course these photos are staged to embarrass the government,' he replied.

'It is a pack of lies,' Anna added.

A footman appeared at the door. 'Minister of the Interior, His Highness Prince Mirskii, Your Majesty,' he announced.

'Thank you, Leonid, send him in,' the Tsar said. Dimitri knew that Nicky would be in no mood to go over the detailing of the lobby of the Tchaikovsky Memorial today.

Mirskii bowed to the Tsar and Tsarina.

'Look at this obscenity.' The Tsar handed the Minister the booklet.

'I made inquiries immediately after you summoned me. There are thousands of them spread through St Petersburg, Moscow, and many other cities, Your Majesty.'

'What!?' The Tsar was furious.

'It seems to be a very well-planned propaganda campaign. A most professionally printed book, too. Not at all like the usual crude pamphlets strewn about.'

At that moment, Baron General Moncransky was announced.

'Moncransky, the Okhrana knew nothing about the printing of such a huge number of things? I can't believe it,' Nicky said.

The Minister handed the General the booklet. It was apparent from his expression that this was the first time he'd seen it.

'No, Your Majesty, we knew nothing of this,' the General said in a whiny voice.

'This is an outrage,' the Tsarina chimed in.

Moncransky's broad face reddened, and Dimitri almost broke out into a smile.

'General, you must find the printing press that is producing these,' the Minister said. 'Make the printer tell you who is responsible, then round them up – and destroy the printing plates.'

Dimitri envisioned the Okhrana beating the printer's head with a lead pipe until he talked.

'Do you understand, Moncransky?' shouted the Tsar. 'You'd better not fail. I'm very disappointed with you, sir.' It was rare to see the Tsar lose his temper and address a general in such a way.

If Moncransky could have shrunk down to the size of an ant and crawled under the floorboards, he would have done it.

Moncransky bowed to take his leave, then caught sight of Dimitri, and his eyes widened slightly.

FORTY-THREE

Unlike the arts circle, the cell meetings were no longer discussions about the polemics of revolution. No arguments, manifestoes, or preaching. Short and to the point, they now centered on the concrete workings of carrying out revolution. Evigenia ran a taut ship, issuing instructions with no backtalk. Members were expected to do as they were told. Occasionally, Dimitri would be given messages to conceal in the eggs, but the cell with Evigenia and Ilya concentrated on printing and distribution the book of photos. A brand new one with all new photos would be coming out soon, double the number of pages. So far, they had been very lucky that their underground printing press hadn't been discovered by the Okhrana. Informers were everywhere. Last month, Grigory had vanished. Dimitri had been certain that Grigory had informed on him about the Mikhailovsky Theater flyers. He thought he would be arrested at any second but nothing had happened.

'Two parcels to our international agents in Brussels and Prague were intercepted by the Okhrana,' Evigenia said sadly.

'It's become impossible to relay coded information to the outside.'

Besides revolutionary agents in Russia, there was a network of them in Europe and in America. Their main responsibilities were to secure funds from sympathetic sources and get newspaper coverage of the misery in Russia. The more bad press the Tsar and the government got, the more support for the rebellion. Jews in America were especially generous. American and British newspapers loved stories about Tsarist oppression since the Kishinev pogrom.

'The messages we planted in those soup cans seemed foolproof,' Evigenia said. 'The codes are crucial to tell people what's happening. I don't know what to do now.'

The cell meeting, which was held in one of many secret apartments, went on for another twenty minutes. When it adjourned, Dimitri approached Evigenia.

'Do you have the next set of codes to go out?' he asked.

Dimitri dipped his crow-quill pen in the ink well. He now was ready to add the facade ornamentation to the drawing of his new bank building. His switch to the Style Moderne had become complete, and he loved his new creative path. He began to draw in the minute organic detailing carved into the stones on the front elevation. Long, swirling lines spread across the front of the building like vines. He loved doing this dynamic undulating, flowing linework. Working from a rough pencil sketch, he would improvise as he went. He would also add ink washes to give openings shadows for depth. Unlike classicism, there were no strict rules to follow, only what the imagination allowed. Drawing was the best part of architecture for him; getting the building constructed was the absolute worst.

After an hour, he had all the detailing down. On the side of his drawing table was the sheet of codes Evigenia had given him. They were all series of numbers. He began to incorporate the first four characters into the sinuous, curving linework. He made them a part of the design so that they were invisible to anyone looking at the elevation – except agents who knew what to see. He added another four characters to a section, then another until all the code was imbedded, in left to right order throughout the drawing.

After the triumphal exhibit of the Tchaikovsky Memorial drawings, he had taken up IARA's offer to submit one drawing a week to their professional publication – which happened to be distributed internationally. Just like architectural weeklies from other countries such as America and Germany, Russia's publications could be purchased in any bookshop abroad. The drawing would be reduced in size for the magazine, which was a good thing for concealing the information. Dimitri accounted for that, and made sure the agents could easily read the code with a magnifying glass.

When he had completed the finishing touches, he gave the drawing a final look and labeled it with the name of the bank and the date. He was quite pleased with the result; the numbers actually added to the richness of the linework. He couldn't wait until he got the new set of codes to hide in the Petrov Cable Company's new headquarters next week.

FORTY-FOUR

As she traveled on the train back to the Alexander Palace, Miss O'Brian felt very chipper, despite the cold rainy fall day. That morning, she'd met Azref and delivered intelligence on Port Arthur's new gun emplacements. Because the city was on a hill, the Japanese infantry had charged it time and again without success. The Russian Army was putting up a brave fight. The pounding of the city by the guns of Japanese battleships had destroyed Russian cannon, but the base did not fall. Her new information could finally turn the tide of battle against the Russians. As the mounting dead and wounded traveled back to the Russian cities, there had been angry public protests about the war and the government's mishandling of it. Last week, thousands held a peaceful rally. Azref had been right; the war would be a catalyst for revolution. Russia was a giant powder keg with a long fuse ready to be lit. He had also told her that there probably was an Okhrana agent planted in the Imperial household, and to be on her guard.

Miss O'Brian had been born a child of the revolution and indoctrinated from childhood by her father. She had accepted this assignment because she thought she could truly change things for the workers. It was also exciting, especially for a fifty-year-old spinster who'd spent her life raising other people's children. She had led a passive existence, agitating for revolution only by spreading handbills and attending secret meetings. Now she was in a unique position to actually make a difference. And according to Azref, she was doing an excellent job.

The train passed long stretches of muddy fields, interrupted by little villages populated by pitiful-looking peasants dressed in gray. They were still basically slaves. Millions of them had been cheated out of their land by the government at the Emancipation. The land, Miss O'Brian fervently believed, belonged to the people free of charge. These villages all resembled one another: a church with a bulbous steeple, a scattering of log cabins with chicken and geese scratching in the dirt roads. The Tsar and the Tsarina had this ridiculous romanticized image of a simple but happy peasant. They had no idea of the miserable reality. She was thrilled when she saw the book with the photos the Tsar was so angry about. Whoever thought of that was brilliant; one photo did more than a thousand pamphlets. Miss O'Brian realized she must find out whether the Okhrana had discovered the printing press. They were sure to tell the Tsar before they made the raid, and she could warn Azref.

Because she had time before she was expected back, Miss O'Brian decided to walk from the station to the palace. She was so conflicted; she was doing the right thing by helping the revolutionaries, but no harm could come to the Imperial Family. There had been four attempts on their lives, including the plague-infected cloth. An agent from the terrorist faction had certainly set up the assassination attempts, and she had to find out who he was before the next one. Miss O'Brian's mood brightened when she realized she would be playing with the Tsarevich soon. The news about Alexis's hemophilia had shocked her, but it didn't make her lose sight of her mission. Personal feeling wasn't allowed in a revolutionary. But Miss O'Brian knew the Imperial Couple was in torment over the child, and she would do anything she could to ease their pain – she hadn't ceased to be a human being.

The great mansions of the courtiers lined the tree-lined boulevard from the station to the palace. About fifty yards ahead, she saw Prince Dimitri getting out of his carriage and walking up to his front door. The prince was very close to the Imperial Family, the children adored him and that silly wife of his. The other day, Miss O'Brian had noticed Dimitri was watching her in a most curious manner as she walked down the corridor past the display room. One day, he had come into the Tsar's private study just as she was coming out – almost as if he wished to catch her snooping around the Tsar's desk. Miss O'Brian stopped walking. Prince Dimitri would be the perfect Okhrana agent, she realized. He knew everything about the Imperial Family and with whom they were in contact. Maybe the Okhrana was already suspicious of her and wanted him to keep an eye on her. Prince Dimitri would be a trusted and valued agent for the Okhrana. *Yes, he has to be the one*, thought Miss O'Brian.

FORTY-FIVE

The crisp fall breeze coming off the Gulf of Finland through the open windows felt so refreshing. It dried the perspiration on Dimitri's and Katya's bodies from two non-stop hours of lovemaking. They cooled off as they lay naked on top of the white silk sheets. Their breathing returned to normal as well. They looked up at the ornamental plaster ceiling above them and smoked cigarettes.

'The photo book was an idea of genius, my love,' Katya said while stroking Dimitri's chest. 'You have the mind of a revolutionary.'

Dimitri smiled. 'Please don't tell the Tsar that.' Then he added with a touch of pride, 'There's going to be a brand-new edition soon and another one after that.'

'It's really opened the entire world's eyes, Dimitri.' She leaned over and kissed his chest.

'All the credit goes to Ilya. I just distribute the book.'

'Printing and distributing the book is the dangerous part.'

'Yes, we have to vary the means of transporting it out of the city to avoid the Okhrana. And I still personally distribute some myself when the opportunity arises.'

'The revolution is about to erupt. Peasants and workers are stirred up. The educated classes are agitating for a constitution,' Katya said enthusiastically.

'And the war in the Far East is going very badly,' Dimitri chimed in. 'The waste of life has made a lot of people angry with the Tsar and the government.'

'That's the sad irony. The death and maiming of those poor boys will bring about the revolution and a better life for Russians.'

Dimitri stared out the window. 'I honestly didn't know that people live like that,' he muttered in a sad tone.

'But now you do, and you're doing something about it,' Katya said, raising both of her legs toward the ceiling.

'You have such great little legs,' Dimitri observed.

'That's a compliment, coming from someone who's seen a lot of female legs,' Katya said with a sly smile.

'I bet you've seen quite a few male legs at the hospital.'

'I look at them in a strictly clinical manner, not in an erotic context like you do.'

'Did,' Dimitri added. 'Past tense, please.'

Kaya threw herself on his chest and gave him a long, passionate kiss.

'Katya,' Dimitri asked in an uncertain tone, 'do you ever come across any hemophiliacs at the hospital?'

'Bleeders? It's such a rare disease, one hardly ever does. It's a terrible affliction, though.'

'Is there any research to cure it?'

'Well, a few years back, they discovered that blood can be divided into types or groups. Each person has one of those blood types, so you can give the bleeder the correct blood type in a transfusion,' Katya said in a doctor's voice.

'Is there anything to make the blood clot? That's the problem, right? The blood won't clot.'

'Exactly. No, the Americans have recommended treatments like hydrogen peroxide or lime, but nothing's been effective.'

'What about research at Johns Hopkins, the hospital you're always talking about?'

'It's the most innovative hospital in America, but, no, I don't think they're searching for a cure there,' Katya replied as she took a sip of white wine.

'Americans seem so technologically advanced in all things. Where else in America could they be working on it?'

'There's a hospital in Boston, and then one called the Mayo Clinic out in the middle of America. I'll search through my journals for anything on it.'

'Yes, that would be nice of you,' Dimitri replied, lighting up another cigarette.

Katya propped herself on an elbow and looked at him with a puzzled expression.

'Why the interest in hemophilia?'

'It's just an odd disease.'

Katya snuffed out her cigarette. 'Medical school is officially over,' she announced as she straddled him.

Although Katya hated to leave the apartment, she enjoyed thinking about their lovemaking as she walked home. Her mind could replay every second like those new cinema projectors. The thoughts always put a smile on her face, and she glowed from within. She could have floated over the sidewalks and streets to her house. It was like walking in a dream but knowing she wasn't dreaming. Being with Dimitri, whether making love or talking about Tchaikovsky, was bliss. She hated to be away from him, and made sure she spent as much of her day with him as possible. She knew she was over the moon in love with him, because it became harder and harder for her to focus at the hospital. That had never been a problem before. She would catch herself thinking of him. Dr Orlinsky would notice and say, 'Doctor, where's your mind at today?'

Katya was going home before she worked the evening shift at St Igor's. Dimitri was having dinner with the Imperial Family tonight. He always looked forward to playing with the Tsar's daughters and getting to hold baby Alexis. She was happy it gave him so much pleasure, but she knew he was troubled by his double life. She could sense that the conflict within him had intensified. She tried to imagine how he felt; realizing that his closest friend was destroying Russia and had to be overthrown. He admired the Imperial Couple. He had told her many times that the Tsar and Tsarina's love for each other had increased every day since their wedding. That was what true love was all about, he insisted.

Katya stopped walking and thought for a moment about the odd question Dimitri had asked her this afternoon.

'Queen Victoria,' she said aloud. 'Hemophilia?'

She was thinking back to her medical school days and remembered that females transferred the trait to males, but never suffered from the disease themselves. A British royal family tree was forming in her mind.

Queen Victoria's daughters could inherit the disease from her, Katya realized, then pass it on it to their daughters, who would transfer it to their sons. Alexandra was a granddaughter . . . who'd just had a son, the Tsarevich, Alexis. The puzzle pieces all fell into place. She gasped and held her hand to her mouth.

'Oh, Dimitri.' Her first thought was that Dimitri would change his mind about the revolution.

FORTY-SIX

'I think the pink color would suit you better, Larissa,' Baron General Moncransky said in a confident tone of voice.

Lara turned to find Moncransky standing next to her in Madame Fournier's hat shop on the Nevsky. He was wearing his deep blue, gold-braided uniform and smoking a fat cigar.

'Yes, the pink hat will do quite well,' Moncransky declared. He summoned a sales lady to wrap it up for Lara.

'My present to you, my dear,' the General said with a bow.

Lara gave him an icy smile. 'Thank you, Igor. Odd to meet you in a ladies' hat store.'

'Always so sharp.'

'I take that as a real compliment, Igor.'

'I just happen to know that you're as intelligent as you are beautiful, that's all,' Moncransky replied. The sales lady gave the General the package to carry. 'Come, Larissa, let us chat a bit.'

Lara walked with him along the Nevsky. He talked about the weather, the racing season, and upcoming social events. Lara remained silent.

'Why don't we step in here for some refreshments?' Moncransky suggested, pointing to the storefront of a little cafe. They took a table in the rear.

Once seated, Lara glared at him. 'What's on your mind?'

'You know, I always find it interesting that commoners think the aristocracy lead such care-free lives. Like we can do any damn thing we want without fear of consequences,' the General said in a jovial voice. The waiter brought their glasses of tea with a plate of pastries. He offered Lara the plate, but she just stared at him. Her cold attitude didn't ruffle him a bit, and he continued talking in a most pleasant manner.

'But people like us *can't* do anything we want,' he exclaimed. 'The commoners don't understand that the aristocracy and the members of Court must obey an iron-clad set of incredibly strict rules that govern every damn aspect of our lives. *We aren't free at all!* But you know that already.'

He sipped his tea and wolfed down a scone.

'Your tea is getting cold, Larissa.'

Lara didn't touch her tea. She just continued staring at him.

'And if we break these rules, there's no second chance – no mercy in our little world. You're cast out of society as though you're a leper. Everyone turns their back on you, never to speak to you again.' Moncransky helped himself to a pastry.

After the last swallow and a sip of tea to wash it down, he asked in a very breezy manner, 'Larissa, does anyone know that you and Count Nagrov's very handsome footman had that little tête-à-tête last summer in the Crimea?'

Lara's eyes narrowed to slits. She clenched her fists.

'You know the rules of the game – hands off the help,' the General said, patting his lips with a linen napkin. 'Think what people would say if they found out. This revelation would definitely set Court tongues wagging. A mere footman and the beautiful Princess Lara? How could she lower herself like that?'

'It was just once!'

'Times three, I've discovered.'

'I have the feeling you're going to tell me my little indiscretion isn't going to remain a secret for long.'

Moncransky just smiled. Lara's expression told him that she understood the severity of her situation.

'You wouldn't,' snapped Lara.

'Rule Number One: a girl can never get herself talked about,' lectured the General. 'I know you *adore* scandal about others, but you'll find scandal about yourself not so amusing.'

'So, in exchange for your silence, I have to let you fuck me a few times. Is that the deal?' Lara asked scornfully. 'Because Dimitri has been fucking your wife on and off.'

'Well, that . . . and something else.'

Lara crinkled her brow.

'I need you to do some detective work on Dimitri. I believe he's part of the revolutionary movement.'

Lara burst out laughing. 'Dimitri!? He's no more revolutionary than my borzoi!'

'My original contact was retired to Siberia. I'm hoping you'll be more effective.'

'Is there something I can get you, madame?' asked the waiter with a look of alarm. 'You don't seem well.'

Lara had remained at the table after Moncransky left. Her mind was dazed. For a moment, she thought she was going to throw up.

'No thank you, I'll be fine in a minute.' She took a sip of her cold tea.

Moncransky was right; she'd broken the rules. It was hubris

that made her think she could have Count Nagrov's tall, good-looking footman and get away with it. Now, she knew her whole world was about to disappear; the only one she'd ever known. She wouldn't be forgiven for such a small infraction. On the contrary, because her gossip and innuendo had caused many women to be cast out of society, people would be eager to see her fall. Society would cheer to see the great Lara Markhov finally receive her comeuppance. But that wasn't going to happen.

Lara stared down at the tabletop. She would have to do what Moncransky wanted. It filled her with disgust that she had to sleep with that pig, but she was even more furious with Dimitri. At first, she'd thought it total nonsense that he was a revolutionary; Moncransky just wanted to get her in the sack for revenge. The General had explained further, how her husband had gotten mixed up in the revolutionary movement through Doctor Golitsyn and her arts circle soirees. A choice lay before her: to betray Dimitri, or become a social leper. The decision was simple: she'd be damned if she'd allow Dimitri's folly to get her kicked out of society.

There was one more reason she would do Moncransky's bidding. Lara and Dimitri were no longer in love, but she was still fond of him. Their marriage was for appearances only because divorce was out of the question. She didn't care about his infidelity, but now it was a matter of principle: he'd committed class betrayal; worse than selling out one's country to the enemy in a war. She felt he had betrayed her, his best friend, Nicky, and the entire aristocracy. Dimitri had done something unforgivable, and he would have to pay.

FORTY-SEVEN

Dimitri believed that Princess Betsey gave the best balls of the season; better even than Lara's. She truly had a God-given talent for social functions. Bacchus would have envied her parties. Betsey didn't put on entertainment, but spectacles. Besides the dozen Imperial Balls given in the Season, there were the private ones given by the courtiers – and there was Betsey's. An invitation in embossed gold letters on stiff white vellum delivered by her couriers in dark blue jackets was highly coveted. Only five hundred of the crème de la crème of St Petersburg society were invited on January 2 to her magnificent light-blue Italian Renaissance palace overlooking the Fontanka Canal. Sleds pulled by horses with bells jingling on their harnesses brought her guests, wrapped in ermine and mink blankets, over the snow-packed streets.

Dimitri was dancing a Strauss waltz with Lara (a husband was required by custom to dance with his wife once). All around them, people were twirling around the parquet ballroom floor in their own happy magical world. The young officers in brilliant uniforms led happy young girls in flowing gowns and diamonds, their faces flushed red from excitement and the excessive heat. A few times tonight, some middle-aged lady had fainted from the heat and had to be carried away by footmen to lie down. Once recovered, they always returned to dance; it was an unspoken rule of society. Along the great mirrored walls lined with displays of exotic flowers from the Crimea sat grandes dames fluttering fans, members of the Diplomatic Corps, government ministers, and even a few long-bearded bishops in black and purple robes. Officers liked private balls because they could drink, unlike at the Imperial Balls.

Betsey liked to vary the music. First a symphony orchestra played Strauss, Rimsky-Korsakov, and Tchaikovsky, reminding Dimitri that the laying of the cornerstone for his Memorial was coming up. Then gypsies in colorful native garb played, followed by a balalaika orchestra. The musical styles alternated during the evening. Dimitri and Katya finished their dance, and he escorted her to the side of the room. Colonel Rassisky came up to Lara.

'I believe this our dance, Princess Lara,' he said with a bow, extending his hand. They spun out onto the floor and effort-lessly blended in with the dancing couples.

As Dimitri watched them, a voice from behind whispered in his ear.

'Hello, Dimitri. We never caught up after you returned from Spała.'

'Why, hello Kate. How beautiful you look tonight. My wife, Lara, was admiring your gown.'

Mrs King was wearing a stunning scarlet gown, whose low neckline accentuating her beautiful full breasts was trimmed in alternating blue diamonds and green emeralds. A single large pendant diamond set against an emerald hung around her long neck.

'Thanks, Dimitri, but I'd rather you say how beautiful I look naked.'

Dimitri smiled but didn't respond.

'I'm getting my Fabergé egg, a copy of the "Pine Cone Egg,"' she said with great satisfaction.

'Ah, that's the one with the automaton elephant. Quite charming. And I suppose you bought out the Moscow Fabergé store for gifts to take back home.'

'You bet I did.'

Dimitri didn't keep up the conversation, he just watched the dancers in silence.

'So, can you call on me this coming week?'

'I have my work on the Tchaikovsky Memorial I told you about, and then there is the crush of these events for the season. I'm so busy.'

Mrs King frowned. 'Certainly, you can find a little time for little ol' me, Dimitri,' she said in a sing-song child-like voice.

'I really don't think I can get away, Kate. Maybe tea at the end of the month,' Dimitri said apologetically.

Her face became flushed, and she looked irritated.

'But if you're free now, let's dance the quadrille coming up,' Dimitri said.

'No thanks. It's too damn hot in here, and I thought it was hot in Alabama,' Mrs King replied testily. She began to walk away.

'You still have to come to the palace and meet Jim,' he called out after her.

She turned to him and glared. 'I didn't come to Russia to talk to some darkie.'

He frowned. He realized that people had started streaming

into the adjacent banquet hall for supper, and followed them in. A woman let out a gasp, and loud shouting broke out.

Guests were standing or sitting at their places at the table designated by place cards. But everyone was lifting the Sèvres dinner plates to find a copy of the *Misery of Russia* booklet hidden underneath. It was if they'd found a dead rat. People began flipping through the pages.

'I've heard about these,' exclaimed Monsieur Blerot, the ambassador from Belgium.

'Thousands of them have been showing up all over Russia for the last few months,' complained a general of Chevalier Guards. 'The Okhrana can't keep up with confiscating all of them. They say they've turned up in Paris and Berlin; even in New York.'

'This is revolting,' cried a woman who threw her copy on the floor.

But most of the guests were absorbed in the photos.

Princess Betsey charged in. 'What is the meaning of this outrage?' she screamed at her head butler. He was flabbergasted and couldn't get the words out.

'Your Highness, when we set the table last night, there were no books under the plates, I swear to you.'

'I apologize, my friends,' Betsey said frantically. 'Collect this filth,' she ordered the footmen. But most guests didn't hand them over. Even Lara didn't give up her copy.

Finally, order was restored, and guests settled in to eat the sumptuous seven-course meal served with French wines and champagne. Conversation was humming while an orchestra played quietly. Then people's heads cocked in reaction to a sound in the distance. Talking trailed off until there was complete silence in the banquet hall. The orchestra had stopped playing. The commotion was coming from the street, and guests got up to look out the tall windows. Some opened them.

'Port Arthur has surrendered! Port Arthur has surrendered!' screamed the crowd in the street outside the palace. 'Russia has lost the war!'

A huge mob had gathered on the Nevsky Prospect, and now was heading north toward the Neva River. People seemed to come out of nowhere to join the crowd, swelling its numbers to what seemed like thousands.

'My son died for nothing!' yelled a woman. '*My* son died in vain,' countered another woman. 'Russia has been beaten by yellow monkeys!'

Most of the guests were in disbelief. One woman began crying. The military men bowed their heads. Some covered their faces with their hands in grief. People began walking back to the table to resume eating, but others walked out of the hall. No one talked while they ate.

Dimitri stood by the window, listening to the shouting. 'This is the beginning,' he said to himself.

Azref was marching along with the crowd on the Nevsky, screaming that Russia had been whipped and humiliated in front of the world. But he had a hard time suppressing a smile, he was feeling so happy.

FORTY-EIGHT

Miss O'Brian was walking back to the train station after attending the Sunday service at the English High Episcopal Church of St Petersburg. With all the British diplomats, their staff, nannies, and governesses in the capital city, they had their own church designed after the High Victorian ones back in England. Because of the Tsarina's fear of gossip, the nanny made the barest of conversation with her fellow parishioners after the service. She actually was held in very high esteem by the British community because she took care of the Tsar's children. They were proud that the Tsarina had been brought up by her grandmother, Queen Victoria, and was English to the bone. She knew British nannies were the very best.

Bundled up in a sable coat the Tsarina had given her as a Christmas gift two years ago, Miss O'Brian trudged on through the bitter January cold. She couldn't wait to get to the station to have a glass of tea there before her train left for Tsarskoe Selo. The nanny still found it odd that Russians drank their tea in clear glasses held in metal holders, instead of china cups. She heard someone shouting in the distance, and when she turned the corner, was surprised to see hundreds of people huddled in a square listening to someone. Since the news of Port Arthur, there had been scores of angry gatherings like this. She stopped to listen to a young priest shouting from a balcony.

'Millions that should have gone to take care of the people were wasted on a war that made Russia a laughing-stock in the world!'

The Assembly of Russian Workingmen standing shoulder-to-shoulder in the square howled their lungs out at that observation.

'End the war!' the crowd shouted over and over again.

Miss O'Brian knew from Azref that the young priest was named Father George Gapon. The charismatic leader of the Assembly had been whipping up support for his grand plan for the rights of the common working man. He was waving a large piece of paper about. Then he raised his other hand, and there was complete silence.

'This petition will free the people from their evil oppressors – the despotic and indifferent government, the capitalistic exploiters who constantly rob the Russian people.'

The crowd went into a frenzy. Men were jumping up and down, grabbing the man next to him and giving him a great bear hug.

'Next Sunday, I will lead you on a mass march to the Winter Palace, where I will hand this petition personally to our Tsar, our Little Father, who will deliver us from oppression. This petition demands a constitution, universal suffrage, universal education, separation of Church and state, amnesty for political prisoners, a minimum wage, and an eight-hour day. And he will end this hopeless war!'

Miss O'Brian smiled at what she had wrought. After the horrible news came that Port Arthur had fallen to the Japanese, all of Russia was humiliated. A wave of protest had swept across the country damning the Tsar and the military for the

disaster. The mismanagement of the war revealed the rotten-
ness of the autocracy. It seemed that all Russians had had a
relative or friend who had died in the Far East. Strikes had
begun to pop up all over the country. Tens of thousands of
workers walked off their jobs; over one hundred thousand
workers in St Petersburg alone. Losing the war was like a
match that lit the fuse of the powder keg, that was setting off
a revolution as Azref predicted. The Tsar hadn't officially
capitulated; he was hoping the Baltic Fleet, which had set sail
in October on an eighteen-thousand-mile voyage to Japan,
might perform a last-minute miracle. But it was doomed to
fail.

'I will see you on Sunday, my brothers,' shouted Gapon.
The crowd cheered wildly and began to break up.

Miss O'Brian shook her head. She had helped to bring about
the revolution she'd dreamed of, but to march on the Winter
Palace was sheer folly. The Imperial Family had permanently
moved to the Alexander Palace, so the Tsar wouldn't even be
there. The crowd here was probably full of Okhrana spies, so
the Tsar would know what was going to happen.

'Damnit, where's my shoe?'

Fedor had the habit of carrying around Lara's shoes. The
borzoi wouldn't chew it up, but just take it to another part of
the palace and drop it. Many a time, servants had to search the
place to find shoes, especially if they were ball slippers, like
she needed tonight. Lara looked at Fedor asleep on her bed.
Next to him was Dimitri's cat, Tolstoy. At first, Lara was
angry that the cat kept coming into her bedroom suite and
sleeping on her silk pillows. She kept tossing it out, but it
always came back. She even thought of chucking it into the
Neva. But after a few months, she gave up and got used to it.
She had to admit, it was a comforting sight to see Fedor and
Tolstoy, who had become good friends, sleeping together
peacefully. Fedor liked to lick Tolstoy's head as though he
was grooming him.

Lara looked around her bedroom, then went into Dimitri's.
He had left to go to his office downstairs. She got down on
her knees to look under the bed. Between the slats of the frame

and the mattress was a booklet. She smiled and pulled the thing out, assuming it was pornography. She had seen lots of pornographic material that courtiers had collected over the years. When she saw the cover, she frowned. It was the book of photos from Princess Betsey's ball. Dimitri must have kept his copy, but when Lara leafed through the booklet, it was marked up in a red ink: 'Shift up, add photo of starving child.' 'Delete peasant picture of hut, put in worker asleep under his machine.'

Lara's eyes widened in disbelief.

'Goddamn you, Dimitri!' she yelled.

It was obvious that Dimitri was revising the layout of the pictures. He *was* a dirty revolutionary. She thought for a moment about how she could get this to Moncransky. The ballet was tonight, so she might talk to him if he was there. Or she would call him in the morning to arrange a meeting. Brimming with anger, she carefully returned the booklet to its hiding place.

'Shit!' When Lara went to retrieve the book the next morning, it was gone.

FORTY-NINE

'What are all these people doing here?' Dimitri asked. Normally, the streets on Sunday mornings in the winter in St Petersburg were empty. Except for going to church, people stayed out of the fierce cold on their day off. But on this windy, cloudy day with the snow swirling about, masses of men, women, and children holding ikons, crosses, and portraits of the Tsar walked slowly down the streets from all directions. Many were singing hymns. They were a ragged lot; peasants and workers, women in babushkas and men in felt visor caps. All had ruddy faces from the cutting wind. It was almost ten, and Dimitri and Katya were on their way to a luncheon and a musicale at a mansion on the quay.

They stood in the doorway of a bookseller and watched the procession pass by.

Katya didn't seem surprised at the crowds. 'It's that workingman's group headed by the young priest, Gapon,' she said. 'I remember Evigenia mentioning it in a cell meeting.'

'Yes . . . but I didn't realize it had such a huge following. Look at all these people.'

Revolution had spread across Russia like wildfire in the weeks after Port Arthur fell. There was no violence yet in the cities, but out in the countryside, peasants had gone berserk, killing landowners, burning and looting property.

'Where are they going?' Dimitri asked in an amazed voice.

'I heard that they'll meet Gapon at one place and then march to the Winter Palace, where he'll hand their demand of rights to the Tsar personally.'

'What?' Dimitri shouted. 'The Tsar isn't even at the Winter Palace today, he's at Tsarskoe Selo. He hates living in the Winter Palace in the winter, it's too damn cold!'

'Grandmother,' Katya called to an old crone passing them. 'Where are you all off to?'

'To see the Tsar and ask him to help us,' the woman cried in a hoarse but happy voice. 'Our Little Father is going to come out of his palace and talk to us.'

'He will listen to our pleas,' said a middle-aged man behind her. 'Over a hundred fifty thousand have signed Father Gapon's petition.'

Dimitri looked at Katya in horror. 'I don't think the Tsar knows anything about this.'

'The poor devils actually believe their beloved Tsar will take care of them,' said Katya with a pitying laugh. 'They don't realize that *he's* the one responsible for their misery.'

'This is madness,' Dimitri muttered.

Dimitri and Katya tagged along at the edge of the crowd, which was now singing patriotic songs like 'God Bless the Tsar.' There was no shouting, no violent threats; just a solemn march. They walked beside a couple with two children, bundled up in what they considered their Sunday best. The mother was carrying a long stick that had a portrait of the Imperial Couple nailed to it. Ahead of them, an old man carried a homemade

Orthodox cross. None of the marchers talked to one another; they just looked straight ahead with dead serious expressions. They had marched down Gorokhovaya Avenue and were now approaching the Alexander Garden, where they would take a right to the Winter Palace.

Except for the low murmuring of hymns, it was eerily silent. Suddenly, Dimitri began to hear the distant sounds of boots running and the clatter of horses' hooves on the cobblestones. To his horror, he could see over the heads of the marchers mounted troops off in the distance. His eyes widened. They were Cossacks with drawn swords. That could mean only one thing – they and the infantry were here to put a stop to the protest.

'Wait, don't go any further, there are soldiers up ahead!' he yelled. With a look of terror on her face, Katya grabbed him and pulled him out of the procession.

'Stop! Stop right where you are!' he shouted at the marchers. 'Turn back!'

An old man replied, 'The Tsar is waiting for us. We can't be late.'

'No, he's not there!' Dimitri called out frantically. 'Please stop! There are Cossacks and soldiers with guns waiting for you! Don't go on!'

'This is a peaceful march, we're not here to hurt anyone,' said a young man to Dimitri's right.

'We're carrying no weapons,' added the woman walking next to him.

'He's right, stop!' Katya yelled. 'The Tsar has sent—'

Katya's warning was interrupted by a deafening volley of bullets that ripped through the crowd. Men, women, and children crumpled in agony. Their banners and ikons dropped to the ground. The air was filled with ear-piercing screams and moans. The trusting marchers were now panic-stricken, and tried to run away in any direction. The wounded lying in the street were trampled. Dimitri pushed Katya into a shop doorway and shielded her with his body as the next volley of bullets whizzed by like angry bees. He twisted his head around to see more bodies drop to the snow-covered street. Then he heard the roar of another volley slice through the cold air, and more people were mowed down. The gunfire stopped. He thought the action was over, but when he looked up the street, he saw an even more horrifying sight. Long, curved sabers raised high, the Cossacks in their black and scarlet coats charged the crowd. It was to be a massacre. The front ranks of the marchers that were still standing broke to the left and right, providing a lane down which the Cossacks drove their horses, steam churning from their nostrils. As the Cossacks charged, they slashed anyone on both sides, showing no mercy for women and children. Dimitri and Katya saw the continuous lifting and falling of the sabers dropping people like logs to the street. Curses, screams, and moans filled the air. When Dimitri saw the pools of scarlet blood on the white snow, it immediately reminded him of the pogrom in Sebezh. In front of him, people were being cut down by the Cossacks and bleeding out into the snow. He unbuttoned his wool coat, took his muffler off, and wrapped it around the sliced neck of a man, tying it tightly.

'This will stop the bleeding,' he said to the man, who was still conscious. Katya had leapt into action as well. Though she didn't have her doctor's bag, she used her wool shawl to bandage the shoulder of an old woman. She began tearing the hem of her dress to make a bandage for a man shot through the shoulder. Between screams of pain, he kept asking about his daughter. More volleys of rifle fire rang out.

Dimitri looked behind him, and saw the Cossacks preparing for another charge from the opposite direction. He dragged the man into a shop doorway. He then went over to a woman had a terrible slash across her face from her eye down to her chin. While tying his silk handkerchief across the hideous wound, he saw that her right eye was gone. Instinctively, he looked about the snow for the eye, but didn't see it. After pulling her out of the way, he turned his attention to a boy of about twelve. By the time he got to him, the Cossacks had begun their charge and were coming right at him. For a second, he thought of ordering them to halt, but the Cossacks didn't seem to take into account social standing. They would just as well kill a grand prince as a factory worker today. He dragged the boy to the base of a storefront just as the soldiers stormed by. A horse trampled a man, and he screamed in agony. When

Dimitri bent over to tend to the boy, his gray-blue eyes were open as though he was gazing up at the cloudy sky. Blood trickled out of his mouth and his head flopped to the side; he was almost completely beheaded. Dimitri went to Katya's side while she treated a young woman whose scalp had been slashed.

'The Tsar did not help us . . .' murmured the girl in a state of shock.

'Don't talk any more, just stay still,' Katya said in a kind quiet voice.

'He's a murderer,' the girl gasped, sitting up. 'My grandmother is dead. Why would the Little Father do this to us?'

Katya wound strips of cloth around the girl's head and gently laid her down in the snow. For the first time, Dimitri realized his coat was covered with blood, and his hands looked as though they had been dipped in red paint. He raised them to his face and stared at them. Bodies were strewn in the snow along with banners and portraits of the Tsar. Tears stung his eyes, and he clenched his fists. At the end of the street by the Alexander Garden, he could make out Cossacks still chasing after people, their swords slashing. He went over to a canvas banner crumpled in the snow that had the words 'God Bless Our Tsar' painted in crude letters. He knew that besides these people laying in the blood-drenched snow, the Tsar had killed something far greater this morning – the workers' devout belief that they could receive justice and help from their Little Father. *He has killed their love for him*, Dimitri thought. After today, nothing in Russia would be the same. Mad with rage, he placed his blood-soaked hands on the side of his head, and let out a scream.

Katya was sitting on the ground, holding the head of an old bearded man in her lap. She knew there was nothing she could do for him; many times she'd seen people minutes from death. The only thing left was to give him a little comfort. Stroking his mane of white hair, she whispered to him that God was waiting to welcome him.

With his eyes closed, he mumbled, 'I'm food for the worms.'

Surprised at his blunt honesty, she leaned over and kissed his forehead.

With great difficulty, the old man wheezed out some words.
'I'm a Jew. Please have someone say Kaddish for me.' She
held his limp body closer as he took his last breath.

Dimitri stood over her and the dead man. Katya looked up
at him. Gazing at the carnage in the street, he said, 'Like I
said, there are things bigger than oneself. If I do nothing . . .
then I am nothing.'

Katya reached up and grasped his blood-spattered hand.

FIFTY

'**B**ut, Dimitri, I didn't order the troops to fire at the
demonstrators.'

'All of Russia thinks you did, Nicky,' Dimitri replied
calmly. He had to control himself from shouting at the Tsar.
Even though they'd been friends for years, one never raised
their voice to a royal, no matter how furious one was.

'The whole incident is so incredibly painful and sad. I
was stunned when Mirskii told me what had happened. It was
the first I heard of it. But the troops were obliged to fire.
The crowd were told repeatedly to halt, but they kept on
coming.'

Nicky took a seat next to Dimitri in his study.

'I was there, Nicky. It was a peaceful march,' Dimitri said
in a tense voice.

The Tsar lit a cigarette and offered one to Dimitri. '*You*
were there? Not as a demonstrator, I hope,' he said with
amusement.

'I saw it with my own eyes. Women and children were
slaughtered. It was a bloodbath.'

'I know, it's most unfortunate. Over a hundred were killed,
and hundreds more wounded,' Nicky said in annoyed tone.

'Unfortunate' wouldn't have been Dimitri's description of
the event. He was incensed by his friend's response but didn't
show it.

'When I met with my ministers, they suggested that I isolate myself from the tragedy by saying the army fired without orders from me. But I refused.'

Dimitri couldn't believe what he was hearing. 'Why?'

The Tsar was vexed by the question.

'I refuse to cast unfair aspersions on the army.'

'But they did a terrible thing, Nicky!'

The Tsar shook his head. 'At heart, I'm a military man. I could never betray the army or the navy. They are the backbone of Mother Russia.'

Crestfallen, Dimitri slumped back into his chair. 'Nicky, your security was the love of your people. Now it's gone. They think you betrayed them.'

'They *still* love me,' Nicholas snapped. 'And I did take action. I immediately met with a delegation of thirty-four workers at Tsarskoe Selo. Like father to son, I advised them to support the army, and never listen to the lies of the wicked Jewish revolutionaries. They all agreed that they would remain loyal to me and fight the radical traitors.'

Downhearted, Dimitri blew smoke rings and watched them float away. There was nothing he could do to help his friend. You couldn't talk to a sleepwalker. Nicky was a man trapped in the past. He had the unshakable belief that he was the ruler chosen by God, answerable only to God and his own conscience. While he waffled on every decision in government, on this point, he never, ever wavered. And Dimitri had to face the fact that Nicky hated Jews. He had been brought up by his father, Alexander III, to despise them, and Jews supposedly had plotted his grandfather's assassination. To curry favor with him, his ministers pushed for more Jewish restrictions and promoted anti-Semitism in Russia. No one in the government except Mirskii had the moral courage to stand up for the persecuted group.

'Let's go over the Tchaikovsky drawings. I want to make a change in the paneling in the music library. It should be malachite instead of wood,' the Tsar said, always eager to avoid unpleasant subjects. 'You must be excited; the laying of the cornerstone is coming up soon. I know I am.'

Alexandra came into the study. How tired and worn out she looked, as though she'd aged twenty years. Dimitri stood and bowed, and she kissed him lightly on the cheek. Worry over the Tsarevich's disease had left a look of permanent sadness on her beautiful face.

'You've been a stranger when we need you most,' she said in an almost pleading voice. 'My poor Nicky's cross is heavy to bear, and he has no one to rely on except true friends like you, Dimitri. I pray on my knees every day to God to give me wisdom to help him in these terrible times.'

Dimitri smiled wanly at her.

'We were discussing the demonstrators,' the Tsar said grimly.

'It was ghastly, but the crowd would not listen, and the army *had* to shoot,' Alexandra insisted. 'The crowd would have grown colossal, and thousands would have been trampled to death. Like at the coronation celebration.'

Dimitri remembered the huge open-air festival scheduled for the people in the Khodynka Field outside Moscow, back in 1896, the day after Nicholas was crowned Tsar. Free packets of treats, gifts, and beer from the Imperial Couple to the people were to be given out. Thousands assembled in the field the night before, but a stampede broke out, and fifteen hundred men, women, and children were trampled to death. The dead were buried in a mass grave.

But as horrible as the Khodynka Field disaster was, at least it was an *accident*. Dimitri knew that 'Bloody Sunday' – what the January 22 massacre was now called – was a deliberate act of slaughter.

'They just wanted to present a petition to Nicky, to improve conditions for the working man,' Dimitri said quietly.

'That petition had only two questions concerning the workers. The rest was sheer nonsense; separation of Church and state, a constitution, an elected assembly,' the Tsarina shot back.

'Ridiculous,' Nicky agreed. 'If anyone is to blame for this, it's the Jewish radicals that filled their heads with such nonsense.'

'Gapon, the man who led the march, was an Orthodox priest, not a Jew,' Dimitri replied.

'Then he should be excommunicated,' Alexandra snapped. 'I'm going to see to it.'

'But, Nicky, the people believe that you're a murderer,' Dimitri said in a beseeching tone. He couldn't let it go; he desperately wanted to help his friend understand the significance of what had happened.

'The Russian people are deeply and truly devoted to me. You saw them cheering me at the Blessing of the Waters just a few days earlier,' Nicky replied in a loud voice.

Every January 19, the Tsar came to the bank of the Neva for a traditional religious service of the Blessing of the Waters. Dimitri knew full well that it was a tightly stage-managed event, with hundreds cheering the Tsar as he rode by. Of course, it looked like everyone loved him. Nicholas and Alexandra lived in their own fantasy world, a million miles from reality. They simply couldn't understand the truth. This saddened him because he was so fond of both of them. What would happen to the Imperial Family, when their world was taken from them? And very soon, the revolution would sweep away Romanov rule.

He changed the subject, albeit to an even sadder matter.

'How is Alexis?' he asked.

'He was in agony the day before yesterday. But the bleeding finally stopped, and he's our happy baby boy now,' the Tsarina said with a smile.

'Have more specialists been to see him?' Dimitri truly hoped there would be one doctor in the world who could save the boy. He loved playing with him on the thick white and mauve carpet of Alexandra's boudoir. Alexis had a golden smile and such beautiful deep blue eyes. It killed Dimitri to picture the boy lying in bed, groaning piteously for hours on end.

'Yes, but it's always the same answer,' Nicky said in a subdued voice. 'Sometimes, I believe that because I was born on the feast day of Job, I'm destined for unhappiness and tragedy,' he added, staring out into space.

Dimitri had noticed an increasing tone of fatalism in his friend since the beginning of the Japanese war and the discovery that Alexis was ill.

'There is more to healing than doctors,' Alexandra said. 'Anna Vyrubova tells me there are holy men who can work miracles.'

Dimitri's head snapped up at this remark. He knew that after Alexis's diagnosis, Alexandra had built a small chapel in a church in the Imperial Park and prayed for hours every day, asking for God's help in curing Alexis. She was such a devout woman that she couldn't believe God had deserted her. But this was the first he'd heard of miracle-workers. Alexandra could never give up hope; she would naturally turn to unconventional solutions. The Tsarevich's disease was still a secret to most of those in the Imperial Court, since his parents didn't want them or the Russian people to know that the future Tsar was an invalid under the constant shadow of death. But members of the Court now had the feeling something was amiss in the Imperial Family. The boy would be out of sight for weeks, then briefly reappear. No children of court members were ever invited to play with him.

'Holy men?' Dimitri said. He remembered the day Nicky told him of his son's illness. There was a mention of healers, but he didn't take it seriously.

'Anna has told me of a Siberian peasant named Rasputin, who is now visiting Bishop Sergei at the Theological Seminary. It is said that he has special powers of healing. One day I must meet him,' Alexandra replied.

FIFTY-ONE

'The empire is in crisis.'

The Tsar said this more to the plate of chicken Kiev in front of him than to his dinner guests.

'Your army is at the ready,' replied Grand Duke Alexis, the Tsar's uncle. He crammed a fork full of chicken into his gray mustached mouth.

Dimitri waited for the Tsar's response. Nicky looked exhausted and drained of blood, as did the Tsarina, which meant they had been up all night with Alexis. Dimitri knew he'd had some falls recently. Whenever he was playing with the Tsarevich, he was constantly on edge that the boy would fall and start bleeding. It reminded him of building a house of cards; the slightest jiggle would bring it tumbling down. The Russian Empire, too, now seemed like that – on the verge of collapsing.

Dimitri had been invited to dine with the Imperial Couple. The two oldest children were eating with them also, because the Tsarina thought they would cheer up their father. Yet Nicky remained in an uncharacteristically gloomy mood.

'It makes me sick to read the news about the strikes in factories, riots, peasants killing their landlords, the murdered policemen,' said the Tsar. 'Life in all of Russia has ground to a halt, and my ministers take no action. They just cackle like frightened hens.'

Dimitri was about to say something, but the Tsar continued speaking. 'Then we lost the war.'

There was a silence in the dining room that one could cut with a knife. Crushed by the news, Nicholas had no choice but to give up and sue for peace. Even the most patriotic Russians admitted that the war with Japan was an unnecessary disaster that had made the country a laughing-stock in the eyes of the world. Many sons, brothers, and fathers died in the conflict – all for nothing. The government and the Tsar were seen as totally inept and stupid. The defeat had invigorated the revolution like petrol thrown on a fire.

Of course, Dimitri was secretly happy that revolution had swept across the country. For months, he had been financing revolutionary activities and coordinating the distribution of the photo book, which had been immensely successful. But again, the realization of the revolt was like a double-edged sword: at the same time that he was working for Evigenia's cell, he was sad for his friend. Nicholas's world was toppling around him, although Dimitri had tried to warn him. Perhaps he could still help him.

All hell had broken loose after Bloody Sunday. The strife had become much worse; strikes had increased almost exponentially. They had shut down parts of the country including St Petersburg and all of Russia's big cities like Moscow, Kiev, and Minsk. When the railway workers walked off the job, every single worker in the country went on strike. Russia was now totally paralyzed. Ships lay idle in port, the trains didn't move, factories were closed down. All schools and universities had closed in St Petersburg and the rest of the cities. There were no newspapers, and the electricity was out most of the time. Coal, the most basic necessity in a Russian winter, went undelivered. Even Katya's hospital had closed. But instead of being sad and dispirited, the common people were deliriously happy – marching through the streets cheering, singing, and waving red flags, which had become the symbol of the revolution. Revolutionist orators spoke to thousands gathered in parks.

The Tsar continued. 'The odd thing is that there is complete order in the streets . . . but something will happen. It's like that ominous quiet right before a summer thunderstorm.'

Dimitri understood what he meant. Though there were marches and protests daily in the cities, no actual violence had erupted between the army and the demonstrators. The troops stood by and watched. Everyone was waiting for a spark to ignite the fighting. But the countryside was another story; it was ravaged by constant violence. The peasants had gone on a rampage, looting and burning the estates like Huns. As they pillaged, they shouted, 'We should get back what is rightfully ours!' and 'The land belongs to us!' Landowners and estate stewards were murdered. Soldiers and Cossacks had to be called out to quell the violence, but it wouldn't stop.

'We need to crush the rebellion by force,' interrupted Grand Duke Alexis.

Dimitri knew he shouldn't, but he had to speak up. 'The other option is to give the people a constitution,' he said in a loud, clear voice. 'Setting the troops on the protestors and strikers might stop them for a while, but they'd be sure to start up again in a few months. You can't shoot a hundred thirty million people.' He directed the last comment to the Grand Dukes.

'Nicky is the ruler ordained by God to rule Russia. You know that,' Alexandra said in a scolding tone.

'A lot of people would agree with Dimitri,' said the Tsar solemnly. The Tsarina frowned and put down her fork.

'Leonid, please take my plate away,' she said to the blond servant.

'The revolutionaries have set up their own elected government with these *soviets*,' said the Grand Duke in disgust.
'Soon, they'll be running Russia instead of you, Nicky!'

The Tsar took a sip of water, then patted his lips with the
linen napkin.

'There's one thing *all* Russian people can agree on – they
love Tchaikovsky,' he suddenly said in a jolly voice. 'And next
week is the laying of the cornerstone for Dimitri's Tchaikovsky
Memorial.'

The Tsar stood up from the dinner table and smiled at
Dimitri.

'We have a new gramophone disk. It's Tchaikovsky's
"Fantasy Overture" from *Romeo and Juliet*. Will you join us
in the study, Dimitri?'

'Oh, please come,' Grand Duchess Tatiana cried, as she
took the last bite of her raspberry tart. 'We can play cards
while we listen.'

Dimitri bent over and kissed Tatiana on her cheek.

'As you wish, my little Highness. I'll be along in a few
minutes.'

There was still enough light coming from the window, so
Dimitri could see everything on the shelves in the display
room very clearly. He pursed his lips, then made his decision.
This time it would be the 'Coronation Egg,' the third Fabergé
Easter Egg Nicholas had given to Alexandra. He picked it up
and opened the hinged yellow-enameled shell. Inside was an
exact gold and diamond-encrusted replica of the carriage the
Imperial Couple rode in for their coronation. Pulling it carefully
out of the egg, he marveled at the incredible workmanship.
Even the platinum wheels and the strawberry-red upholstery
were exactly like the real thing. He opened its little door and
placed a tiny piece of folded paper on the floor of the carriage,
then put it back into the egg. As usual, he set it slightly forward
from the line of the other eggs and gifts to let his fellow agents
know which object held the message. He opened the door of
the display room a crack to see if anyone was about, then
hurried down the marble hallway to the Tsar's study.

FIFTY-TWO

'What an insult to the Russian Imperial Army! To have a decorated officer from a fine family want to overthrow our beloved Tsar!'

General Moncransky nodded to the lieutenant, who smiled and turned the wooden handle of the vise attached to the end of the long table. Azref, whose head was face-down in the vise, screamed in agony. This was the Okhrana's most reliable method of persuasion: cheap, simple, and effective.

'I think I'm going to have you shot in front of a firing squad for being a traitor. No Siberia for you, Captain!' Moncransky said in a solemn voice. The man merely groaned. Moncransky was glad in a way he was so tough to break, being a soldier.

Azref burbled something.

'What was that, Captain?'

'Fuck the Tsar,' was what it sounded like. At that, the vise was tightened another quarter-turn, producing an ear-piercing scream.

'Once again, who are your confederates in the Imperial Palaces? Is one of them Prince Dimitri Markhov?'

Gurgling and moaning were the reply. The vise was tightened an eighth of a turn.

Moncransky knew when the bravest man was at his breaking point. He was almost there with Azref. He nodded for an eighth more.

This produced a cracking sound, like someone breaking open a walnut. Azref screamed non-stop. Moncransky thought he heard him say something, and knelt down to look up at Azref's face. It was red as a beet, and his eyes were open and bulging. Azref croaked the word again, and then went silent.

Moncransky stood up with a puzzled expression. 'Sounded like "ninny." He called me a ninny!' the General said incredulously.

A captain knocked on the door and entered. He saluted and said in a stentorian voice, 'The others are assembled downstairs, Your Super-Excellency.'

The lieutenant stepped forward and felt for a pulse on Azref's neck, then nodded.

'It's a shame, Your Super-Excellency, we got nothing out of him. Except finding this code book in his room,' the lieutenant said in a resigned tone of voice.

'Have an orderly clean up this mess,' the General growled. He slapped Azref on the back.

'You did yourself proud, Captain. Most men and women talk at the very first turn of the handle.'

The General walked into a small office adjoining the interrogation room. A doughy woman rose from a chair and walked up to him.

'Did he tell you that Prince Dimitri was the traitor?' Anna Vyrubova asked in an eager voice.

'No, I'm afraid not. Azref "cracked," but not in the way we wanted him to,' the General said. Moncransky didn't take her seriously as an Okhrana agent because she was a woman, but he pretended to. Anna scowled at him.

'He *is* the traitor who's betraying the Tsar. For months, he's been hectoring His Majesty about establishing a constitutional monarchy,' Anna snapped. 'His movements have been very suspicious, especially around the display rooms. I've been watching him.'

'Rest assured, Mademoiselle Vyrubova, I will have proof that Prince Dimitri is a revolutionary agent. You needn't worry yourself. We know how dedicated you are to the Imperial Family. The Okhrana is very appreciative of your work, and we'll keep you on as an operative. Now, if you would excuse me, I have to attend a meeting.'

'Prince Dimitri is a revolutionary working right under your noses!' Anna yelled after Moncransky. 'Arrest him!'

When Moncransky entered the room downstairs, men were smoking and chatting around a long wooden conference table. He took a seat at the head and rapped his ring on the table.

'Gentlemen, there are millions of Russians who still love and obey our great Tsar. The Union of Russian People, or the Black Hundred, as it's popularly known, is the Tsar's largest and most important loyalist group. It will be organizing many patriotic parades throughout Russia to show support for the Romanov Dynasty. This gives us a splendid opportunity to put into place a counter-revolutionary action to draw the workers' and peasants' attention from the revolution. We intend to ignite hundreds of pogroms across Russia *on the very same day.*'

Isvoltsky took up the narrative. 'In Odessa and in three hundred other cities and towns, large patriotic processions supporting our beloved Tsar will take place, one week from today,' he explained in a businesslike tone. 'We will have a sharpshooter in position to kill the man leading the group in the biggest cities.'

Moncransky continued the explanation. 'The murders will be blamed on Jewish revolutionaries set on destroying the Empire. The Black Hundred will have men and women run through the streets screaming that the Jews killed a Christian.' He smiled. 'We will also scatter the usual handbills.'

'All hell will break loose in Russia, and a lot of Yids will die,' Isvoltsky added.

'Good show.' 'Excellent.' 'Splendid,' came the men's reactions.

Moncransky stood up, signaling that the meeting had come to an end.

'A super pogrom!' he crowed with great pride. 'Wonderful.'

FIFTY-THREE

'We're going to get in trouble,' whined Marie.

'Must you be such a goody-two-shoes?' replied Olga in an annoyed voice. She was pushing the button repeatedly on the 'Cuckoo' Imperial Easter Egg to make the rooster pop up and down. Tatiana was lying on the floor of the display room winding up the gold train from the 'Trans-Siberian Egg.'

'Papa doesn't mind if we look at the eggs,' Tatiana snapped.
'Only when he's with us, I thought,' Marie replied.

Though their days were strictly scheduled, there was time
when the Grand Duchesses could roam through the palace
without supervision. The girls were in the display room of
the Alexander Palace all by themselves. They liked opening the
Imperial Easter Eggs, and pulling out the surprises.

'Well, you thought wrong,' Olga said. 'We're old enough
to play with them if we're careful – except for her.' Anastasia
was sitting on the carpet examining an enameled pearl cigarette
case. 'She'd break one for sure.'

Tatiana tired of the train and picked up the 'Peter the Great
Egg.' She ran her finger over the tiny statue inside.

'Then I'm going to play with one,' Marie said and walked
over to the shelves.

Olga had put away the 'Cuckoo' and moved on to the
'Pine Cone Egg.' She enjoyed playing with its windup
elephant.

'Why don't we wind up the train and the elephant and run
them into one another?' Olga said with glee. Tatiana giggled
and nodded.

As her sisters were preparing to do that, Marie went over
to the pink pearl-encrusted 'Lilies of the Valley Egg.' She sat
on the carpet and pressed its button to pop up the miniature
portraits of her father, Olga, and Tatiana. Marie repeated the
operation four more times until a little piece of folded paper
fell out from behind the portrait of her father onto the floor.
She set the egg down and examined the paper closely.

'What's this?' Marie asked Olga.

At first Olga ignored her little sister, but she glanced over
and saw the paper in Marie's hand.

'Where did that come from?'

'It fell out of the egg.'

Tatiana now saw it. 'I know what that is. It's a price tag.'

Marie crinkled her nose in puzzlement.

'Remember when we go with Nanny to the stores on the
Nevsky and each thing has a piece of paper attached to it that
tells you how much it costs? Like two rubles or six kopecks,'
Tatiana said.

'Let me look at that,' ordered Olga. She snatched the paper from her sister's hand.

'It doesn't look like a price tag. It has no numbers, just a bunch of letters.'

'What do they say?' Marie asked.

'Nothing, it's just a gobbly-kook of letters.' Olga handed the paper back to her sister and resumed readying the elephant for its crash into the train.

The girls played for another twenty minutes until Olga announced it was almost teatime and ordered her sisters to put every egg back where they found it. She knew this because she was old enough to have a pin watch attached to the front of her dress.

At tea, the girls chattered away to their mother and father about their day and what they learned in class. Nicholas enjoyed quizzing them on their French and English.

The only daughter not talking was Marie; she was idly playing with a little piece of paper by her teacup.

'What do you have there?' her father asked.

'It's not a price tag,' Marie answered confidently.

Nicholas smiled at his wife. 'Let me see it, my sweet.'

Marie first took a bite of her ginger cookie then got up and brought the paper to her father who was sitting at the head of the table.

'It's just a lot of letters strung together, not words,' Nicholas said in an amused voice.

The Tsar was interrupted by the sound of breaking crockery. Everyone at the table turned their heads toward its source.

'Nanny,' shouted Tatiana, 'you've dropped your cup and splattered tea all over the front of your frock.'

Olga took her linen napkin and started dabbing Miss O'Brian's dress.

'Leonid, bring a dish of cold water,' commanded the Tsarina. 'We want to blot up these tea stains before they set.'

Miss O'Brian had a dazed look on her face.

'Don't look so worried, Nanny, these stains will come out,' Olga assured her as she dabbed away.

As if coming out of a trance, Miss O'Brian spoke haltingly.

'No, Leonid needn't bother. I'll change out of my frock. Will you excuse me, Your Majesty?' she asked the Tsarina.

'Why certainly, dearest Nanny.'

Miss O'Brian rose shakily from her seat and left the room. With the commotion over, the Tsar resumed his interest in Marie's find.

'Did you write these letters?'

'No, I found it.'

'Where?' asked the Tsarina.

Marie glanced at Olga before answering.

'On the floor.'

'Someone must have dropped it,' observed Olga.

Dr Botkin, the family's personal physician, who had been invited to tea, took the paper from the Tsar. 'It looks like a code of some sort, Your Majesty. I've seen these things back when I was a doctor in the army.'

This interested the Tsar. 'Well, just for fun, I'll pass it on to the Okhrana.'

'Read it to me again!' General Moncransky said in a jolly voice.

Captain Odin of the cryptology section cleared his voice.

'Markhov to leave new book in regular spot. Proceed with plan.'

'One more time!'

'Markhov to leave new book in regular spot. Proceed with plan.'

To Captain Odin's astonishment, the General, grinning from ear to ear, did a little jig, kicking out his legs and clapping his hands. The fat old general had been transformed into a child.

'Isvoltsky,' Moncransky yelled to his adjutant, 'when is the groundbreaking ceremony for that memorial?'

'We're not picking him up now?'

'No,' Moncransky said with a sly smile, 'I want to wait for a special time to show the Tsar that his best friend is a fucking traitor.'

FIFTY-FOUR

'What's America like, Madame Doctor?' Nadia asked in a quiet, scared voice.

'It's got buffaloes and wild Indians with red-painted faces,' her brother Mendel shouted with glee. 'And they scalp people!' Four-year-old Nadia began to whimper and hang onto her mother's long overcoat.

'You shut your trap, boy,' his mother yelled.

Katya and the Mandel family stood together on Wharf Seven on a quay on the Neva. They were waiting for the transfer boat that would take the mother and two children out to their schooner.

Katya knelt down to Nadia and wiped her tears with a white hankie. 'It's a wonderful place with all kinds of things: mountains, big cities like St Petersburg, countryside as far as the eye can see,' she explained. 'And the Indians are all peaceful,' she added, casting a sidelong glance at Mendel.

Mrs Mandel took Katya's hand. 'Thank you again for what you've done, Madame Doctor.'

'With your husband gone, America is the best place to be,' Katya said in a confident tone.

'To tell you the truth, I'm as scared as Nadia. But Mrs Tannenbaum, whom you also helped, wrote me to say how wonderful things were in New York. She lives in a three-room apartment that she doesn't share with any other families, and it has steam heat. Can you imagine that?' Mrs Mandel asked.

'Check one last time before you get into the boat that you have all your documents,' Katya advised. 'When you get to Ellis Island, be sure to show them that you have a sponsor who'll give you a job, or they'll send you back. And for heaven's sake, don't say any of the children are sick.'

Mendel was playing too close to the edge of the wharf. His mother shouted at him to stand back.

'Mrs Tannenbaum says the United States is the new promised

land,' Mrs Mandel said happily. 'They leave Jews alone; the goys don't crash into your house and beat your head in like they did my poor Abraham.'

'I am sure that America will seem like heaven, after what you've gone through in Kishinev,' Katya reassured her.

With a big smile on her haggard face, Mrs Mandel said, 'We've been studying English – to learn the language of a country where people are treated like human beings.'

Katya nodded approvingly. 'The more English you know, the easier it will be.'

The recent wave of new pogroms across Russia had left many dead and families destitute. Thousands of Jews were desperate to leave, selling their belongings for next to nothing to buy exit certificates and steamship tickets to America or the Argentine. Katya was furious when she heard that men posing as emigration contractors for the Jewish Colonization Society took money from families and absconded with it, leaving the Jews helpless. With the Baron's assistance, she was sponsoring several families who had been ruined in the pogroms. The thought haunted her: if her great-grandfather hadn't converted to the Orthodox Church, she might be one of these victims – raped or dead.

But Katya soon discovered that it was an incredibly compli-cated process, especially if the family didn't have the proper papers: a police certificate, an exit certificate, a passport along with the passport tax. A missing birth certificate was disastrous. Proof that the children were biologically connected to the parents was extremely important. If an emigrant's relative had evaded military service by escaping the country, the state held them personally responsible for the three-hundred-ruble fine. It was the Society's job to approve or disapprove the Jews' applications. To Katya's consternation, the decision came down to whether they could work. She had to go before the Society and plead for her families' approvals. But the Russian govern-ment had to concur, and it took ages to decide. Katya soon learned that large bribes to bureaucrats were most effective. She was lucky she came from a wealthy family, although her father and siblings knew nothing of this.

'Here it comes!' Mendel cried out when the transport boat

pulled up along the wharf. Katya smiled; for most of the children, it was a great adventure. She helped Mrs Mandel with the bags.

With everyone aboard, Katya handed her a card. 'Once you settle in, you write me to tell me how you are. Promise?'

With tears in her eyes, the woman reached out and kissed Katya's hand.

'That Church of yours should make you a saint,' she cried out as the boat chugged away.

Katya kept waving until they reached the ship which would take them to Bremen. There, they'd catch a steamship to New York.

Walking back to the carriage, she lit a cigarette and turned one last time to look out at the harbor. The Baron was waiting for her in his carriage.

'You've just done what my people call a "mitzvah." An act of extraordinary kindness,' he said.

Katya smiled at him. 'I had no choice. After the latest pogroms, I wasn't going to stand by and do nothing.'

'These people will always remember your kindness,' the Baron added, patting her hand. 'Your willingness to do the right thing.'

'I intend to do many more mitzlas.'

'Mitzvahs,' corrected the Baron.

'The Pinskys leave next Tuesday.'

'You're still coming next week to my home for Passover?' asked the Baron as the carriage rattled along. 'There'll be lots of *challah*.'

'To commemorate God's liberation of the Israelites from slavery in Egypt.'

'Precisely,' the Baron answered.

'I'll be there. But I dislike your Jewish holidays,' Katya grumbled.

Her comment amused the Baron. 'On what grounds, Doctor?'

'Jews may have been freed back then, but they're still in slavery in Russia, and other places around the world. Treated like shit,' Katya snapped in an angry voice.

'That's not a fair comparison. Jews are terribly mistreated, but not like the slaves of Egypt.'

'Well . . . maybe,' Katya retorted.

'So, is it just Passover with which you have a problem?'

'Yom Kippur also bothers me,' Katya said. She had joined the Baron's family to celebrate the holiday last fall. 'It's supposed to be a day of atonement for Jews' sins. But their sins are *nothing*, compared to the way the world sins against them.'

'It's our most important holiday. To ask forgiveness from those we've sinned against,' the Baron replied in a patient voice.

'Yes, I know. But where's the high holiday for the world to ask forgiveness for what they've done to the Jews? Like these recent pogroms across the Empire. Four hundred killed in Odessa alone.'

'I agree, it was shocking. To have one isolated pogrom is normal, but scores across the country at the same time is horrendous,' the Baron said in a troubled voice.

'It's clear: the Tsar and the government have been instigating all these pogroms as a way to counter the revolution that's exploded,' Katya said, raising her voice. 'It's an old strategy – blame the Jews for all of a nation's ills.'

'Yes, I've heard the rumor that the Black Hundred and the government planned it all.'

'And we are powerless to stop them.' Katya sighed.

'*We?*' the Baron said with a wry smile. He held up his gloved hand, as a signal that she didn't have to explain. The carriage pulled up to her house.

'See you at Passover,' Katya called out.

FIFTY-FIVE

The Grand Duchesses and their nanny were gathered on a little island in a man-made lake near the Alexander Palace. Miss O'Brian had rowed the children over in a small boat. The island had an ornate open-air wooden pavilion that served as playhouse for the children. Behind it was the children's pet cemetery, where cats, birds, mice, rabbits, and one dog had been laid to rest by the children. A burial service for a rabbit was now taking place.

Miss O'Brian welcomed this little excursion to get out of the palace. She'd been on pins and needles since Marie had found the code. She'd seriously considered making a run for it. Then she'd decided that because she was a lifelong revolutionary, she must be brave enough to take the consequences for her actions – banishment for life to Siberia. Miss O'Brian had nothing to be ashamed of; she was proud of what she'd done. When the Okhrana did burst into her room to arrest her, the nanny would proudly confess, although she'd be quite sad never to see her girls again. But four weeks had passed and nothing happened.

'O dear Lord, please take our beloved Pavlova and take good care of her. She loves tiny pieces of cut-up carrots and cucumbers,' Tatiana said.

'Pavlova was a very good bunny,' added Olga in a sad voice. 'So soft and warm.' She stroked the small wooden box that held the rabbit's body.

'Why do bunnies die, Nanny?' Marie asked.

Miss O'Brian was touched by the innocent question.

'God decides it's time for bunnies to come up and be with him. He has millions of bunnies and pets in heaven.'

'Say hello to God for me, Pavlova,' Tatiana said. 'Tell him I always say my prayers.'

Olga placed the box in a hole that a groundskeeper had dug for them earlier that day. After the burial, a staff carpenter would make a white cross engraved with the pet's name. There were now eleven crosses, including Pavlova's, who was named after the famous ballerina.

The Grand Duchesses filled the grave with the mound of excavated dirt. Anastasia helped, but lost her footing and fell into the shallow hole, to the delight of her sisters. The nanny lifted her out and brushed off her dress. Afterwards, they retired to the pavilion to snack on the cookies, sweets, and cold tea that Miss O'Brian had packed for the occasion.

'It's so sad to lose a pet,' Olga said.

'It breaks your heart, it really does,' Tatiana said sadly.

'Leonid's heart was broken when Mikhail, his bird, died,' Marie added.

Because the children had few outside playmates, they forged friendships with the immediate household staff, like Jim and Leonid the footman.

'Leonid had a bird?' Miss O'Brian asked. She knew the tall blond footman only slightly.

'Yes, he kept him in a cage in his room. He brought him to St Petersburg when he got the job as footman,' Olga explained while breaking her cookie into small pieces.

'Leonid is so good looking and tall. I hope I marry someone who's as handsome as he is,' Marie said wistfully.

'Baroness Sophie Gurko told me the taller and more handsome the footman is, the higher his pay,' Olga announced, proud of possessing this inside information. 'And Monsieur Cubat, our master chef, is the highest paid person in the household – although Papa doesn't like his French cooking.'

Miss O'Brian giggled at this, causing the girls to laugh with her.

'Leonid was so sad. We said he could bury Mikhail in our cemetery,' Marie said.

This caught Miss O'Brian's attention. She put down her glass of tea on the floor of the pavilion.

'I don't remember a burial service for his bird.'

'We wanted to have a ceremony, but Leonid said he was too sad, and would rather bury his bird alone. So, we said that he could row out and bury Mikhail on his own. He brought a shovel and dug his own hole, then he got the carpenter to make a cross like the rest,' Olga explained in a matter-of-fact voice.

'Rest in peace, Mikhail,' Tatiana said, looking up to the sky.

'Finish your cookies, girls. I'll be right back,' Miss O'Brian said.

The nanny walked over to the cemetery, searching the crosses until she found Leonid's bird. Something seemed slightly different about this grave. She knelt down to take a closer look. Unlike the other graves, which had been feathered in with grass, this one had a thin but distinct line

outlining a rectilinear hole. Using both hands, she dug her
fingers into the earth and pulled out a wooden box mounded
with grass.

Miss O'Brian set the little coffin on the grass. She removed
the lid, and sure enough, there was a body of a decomposed
bird. But the coffin was much deeper than it had to be for a
tiny bird. She poked at the panel on which the bird was lying,
and it moved. The coffin, she realized, had a false bottom.

When she lifted the panel up, her eyes widened in horror.
'Leonid?!'

There, below it, lay odds and ends of what looked like the
left-over ingredients for making a bomb – a fuse, a roll of
wire, and a timer. A short reddish-brown cylinder could have
been a stick of dynamite. Because the servants' quarters were
being randomly searched after the assassination attempt in
the dining room, Leonid couldn't keep these things in his room
anymore. She turned to see if the girls were watching, but
they were absorbed in their snacks. Picking up the box very
gingerly, she walked it over to the edge of the lake, and
dumped the bomb-making items into the water. Then she
returned to the grave and put back everything as she'd found
it, kneeling and patting down the joints of the hole so they
didn't look disturbed. As she stood up, she realized she'd been
sweating like an open faucet.

'Finish up, my little bears!' she called out to the girls. 'Time
to get back.'

As she rowed back to shore, the nanny boiled with anger.

Miss O'Brian stood patiently inside a room in the private
apartments, peering out into the corridor from a crack in the
open door. Her breathing was steady and controlled. To her
surprise, her hands weren't sweating. Ten minutes passed, then
suddenly, her body stiffened. She closed her eyes and counted
to ten, then flung open the door.

'Please help me!' she cried out to Leonid, who was alone
in the corridor. He turned around and saw her wide-eyed look
of terror.

'What has happened, Madame?' he asked, coming toward
her.

'Little Anastasia has had an accident. You must come with me now!'

Miss O'Brian ran back into the room, followed by Leonid. They came to an alcove outside the Tsarina's dressing room.

'The elevator didn't come all the way down to the floor! Anastasia looked into the gap and fell in. Help me get her out!'

The open elevator platform was about three feet higher than the first floor. Leonid flattened his body on the floor and stuck his head into the gap. Quick as a flash, Miss O'Brian reached up and yanked the metal handle forward. The elevator dropped, producing a sickening, crushing sound.

The nanny ran into the corridor, and shrieked at the top of her lungs.

'Help, there's been a terrible accident! For God's sake, please help me!'

Miss O'Brian was in her sitting room of her private suite, drinking a glass of tea with Baroness Sophie Gurko. The Tsarina's lady-in-waiting patted the nanny's hand.

'This has been such a horrible experience for you my dear,' the Baroness said sadly.

'We can't tell the children; they liked Leonid,' Miss O'Brian said.

'As did the Tsarina. She was so fond of the boy,' added the Baroness.

'She'll be heartbroken when she gets back from the ceremony.'

'What ceremony is that?' In all the commotion, Miss O'Brian had uncharacteristically lost track of the day's schedule.

'The laying of the cornerstone for the Tchaikovsky Memorial is at two, remember? And I found out,' the Baroness exclaimed with delight, 'that the Tsarina had Prince Dimitri design a surprise gift for the Tsar commemorating the occasion. The prince just picked it up. He'll be presenting the gift personally to His Majesty.'

'What kind of gift? Like a Fabergé egg?' the nanny asked.

'No. It's basically a big box to put odds and ends. When

the lid opens, it plays a tune,' the Baroness explained. 'It's quite charming. The Tsar will be very pleased.'

'How big is this box?'

'Oh, I'd say about this tall and about this wide,' the Baroness replied, holding her hands apart to give the nanny an idea of its size.

Miss O'Brian bolted out of the room.

FIFTY-SIX

I t was an unusually sunny and warm March day. Thousands had turned up for the cornerstone-laying ceremony. Shoulder to shoulder, they crowded both sides of the street along the Griboedova Canal. People even filled up Plekhanova Avenue a block north. From the surrounding buildings, the public looked out from windows and rooftops. The Tsar was right, thought Dimitri; revolutionaries and non-revolutionaries alike loved Tchaikovsky. The event would temporarily take people's minds off the insurgent fervor that was increasing by the day. On the empty lot where the Memorial would be built sat a five-tiered grandstand with wooden chairs. At its center was an Imperial Box adorned with gold double-headed eagles and white-blue-red bunting. Directly behind the grandstand was assembled the St Petersburg Symphony, which was playing Tchaikovsky's Concerto Number One. Cossacks with grim expressions were mounted around the perimeter of the crowd.

Dimitri and Lara, who came for the purpose of showing off her new hat and dress, and Peter Carl Fabergé took their places on the grandstand, along with the Grand Dukes – the Tsar's uncles and cousins, ministers, courtiers, and guests. To Dimitri's surprise, General Moncransky and some officers were sitting two rows behind him. The General smiled and bowed to Dimitri. In his lap, Dimitri held the Tsar's gift in a specially made mahogany box. He was more excited to present the gift than seeing the cornerstone of his building laid.

The orchestra began playing 'God Save the Tsar,' which

was the signal the emperor had arrived. Everyone stood up and began singing. People cheered when the Tsar and Tsarina waved as they took their places in the box. Dimitri was a bit disappointed that the children could not attend; Alexandra thought they'd be too restless and distracting. He would bring them to the site as construction progressed; it would be much more interesting for them. The program called for a short concert of Tchaikovsky highlights before the actual ceremony.

Dimitri looked over at the Tsar, who sat listening to the Tchaikovsky piece. He was in his own world, smiling as the beautiful music took him far away from his enormous troubles. 'His heavy cross to bear,' as the Tsarina would say. Nicky's head swayed and his toe tapped to the rhythm of *The March Slav*.

Dimitri's beloved *Capriccio Italien* came next, but his mind began to wander, and he didn't hear a note. He kept looking over at Nicky. With his whole heart, he didn't want to believe what Katya had said – that the Tsar and the government had orchestrated the pogroms all along. She'd told him that the recent wave of violence across the country had been a counter-revolutionary action, instigated through blaming the Jews for the peasants' misery. Hundreds had been murdered. And Katya was right. His old friend was responsible for Russia's misery, but Nicky didn't have the faintest idea he was to blame – or even know of the abject misery. Dimitri felt angry – and sorry for him.

The orchestra segued into the last two minutes of the *1812 Overture*, the Tsar's favorite Tchaikovsky piece. The crowds started cheering like mad. If all Russians loved Tchaikovsky, then this was their favorite piece, which commemorated the great victory over Napoleon. Dimitri continued to look for Katya, expecting to see her squirming through the audience to stand at the very front. A dramatic crescendo ended the piece. When it was finished, he would walk down to the Imperial Box and present his Fabergé design to the Tsar.

Dimitri unwrapped it from its green velvet cloth. The blue enamel and gold music box glowed in the afternoon sun. He smiled with pride at his creation. He had shown it to the Tsarina yesterday morning, and she'd absolutely loved it. The gift had been left in the palace for safekeeping, and he had picked it up this morning.

As the final notes were dying out, he made his way down. He didn't see Moncransky and his entourage following right behind him. He was at the bottom tier, when he saw a figure moving forward through the crowd. He looked down so he wouldn't lose his footing and trip. When he looked up, to his delight, he saw Katya standing there. He'd known she would never miss this special moment and would steal away from the hospital to see it. He beamed a big smile at her. Then a woman in a light blue dress shoved roughly past Katya and came running straight at him.

'Miss O'Brian?' Dimitri stammered.

The nanny had a wide-eyed look of horror on her face that frightened him.

'It's a bomb,' Miss O'Brian said in hushed voice. He followed her eyes down to the box. For a few seconds that seemed like two months, he stood paralyzed with fear. Listening closely, he could hear the faintest ticking coming from the gift. Slowly, the cobweb of panic cleared from his head, and he knew what he had to do. From his left, he could see Moncransky was approaching. Dimitri was about to take off with the box when the General clamped his hand on his shoulder.

'Prince Dimitri,' the General shouted in a voice all could hear, 'in the name of the Tsar, I am . . .'

'It's after two,' shrieked the nanny.

Before Moncransky could say another word, Dimitri twisted away from his grasp and began to run. He had taken just two steps when Miss O'Brian snatched the gift out of his hands and started running away from him. With confused expressions, the Tsar and Tsarina watched the goings-on taking place right in front of them. There was a ten-foot-wide space on Griboedova Street between the crowd and the grandstand for security, and she ran down the middle of it. Policemen in plain clothes started chasing after her.

Dimitri watched her figure become smaller in the distance. Ten seconds later, there was the sound of a muffled explosion. The crowd screamed as a cloud of smoke erupted, and Miss

O'Brian was gone from view. The police ran up to a blackened spot that was spattered with pieces of flesh among fragments of light blue cloth.

Dimitri just stood there stunned watching in amazement.

'Prince Dimitri is an assassin! He tried to kill our Tsar!' Anna Vyrubova screamed.

'Murderer!' shouted someone else.

'Revolutionary!'

'Seize him!' Anna Vyrubova yelled at the top of her lungs.

'No! That's not true!' Dimitri shouted back at his accusers in the grandstand. His eyes locked with Nicky's, who was standing in the box staring at him with an astonished look.

The crowd began to panic, screaming and scattering like mad in all directions. Katya fought her way through the mob to get to him.

'Dimitri, what's going on?' she asked in a stricken voice. 'Who was that woman that grabbed the gift from you?'

As Dimitri was about to answer, he saw Moncransky and his men. They had been caught up in the panicked crowd, but now had regrouped and were heading his way.

'We have to get the hell out of here!' he yelled, yanking Katya by the arm. In the chaos, they were able to push their way through the crowd, leaving Moncransky behind. At the edge of the mob, they burst free and ran to the next street over. Dimitri spied a man about to get into a carriage. He ran up to him and shoved him aside.

'Go!' he shouted to the driver as he pulled Katya in behind him and slammed the door.

'What are we going to do?' Katya said in a frightened voice. She was sitting across from him with a look of dread on her face.

'I didn't try to kill the Tsar,' Dimitri gasped, catching his breath. 'But once the Okhrana find out I'm part of the revolution, they'll say I did. And you'll be connected too.'

'You'll be hanged! We've got to get out of the country. We have no choice!' Katya cried.

Dimitri stuck his head out of the carriage window. 'Faster!' he yelled to the driver.

*   *   *

In the middle of a swarm of frightened people, Asher Blokh stood as still as a statue with his head bent. This had to be a nightmare, he thought. The bizarre scene he'd witnessed was just a bad dream that he would wake up from. The assassination was mere seconds from being carried out, when this crazy woman came out of the crowd to thwart it. He started walking away from the mob as if in a trance. What the hell happened?

Blokh shuffled over to the stone parapet of the Griboedova Canal and stared into the still, gray water which was partially frozen. The woman was obviously trying to ditch the bomb in the canal, but she didn't make it. He couldn't believe his bad luck. Feeling like a whipped dog, he walked along the parapet. He was still convinced he'd been doing the right thing. The Tsar was a dictator destroying the lives of millions, especially his own people. If he died, Russia would be free. But after four unsuccessful assassination attempts, maybe the old Russian saying that 'the eviler a man is, the longer he lives' was true.

Shaking his head in disbelief, he lit a cigarette and walked home. He was going to do something he'd never imagined: he was giving up. He tried to remember where he'd put Hersch's American address.

FIFTY-SEVEN

When his bedroom door burst open, Dimitri felt as though he would faint. He expected a volley of gunfire from the Imperial Police. Lara rushed into the room.

'Dimitri, you idiot, do you know what you've done?' she screamed at him. 'And what you've done to me?'

Dimitri, who had been packing a bag on the bed, gaped at his wife.

'And you, little doctor. Did you think you would get away with your lover?'

Dimitri and Katya gave Lara puzzled looks.

Lara smiled at her husband. 'Dimitri, my love, I could sense what was going on between you two when you introduced me at our ball. *No one* has better intuition about these things than me!'

Dimitri took a step forward. 'I'm sure you won't understand this, Lara, but I've given up my life of privilege to stand up for the oppressed.'

'No, I *don't* understand. The only explanation is that you've gone insane,' Lara spat out in disgust. 'You're a goddamn traitor to our class. You're a shit to turn against us – and Nicky, your best friend. And all for a bunch of ignorant peasants and Jews. How could you do such a rotten thing?' she yelled, her face red.

'I did feel like a shit to turn against him, but I had no choice,' Dimitri said. 'Nicky is a good-hearted person, but a terrible Tsar. His head is stuck in the sand, and millions have suffered for it. I just couldn't stand by. It's all about a belief in something bigger than oneself.'

Lara shook her head in repulsion. 'What a load of horse manure!'

There came a fierce pounding on the front door downstairs. Voices shouted to open up and let them in.

'Ah, they were looking for you around the grandstand. I knew the police would be here soon,' Lara said with a smile.

She dashed out of the room and ran down the curving marble stair. She waved off the footman to open the door herself. There stood General Moncransky, along with a half-dozen policemen. Two had revolvers in their hands.

'Your Highness, we've come to arrest Prince Dimitri Markhov for attempting to murder the Tsar, and for revolutionary activity against the Imperial government,' the General announced in a stentorian voice, a look of triumph on his ruddy face.

'Yes, he *is* a traitor! I want him to hang!' Lara said in a loud, angry voice. The General smiled at her.

Upstairs, Dimitri could hear Lara from the bedroom. He went over to Katya and put his arms around her.

'This is it, my sweet,' Dimitri whispered, looking deep into her blue eyes. 'Always know that I loved you.'

Suddenly, Katya put her index finger up to her lips, motioning for him to be quiet.

'But you're too late,' Lara announced in a frantic voice. 'Prince Dimitri has left the city, but I know his plan. He's on his way by train to the Black Sea, to catch a boat to Constantinople, arranged by his fellow conspirators. He's dressed like a peasant in a black cap and dark green jacket. And he's carrying a cat.'

Moncransky's eyes widened in surprise.

'You must hurry! There's not a moment to lose,' Lara shrieked.

The last detail about the cat seemed to flummox the police, but they and the General ran back to their carriage. 'Get the bastard!' Lara yelled after them.

Dimitri and Katya heard the front door close, then footsteps coming slowly up the stair.

Lara strode into the bedroom.

'Do you have everything you need?' Lara asked in a matter-of-fact tone. 'What about Katya? She can take some of my things.'

Dimitri and Katya stood still, jaws dropped in disbelief. Dimitri tried to speak, but no words came out of his mouth.

'I called my servant . . . he's on his way with my bag and passport,' Katya said in a halting voice.

Lara looked down at Tolstoy sleeping on the bed through all the commotion.

'Dimitri, I'll take care of your cat. I promise, I won't drown it in the Neva,' Lara said. 'You can get another one where you're going. By the way, do you know where you *are* going?'

'Well, all this has happened quite suddenly, so I haven't exactly made definite travel plans.' He was still having trouble comprehending this turn of events.

Lara regarded him coolly. 'You can't escape by the Black Sea, that's where they'll be looking. You have to go north.'

She walked over to the window and thought for a moment.

'You have to cross the Gulf of Finland by boat to Stockholm,' she said in an authoritative voice. 'Then to America.'

'America?' he repeated.

'Yes, New York. Isn't that where all the Jews are heading these days? It's the new promised land, I hear. I don't picture you in Palestine, Dimitri, sitting on a camel.' She smirked.

A servant knocked on the door and brought in Katya's suitcase and her black doctor's bag.

'We've been to New York a few times,' Lara continued. 'There are friends there to help you. You two stay down in the wine cellar while I make the arrangements for your passage. You must be out of here in a few hours, before the police come back – and they will.'

'But what about you?' asked Katya.

'Oh, my husband will cause me a lot of embarrassment in Court, but nothing I can't handle. I'll say I'd been duped, and everyone will feel sorry for me. And if this isn't grounds for divorce, I don't know what is,' she replied with a laugh.

She crinkled her brow. 'Do you have enough cash?'

'Not much, but it will do. I have funds in Zurich,' Dimitri said.

'Here, take this just in case.' Lara unfastened her favorite pearl and diamond necklace and placed it in his bag. 'You can use it to set yourselves up in America. Take those Fabergé trinkets on the mantel; they could be worth something.'

Dimitri went over to Lara and grasped her hand.

'Larissa, have you grown a woman's heart?'

'No, I'm still just a monstrously vain aristocrat. But coming back in the carriage from the ceremony, I realized that you must *really* believe in what you're doing, to throw your whole life away for it. You're sacrificing *everything*. But you always were such a blockhead.' She placed her arms around Dimitri and kissed him on the cheek.

'We had some good times together, Prince Dimitri. On my list of my ten best lovers, you rank number three,' she added with a smile.

'I'm honored.'

'Good luck to you, my handsome prince, and to you, little doctor,' Lara said. With a wave, she strode out of the room.

'Lara,' Dimitri called out, and she stopped in the stair hall. 'Take care of yourself.'

'You know I will,' Lara replied with a sly smile.

Dimitri gave her hand a squeeze, and Lara turned to go down the stairs.

'I'm happy you're in love again, Dimitri,' she called over her shoulder.

He ran back to the room and finished packing his bag with Katya's help. Just before he left, he grabbed his framed architectural degree off the wall and tossed it in.

FIFTY-EIGHT

'Your Highness, it's time to leave. Please follow me.'

'Thank you, Firs.'

Katya and Dimitri grabbed their bags and followed the servant through the cavernous cellar to the rear courtyard. A wagon loaded with a huge pile of hay, hitched to a single horse, was backed up to the mansion. It was still a sunny afternoon.

'Thank you, Firs,' Dimitri whispered while embracing him.

Josef, the Markhovs' old coachman, waved for them to come forward.

'Lie flat on the bed of the wagon, Your Highness, with your heads pointing toward the back,' he whispered. Dimitri and Katya did as they were told. Josef and Firs buried them and their bags with thick layers of hay. Then they placed several wooden crates and sacks of meal on top of the hay. Firs raised the backboard of the wagon, and they rumbled off. Dimitri tried to get a sense of the direction they were headed, but Josef was going in and out of a maze of streets.

'You there! Halt!' came a command ten minutes later.

'Halt, damn you!' a different voice yelled.

Dimitri couldn't see Katya's face because of the hay, but he reached out and grasped her hand. Dimitri's heart was in his throat when he heard the clatter of horses' hooves coming toward them. The horses pulled up alongside the wagon.

'You old idiot. Didn't you hear me tell you to stop?'

Josef turned to his right to face a large Cossack in a scarlet tunic on a dappled gray horse. On his left was another Cossack on a chestnut mount.

'One of your crates fell off the wagon. It's lying back there in the middle of the street,' the Cossack on the right said in a gruff, impatient voice.

Josef with his leathery face and white mustache stared at the Cossack.

The soldier got angry when Josef didn't respond.

'Did you expect me to go back and fetch it for you, you stupid fool?' thundered the Cossack.

'Get down from the wagon and go get it!' the other Cossack yelled. 'You can't leave it in the road!'

Josef looked behind him and saw the crate about thirty yards away. Slowly he got down from the wagon.

'Don't worry, grandfather. We won't let your horse walk off.'

Josef trudged off to retrieve the crate.

The two Cossacks began talking across the wagon bed.

'So, what did you think of Andrushka?' the one on the left asked.

'Splendid pair of jugs on the girl.'

'You should see her ass, it's a work of art.'

The soldiers laughed hilariously.

As they talked, their horses smelled the hay in the wagon. They stretched out their necks and began eating it. The Cossacks took no notice and continued talking.

'Remember Eva? Now she had a great set. All girls from Kiev do,' announced the Cossack on the left.

'I was garrisoned in Kiev for six years, and I never noticed that,' said the other soldier.

Josef was only halfway to the crate. The two horses had begun gorging themselves on the hay, their heads sticking into the wagon bed as though it was a trough. Because he owned horses, Dimitri knew that chomping sound well. Their mouths seemed just inches away from them. Sweat poured off his body. The hay between the sacks and crates was being devoured. Josef was now trudging back with the fallen crate.

'When are you going on leave?' one Cossack asked.

'In three weeks. I can't wait. Going home first to Minsk,
then to the Black Sea.'

'Had a girl once in Minsk. Nice little thing.'

Huffing and puffing, Josef finally made it back to the wagon.
The thick pile of hay was thinning out in places. Dimitri and
Katya scrunched closer to the middle of the wagon bed. The
Cossacks' horses were like eating machines; looking up
through the hay, Dimitri could see glimpses of the chestnut's
muzzle.

'Give me the crate, I'll set it back on,' volunteered the
Cossack on the right. He backed his horse up a few steps and
reached out for the crate, which Josef reluctantly handed over.

'The problem is, old man, you don't have the load properly
distributed. No wonder it fell out. Here, let me show you how
it should be done.'

Leaning out from his horse, the soldier began moving sacks
and crates around. The chestnut horse kept eating away. The
right sleeve of Dimitri's jacket and the bottom of Katya's blue
dress were now discernible. Sensing this, Dimitri eased Katya
even closer and squeezed his eyes tight.

'There you go, old-timer,' the Cossack said in a pleasant
tone of voice.

'Now off with you,' said the other Cossack. He yanked his
horse away from the wagon bed.

Instead of going in the opposite direction, the Cossacks rode
along with the wagon, chatting about the proper sharpening
method for their swords. Dimitri listened to the banter, gritting
his teeth. After a few more nerve-wracking minutes, the
soldiers took a right onto another street.

'Are you all right, Your Highness?' Josef asked in a low
voice.

'Yes, Josef. When will we get there?' Dimitri asked.

'Just a few more minutes, Your Highness.'

The wagon finally stopped. It was very quiet, but Dimitri
could hear water lapping gently against stone. He knew they
were somewhere along the Embankment overlooking the Gulf
of Finland. Josef shifted the load to the back of the wagon,
to make it easier for them to slide out.

'Quickly, Your Highness,' Josef whispered.

The coachman pulled out Dimitri by his arms, then Katya. Hay clung to their clothes and hair. They were at the red granite wall of the quay on the Embankment. A fishing boat moored below awaited them. The boatman caught the bags Josef tossed down. Then Josef took hold of Katya's waist, and lowered her down. Dimitri had swung his leg over the ledge when a voice called out.

'You there! What do you think you're doing?'

A city policeman ran toward them. He glanced over the quay wall and saw the boat below, then turned to Dimitri, who still had one leg over the wall.

'It's against the law to board a boat like that. You must do it at an official customs dock,' the policeman snarled. 'You could be smuggling illegal goods. Let me see your papers.'

'Certainly, your honor.' Dimitri smiled at the young man, then hurled himself off the wall. He crashed down onto the deck of the boat. At that moment, the vessel revved its engine and chugged off at full speed.

Enraged, the constable started screaming at the boat to halt.

'Smugglers!' he shouted. 'Stop!'

The boat was now about forty yards away. When he saw that it wasn't going to stop, the policeman drew a revolver from his holster.

'Stop, I said!' he yelled as he fired a shot at the boat, then took better aim and prepared to shoot again.

Meanwhile, Josef had circled around the young policeman. He grabbed him from behind by his collar and the seat of his pants, then tossed him like a bag of flour over the quay wall.

The boatman, a gray-haired, grizzled seaman, led Dimitri and Katya to the cabin below. He hid them in an opening in the wall, placing a false panel over it.

'As a matter of fact, I am a smuggler,' the boatman told them with a smile.

In the total darkness of the recess, Dimitri and Katya held hands. They didn't say a word to each other; both were lost in thought. For the first time in hours, Dimitri was able to sit quietly and think clearly. The hum of the boat's engine and the constant rush of the water against the hull were the only sounds he heard. He realized that Nicky finally knew he was a revolutionary, which was true – and he also believed he was an assassin, which wasn't true. He'd never forget the look in his friend's eyes. Sadness engulfed Dimitri as he thought of the Grand Duchesses hearing that he had tried to kill their mother and father. He knew the time would come when the Tsar discovered his involvement in the revolution, and they would have parted as friends forever. But he certainly didn't want it to happen the way it did today. Still, he'd had made the right decision to join the revolt. He just couldn't stand by any longer. He thought of writing Nicky a letter after he was settled in New York, explaining why he'd distributed the books and fliers, and that he hadn't known about the bomb in the gift. But it would be of no use. He knew Nicholas and Alexandra would never forgive him for what he did.

Dimitri heard Katya sobbing quietly. He knew she was thinking that she would never see her homeland again. It broke her heart to leave her family. Who would look after her father? She'd never see Noskey again. Dimitri would never see Russia again, either. The minute he set foot back in the country, he'd be arrested.

Dimitri wrapped his arm around Katya. They sat there in silence. He thought back to the bizarre events of the ground-breaking ceremony earlier that day. It suddenly dawned on him that the Tchaikovsky Memorial would never be built – since it had been designed by a revolutionary assassin. None of his buildings done in the Style Moderne would ever be constructed. His heart sank at the thought. He had made a great creative breakthrough, and now it was over.

He could feel Katya's shallow breathing. He pulled her closer and rested his cheek against her hair and took in the sweet scent. He smiled. What did it matter? His buildings had been the most important thing to him, but he'd just been fooling himself – they'd only been a substitute for the emotional void in his life since the failure of his marriage. What was truly most important was sitting right next to him.

'We made it, my darling,' he whispered in Katya's ear.

FIFTY-NINE

The steamship's black hull sliced through the North Atlantic waves with ease. Dimitri always thought of these great ships as buildings traveling on their sides. The three blue-and-white smokestacks soaring above the top deck reminded him of American skyscrapers. He loved to stand at the rail of the bows and feel the cool breeze and spray. After two days at sea from Stockholm, his mood had brightened. The unpleasant memories of the last few days were still there, although they didn't cut him as sharply. But the sadness at having to flee Russia hadn't diminished in the least. He was now homeless, uprooted from the place he'd loved.

He felt a tap on his arm. Katya snuggled up to him and rested her head on his shoulder.

'A kopeck for your thoughts,' she said.

'That's about all they're worth,' he replied.

'The Yanks say they're worth a penny,' Katya said, gazing out at the vastness of the Atlantic Ocean.

'We'll have to get jobs in the New World. You as a doctor, me as an architect,' Dimitri said in a wistful voice.

'Yes, it may be a struggle at first. You'll have to give up the caviar for your horse for a while.' Katya smiled.

'Such a shame,' Dimitri replied.

They stood at the bows in silence for a few minutes.

'I was thinking of Lara,' he said with a smile. 'You really don't know the good there can be in a person.'

'Then, Lara, if it's a girl,' Katya said cheerfully.

With a puzzled expression, Dimitri gazed into the cornflower-blue eyes he'd loved ever since the first time he met her at the Catherine Palace ball.

Katya looked down and she patted her belly.

With inexpressible happiness, he pulled her to him and kissed her deeply.

Arms entwined, together they turned to face toward the bows of the boat, the immense sea and their future rushing toward them.

'Yes, Lara, if it's a girl.'